James H. Graff

Barren Honour

A tale

James H. Graff

Barren Honour
A tale

ISBN/EAN: 9783337411848

Printed in Europe, USA, Canada, Australia, Japan

Cover: Foto ©Andreas Hilbeck / pixelio.de

More available books at **www.hansebooks.com**

BARREN HONOUR.

A Tale.

BY THE AUTHOR OF

"GUY LIVINGSTONE," "BRAKESPEARE,"

"SWORD AND GOWN," &c.

LONDON :

TINSLEY BROTHERS, 18, CATHERINE ST., STRAND.

1868.

JOHN CHILDS AND SON, PRINTERS.

CONTENTS.

CONTENTS.

BARREN HONOUR.

CHAPTER I.

NEW AND OLD.

A VERY central place is Newmanham, both by local and commercial position—a big black busy town, waxing bigger and blacker and busier day by day. For more than a century that Queen of Trade has worn her iron crown right worthily; her pulse beats, now, sonorously with the clang of a myriad of steam-hammers; her veins swell almost to bursting with the ceaseless currents of molten metals; and her breath goes up to heaven, heavy and vaporous with the blasts of many furnaces.

Whenever I pass that way, as a born Briton, an unit of a great mercantile nation, I feel, or suppose myself to feel, a certain amount of pride and satisfaction in witnessing so many evidences of my country's wealth and prosperity; they are very palpable indeed, those evidences, and not one of the senses will be inclined to dispute their existence. If I chance to have an exiled Neapolitan prince, or a deposed grand-duke, or any other potentate in difficulties, staying with me (which, of course, happens constantly), I make a point of beguiling the illustrious foreigner into the dingy labyrinth of Newmanham, from which he escapes not till he has done justice to every one of its marvels. Nevertheless, as an individual whose only relations with commerce consist in always wanting to buy more things than one can possibly afford, and in never by any chance having anything to sell, except now and then a horse or two, more or less "screwed," or a parcel of ideas, more or less trivial—as such an one, I say, I am free to confess, that my first and abiding emotion, after being 10 minutes in that great emporium, is a desolate sense of having no earthly business there, and of being very much in everybody's way—a sentiment which the natives seem perfectly to fathom and coincide with.

It is not that they make themselves in any wise disagreeable, or cast you forth with contumely from their hive. The operative element does not greet the stranger with the "'eave of a arf-brick," after the genial custom of the mining districts; neither is he put to confusion by a broad stare, breaking up into a broader grin, as sometimes occurs in our polite seaport towns. A quick careless glance, as if the gazer had no time even for curiosity, is the worst ordeal you will have to encounter in passing a group of the inhabitants, whether at work, or, by a rare chance, resting from their labours. There are "roughs" to be found there more dangerous, they say, than in most places; but these do not show much in daylight or frequented thoroughfares. They have their own haunts, and when the sun arises they lie down in their dens. Indeed, the upper Ten Thousand—the great manufacturers and iron-founders or their representatives

—will treat you with no small kindness, especially if you have letters of introduction: they will show you over their vast works and endless factories, adapting their conversation always to your limited capacity, becoming affably explanatory or blandly statistical, as the occasion demands, only indulging in a mild and discreet triumph, as they point out some unutterably hideous combination of steel and iron peculiar to their own establishment, which produces results as unexpected as a conjuring trick. Even so have we seen Mr Ambrose Areturus, the stout and intrepid voyager, beguile a Sabbath afternoon in exhibiting to a friend's child—to the officer of the day from the contiguous barracks—to a fair country cousin—or some other equally innocent and inquisitive creature—the treasures of the Zoological Society, not a few of which are the captives of his own bow and spear; lingering, perhaps fondly, for a moment, opposite a gigantic bivalve or mollusca which he is reported to have vanquished in single combat.

But, in spite of all this hospitality, the consciousness of being in a false position, of taking up people's time where time is money—in fact, of being rather a nuisance than otherwise—cannot easily be shaken off: the eye grows weary with seeking a resting-place where everything illustrates perpetual motion, and the brain dizzy with the everlasting tremor and whirr of wheels. It is a positive relief, when we find ourselves starting on one of the lines that radiate from Newmanham to every point of the compass, like the feelers of a cuttle-fish, always dragging in "raw material" to the voracious centre: it is an absolute luxury, an hour afterwards, to sweep on through the great grazing-grounds again, and to see 40 acres of sound, undulating pasture stretching away up to the black 'bullfinch' that cuts the sky-line.

You may easily guess what the political tone of such a borough must be: Liberalism of the most enlightened description flourishes there unchecked and unrivalled; for no Conservative candidate has yet been found so self-sacrificing as to solicit the suffrages of Newmauham. Were such an one to present himself, it is scarcely probable that the free and independent electors would content themselves with such playful missiles as graveolent eggs or decomposed cabbage-stalks: they would be more likely to revive for his especial benefit that almost obsolete *argumentum a lapide* which has silenced, if it did not convince, many obstinate enthusiasts—who, nevertheless, were not far from the truth, after all. In no other town of England are Mr Bright's harangues received with such favour and sincere sympathy. When the santon-fit is on that meek Man of Peace, and carries him away in a flood of furious diatribe against "those who sit in high places and grind the faces of the poor," it is curious to remark how willingly and completely his audience surrender themselves to the influence of the hour. You may see the ground-swell of passion swaying and surging through the mass of operatives that pack the body of the hall, till every gaunt grimed face becomes picturesque in its savage energy; you have only to look round to be aware that education, and property, and outward respectability, are no safeguards against the contagion; it is spreading fast now through that phalanx of decent broad-clothed burghers on the platform, and—listen—their voices chime in with ominous alacrity in the cheer that rewards a peroration that in old days would have brought the speaker to the pillory.

That same cheer, once heard, is not easily forgotten: there is not the faintest echo of anything joyous, or kindly, or hopeful, in its accent; one feels that it issues from the depths of hearts that are more than dissatisfied— through lips parched with a fiery longing and thirst for something never yet attained. For what? God help them! *they* could not tell you—if they dared. Go to an agricultural dinner (farmers are the most discontented race alive, you know), mark the tumult among the yeomen when the health of the county favourite has been given, or rather intimated, for they know what the speaker would say, and before he could finish, the storm of great, healthy voices broke in. Those two acclamations differ from each other more strikingly than does the full round shout of a Highland regiment "doubling" to charge, from the hoarse, cracked "hourra" of a squadron of Don Cossacks.

With these dispositions, you may conceive that, albeit Newmanham rather covets land as an investment (they make very fair and not unkindly seigneurs, those *Novi homines*), she cherishes little love or respect for the landed interest, its representatives, and traditions. Yet, when a brother magnate from Tarenton or New Byrsa comes to visit one of these mighty burghers, to what object of interest does the host invariably first direct the attention of his honoured guest? Deferring to another day the inspection of his own factory, and of all other town wonders, he orders round the gorgeous barouche, with the high-stepping greys overlaid with as much precious metal as the Beautiful Gate, and takes the stranger 15 miles away, to view the demesne which, through the vicissitudes of six centuries, has been the abiding-place of the Vavasours of Dene.

The house is not so ancient, nor does it stand on the site of the old Castle. All that would burn of *that* crumbled down in a whirlwind of flame, one black winter's night during the Wars of the Roses. There had long been a feud between the Vavasours and a neighbouring family nearly as powerful and overbearing. Sir Hugh Mauleverer was a shrewd, provident man, and cool even in his desperation. When he saw signs of the tide turning against Lancaster, he determined to settle one score, at least, before he went to the wall. So, on New-year's eve, when the drinking was deep, and they kept careless watch at Dene Castle, the Lancastrians came down in force, and made their way almost into the banqueting-hall unopposed. Then there was a struggle—short, but very sharp. The retainers of the Vavasour, though taken by surprise, were all fully armed, and, partly from fidelity, partly because they feared their stern master more than any power of heaven or hell, partly because they had no other chance, fought like mad wild-cats. However, three to one are heavy odds. All his four sons had gone down before him, and not a dozen men were left at his back, when Simon Vavasour struck his last blow. It was a good, honest, bitter blow, well-meant and well-delivered, for it went through steel and bone so deep into Hugh Mauleverer's brain that his slayer could not draw out the blade: the grey old wolf never stirred a finger after that to help himself, and never uttered a sound, except one low, savage laugh as they hewed him in pieces on his own hearth-stone. When the slaughter was over, the sack, of course, began, but the young Mauleverer, though heated by the fight, and somewhat discomposed by his father's death, could not forget the courtesy and charity on which he rather prided himself. So, when every living thing that had down on its lip was put out of pain, he would not suffer the women and children to be outraged or tortured, magnanimously dismissing them to wander where they would into the wild weather, with the flames of Dene Castle to light them on their way. Most of them perished before daybreak; but one child, a grandson of the baron's, was saved at the price of its mother's life. She stripped herself of nearly her last garment to cover the heir of her house, and kissed him once as she gave him to the strongest of the women to carry, and then lay down wearily in the snow-drift to die.

When Walter Vavasour came to manhood, the House of York was firm on the throne, and another manor or two rewarded his family for what it had suffered in their cause. He commenced building on the site of the present mansion; but it was reserved for his grandson (who married one of the greatest heiresses at the court of Henry VIII.) to complete the stately edifice as it now stands, at the cost of all his wife's fortune, and a good part of his own.

There are more dangerous follies than a building mania; and perhaps it would have been well for Fulke Vavasour if he had ruined himself more utterly in its indulgence. Poverty might have kept him out of worse scrapes. If he resembled his portrait, his personal beauty must have been very remarkable, though of a character more often found in Southern Europe than in England. The Saxon

and Norman races rarely produce those long, dark, languid
eyes, and smooth, pale cheeks, contrasted with scarlet lips,
and black masses of silky hair.   Fair form and face were
fatal endowments in those hot-blooded days. when lovers
set no bounds to their ambition, and *une caprice de grande
dame* would have its way in spite of—or by means of—
poison, cord, and steel.   All sorts of vague rumours were
current as to the real cause which brought the last Lord
Vavasour to the scaffold.   The truth can never be known ;
for on the same night that he was arrested, a cavalier
(whom no one recognized) came to the Dene ; he showed
the Baron's signet-ring, and required to be left alone in
his private chamber.   The day was breaking when the
stranger rode away ; and an hour afterwards a pursuivant
was in possession of the house, making, as is the fashion
of his kind, minute perquisitions when there was nothing
left to search for.   Doubtless all clue to the mystery
was destroyed or removed before he came.   But it may
well be, that, if Fulke Vavasour was innocent of the plot
for which he died, he was not guiltless of a darker one,
with which statecraft had nothing to do.   It is certain
that his widow—a most excellent and pious young woman,
one of the earliest Protestant converts, and a great friend
of the Bishops—made little moan over the husband whom
she had long wearied with her fondness; she never indeed mentioned his name, except from necessity, and then,
with a groan of reprobation.   They will endure neglect
like angels, and cruelty like martyrs ; but what *dévote* ever
forgot or forgave an infidelity ?

Let it be understood, that I quote this fact of the
widow's scant regret just for what it is worth—a piece of
presumptive evidence bearing upon a particular case, and

in no wise illustrating a general principle. I am not prepared to allow, that a fair gauge of any deceased person's moral worth is invariably the depth or duration of the affliction manifested by his nearest and dearest.

The barony of course became extinct with the attainted traitor; but the broad lands remained; for the Tiger, in a fit of ultra-leonine generosity, not only disdained himself to batten on his victim, but even kept off the jackals. Perhaps, the contracting heart of the unhappy jealous old tyrant was touched by some dim recollection of early chivalrous days, when he took no royal road to win the favour of woman or fortune, but met his rivals frankly and fairly, and either beat them on their merits, or yielded the prize.

The sins of the unlucky reprobate were not visited on his children. The estate gradually shook off the burden he had laid upon it, and during the four succeeding generations the prosperity of the Vavasour rather waxed than waned. Like the rest of the Cavaliers, they had to bear their share of trouble about the time of the Commonwealth; but they were too powerful to be forgotten when the King came to his own again. Indeed, there was a good deal of vitality about the family, though individually its members came curiously often to violent or untimely ends; and the domain had descended in unbroken male succession to its present owner with scarcely diminished acreage. Yet from a period far beyond the memory of man, there had been no stint or stay in the lavish expense and stately hospitality which had always been maintained at Dene. Twice in the last 100 years the offer had been made of reversing the attainder, and reviving the ancient barony, and each time, from whim or

some wiser motive, rejected.   No minister had yet been
found cool enough to proffer a baronetcy to those princes
of the Squirearchy

It is not worth while describing the house minutely.
It was a huge, irregular mass of building, in the Tudor
style, with rather an unusual amount of ornamental
stonework; well-placed near the centre of a very extensive park, and on the verge of an abrupt declivity.
The most remarkable features in it were the great hall
—50 feet square, going right up to the vaulted roof, and
girdled by two tiers of elaborately carved galleries in
black oak—and the garden-front. The architect had availed himself right well of the advantages of the ground,
which (as I have said) sloped steeply down, almost from
the windows; so that you looked out upon a succession of
terraces—each framed in its setting of curiously wrought
balustrades—connected by broad flights of steps leading
down to a quaint stone bridge spanning a clear, shallow
stream. Beyond this lay the Plaisance, with its smooth-
shaven grass, studded with islets of evergreens, and endless winding walks through shady shrubberies, issuing
from which, after crossing a deep-sunk fence, you found
yourself again among the great oaks and elms of the deer-
park. If there had been no other attraction at Dene, the
trees would have been worth going miles to see; indeed,
the staunch adherents of the Vavasours always brought
the timber forward, as a complete and crushing refutation
of any blasphemer who should presume to hint that the
family ever had been, or could be, embarrassed. The stables
were of comparatively modern date, and quite perfect in
their way; they harmonized with the style of the main
building, though this was not of much importance, for

the belt of firs round them was so dense, that a stranger was only made aware of their existence by a slender spire of delicate stonework shooting over the tree-tops, the pinnacle of a fountain in the centre of a court. The best point of view was from the farther end of the Plaisance. Looking back from thence, you saw a picture hardly to be matched even amongst the "stately homes of England," and to which the Continent could show no parallel, if you traversed it from Madrid to Moscow. The grand old house, rising, gray and solemn, over the long sloping estrado of bright flowers, reminded one of some aged Eastern king reclining on his divan of purple, and silver, and pearl. No wonder that Dene was a favourite resort of the *haute bourgeoisie* of Newmanham on Mondays, when the public was admitted to the gardens, the state apartments, and the picture-gallery; indeed, on any other day it was easy to gain admission if the Squire was at home, for Hubert Vavasour, from his youth upwards, had always been incapable of refusing anybody anything in reason. If "my lady" happened to be mistress of the position, success was not quite such a certainty.

I think we have done our duty by the mansion; it is almost time to say something about its inmates.

CHAPTER II.

MEA CULPA.

THERE were all sorts of rooms at Dene, ranging through all degrees of luxury, from magnificence down to comfort. To the last class certainly belonged one especial apart-ment, which from time immemorial had been called "the Squire's own." For many generations this had repre-sented the withdrawing-room, the council-chamber, the study, and the divan of the easy-going potentates who had ruled the destinies of the house of Vavasour; if their authority over the rest of the mansion was sometimes disputed, *here* at least they reigned supreme. There was easy access from without, by a door opening on a narrow winding walk that led through thick shrubberies into the stables, so that the Squires were enabled to welcome in their sanctum, unobserved, such modest and retiring com-rades as, from the state of their apparel or of their nerves, did not feel equal to the terrors of the grand entrance. Hither also they were wont to resort as a sure refuge, whenever they chanced to be worsted in any domestic skirmish: though tradition preserves the names of several imperious and powerful Chatelaines, and chronicles their prowess, not one appears to have forced or even assailed these entrenchments. It almost seemed as if provision had been made against a sudden surprise; for, at the extremity of the passage leading to the main part of the building, were two innocent-looking green-baized doors, with great weights so cunningly adjusted, that one, if not both of them, was sure to escape from weak or unwary hands, and to close with an awful thunderous bang, that went rolling along the vaulted stone roof, till even a Dutch garrison would have been roused from its slumbers. Very, very rarely had the rustle of feminine garments been heard within these sacred precincts; hardly ever, indeed, since the times of wild Philip Vavasour—"The Red Squire"—who, if all tales are true, entertained singularly limited notions as to his own marital duties, and enormously extensive ones as to *les droits de seigneurie*.

It was a large, square, low-browed room, lined on two sides with presses and bookcases of black walnut wood, that, from their appearance, might have been placed there when it was built. The furniture all matched these, though evidently of quite recent date; the chairs, at least, being constructed to meet every requirement of modern laziness or lassitude. An immense mantelpiece of carved white marble, slightly discoloured by wood-smoke, rose nearly to the vaulted ceiling, in the centre of which were the crest and arms of the family, wrought in porphyry. There were two windows, large enough to let in ample light, in spite of heavy stone mullions and armorial shields on every other pane—the south one looking to the garden-front, the west into a quiet old-fashioned bowling-green, enclosed by yew hedges thick and even as an ancient rampart, and trained at the corners into the shape of pillars crowned with vases. Not a feature of the

place seems to have been altered since the times when
some stout elderly Cavalier may have smoked a digestive
pipe in that centre arbour; or later, when some gallant
of Queen Anne's court may have doffed delicately his
velvet coat, laying it like an offering at Sacharissa's feet,
ere he proceeded to win her father's favour by losing any
number of games.

A pleasant room at all hours, it is unusually picturesque
at the moment we speak of, from the effects of many-co-
loured light and shade. A hot August day is fast drawing
to its close; the sun is so level, that it only just clears
the yews sufficiently to throw into strong relief, against
a dark background, the *torso* of a sitting figure which is
well worth a second glance.

You look upon a man past middle age, large-limbed,
vast-chested, and evidently of commanding stature, with
proportions not yet too massive for activity; indeed, his
bearing may well have gained in dignity what it has lost
in grace. The face is still more remarkable. Searching
through the numberless portraits that line the picture-
gallery, you will hardly find a dozen where the personal
beauty for which the Vavasours have long been proverbial
is more strikingly exemplified than in their present re-
presentative. There are lines of silver—not unfrequent
—in the abundant chestnut hair and bushy whiskers; but
54 years have not traced 10 wrinkles on the high white
forehead, nor filled the outline of the well-cut aquiline
features, nor altered the clearness of the healthy, bright
complexion, nor dimmed the pleasant light of the large
frank blue eyes. There is a fault, certainly—the want of
decision, about the mouth and all the lower part of the
face; but even this you are not disposed to cavil much

at, after hearing once or twice Hubert Vavasour's ready, ringing laugh, and watching his kindly smile. His manner had that rare blending of gentle courtesy with honest cordiality, that the rudest stoic finds irresistibly attractive: you never could trace in it the faintest shade of condescension, or aggravating affability. Presiding at his own table, talking to a tenant at the cover-side, discussing the last opera with the fair Duchess of Darlington, or smoking the peaceful midnight cigar with an old comrade, the Squire of Dene seemed to be, and really was, equally happy, natural, and *at home*.

At this particular moment the expression of his pleasant face was unusually grave, and there was a cloud on his open brow, not of anger or vexation, but decidedly betokening perplexity. He was evidently pondering deeply over words that had just been addressed to him by the only other occupant of the "study."

The latter was a tall man, slightly and gracefully built, apparently about 30; his pale, quiet face had no remarkable points of beauty, except very brilliant dark eyes, looking larger and brighter from the half-circles under them, and a mouth, which was simply perfect. You could not glance at him, however, without being reminded of all those stories of unfortunate patricians, foiled in their endeavours to escape because they *could* not look the coal-heaver, or rag-merchant, or clerk, whose clothes they wore. If the whim had possessed Sir Alan Wyverne to array himself, for the nonce, in the loudest and worst-assorted colours that ever lent additional vulgarity to the person of a Manchester "tiger," it is probable that the travestie would have been too palpable to be amusing; he would still have looked precisely as he did, now and ever—from the crown of his small head to the sole of his slender foot—"thoroughbred all through."

The intelligence, which seemed to have involved the Squire in doubt and disquietude, was just this. Five minutes ago he had looked upon Wyverne only as his favourite nephew: he had scarcely had time to get accustomed to him in the new light of a possible son-in-law; for the substance of Alan's brief confession was, that, in the course of their afternoon's ride, he had wooed and (provisionally) won his fair cousin Helen.

Now, when the head of a family has five or six marriageable females to dispose of, forming a beautiful sliding-scale from "thirty off" downwards, his feelings, on hearing that one is to be taken off his hands, are generally those of unmixed exhilaration. Under such circumstances, the most prudent of "parents" is apt to look rather hopefully than captiously into the chances of the future *ménage:* he is fain to cry out, like the "heavy father," "Take her, you rascal, and make her happy!" and indeed acts up to every part of the stage direction, with the trifling exception of omitting to hand over the bulky note-case or the "property" purse of gold. But it is rather a different affair when the damsel in question is an only daughter, fair to look upon, and just in her nineteenth summer. *Then* it will be seen, how a man of average intellect can approve himself at need, keenly calculating in foresight, unassailable in arguments, and grandiloquent on the duties of paternity. His stern sagacity tramples on the roses, with which our romance would surround Love in a Cottage. It is no use trying to put castles in Spain into settlements, when even Irish estates are narrowly scrutinized. Perhaps we never were very sanguine about our expectancies, but till this instant we never regarded them with such utter depression and humility of spirit. Our cheery host of yesternight— he who was so convivially determined on that "other bottle before we join tho ladies"—has vanished suddenly. In his stead there sits One, filling his arm-chair as though it were a judgment-seat, and freezing our guilty hearts with his awful eye. Our hopes are blighted so rapidly, that, before tho hour is out, not one poor leaf is left of the garland that late bloomed so freshly. We have only one aim and object in life now—to flee from that dread presence as quickly as we may, albeit in worse plight than that of Sceva's sons. How sorry we are that we spoke!

But Hubert Vavasour's voice was not angry, nor even cold. If there was the faintest accent of reproach there, it surely was unintentional; but in its gravity was something of sadness.

"Alan, would it not have been better to have spoken first to me?"

His own conscience, more than that simple question or the tone in which it was uttered, made Wyverne's cheek flush as he answered it.

"Dear Uncle Hubert, I own it was a great fault. I am so sorry for not having told you the secret first, that I hardly know how to ask even *you* to forgive me. But will you believe that there was no *malice prepense?* I swear, that, when I went out this afternoon, I had no more idea of betraying myself to Helen than I had of proposing to any Princess-Royal. I am sure I have no more right to aspire to one than the other. But wo were riding fast and carelessly through Holmo Wood; a branch caught Helen's *sombrero*, and held it fast. I went back

for it—we could not pull up for a second or two. When
I joined her again, she was trying to put in order some
rebellious tresses which had escaped from their net; the
light shot down through the leaves on the dark ripples
of hair; there was the most delicious flush you can
fancy on her cheek, and her lips and eyes were laughing—so merrily! I don't believe that the luck of painters
ever let them dream of anything half so lovely. I suppose
I've seen as many fair faces as most men of my age, and
I ought to be able to keep my head (if not my heart) by
this time. Well—*it went*, on the instant. I had no more
self-control or forethought than a schoolboy in his first
love. Before I was aware, I had said words that I ought
never to have spoken, but which are very, very hard to
unsay. Don't ask me what she answered. I should have
been still unworthy of those words, if, since my manhood
began, I had never done one ill deed, never thrown one
chance away. Uncle Hubert, you can't blame me as
much as I despise myself. The idea of a man's having
got through a good fortune and the best years of his life,
without having learnt—when to hold his tongue!"

The clouds had been clearing fast on Vavasour's face
while the other was speaking, and the sun broke out, suddenly, in a kind, pleasant smile. Probably more than one
feeling was busy with him then, which it would have been
hard to separate or analyze. The father's heart swelled
with pride and love as he heard of this last crowning
triumph of a beauty, that, from childhood upwards, he
had held to be peerless. Indeed, he was absurdly fond of
Helen, and had spoiled her so consistently, that no one
could understand why the *demoiselle* (who certainly *had* a
will of her own) was not more imperious and wayward.

Besides this, the Squire's strong natural sense of humour
was gratified. It amused him unspeakably to see his
calm, impassible nephew for once so embarrassed as actually to have been betrayed into blushing. More than all,
gay memories of his own youth and manhood came troop-
ing up fast, some faint and distant, some so near and
brightly-coloured that they almost seemed tangible—
vanishing and reappearing capriciously, as one fair vision
chased another from light into shade, like elves holding
revel under a midsummer moon.

True, the days of his gipsyhood were past and gone;
but the spirit of the Zingaro had tarried with Vavasour
longer than with most men, if indeed it was even yet
extinct. He could not help owning that, if the same
temptation had assailed himself at the same age, he would
have yielded quite as easily as Wyverne had done that
day, with perhaps rather less of prudent scruple, and with
more utter contempt of consequences. Though he had
seldom given grounds to Lady Mildred for grave accusa-
tion or even suspicion, gayer gallant never breathed since
Sir Gawaine died. A chivalrous delicacy and high sense
of honour had borne him (and others) scathless through
many fiery trials; yet—not so long ago—hearts had
quivered at the sound of his musical voice, like reeds
shaken by the wind. Few men had achieved more con-
quests with less loss to victor and vanquished; for he was
satisfied with the surrender of a beleaguered city without
giving it up to pillage. Flesh is weak, we know: it would
be rash to assert that, in his hot youth, Hubert Vavasour
had never regretted a lost opportunity; but perhaps he
did not sleep less soundly now, because of all the lost
souls who, on either side of the grave, live in torment, not

one could lay its ruin at his door. Two or three reputations slightly compromised is surely not an immoderate allowance for a *viveur* of five-and-thirty years' standing, and need scarcely entail indulgence in poppies or mandragora. I think it speaks well for the presiding judge if, when a young offender is brought up before the Council of the Elders, those ancient memories stand forth as witnesses for the defence.

So the Squire's tone was cheery and hearty as ever, when he replied to Alan's rather unsatisfactory explanation, and there was a laugh in his eyes.

"It must have been a terrible temptation, for the mere recollection of it makes you poetical. That period about 'the sunlight on the rippled hair' would have done credit to a laureate in love. Seriously, my dear boy, I'm not angry with you; and I don't feel inclined to blame you much. I only meant that if you had spoken first to me, you would have heard one or two things not pleasant to hear, which *must* be told you now, and which had better have been said earlier."

"Uncle Hubert," Wyverne said, gently, "don't worry yourself with going through all the objections which make the affair impracticable. I know them so well. It is easy to give up hopes that one never had any right to cherish. Of course it is clear what you and Aunt Mildred ought to say. See, I accept your decision beforehand. I promise you that I won't murmur at it, even to myself, and I shall not like any one of you a bit the worse. It was written that Helen should be my first serious love, and my last too, I fancy. *Kismet*—it is my fate; but that is no reason why *hers* should be bound up with it."

The ruffle of brief emotion had passed away from his

quiet face, and it had settled into its wonted calmness; though at that instant the happiness of two lives was swaying in the balance, it betrayed no disquietude by the shadow of a sign.

Hubert Vavasour rose and laid his hand upon the speaker's shoulder. There was nothing of mirth left now in the expression of his features; all their grand outline was softened in a solemn tenderness, and his strong voice was low and tremulous as a woman's.

"I have not deserved to be so misunderstood, and—by you. Alan, you are my only sister's son, and I have loved you all your life long like my own. You were too young when your mother died to remember how I mourned her. You never knew either that, when I said good-bye to her, after the last Sacrament, I promised her, as plainly as I could speak for tears, that I would always stand fast by you and Gracie. I wish other promises were as easy to keep faithfully. Do you suppose that my interest in you ceased with my guardianship, though my right of interference did? In spite of everything that has happened, there is no man living to whom I would give Helen so readily as to yourself. I am not going to trifle with you. As far as my consent to your marriage can help you, you have it freely; God's blessing go with it. Now —will you listen patiently while I tell you of difficulties in the way?"

If a life dearer than his own had depended on Alan Wyverne's saying anything intelligible at that moment, he could not have saved it by the utterance of one word; but there was eloquence enough in the long white fingers, which closed round his uncle's with the gripe of a giant.

The Squire sate down again, leaning his forehead on his

hand that shook ever so little, keeping his face, so, half shaded. He was a bad dissembler, and the effort to speak cheerfully was painfully apparent.

"Alan, have you any idea how the account stands between the world—taking it as a commercial world—and the Vavasours of Dene? I don't see how you should have; for, besides your aunt, your cousin Max, and myself, not half-a-dozen people, I believe and hope, know the real state of affairs. There is no bankruptcy court for *us*, or I should have been in it years ago. There were very, very heavy encumbrances on the property when I came into it, and—see—I dare not look you in the face—they are nearly doubled now. I can give no account of my stewardship; but I suppose play is about the only extravagance I have not indulged in; and "my lady"—mind. I don't blame her—is not a much better economist. I wonder our family has lasted so long. It has never produced a clever *financier*, I need hardly say; but, more than that, not one Vavasour for the last seven generations has had the common sense or courage to look his difficulties in the face, and retrench accordingly. Unluckily, rolling debts are not like rolling stones; they *do* increase in volume, diabolically. Well, it's no use beating about the bush or making half confessions. Here is the truth in six words: a quarter of a million would hardly clear us. They said I gave up the hounds because I had got too heavy to ride up to them; perhaps you will guess if *that* was the real reason. It was more as a sop to keep my conscience quiet than anything else though; for £3000 a year saved only keeps a little interest down, and leaves the principal as big and black as ever. When Max came of age, it was absolutely necessary to make some arrangement. We cut off the entail of all property, sold some outlying farms, and replaced the old mortgages by new ones on rather better terms. But—we raised more money. Max owed seven or eight thousand, and I wanted nearly as much to go on with. He behaved very well about it, only binding me down by one stipulation—that I should cut no timber; for it was suggested then that £30,000 worth might be felled and scarcely missed. He had a fancy, that whether Dene stayed with us or passed away to others, it should keep its green wreath unshorn. It looks as if there were some sympathetic link between our fortunes and our forests—we have cherished and spared them so for centuries: if any White Lady (like her of Avenel) watches over our house, I am very sure she is a Dryad. Alan, the worst is still to tell."

He paused for a minute or so, clearing his throat once or twice nervously, all to no purpose, for when he spoke again his voice was strangely husky and uncertain.

"You don't know much of Newmanham? The greatest iron-founder there is one Schmidt, a German Jew, whose father was naturalized. They say he is worth half a million. When a man of the people has made money up to that mark, he is always mad to invest in land. Only six months ago, I found out that Schmidt had bought up every shilling of mortgage on this property, and—and—by G—d, I believe he means to foreclose."

The Squire stopped again, and then broke out into a harsh unnatural laugh.

"The patriarch knows where to pitch his tent, doesn't he, Alan? His spies have searched out the length and breadth of the land already, and I dare say he knows as much about the woods now as I do. His lines will fall in

pleasant places when he has cast out the Hittite. Dene
would be no bad spot to found a family in. Twenty
quarterings ought to leave savour enough about the grey
walls, to drown somewhat of the Newmanham *fumier*.
Leah has been prolific, they tell me. The picture-gallery
will be a nice place for the little Israelites to disport
themselves in in bad weather, and the Crusaders and Cavaliers will look down benevolently 'on the young Caucasians
all at play.' Perhaps he will offer something handsome, to
be allowed to take our name. Faith, he may have it! I
don't see why we should keep *that* to ourselves, when all
the rest is gone."

The bitter laugh ended in something like a sob, and the
lofty head sank down lower still. Looking on Wyverne's
colourless face, you would not have guessed that its pallor
could deepen so intensely as it did when any strong emotion possessed him. During the last five minutes it had
grown whiter by several shades.

"It is punishment enough for all my faults and follies,"
he said, "to be forced to listen to such words as these, and
to feel myself utterly helpless and useless. Uncle Hubert,
I remember, when every one thought my ruin was complete, you came the first to offer help, and you never
dreamt of taking interest by making me listen to advice
or reproaches. Now, I hear of *your* troubles for the first
time, and I find that I have come in, seasonably, to add
another grave embarrassment. What a luxury benevolence
must be, when it meets with such a prompt return. If
you knew how I hate myself!"

The elasticity of Vavasour's gallant spirit had quite
shaken off by this time the momentary depression, of
which he was already heartily ashamed. He threw back

his stately head with a gesture full of haughty grace, as if about to confront a palpable enemy or physical danger, and his voice rang out again, bold and musical and clear.

"Don't speak so despondingly, Alan. My weakness has infected you, I suppose? I don't wonder at it. I am not often so cowardly; indeed it is the first time I have broken down so, and I think it will be long before I disgrace myself so again. Yes, you would help me if you could, just as I would help you. I know you, boy, and the race you come of. *Bon sang ne peut metir.* Whatever happens, I shall never repent having given you Helen. But I want you to see your line clearly; it isn't all open country before you. Listen. I am certain "my lady" has some projects in her head. She thinks her daughter fair enough to be made the pillar and prop of our family edifice. Poor child! that slender neck would break under half such a burden. Now, if either of the young ones is to be turned into an Atlas, surely Max ought to take the part. But he is too proud, or too indolent, or too fond of his comforts, to give himself any trouble in the matter. Faith, I like him the better for it. I think I would rather see the old house go to ruin respectably than propped by Manchester money-bags. *Que diable!* Each one to his taste. I don't imagine that your aunt's visions have assumed shape or substance yet. The coming son-in-law and his millions are still in cloud-land, where I hope for all our sakes they will remain. For my own part, if Crœsus were to woo and win Helen to-morrow, I don't see how it would help us much; besides, it is quite probable that he would have gone away rejected. If you had never spoken, you cannot suppose that I would have seen her sacrificed. Still, I warn you that her ladyship has some ideas of the sort floating on her diplomatic brain, so you must not be disappointed if her consent and concurrence are not quite so heartily given as mine."

"I have a great respect for Aunt Mildred's sagacity," Wyverne answered, gravely; "whatever policy she might adopt I am sure would be founded on sound principles, and carried out wisely and well. It is very rash to run counter to any plan of hers, even if it be in embryo; I doubt if one ought even to hope for success. My dear uncle, every word you say makes me feel more keenly how wrongly I acted this unlucky afternoon."

The Squire held out his hand again; the strong, honest grasp tingled through every fibre of the other's frame, bringing hope and encouragement with it, like a draught of some rare cordial.

"Alan, I have heard of many rash and wild deeds of yours, never of one that made you unworthy of your blood or mine. It would be rather too good if *I* were to cast mere extravagance in your teeth. I won't hear any more evil auguries or self-reproaches. My word is passed, and I shall not take it back again till you or Helen ask me to do so. We will talk more of your prospects another time. As long as I live you will do well enough; afterwards we shall see. Thank God, she is the only child I have to provide for. Don't be down-hearted, boy! The Vavasours of Dene are a tough, tenacious race, and die hard, if all tales are true; we are not *aux abois* yet. "Vast are the resources of futurity," as some great and good man observed; perhaps we shall pull through, after all. At any rate, we will not be tormented before our time. The thing which is most on my mind at this moment is— who is to tell this afternoon's work to 'my lady?'"

The Squire's bright blue eyes were glittering with suppressed humour as he said the last words, merrily, as if he had never heard of such things as troubles or mortgages. Alan could not help smiling at his uncle's evident eagerness to be spared the responsibility of ambassador.

"I fancy the worst is known to my poor aunt an hour ago. Helen went straight to the *boudoir* when we came in; she wished to tell everything herself, and immediately. It is the best way. Poor child! I hope she has had half the success that I have met with; one cannot count on such good fortune, though."

Vavasour's face was radiant with satisfaction, it was an unspeakable relief to him to hear that the official communication had been made.

"What a brave girl that is!" he said, with profound admiration; "she has 10 times her father's courage. Alan, confess now, you didn't try to be first—*there?* Well, let us pray for light winds, for we may have to tack more than once before we fetch the haven where we would be. But, as the sailors say, 'we can't tell what the weather will be till we get outside,' so—*vogue la galère!* Hark! there goes the dinner gong; go and dress directly; of all days in the year this is the last on which to keep her ladyship waiting."

CHAPTER III.

A "MOTHER OF ENGLAND."

IF the Squire's study was the most comfortable room in the Dene, the prettiest. and to a refined taste the most attractive, without contradiction, was "my lady's chamber." It was of moderate size, on the first floor, at an angle of the building; two deep oriels to the south and east caught every available gleam of sunshine in winter, while in summer-time many cunning devices within and without kept heat and glare at bay The walls were hung with dark purple silk, each panel set in a frame of polished oak; bright borderings and bouquets of flowers inwoven, prevented the effect from being sombre; the damask of the furniture, as well as the velvet of the *portières* and curtains (these last almost hidden, now, in clouds of muslin and lace), matched the hangings exactly. There was as much of buhl and marqueterie and mosaic in the room as it could *well* hold—no more; no appearance of crowding or redundance of ornament. On each of the panels was one picture, of the smallest cabinet size, and on three of the tables lay cases of miniatures, priceless from their extreme rarity or intrinsic beauty; and all sorts of costly trifles, jewelled, enamelled, and chased, were scattered about with a studied artistic carelessness. The delicate *mignardise* pervading every object around you was very agreeable at first, and finished by producing the oppressive, unhealthy effect of an atmosphere over-laden with rare perfumes. Such an impression of un-reality was left, that you fancied all the pretty vision would vanish, like a scene of fairy-land, at the intrusion of any rude unauthorized mortal, such as some "mighty hunter," bearing traces of field and flood from cap to spur. That the hallowed precincts had never been profaned by so incongruous an apparition since Lady Mildred Vava-sour began to reign, it is unnecessary to say. Her hus-band came there very seldom; her son, rather often, when he was at home. With these two exceptions, the threshold had remained for years inviolated by masculine footstep, as that of the Taurian Artemis. Few even of her own sex had the *entrée*, and of these, only three or four ventured to penetrate there uninvited. It was a privilege more difficult to obtain than the gold key of the *petits apparte-mens* at Trianon.

The whole tone and aspect of the *boudoir* was marvel-lously in keeping with the exterior of its mistress. She occupied it on that August evening, alone, if we might except a Maltese lion-dog, sleeping in lazy beatitude, half buried in a purple velvet cushion, like a small snow-ball. It may be as well to say, at once, that this latter personage, though a very important one in his own sphere, gifted with remarkable intelligence, and capable of strong attachments, has nothing on earth to do with the story

It would be difficult as well as uncourteous to guess at Lady Mildred Vavasour's precise age; her dark hair has lost perhaps somewhat of its luxuriance, but little of its glossy

o 2

shcen; her pale cheek—tinged with a faint colour (either
by nature or art) exactly in the right place—and white
brow, are still polished and smooth as Carrara marble;
and her small, slight, delicate figure, with which the tiniest
of hands and feet harmonize so perfectly, retains its graceful roundness of outline.

Why is it that, after one brief glance—giving the lady
credit for all these advantages—we feel sure that she has
advanced already far into the maturity of matronhood?
Perhaps, when the mind has been restless and the thoughts
busy for a certain number of years, those years *will* not be
dissembled, and, however carefully the exterior may have
been conserved, traces of toil, sensible, if not visible, remain.   There is no short cut to Political science any
more than to Pure mathematics; not without labour and
anxiety, which must tell hereafter, can their crowns be
won; and Foresight, though certainly the more useful
faculty of the two, is sometimes more wearing than
Memory.

Now, in her own line, Lady Mildred Vavasour stood
unrivalled; she was the very Talleyrand of domestic
diplomacy.   I do not mean to infer that she was pre-
eminent among those Machiavels in miniature, who
glide into supremacy over their own families impercep-
tibly, and maintain their position by apparent non-resistance, commanding always, while they seem to obey.   In
her own case such cleverness would have been wasted.
She no more dreamt of interfering with any of the Squire's
tastes or pursuits, than he did with hers; and was perfectly content with complete freedom of action, sure of
having every whim gratified.   Indeed, up to the present
time her talent had been employed in singularly disin-

terested ways. Very, very seldom had she acted with her
own advantage, or that of any one closely connected with
her, in view. The position of the Vavasours was such as
never to tempt them to look for aggrandizement; the
Squire represented his county, as a matter of course, but
there was not a particle of ambition in his nature; and
her son had always steadily refused to allow his mother's
talents or influence to be exercised on his behalf. But
she had a vast circle of acquaintance, both male and
female, and when any one of these was in a difficulty, he
or she constantly resorted to Lady Mildred, sure of her
counsel, if not of her co-operation. She gave one or both,
not in the least because she was good-natured, but because she liked it. She liked to hold in her little white
hand the threads of a dozen at once of those innocent
plots and conspiracies, which are carried on so satisfactorily
beneath the smooth, smiling surface of this pleasant world
of ours. Granting that the means were trivial, and the
end unworthy—it was almost grand to see how her cool
calculation, fertile invention, and dauntless courage, rose
up to battle with difficulty or danger. She loved a com-
plicated affair, and went into it heart and soul; no one
could say how many cases that had been given up as hopeless, she had carried through auspiciously, with an exceptional good fortune. With mere politics she meddled
very seldom (though she never sought for a place or pro-
motion for one of her own favourites, or an adopted *protégé*,
without obtaining it), but in her own circle there scarcely
was a marriage made or marred of which the result might
not have been traced to the secret police of Lady Mildred's *boudoir*. If she had a *specialité*, it was the knack
of utterly crushing and abolishing—in a pleasant, noise-

less way—a dangerous Detrimental. The victim scarcely ever suspected from what quarter the arrow came, but often entertained, in after-days, a great respect and regard for the fatal Atalantè.

Yes, the work had told even on that calm, well-regulated nature: Lady Mildred's smile was still perilously fascinating; but a certain covert subtlety, when you looked closer, half neutralized its power; and the bright, dark eyes were now and then disagreeably searching and keen. At such times you could only marvel at the manifest contradiction; with all the outward and visible signs of youth about her, she looked unnaturally older than her age.

In all probability, at no one period of her life had she been more attractive than at the present moment. There was extant a miniature taken before she was 20, and the resemblance of that portrait to the living original was very striking. One charm she certainly never could have possessed—*La beauté du Diable.*

Now we are on the subject, I wish some one would explain this same paradox or misnomer. Do we take it in a passive sense, and suppose that, if any emotion of love could fall on "the blasted heart"—like water on molten iron—it would be stirred by that especial type of loveliness—seen now so seldom, but remembered so well? It may well be so. *Væ miseris!* Every other phase of mortal and immortal beauty has 10,000 representatives in Gehenna, save only *this.* Surely few lost spirits carry the stamp of innocence on their brows, even so far as the broad gate with the dreary legend over its door—"Leave hope behind you." Seen very seldom—only when across the great Gulf, the souls in torment catch a glimpse of angelic features melting in intense, unavailing pity; but, perchance, well remembered, for where should freshness and innocence be found, if not in the faces of the Cherubim? And his punishment would be incomplete, if it were given to the Prince of Hell to forget sights and sounds familiar to the Son of the Morning.

It is worth while to realize how dwarfed, and trivial, and childish, appear all tales of human ruin and shame and sorrow, by the side of the weird primeval tragedy. Well: the brute creation sympathizes with *us* in our pain; but who are we, that we should presume to pity a fallen archangel? Truly, pious and right-minded men have done so, in all simplicity and sincerity. The story of the Perthshire minister is always quoted among the *Traits of Scotch Humour;* but I am sure the amiable zealot intended nothing irreverent, and saw nothing grotesque in his prayer. He had exhausted, you know, his memory and imagination in interceding not only for his own species and the lower orders of animals, but for "every green thing upon the earth" besides. He paused at last and took breath; then he went on—rather diffidently, as if conscious of treading on perilous gound, but in an accent plaintively persuasive—

"An' noo, ma freends, let us praigh for the De'il ; naebody praighs for the puir De'il!"

That is not a bad digression—taking it *as* a digression —from the boudoir of a *petite maîtresse* to the bottomless pit. Whatever connection may ultimately be established between the two, I am aware that it is neither usual nor justifiable to place them in such close proximity.

But, here, I make my first and last act of contrition for all such divagations, in season or out of season, past, pre-

sent, and to come.   Reader of mine! you have always the
resource (which I would were available in society) of
banishing your interlocutor when he bores you, by skip-
ping the paragraph or throwing the book aside.   I may
not hope to instruct you; it is quite enough if your interest and yourself are kept awake.   Whether this object
would be promoted by writing "to order," is more than
doubtful.   If one's movements are naturally awkward and
slow, they will scarcely gain in grace with the fetters on.
Let us not force our talent, such as it is.   Few qualities
are more useful or estimable than that grave pertinacity
of purpose which never loses sight for a moment of the
end it has had in view all along.   But then, one must
have a purpose to start with; and up to the present point,
this volume is guiltless of any such element of success.
It is in the nature of some to be desultory; and there are
heretics who think that the prizes of Life—let alone those
of authorship—would hardly be worth the winning, if one
were bound down under heavy penalties to go on straight
to the goal, never turning aside for refreshment by the
way.

Peccavimus, et peccabimus.   If this literary ship must
be shattered on rocks ahead, we will, at least, make no
obeisance to the powers that have ordained the wreck.
O younger son of Telamon! you have spoken well, if not
wisely.   The wrath of adverse gods is mighty, and hath
prevailed; but let us die as we have lived—impenitent
and self-reliant, without benefit of Athène.

It is nearly time, though, to go back to Lady Mildred.
She is still sitting where we left her—I am ashamed to
say how long ago—in the same attitude of indolent grace;
a very refreshing picture to look upon after such a sultry

day, the ideal of repose and comfortable coolness. No mortal eye had ever seen "my lady's" cheek unbecomingly flushed, or her lips blue with cold; it must be confessed that she seldom threw a chance away in taking care of herself, and had a wholesome dread of the caprices of our English atmosphere. She had been amusing herself for the last two hours with one of the pleasant paper-covered *novelettes* which flow in a stream (happily) perennial from that modest fountain-head in the Burlington Arcade, mollifying our insular manners, and not permitting us to be brutified. The labour of perusing even this unremittingly, seemed to be too much for the fair student, for ever and anon the volume would sink down on her lap, and she would pause for several minutes, musing on its philosophy —or on graver things—with half-closed eyes.

While she was indulging in one of these reveries or semi-siestas, a quick, elastic step came down the long corridor. Lady Mildred could not have been dozing (nobody ever does allow that they have been sleeping— out of their beds), for she recognized the footfall instantly, though it brushed the deep-piled carpet so lightly as to have been to most ears inaudible: simultaneously with the timid knock that seemed to linger on the panel, her clear quiet voice said—

" Come in, my Helen ! "

In these prosaic days of Realism, when Oreads and Undines, and other daughters of the elements, have become somewhat coy and unattainable, it would be hard to conjure up a fairer vision than that which now stood hesitating on the threshold. I will try to give you a faint idea of Helen Vavasour as she appeared then, in the spring-tide of her marvellous loveliness.

She had inherited the magnificent stature for which her
family had for centuries been remarkable, united to the
excessive refinement of contour and delicacy of feature
which had made "the Dene beauties" world-renowned.
Her figure, though very slight, betrayed no signs of fragility, and you guessed that the development that three
more years must bring would make it quite faultless.
Her hair was darker than her mother's by many shades—
equally fine and silky, but thrice as luxuriant; its intense
black was relieved by a sheen of deep glossy blue, such
as Loxias may have worshipped in the tresses of the
violet-haired daughter of Pitané. Her complexion was
much fairer than is often found where all the other points
are so decidedly a brunette's; dazzling from its transparent
purity, it was never brilliant, except when some passing
emotion deepened the subdued shade of delicate, tender
pink into the fuller rose-tint that lines a rare Indian shell.
So with her eyes—long, large, and velvet-soft, they stole
upon you at first with a languid, dreamy fascination; but
you never realized their hidden treasures till amusement,
or love, or anger made them glitter like the Southern
Cross. It was one of those faces bearing even in childhood the impress of pride and decision, over which half a
century may pass without rendering one line in them
harsher or harder.

If ever you have taken up a plain photograph, untouched
by the miniature-painter, of the form and features (for the
moment) deemed fairest of all, you will sympathize with
my utter dissatisfaction in reviewing this abortive attempt at portraiture. The stereoscope brings out a certain similitude; but what a cold colourless parody on the
glorious reality! That very fixedness of expression—in

the original so perpetually varied—makes it an insult to
our incarnate idol.

Long and attentive study, for her own or her friends'
benefit, had taught Lady Mildred to read very fluently
the language of eyes; the glance of the Expert drew their
secret from Helen's, during those few seconds while she
stood hesitating in the doorway; and a shy, conscious
happiness glowing round her like a soft halo, made surmise
certainty.

O laughter-loving daughter of Dioné! your divinity is
trampled in the dust, and none worship now at the shrines
of Aphrodité, Astarte, or Ashtaroth; but one feels tempted
at times to turn Pagan again, were it only to believe in
your presence and power. Other, and younger, and fairer
faces have borne tokens of having met you in the wood,
since your breath left a freshness and radiance on the
swart features of the false sea-rover, that carried Dido's
heart by storm.

Yes, Lady Mildred guessed the truth at once, and all
her self-control was needed to repress a sign of vexation
and impatience, which very nearly escaped her; it bore
her through, though, triumphantly. Nothing could be
more placable and propitious than her smile; nothing
more playfully encouraging than her gesture, as she
beckoned Helen to her side:—

"My darling! what has happened in your ride to agitate
you so? I can see you are not much hurt. Come and
make confession instantly."

This was apparently the young lady's intention, for she
had evidently come straight to the boudoir after dismount-
ing: she was still in her riding-dress, and had only taken
off her Spanish hat. While her mother was speaking she

came near with the swift, springy step which made her
walk inimitable, and knelt down by the low couch, half
concealing her glowing face and sparkling eyes.

If there is any written manual adapted to such rifle-
practice (I mean where a young woman has to fire off at
her parent a piece of intelligence particularly important or
startling), I fancy, here, it would run thus—"At the word
'three,' sink down at once on the right knee, six inches
to the right and 12 inches to the rear of the left heel, and
square with the foot, which is to be under the body and
upright"—the great difference being that the fair re-
cruit is "*not* to fix the eye steadfastly on an object in
front."

So far, certainly, Helen acted up to the formula provided for her case; but she had not been much drilled,
and was indeed singularly exempt from most of the little
weaknesses, conventionalisms, and *minauderies* which are,
justly or unjustly, attributed to modern damosels. Natures like hers affect, as a rule, no more diffidence than
they feel, and are seldom unnecessarily demonstrative,
however small and select their audience, and however
dramatic the piece they are playing. So, after a few
minutes' silence, she looked up and said, quite quietly
and simply—

"Mamma, Alan asked me this afternoon to marry him;
and—I love him dearly."

The two voices were strangely alike in their accent and
inflexions; but the girl's voice, even when, as now, somewhat tremulous and uncertain, was mellower in its rich
cadences, fuller and rounder in its music.

Lady Mildred clasped her daughter's waist, and bent
down to kiss her, repeatedly, with passionate tenderness.

When the close embrace was ended, she lingered yet for a few seconds with her cheek pillowed on Helen's forehead; during those seconds her features were set, and her lips tense and rigid; that brief interval of self-indulgence lasted just so long as it would have taken her to mutter the words—"It shall never be."

Now, mark; the daughter was kneeling at her mother's feet, as she might have knelt to say the first prayer of infancy; she had just told the secret which involved her life's hope of happiness—whether wrongly or rightly founded it matters not; the mother sate there, with firm, cool resolve at her heart to crush the hope and frustrate the purpose; and yet she kissed her child without shivering or shrinking. To our rough common-sense it would seem, that caress more cruel in its falsehood, more base in its deliberate treachery, never was bestowed since that one over which angels wept and devils shouted for joy—the kiss given in the Garden of Gethsemane.

But who are we, that we should criticise the policy of a Mother of England, cavil at her concessions to expediency, or question the rectitude of her intentions? They are white-hot Protestants, many of them, but none the less do they cherish and act upon the good old Jesuit maxim—"The end justifies the means." Unluckily, sometimes even *their* sagacity and foresight are baffled in guessing what the end of all will be. You have read *Aspen Court*, of course? Do you remember Cyprian Heywood's definition of a parable?—"A falsehood in illustration of truth." "My lady" affected this convenient figure of speech a good deal; her first words now were decidedly parabolical.

"My dearest child, you have quite taken my breath

away. I cannot tell yet whether I am sorry or glad to hear this. It comes so very suddenly!"

"Ah, mamma, say at least that you are not angry—with Alan," the soft voice pleaded.

Lady Mildred did not think it necessary to remain long astounded, being always averse to unnecessary expenditure of time or trouble. So she answered, after drawing one or two deep, agitated breaths (wonderfully well done), with intense gentleness of manner and tone—

"How could I be angry, darling? Next to Max, and yourself, and your father, I think I love Alan better than anything in the world. He has been rash and wild, of course; but I believe he is quite good and steady now. I am sure he will try and make you happy. Every one will exclaim against your imprudence, and mine; but we will not look forward despondently. Only you must not be impatient; you *must* wait and hope. You don't know as well as I do what difficulties are in the way. Perhaps I ought to have foreseen what was likely to happen, when you and Alan were thrown so much together as you have been lately; but I never dreamt—" she stopped, compressing her lips as if annoyed that a truth, for once, was escaping them. "Well—never mind; confess, Helen, you did not fear that *I* should oppose your wishes? You know my first object in life is to see you happy; and I have not often contradicted you, have I, since you were old enough to have a will of your own?"

I fancy that most damsels, under similar circumstances, would have been of Miss Vavasour's opinion—"That there never was such a darling mother." She did not express it very intelligibly, though; and, indeed, it must be confessed, that the conversation from this point was of a somewhat incoherent and irrational nature. Feminine example is miraculously contagious; if the fountain of tears is once unlocked, the gentle influence of the Naïad will be sure to descend on every womanly bosom within the circle of its spray. I do not mean to imply that upon the present occasion there was any profuse weeping; but they got into a sort of *caressive* and altogether childish frame of mind—a condition very unusual with either mother or daughter. It may be questioned, if the sympathetic weakness displayed by Lady Mildred was altogether assumed. The most accomplished actresses have sometimes so identified themselves with their parts, as to ignore audience and foot-lights, and become natural in real emotion. Five minutes, however, were more than enough to restore one of the parties to her own calm, calculating self. Another yet fonder caress told Helen, as plainly as words could have done, that the audience was ended: as soon as she was alone, Lady Mildred fell back into her old quiet musing attitude. But the French novel was not taken up again; its late reader had a plot, if not a romance, of her own to interest her now. Whether the thoughts that chased one another so rapidly through that busy brain were kindly or angry, whether the glimpses of the future were gloomy or hopeful—the smooth, white brow and steady lips betrayed, neither by frown nor smile.

CHAPTER IV

A WAIF FROM A WRECK.

" Look into a man's Past, if you would understand his Present, or guess at his Future." So spake some sage, name unknown, but probably intermediate in date between the Great King and Mr M. F. Tupper. The rule is not implicitly to be relied on, but perhaps there is as much of truth in it as in most apophthegms of proverbial philosophy.

So it may save some time and trouble hereafter, if we sketch briefly now some of Alan Wyverne's antecedents; for he is to be the chief character in this story, which has no *hero*, properly so-called, nor heroine either.

The main facts are very soon told: his twenty-first birthday saw him in possession of a perfectly unencumbered estate of £12,000 a year, and all the accumulations that two paragon guardians had toiled to amass during an unusually long minority; his twenty-eighth dawned on a comparative pauper.

The last score of centuries have taught us many things; amongst others, to go down-hill with a certain caution and timidity, if not with sobriety. We never hear now of those great disasters to which the very vastness of

their proportions lent a false grandeur; where a colossal
fortune foundered suddenly, leaving on the world's surface a vortex of turbulence and terror, such as surrounds
the spot where a three-decker has gone down. The
Regent and his *roués* were wild in their generation, but
they never quite attained the antique magnificence of
recklessness. The expenses of a contested county elec-
tion 50 years back would have shown poorly by the
Ædile's balance-sheet, A. C. 65, when Cæsar laughed to
see his last *sestertium* vanish in the brilliancy of the
Circensian Games. What modern general would carry
£20,000 of debt as lightly as he did half-a-million, when
he went out to battle with the Lusitanian? If we even
hear now-a-days of a like liability, it is probably in connection with a great commercial " smash," involving
curious disclosures as to the capabilities of stamped
paper, and the extent of public credulity; but the interest of such rarely spreads west of Temple-bar. Truth
to say—however moving the tale may be to the unfor-
tunates ruined by the delinquent, there is still little romance to be extracted out of mercantile atrocities.

Nevertheless, if you only give him time, and don't
hurry him beyond his stride, a dwarf will " go to the
dogs " just as easily and surely as a giant. After our
mesquine fashion, that journey is performed so constantly,
that only some peculiarities in Alan's case make it worth
noting at all.

Few men have trodden the road to ruin with such a
perfectly smooth and even pace; there was no rush or
hurry about it from beginning to end; nothing like a
crash to attract notice or scandal. He was known to bet
high and play deep; but no one spoke of him at the

D

clubs as having lost an extraordinary stake on any one night, nor did the chroniclers of the Turf ever allude to him amongst those "hit hard" on any single event. *One* destructive element never showed itself throughout his career. It must have been gratifying to those much-abused Hetæræ to reflect (do they ever reflect at all?) that none could charge any one of the sisterhood with having aided in Wyverne's downfall. Reckless and extravagant as the son of Clinias, he escaped—at least Timandra. More than one scruple, probably, helped him to maintain a continence which soon became so well known, that the most persevering of feminine fowlers never thought of laying her snares in his way. Something might be ascribed to principles learnt at his dead mother's knee, which all the contagion of Bohemia failed quite to efface—something to a chivalrous reverence for the sex, which withheld him from deliberately abetting in its open degradation—something to the pride of race, with which he was thoroughly imbued. He loved his ancient name too dearly, to see it dragged through the dust past the statue of Achilles, at the chariot-wheels of the fairest Phryne of them all. For once—hearing a story of human folly and frailty, you asked, "*Dove la donna?*" and waited in vain for a reply

If the Sirens failed to seduce Wyverne, that was about the only peril or temptation from which he escaped scathless. Profuse hospitality all the year round in London, Leicestershire, and at his home in the North, cost something; a string of 10 horses in training (besides yearlings and untried two-year-olds), which only won when their owner had backed something else heavily, cost more: backing other men's bills *currente calamo*, receiving no

substantial considerations for so doing, cost most of all.
Alan's bold, careless handwriting was as well known in a
certain branch of commerce as the official signature on the
Bank of England's notes. There was joy in Israel when
they saw his autograph: Ezekiel and Solomon—most
cautious of their tribe (those crack bill-discounters are
always lineally descended, it would seem, from some prophet or king)—smacked their bulbous lips in satisfaction
as they clutched the paper bearing his endorsement:
their keen eyes looked three months forward into futurity,
and saw the spoil of the Egyptian secure. Alan's own
resources, though rapidly diminishing, always sufficed his
own wants; but he never tired of paying these disinter-
ested liabilities so long as his friends could furnish him with
any decent excuse for his doing so: if the defaulter failed
in making out even a shadow of a case, Wyverne still
paid, but never consorted with him afterwards. Then
the dark side of his character came out. Generous and
kind-hearted to a fault, he was at times obstinate to
relentlessness: slow to take offence or to suspect inten-
tional injury, he was yet slower in forgiving or forgetting
either: he did not trouble himself to detect the falsehood
at the bottom of any tale of distress, but against imposture
carried with a high hand he set his face as it were a millstone.

Hercules St Levant (of the Chilian Cuirassiers) would
tell you—if he could be brought to speak coherently on
the subject—that he dates his ruin from the day when he
miscalculated the extent of Sir Alan Wyverne's long-suffering or laziness. Surely, some of us can remember that
wonderful copper Captain—the round, ringing tones
tempting you with a point over the proper odds—the

scarfs and waistcoats blinding in their gorgeousness, so
"loud" that you *heard* them coming all the way up from
the distance-post—the supernatural whiskers, whose sable
volutes shaded his broad shoulders like the leaves of a
talipat-palm? Hercules was very successful at first he
must have started with a nominal capital, but he had
plenty of courage, some judgment, and more luck; so, by
dint of industry, and now and then picking up crumbs
from the table of those by whom the "good things" of
the turf are shared, he contrived to ruffle it for awhile
with the best of them. Men of mark and high estate
would meet and hold communion with him—as they have
done with deeper and darker villains—on the neutral
ground at "The Corner," without caring to inquire too
closely what Cacique had signed his commission, or on
what foughten-fields the rainbow of his ribbons was won.
With common prudence he might have held his own till
now. But St Levant was a buccaneer to the backbone:
he spent his winnings as lavishly as any one of the young
patricians whom he delighted to honour and imitate; and
took his ease in the sunshine, scorning to make the slightest provision for the season of the rains. It came at last,
in an Epsom Summer Meeting. The adverse Fates had it
all their own way there: several of the Captain's certainties were overturned, and several promising "plants"
were withered in their bud. It was the fourth "day of
rebuke and blasphemy," and still the battle went hard
against the Peruvian plunger. The Oaks dealt him the *coup-
de-grace:* it was won by an extreme outsider. Hercules
saw the number go up, and staggered out of the enclosure
like a drunken man, with hardly breath enough left to
hiss out a curse between his white lips. "Hecuba" was

one of six that Wyverne had taken with him against the field for an even thousand: her name had never been mentioned in the betting at the time, and Alan only selected her because he chanced to know her owner and breeder well.

St Levant was ruined horse-and-foot, without power or hope of redemption: that one bet would just have pulled him through. Some pleasanter engagement had kept Wyverne away from The Corner on the " comparing day," and with his usual carelessness he had even omitted to send his book down by other hands: Hercules saw a last desperate chance, and grasped at it, as drowning men will do. He appeared at the settling with his well-known betting-book (gorgeous, like all his other belongings, in green morocco and gold), but Hecuba's name was replaced by the second favourite's. He chanced to have in his possession a fac-simile of the original volume, and had copied out, in the interim, every bet it contained, with this one trifling alteration. The matter came before the authorities, of course. The discussion that ensued, though stormy (on one side), was very short and decisive: the swindler's foamy asseverations were shivered, like spray, on the granite of the other's calm, contemptuous firmness. The judges did not hesitate long in pronouncing against St Levant their sentence of perpetual banishment. All his piteous petitions addressed to Wyverne in after days to induce the latter to obtain a mitigation of the punishment, remained absolutely unanswered. There still survives—a pale, blurred shadow of his former self—as it were, the *wraith* of the Great Captain. We see occasionally a hirsute head rising above the sea of villanous figures and faces that seethe and serge against the rails of tho en-

closure: we catch glimpses of a meteoric waistcoat flashing through the surrounding seediness; and we hear a
voice, thunderous as that of the elder Ajax, dominating
the din of the meaner *mélée;* but there is no reversal of
his doom.   The poor lost spirit must ramp and roar
among the "welshers" of the outer darkness, for the paradise of the Ring is closed to him for evermore.

Everybody—including the two or three friends who
might hope to ride his horses—was sorry for Wyverne
when a heavy fall over timber laid him up, quite early in
the season, with a broken arm and collar-bone.   The only
pity was, that that fortunate accident should not have
happened three years earlier.   The indoor resources of a
country-town, where all one's associates hunt five days
a-week at least, are limited.   One morning Alan felt so
bored, that the whim seized him to look into his affairs,
and ascertain how he stood with the world: so he sent for
his solicitor (as much for the sake of having some one to
talk to as anything else), and went in at business with
great patience and determination.   The men who sat with
him on the second evening after the lawyer's arrival,
thought Wyverne looking paler and graver than usual,
but he listened to their account of the run with apparently
undiminished interest, and sympathized with his friends'
mishaps or successes as cordially as ever.   Only once his
lips shook a little as he answered in the negative a question—"If he felt in much pain?"   Yet that morning
had been a sore trial both of brain and nerve.   It is
not a pleasant time, when you have to call for the
reckoning of 10,000 follies and faults, and to *pay* it too—
when the bitter *quart d'heure de Rabelais* is prolonged
through days.

Though they arrived then at a tolerably accurate idea of the state of Alan s finances, it took months to complete the final arrangements. When everything in town and country that could well be sold had been disposed of, Wyverne was left with a life income of just as many hundreds a-year as he had started with thousands. But all his personal debts, and liabilities incurred for others, were paid in full. The only absolute luxuries that he retained (with the exception of all the presents that he had ever received) were the two best hunters in his stud, and his grey Arab, "Maimouna." That residue might have been nearly doubled, if Alan would have consented to dismantle the Abbey. But he could not help looking upon its antique furniture and fittings in the light of heirlooms. He had added little to them when he came into his inheritance: he took nothing away when he lost it. So the great, grave mansion still retained its old-fashioned and somewhat faded magnificence; and few changes, so far, were to be seen there, except that the grass grew long on the lawns, and the flowers wandered over the parterres at their own sweet will, and instead of thick reeks of unctuous smoke, only a thin blue line stole out modestly from two or three chimneys now and then in the shooting season. The game was still kept up, and the farmers watched it as jealously and zealously as if they had been keepers in their landlord's pay.

The sternest Stoic alive could scarcely have fallen into his new position more naturally, or adapted himself to its requirements more gracefully, than did that gay, care-less Epicurean. If he had any regrets for the irrevocable Past, he kept them to himself, and never wearied his friends for their sympathy or compassion; he accused no one with reference to his ruin; 1 doubt if he even blamed himself very severely. There was no more of recklessness in his conduct, than there was of despondency in his demeanour; but he comforted himself exactly as you would expect to see a man do, of good birth and breeding, and average steadiness, born to a modest competency. His experience, brief as it was, might have taught him to be somewhat sceptical as to the virtues of our human nature, more especially having regard to such trifles as truth and honesty; but no amount of punishment will beat wisdom or knowledge into a confirmed dunce or idler. His constitutional indolence may have had something to say to it; but to the last hour of his life Alan Wyverne never learnt to be suspicious, or sullen, or cynical.

To be sure, the world in this case broke through an established rule, and behaved better to him when he was at the bottom of the wheel than it had ever done at the culminating point of his fortunes. There seemed to be a general impression that he had been very badly treated by some " person or persons unknown," and it became the fashion to compassionate Wyverne (in his absence) exceedingly. People who in former days met and parted from him quite indifferently, found out suddenly that they had always been very fond of him, and contended as to who should attract him to their house in the hunting or shooting season. The Marquis of Montserrat, for instance, roused himself from where he lay, surrounded by every delight of a Mussulman's paradise, in his summer palace by the Bosphorus, to send a sort of *firman*, giving Alan powers of life and death over the keepers and coverts of all his territory marching with the lands of Wyverne Abbey; an instance of good nature which was the more remarkable, inasmuch as the great Absentee not only carries laziness and selfishness to a pitch of sublimity, but has of late registered a vow against befriending any one under any circumstances whatever. This last and rather superfluous hardening process was brought about in this wise.

Some years ago there appeared suddenly in the firmament of fashion a little star; no one knew whence it came —though it was supposed to have risen in the East; and when, after twinkling brightly for a brief space, it shot down into utter darkness, no one cared to ask whither it went. Mr Richardson had advanced just so far in intimacy with the magnates of the land that they began to call him "Tom" (his Christian name was Walter), when the crash came, and he subsided into nothingness. He lived upon that recollection, and little else, for the remainder of his days. Yet one chance was given him. Wandering about the Continent, he met the Marquis of Montserrat. The mighty golden Crater and the poor shattered Amphora had once floated side by side, for a league or two, down the same stream. After a *tête-à-tête* dinner (the *côtelettes à la Pompadour* were a success), old recollections, or his own Clos Vougeot, made the peer's heart warm, and he bethought himself how he might serve the unlucky pauper. At last he said,

"Tom, there is a regular establishment at Grandmanoir, and there always will be in my time, though I never mean to see it again. Go and live there; you'll be more comfortable than in lodgings, and save rent and firing besides. Make yourself quite at home; slay the venison; eat the fruit of the vine, and drink the juice thereof (the cellar ought to be well filled); and grow as fat as Jeshurun, if you like. I only insist on one thing. Whether matters are going on well or ill in the house or out of it—don't bother *me* about them. I don't want to hear a word on the subject. Is it settled so?"

You may fancy Tom Richardson's profuse thanks and his great joy and gladness at finding himself chatelain of Grandmanoir. The *valetaille* treated him at first with no small kindness (he was a meek little man, averse to giving unnecessary trouble), and for some months all went merrily. But before a year had passed there began to dawn on the stranger's mind suspicions, which soon changed into certainties. There existed at Grandmanoir the most comprehensive and consistent system of robbery that could well be conceived. It would have been harder to find one honest menial there than 10 saints in a City of the Plain. Everybody was in it, from the agent and house-steward, who plundered *en prince*, down to the scullion (fat, but *not* foolish), who peculated *en paysanne*. There was commercial blood in Tom Richardson's veins, and the sight of these enormous misdeeds vexed his righteous soul exceedingly. One day he could withhold himself no longer, but sat down in a fury and wrote,

"My dear lord,—In spite of your prohibition, I feel it my duty," &c.

And so went through all the disagreeable details regularly. The reply came by return of post, though not exactly in the shape that he expected. The steward came in with scant ceremony, an evil smile on his face (he probably guessed at the truth), charged with his lord's commands that the visitor should quit Grandmanoir before sunset and never return there. Thus rudely was broken the last of poor Tom's golden dreams. The Great Marquis, when the circumstances were alluded to, never could be brought to see any harshness in his own conduct, but spoke of his *protégé's* rather plaintively as "an instance of human ingratitude that he was really not prepared for." He did not give the species many chances of surprising him in *that* way again.

If the chiefs of his tribe were ready to comfort and cherish the disabled "brave," now that he could no longer put on paint and plume, and go forth with them on the "war-trail," be sure that the matrons and maidens were yet more active and demonstrative in sympathy. There must be extraordinarily bad features in the case of distress that fails to secure feminine compassion; except in a matrimonial point of view, our sisters rarely consider a man deteriorated because he is ruined. Though he was a general favourite in his set, Wyverne possessed many more real friends of the other sex than of his own. If there is anything in reciprocity, it was only fair that it should be so. Alan's reverence and affection for Womanhood in the abstract were so intense and sincere, as to be almost independent of individual attributes. His companion for the moment might be the homeliest, humblest, least attractive female you can conceive; but with the first word his tone and manner would change and soften in a way that she could not but perceive, even if she did not appreciate. Most of them *did* appreciate it, though, and this was the secret of his invariable and proverbial success. Wyverne could like a woman honestly, and let her know it, without a thought of love, and could always render courtesy where admiration, or even respect, unfortunately, were out of the question. However good the sport might be in other ways, he considered the day com-

paratively lost in which the feminine element was wanting. While his comrades were resting for an hour before
dinner—dead beat with seven hours' hard stalking in the
corries of Ben-mac-Dhui—Alan would be found loitering
about the door of the chief keeper's bothy, carrying on,
under extreme difficulties of dialect, a flirtation on first
principles with his orange-haired daughter. He seemed
to derive some refreshment from the process, though the
absence of a beard, and the (occasional) presence of a
petticoat, were about the only distinctive characteristics
of her sex that the robust Oread could boast of. When
the season was at the flood, he would spend hours of an
afternoon in the quiet twilight of a boudoir in Mayfair,
by the side of an invalid's sofa. Sooth to say, that room
held no ordinary attractions. Lady Rutherglen had been
a famous beauty in the Waterloo year; and though long
illness had somewhat sharpened her delicate features, she
still retained the low sweet voice and winning manner
which had made wild work with the heart of the Great
Czar (the imperial wooing was utterly wasted, for the
witty, wayward Countess could guard her honour as well
as the stupidest of Pamelas) : there was hardly a wrinkle
on the little white hand, and the lovely silver hair looked
softer and silkier now, than it had ever done in its golden
prime.

    Sad and strange shapes of sin and sorrow cross our path
sometimes, as we walk home from club or ball through
the early morning. Saddest perhaps and strangest of all,
is the spectacle of one of God's creatures, unsexed and
deformed by passion and fiery liquor, struggling in blind
undiscriminating rage, and shrieking out defiance alike of
friends and foes. The Menad ceased to be romantic when

the Great Pan died. Erigone may be magnificent on
canvas, but even Béranger failed in making her attractive
on paper: in flesh and blood she is simply repellent.
Public sympathy would side rather with Pentheus now-a-
days than with his cruelly convivial mother; and we hold
the disguise of drink to be the least becoming of all
Myrrha's masquerades. Such a sight affected Wyverne
with a disgust and pain that few men could have fully
appreciated; but he rarely would pass by without an
attempt at mediation. They say that his kind, gentle
voice was almost magical in its soothing power. The
exasperated guardian of the night would relax the rough-
ness of his grasp; and the "strayed reveller" would
subside from shrill fury into murmurs placable and
plaintive, yielding, in spite of the devil that possessed her,
to the charm of his cordial compassion and invincible
courtesy.

All things considered, womankind had rather a better
reason for petting Alan than could be given for most of
their whims. When his resources were almost unlimited,
he was always so perfectly regardless of time and trouble
and cost in endeavouring to gratify even their unexpressed
wishes, that it was no wonder if, when the positions
were reversed, he began to reap his reward, and found
out that he had laid up treasure against the time of
need.

I have said more than enough to give you some insight into a character in which the elements of hardness
and ductility, passionate impulse and consummate coolness, recklessness and self-control, were strangely mingled,
like the gold, brass, iron, and clay in the frame of the

giant Image that stood beside the prophet in his trance, on the banks of "the great river Hiddekel."

With all his faults and failings, Hubert Vavasour would have chosen him out of broad England for a son-in-law. Lady Mildred thought that such a bridal dress would become her daughter worse than a winding-sheet.

Which of the two was right?   Probably neither.   There is little wisdom in extremes.

CHAPTER V

THE GIFTS OF A GREEK.

WHEN Helen came into the cedar drawing-room (the place of assembly before dinner) she found her father alone. His face was rather thoughtful and grave, but it brightened as she came quickly to his side, and nothing but intense love and tenderness remained, when she rested her clasped hands on his shoulder, and looked up at him with a deepened rose colour on her cheek, and a question in her great, earnest eyes. If she had dreaded the meeting. all fear would have vanished even before the strong, true arm circled her waist, and the kind honest voice that had never yet lied to man or woman murmured "God bless you, my own darling!" Helen felt happier and safer then, than when she rose from receiving her mother's more elaborate caress and benediction.

Nothing, surely, can be more natural or justifiable under such circumstances than a paternal embrace; therefore there was no particular reason for those two starting apart, with rather a guilty and conscience-stricken expression of countenance, when the door opened, and Lady Mildred glided in with the even noiseless step and languid grace that all her friends knew so well, and some admired so much. The appearance of things did not greatly please her, neither did it trouble her much. She had a high opinion of her own resources, and a very poor one of the talents against which she meant to contend; so she regarded the signs of coalition before her with the same contemptuous indifference that a minister (with a safe majority) would display, when the Opposition threatens a division, or that a consummate billiard-player would feel, when his antagonist (to whom he gives 10 points under the proper odds) makes a grand but unproductive fluke.

As a rule, unless her adversary was extraordinarily skilful or vicious, that accomplished duellist preferred *taking* his fire; so on this occasion Hubert Vavasour had to speak first. He came to time gallantly, though rather nervously

"You have heard what these foolish children have been doing and saying this afternoon, mamma? I suppose they ought to be scolded or sent to bed supperless, or otherwise chastised; but I cannot play the stern father, and you don't look much like Mother Hubbard. *We* were foolish and childish once, Mildred; surely you remember?"

If his own life or fortunes had been at stake, there would not have been half such pitiful pleading in his eyes and his tone.

Lady Mildred's memory was unusually retentive, but it did not accuse her of any such weakness. Her imagination must have been tasked before she could have pleaded guilty; nevertheless she called up a little conscious look with admirable success, and smiled with infinite sweetness. Perhaps there was the faintest sarcastic inflexion in the first few words of her reply, but it needed a sharper ear to detect it than either her husband or daughter owned.

"Dear Hubert, you are growing romantic yourself again, or you would scarcely call Alan a child. If he is one, he is very wise for his years. But on the principle of love levelling everything, I suppose all ages are the same when people forget to be prudent. Of course it was a great surprise to me. I can hardly realize it yet; but—has not Helen told you? I *do* approve more than I ought to do, and I hope and pray that good may come of it to both of them. I love Alan nearly as well as I do my own Helen, and she and you know how dearly that is."

She wound her arm round her daughter's waist as she spoke, and drew her close till the two soft cheeks met. It was the prettiest *pose* you can fancy—nothing theatrical or affected about it—enough of tender *abandon* to satisfy the most fastidious critic of attitudes—beautifully maternal without being gushingly demonstrative; but not a hair in "my lady's" careful braids was ruffled, nor a fold in her perfect dress disarranged. The embrace was still in progress, when the door opened again and Alan Wyverne joined them, only preceding by a few seconds the announcement of dinner. It is just possible that the caress might have ended more abruptly, if one ear in the cedar drawing-room had not been quick enough to distinguish his footstep from that of the Chief Butler—a portly man, with a grand and goodly presence, in his gait sedate and solemn—who ever bore himself with the decent dignity befitting one long in authority, conscious of virtue, and weighing seventeen stone.

Nevertheless Lady Mildred's knowledge of her nephew's character made her aware that it would not answer to try with him the line of strategy which might succeed with

E

her husband and daughter. It was very unlikely that he would be taken in by the feint of unconditional surrender. Alan had not devoted himself to the society of womankind for so many years, without acquiring a certain insight into their charming wiles. It was very easy to persuade, but wonderfully difficult to delude him. She did not like him the worse for that; indeed she only spoke the truth when she said he was one of her chief favourites. Under any other circumstances she would have grudged neither time nor trouble to serve him, either by gratifying his wishes or advancing his fortunes, and perhaps really regretted the stern political necessity which made it an imperative duty to foil him if possible. Her game now was the temporizing one—to treat, but under protest. She looked up once in Alan's face as she leant on his arm on their way to the dining-room. That glance was meant to combine affection with a slight tinge of reproach, but a gleam of covert amusement in her eyes almost spoilt the intended effect. Lady Mildred had a strong sense of humour, and after the first vexation was over, she could not help laughing at her own carelessness and want of prevision. The fact was, she believed Wyverne capable of any amount of flirtation with any creature wearing a kirtle; but, with regard to serious matrimonial intentions, she had held him safe as if he had been vowed to celibacy; in default of a better, she would have allowed him on an emergency to play chaperon to Helen. Lo, the sheep-dog not only proved faithless to his trust, but was trying to make off with the flower of the flock, leaving its mistress to sing—with the "lass of the Cowdenknowes"—

> "Ere he had taken the lamb he did,
> I had lieve he had taken them a'"

They were rather a quiet quartetto at dinner Helen was by no means sentimental, nor did she think it the least necessary to be nervous, even under the peculiar circumstances; her colour, perhaps, deepened occasionally by a shade or two, without any obvious reason, and the long shadowing lashes swept down over her eyes more frequently than usual, as if desirous of veiling their extraordinary brilliancy; beyond these, there were no outward and visible signs of perturbation, past or present; her accomplice's face was a study for its perfect innocence and calmness. Nevertheless, neither was quite equal to the effort of discussing utterly uninteresting subjects quite unconcernedly; both had a good deal to think of, and *one* had a good deal to prepare for. Hubert Vavasour was cheerful and happy enough, apparently, but he only talked by fits and starts; so that it devolved on "my lady" to defray the expenses of the conversation. She performed her part with infinite tact and delicacy; it was only the fact of her so rarely taking any trouble of the sort in a strictly domestic circle (she thought it quite enough, there, to submit to be amused), that caused the effort to be observable.

It would be just as easy to make a dam-head of sand water-tight, as to prevent the knowledge of an event very interesting to one of its members, percolating through a large household within a few hours after it has happened. You may not see the precise spot where the water soaks through, and you may never discover the precise channel by which the intelligence is circulating; but there is the fact, and a very provoking one too, sometimes. It is unnecessary to say, that the probable engagement of the cousins formed the prominent subject of discussion that night in the steward's room, though of the circumstances of the *fiançailles* everybody was profoundly ignorant. Of course Alan could not be closeted with his uncle, and Helen with her mother, immediately after returning from a *tête-à-tête* ride, without the domestics drawing their own conclusions—to say nothing of the traces of emotion, which perhaps even that haughty demoiselle failed to dissemble from the quick-witted Pauline.

The Chief Butler (before alluded to) during a quarter of a century's servitude in the family had acquired, besides a comfortable competence and considerable corpulence, a certain astrological talent with regard to the signs of the times showing themselves within his limited horizon. He was faithful, too, after his fashion; but—loving his master much—he honoured his mistress more, and was ever especially careful to ascertain how the wind blew from *that* quarter. He was wont to preside over his little parliament like Zeus over the Olympian conclave; hearkening to, encouraging, and, if need were, controlling the opinions of the minor deities; on such occasions his words were few, but full of weight and wisdom. He waited now till, after long discussion, the majority decided that "it would be a very nice match, and suitable everyways" (a feminine voice remarking "What did it matter about fortune? Sir Alan was good enough for a duchess"); then, slowly and solemnly, said the portly Thunderer:

"It may be a match, and it mayn't be a match. I've nothing to say against Sir Alan, and I wish him well; but there'll be some curious games up, or I'm mistaken. I doubt my lady ain't altogether pleased about it—she was so uncommon pleasant at dinner!"

ὣς ἔφαθ', οἱ δ' ἄρα πάντες ἀκὴν ἐγένοντο σιωπῇ
Μῦθον ἀγασσάμενοι· μάλα γὰρ κρατερῶς ἀγόρευσεν.

According to one proverb, "No man is a hero to his own valet;" another tells us, "Bystanders see most of the game." Combining these two, we may guess how it is that the deepest politicians of private life do not always succeed in blinding the eyes of their own domestics, however great an interest they may have in doing so. Perhaps a rash and quite unfounded contempt for the auricular and mental capacities of a most intelligent class may sometimes help to throw them off their guard; though the proudest *lionne* of our democratic day would hardly care to emulate the cynicism of that exalted dame (she was nearly allied to the Great Monarch) who, when discovered in her bath receiving her chocolate from the hands of a gigantic lacquey, replied to her friend's remonstrance— "Et tu appelles *ça* un homme?"

The Squire of Dene was not so clearsighted as his majordomo: indeed, that pleasant habit of contemplating things in general through a roseate medium is apt to lead one into errors with regard to objects distant or near. He thought the aspect of affairs decidedly favourable; so, when they were alone again, he looked across the table at Wyverne with a smile full of hope and intelligence— draining at the same time his first beaker of claret with a gusto not entirely to be ascribed to the flavour of the rare '34.

"I drink to our castle in Spain," he said; "it seems to me the first stone has been laid auspiciously."

The other filled a bumper very slowly, and drained it deliberately, before he replied. Surely it was more that curious presentiment of some counter-balancing evil in the

dim background, which so often accompanies great and
unexpected happiness, than any intuitive knowledge of
the real state of things, which prompted the half-sigh—
not smothered so soon but that Vavasour's ear caught it
" flying."

"It is almost too good to be true, Uncle Hubert. I'm
modest about my own merits; and I think I know pretty
well by this time how much luck I ought to expect.
Would it not be wrong to reckon on winning such a prize
as that, without some trouble, and toil, and anxiety? I
confess I don't like these very 'gay' mornings; the clouds
are strangely apt to gather before noon, and one often gets
drenched before sunset."

During the short interval that had elapsed since the
first confidence was made, the Squire had signed in his
own mind a treaty with his nephew, offensive and de-
fensive; he had identified himself so thoroughly with the
latter's interests, that it provoked him a good deal now to
meet with something like despondency; he had counted on
an exhilaration at least equal to his own.

"Your poetical vein fails you, Alan; you are scarcely
so happy in your similes as you were three hours ago.
That's rather a threadbare one, and certainly not worthy
of the occasion; it isn't true, either, as you would find if
your habits were more matutinal. I don't think you know
much about your own merits, or about 'my lady's' intentions; perhaps you do injustice to both. But—simply to
gratify you—we will suppose the worst; suppose that she
is hostile, and only hiding her game. Well, I believe
there *is* such a thing as paternal authority, though mine
has been in abeyance ever since Max was born: I think I
should be equal to exercising it if we came to extremities.

When all one's other possessions are encumbered, there would be a certain satisfaction in disposing of a daughter. I'm not aware that any one holds a mortgage on Helen."

Now Hubert Vavasour spoke in perfect sincerity and singleness of heart, when he thus purposed to assert a suzerainty quite as unreal as the kingdom of Jerusalem or the bishopric of Westminster. His chances of success in such a reactionary movement would have been about equal to those of a modern French proprietor who, at the marriage of one of his tenants, should attempt to revive those curious seignorial rights, used or abused four centuries ago by Gilles de Rets and his compeers. Alan could not but admire the audacity of the resolve; but his sense of the absurd was touched when he reflected on the utter impossibility of its accomplishment. Perhaps this last feeling helped to dispel the gloom which gathered on his face; at any rate, his smile was gay enough now to satisfy his sanguine confederate.

"I should like to know the man, Uncle Hubert," he said, "who would persist in being suspicious or misanthropical after talking to you for 10 minutes. *I* am not such a natural curiosity. 'Sufficient for the day is the evil thereof:' that's the only sound and remunerative philosophy, after all. There has been nothing but good in this day; so I don't know what ungracious or ungrateful devil possessed me: but you have fairly exorcised him. Let us do as our fathers did—burn our galleys, advance our gonfalon, and cry—'*Dieu nous aide!*'"

"That's more like the old form," Vavasour replied; "say no more about it now. The claret stands with you; don't linger over it to-night, I fancy we are waited for."

Wyverne's first glance on entering the drawing-room searched for his cousin; he was rather relieved than otherwise at not finding her there; he felt that the difficulties of the next half-hour were best encountered alone. Lady Mildred was reclining on her usual sofa; close to it, and just within easy ear-shot of the cushion supporting her head, was placed a very low and luxurious arm-chair. "My lady" was ever considerate as to the personal comfort of her victims, and took especial care that they should not be galled by the ropes that bound them to the stake; acting, I suppose, on the same benevolent principle which prompts the Spaniard to deny nothing to those who must die by the garotte on the morrow.

The proximity was ominous, and far too significant to be unintentional. The instant Alan saw that chair, he guessed for what use it was destined, not without a slight apprehensive thrill. Just so may some forlorn Scottish damsel of the last century, whose flaxen locks snood might never braid again, have shivered in the cold white penance-sheet, recognizing the awful Stool on which she was to "dree her doom." Nevertheless, he accepted the position very gallantly and gracefully, sinking down easily into the *causeuse* and nestling comfortably into its cushions, without any affectation of eagerness or betrayal of reluctance. As he took up Lady Mildred's little soft hand and kissed it, his natural caressing manner was tempered by a shade of old-fashioned courtesy; and even that calm *intrigante* for the moment was not exempt from the influence of a dangerous fascination. Do not, however, do her the injustice to suppose that she once relented in her set purpose, or faltered one whit in its execution.

It would savour somewhat of repetition, and simply

bore you, if all the conversation that ensued were given
in detail. "My lady's" line was perfect frankness and
candour. She alluded pleasantly to the great matrimonial
fortunes that she had projected for Helen, and confessed—
pleasantly, too—her conviction that the alliance now contemplated was perfectly imprudent, and in a worldly point
of view altogether undesirable; she dilated rather more at
length on the affection for Alan, indulgence to Helen, &c.
&c., which induced the parents to overlook all such objections, and to give their conditional consent; but even
on this point she was not oratorical or prosy. Nevertheless her hearer was quite aware that there was some more
serious obstacle kept in the background; all these preliminary observations were so many shots to try the distance; the battery did not take him by surprise when it
opened in earnest.

"Alan, I know it must bore you, now that Helen has
come down-stairs, to be obliged to listen to *Madame Mère;*
it is very good of you not to show it: be patient a little
longer. I must make you look at one side of the question
that has escaped you, so far, I think; it is so important
to the happiness of both of you, that you should see your
way clearly I am not much afraid of your getting into
difficulties again, your lesson has been sharp enough to
cure you of extravagance; but there are embarrassments
worse than any financial ones, which are only tiresome and
annoying, after all. My dear nephew—has it occurred to
you yet, that in changing your *vie de garçon,* you will have
to economize in more ways than one, and wear some
chains, though they may be light and silken?"

"I've hardly had time to realize the position, Aunt
Mildred," Wyverne answered, "but I am conscious of a

perfect flower-show of good resolutions, budding and
blossoming already. While I was dressing, I was considering how I could best get rid of my hunters, and I
have almost decided where to place them."

"You are too eager in beginning self-denial," Lady
Mildred said; "perhaps it will not be necessary to part
with your horses *this* season. But you must settle your
future establishment with Helen and your uncle. *I* was
thinking of some other favourite pursuits of yours—of
handsomer and more dangerous creatures than Red Lancer
—though I suppose he is a picture of a horse, and it always makes me shiver to see him rear. You may be angry
with me, and call me prudish or puritanical if you like;
but I *must* say it. Alan—do you know that I consider
you the most confirmed and incorrigible flirt of my acquaintance?"

To apply to the speaker either of the two epithets she
deprecated would have been simply impossible. Her
bright eyes sparkled with a malicious amusement and gay
triumph as she marked the effects of her words in the
quaint look of contrition mingled with perplexity which
overspread Wyverne's face—usually so imperturbable.
For once in his life, he felt fairly at a loss for a reply.
Those general accusations are remarkably hard to meet,
even when one is conscious of innocence; but woe to the
respondent, if the faintest shadow of self-conviction hangs
over his guilty head! The adverse advocate sees the weak
point in a moment, and bears down on his victim with the
full flood of indignant eloquence, exulting in a verdict
already secured.

On this occasion, however, Lady Mildred did not seem
inclined to press her advantage; she interrupted Alan's

attempt at a disclaimer, before his embarrassment could become painful.

"Don't look so dreadfully penitent: you make me laugh when I am quite determined to be grave. I did not mean to impute to you any dark criminality. Up to the present time, perhaps, that general devotion has been rather useful in keeping you out of serious scrapes: you certainly have been singularly fortunate in that way—or wonderfully discreet. Besides, I don't mean to lecture you: it is a peculiarity in Helen's character, not in yours, that makes me give you this warning. I suppose you have guessed that she is capable of strong attachment; but you have no idea how exacting she is of undivided love in return. She has only had friendships (and very few of these) to deal with so far: but I remember her fretting for days, because her favourite governess would not give up corresponding with some school friend whom Helen had never seen, but had magnified into a rival. It is no use disguising the truth from you, when I cannot disguise it from myself, much as I love my pet. *You* would not like her to be faultless? Helen is not captious or suspicious; but she is absurdly jealous, sometimes. I cannot conceive how she learnt to be so: she certainly did not inherit the weakness from her father or me. I believe she would begin to hate a dog or a horse, if you made it too great a favourite; and words or looks of yours—perhaps quite innocent and meaningless—might make her more miserable than I can bear to think of. Dear Alan, it tires me more to sermonize than it bores you to be forced to listen; but what would you have? If a mother has any duties at all, it must be one of them to speak when danger threatens her own child and another whom she loves almost as dearly."

A peculiarity of "my lady's" *parables* was, that not only were they always plausible and probable, but they generally contained an element of truth and a slight foundation of fact: it made the deception more dangerous, because more difficult to detect. Really scientific coiners do not grudge a certain expense of pure silver to mix with the base metal: it adds so much sharpness to the outline and clearness to the ring.

So, though Alan had never till this moment heard of that defect in his fair cousin's character, he was by no means inclined to disbelieve entirely in its existence now; simply because he knew his aunt too well to suppose that she would venture upon an utter fiction which would refute itself in a very short time. Most men would be somewhat disquieted by the revelation of a phase in their *fiancée's* disposition, which is likely to interfere materially with domestic comfort and peace: but it troubled Wyverne wonderfully little. Whatever her mother might say or insinuate, he could not believe that the proud, beautiful eyes would ever condescend to show signs of unworthy or vulgar passions. He knew that Helen was too frank and impetuous to keep a suspicion concealed for half-an-hour; and he felt that he could rely on himself for not giving her serious cause of uneasiness. It was rather a conviction that he was losing ground every moment, slowly but surely, as his adversary's game developed itself, that made his face very grave as he answered, though he was calm and self-possessed again as ever—

"You don't expect me to be so conceited as to allow all you implicate, Aunt Mildred? Still, I fear I cannot deny that I have found many of your sex very charming, and that I have not always refrained from confiding the fact to the parties most interested in hearing it. (I rather pride myself on that circumlocution!) But, you know, I was never bound over to keep the peace till now. I think I can give fair securities, though not very substantial ones. Remember, I pledge all my hopes of happiness—of happiness greater than I ever dreamt would fall in my way. I don't think I should risk them lightly. I cannot tell *when* I began to love Helen; but I know that for months past the temptation has been growing stronger which vanquished me to-day: for months past it has made me proud to compare her with all the women I have ever admired (you say, Aunt Mildred, their name is legion), and to feel that not one could stand the comparison for an instant. *That* ought to be a safeguard, surely, against other enchantments? I can hardly fancy Helen playing Zara; yet, if the whim should seize her, I think it would be easy to prove to her that the part did not suit her at all. It is not my way to be prodigal of professions; but I am certain of one thing: there is no imaginable friendship or acquaintance—past, present, or to come—that I would not give up to spare that child ten minutes' unhappiness; and I should not call it a sacrifice. You are right to be distrustful when so much is at stake; but, on my faith and honour, *I* have no fears."

The clear dark eyes were fastened on Lady Mildred's inscrutable face very earnestly, as if beseeching that at least truth might be answered by truth. The trained glance of that great diplomatist did not care to meet the challenge: it must needs have quailed. I would not affirm that a momentary compunction did not assail her just then, while she did justice, in thought, to the kind, generous nature of the man she had determined to betray. It be-

hoves the historian to be impartial, and not to attribute
an ideal perfection even to his pet politician. The Prince
of Benevento himself might be pardoned for indulging in a
brief self-reproach, after maligning his own daughter and
lying to her accepted lover, within the same half-hour.
When Lady Mildred spoke again, her voice, always low
and musical, was unusually gentle and subdued.

"I am not so unkind or unjust as you seem to think,
Alan. I do believe thoroughly in your sincerity now, and
I am sure you will try your very utmost at all times to
make Helen happy. I don't mean to say that it will be
necessary to set a watch on your lips, and measure out the
common attentions of civilized life by the phrase: the
constraint would be too absurdly evident. if *you* were to
become formal! Nor can I suggest. at this moment, any
one acquaintance that it would be better you should sacrifice: your own good sense will tell you when and where to
be careful and guarded. But I do wish that both you and
Helen should try how far you are suited to each other,
before you take the one step in life which cannot be recalled. Remember how very young she is. You cannot
call me unreasonable if I ask one year's delay before we
fix the day for your marriage?"

It came at last—that cunning thrust under the guard,
impossible to evade, difficult to parry, which the fair
gladiator had been meditating from the very outset of her
graceful sword-play: all the feints of "breaking ground"
had no end or object but this. At those last words Wyverne set his lips slightly, and drew himself together with
the involuntary movement which is—*not* shrinking, just as
a fencer might do touched sharply in mid-chest by his opponent's foil. Twelve months—not a long delay, surely—

scarcely more than would be required to complete the settlements, *trousseaux*, and other preliminaries for some matches that we wot of, especially if a great house is to bo swept and garnished, before the bride is brought home. Alan might have thought about some such preparations years ago; now—he only thought that, whatever forces Lady Mildred might have in reserve would all be marshalled in their place before half the probationary year had passed.

But her position was perfectly safe and unassailable. When a prospective mother-in-law consents to ignore a suitor's social and finaucial disadvantages, he cannot well quarrel with her for endeavouring to make sure that the damsel's affections are not morally misplaced: of course her domestic prospects ought to be bright, in proportion as her worldly ones are gloomy. The aspirant may have a private surmise, amounting almost to a certainty, that he is being unfairly dealt with. He may murmur to himself that, if he had been a marquis or a millionnaire, the maternal scruples would have been mute; but it would show sad lack of wisdom to express such feelings aloud. If the case were to come on for trial, no judge or jury in England would give the plaintiff a verdict. He would not only lose his cause, but get "committed for contempt of court," and incur all sorts of vague pains and penalties, besides being held up as a phenomenon of ingratitude, and a warning to his fellows for the remainder of his natural life. Most men, who come to grief under such circumstances, will find their position disagreeable enough, even without the perpetual punishment of the pillory.

Yes, reason, if not right, was on "my lady's" side; aud she was perfectly aware of her advantage; for her eyes met Wyverne's steadily enough now as she waited for his reply.

The latter had reckoned so fully on meeting with opposition somewhere in this quarter, that it is doubtful if he was exactly disappointed at the turn the conversation had lately taken : though perhaps, as a matter of taste, he would have preferred more overt antagonism and obstacles more tangible to grapple with. At any rate, there was not a trace of sullenness or vexation in his manner when he spoke.

"I should have thought it unreasonable if you had made my probation as long as Jacob's, Aunt Mildred; simply because the span of life is greatly contracted since the patriarchal times, and everything ought to go by comparison. It would not so much matter to Helen; for, as you say, she *is* very young : she will only be in the prime of her beauty when my hair is grey. But I confess I should like to reap the reward of patience before I pass middle-age. Men seem to appreciate so few things *then*, that I doubt if one would even enjoy domestic happiness thoroughly. No; I don't think you at all exacting or over-cautions; and I will bide my time with a tranquillity that shall be edifying. I never found a year very long yet, and I shall have so much to do and to think of during the present one that I shall have no time to be discontented."

Lady Mildred smiled on the speaker sweetly and gratefully, but the keen, anxious *business-like* look still lingered in her eyes.

"Thank you so very much, dear Alan," she whispered, "you have behaved perfectly throughout, just as I expected you would" (she spoke truth, there.) "You will

promise me, then, that the day of your marriage shall not
be actually fixed till the year has passed? You know
your uncle is rather impetuous, and not very prudent; I
should not wonder if he were to try to precipitate matters,
and that would involve discussions. Now I never could
bear discussions, even when my nerves were stronger than
they are; I think they grow worse every day. If *you*
promise, I shall have nothing of this sort to fear. You
will not refuse me this because it looks like a selfish request?"

I have the pleasure of knowing, very slightly, a Companion of the Order of Valour who carried the colours of
his regiment at the Alma—it was his "baptism of fire."
At the most critical moment of the day, when the troops
were struggling desperately up "the terrible hill-side,"
somewhat disordered by the vineyards and broken ground;
when the Guards were reeling and staggering under the
deadly hail that beat right in their faces; the man I
speak of turned to the comrade nearest to him and remarked,

"Do you suppose they *always* shoot as fast as this,
Charley? I dare say it's the correct thing, though."

They say his manner was as listless and unconcerned
as usual, with just a shade of diffidence and doubt, as if he
had been consulting a diplomatic friend on some point
of etiquette at a foreign Court. I have the happiness of
knowing, very well, an officer in the sister service who
has received a medal scarcely less glorious, for rescuing
a sailor from drowning in the Indian Sea. They had
had a continuance of bad weather, and worse was coming
up all round; great lead-coloured billows weltered and
heaved under their lee—foam-wreaths breaking here and

F

there, to show where the strong ship had cloven a path
through the sullen surges; there was the chance, too, of
encountering one of two sharks which had been haunting
them for days; but I have heard that on Cis Hazlewood's
face when he went over the bulwarks, there was the same
expression of cheery confidence as it might have worn
when he was diving for eggs at The Weirs.

Now it is fair to presume, that both these men were
endowed with courage and coolness to an exceptional
degree; but I very much doubt if, in perfect exemption
from moral or physical fear, and in contempt for danger
either in this world or the next (if the said peril stood in
her path), Lady Mildred might not have matched the pair.
When the Vavasours were travelling in Wales, soon after
their marriage, something broke as they were descending a
long steep hill, and the horses bolted; it was a very close
question between life and death till they were stopped by
a couple of quarrymen just at the spot where the road
turned sharp to the left over a high narrow archway; no
carriage going that pace could have weathered that corner,
and the fall was 30 feet clear. The poor Welshmen certainly earned their rich reward, for they both went down,
and were much bruised in the struggle, and one got up
with a broken collar-bone. When the horses first broke
away, "my lady" deigned to lay aside the book she was
reading, but showed no other sign of interest in the proceedings, far less of discomposure. The Squire was once
asked "how his wife behaved after it was all over?" (that
is generally considered the most trying time). "She
looked," was the answer, "precisely as if she had expected
the episode all along; as if it had formed part of the
programme of our wedding tour that the horses should

bolt on that particular hill, and be stopped at that very critical spot by those identical quarrymen. It struck me that she praised and compassionated the poor fellow who was hurt, exactly as one might an acrobat who had met with an accident while performing for our amusement."

You may judge from this fact, whether "my lady's" nerves were as weak and sensitive as she was pleased to represent them. But with all her wile and wariness, she was a thorough woman at heart; and, as such, was not disposed to let a chance slip of turning to account the apparent bodily fragility which dissembled a very good constitution. Seldom, indeed, does maid or matron allow any small capital of the sort to lie long idle or profitless. Throughout all ages, despots have been found, anxious to drape their acts of oppression with a veil of reason and legality just dense enough for decency. In the present case, Lady Mildred brought forward a convenient and colourable pretext for a fresh exaction; she was rather indifferent as to its being received with implicit credit, for she knew that Alan was too kindly and courteous to contradict her.

As it happened, Wyverne was not deceived for a moment; but as the really important points of the hollow treaty were already decided, he did not think it worth while to hesitate over minor details.

"You shall have all you ask without reservation," he said, "and 'thereto I plight my troth.'"

So they locked hands there—faith and falsehood—truth and treachery—the one, harbouring no thought that was not honest and tender; the other, consistent to the last in her dark, pitiless scheming. Yet the woman's fingers

were most cordial in their pressure, and they never shrank
or trembled.

It is pleasant to read of the retribution that descended
on Brian de Bois-Guilbert, or Sir Aldinger; but poetical
justice does not always assert itself so conveniently as
in the lists at Templestowe. I wonder how often in the
ordeal of battle, honour has gone down before dishonour,
to the mocking echo of the herald's cry—" God defend the
right ! "

Lady Mildred lay back on her sofa, with a long sigh of
weariness which was not altogether feigned.

"I will not keep you another instant," she whispered.
"Go to Helen, and be as happy as you like; you have
earned that reward."

Miss Vavasour had been sitting all this while close
to her father's side. The chair she had chosen was so
low that her head could rest against his hand as it lay
on the arm of the vast *fauteuil*. They had been very
quiet, those two, while the conference was proceeding,
scarcely venturing to glance twice or thrice furtively in
the direction of the dread divan; but their whispered
confidences were pleasant enough, if one might judge
from Helen's beautiful blushes and the Squire's musical
laugh breaking in at intervals, discreetly modulated and
subdued. Both gazed anxiously in Alan's face as he drew
near, trying to augur from its expression how he had
sped. It told no tales; for his brow was smooth and his
smile serene, as if there were no such things in this
world of ours as doubt, or distrust, or despondency If
he could not hope to clear away all troublesome thorns
from the path of the fair girl who had promised that day
to trust him, he could at least spare her the pains of

anticipation; for her sake as well as his own he was determined to make the most of every hour of sunshine.
Without going into particulars then, he succeeded in
leaving an impression that Lady Mildred had shown
herself more favourable to their wishes than could have
been hoped for. Helen went to rest that eventful night,
when childhood ended and her womanhood began, in a
flutter of happiness which lasted through her dreams.

"While we live let us live." How is this agreeable
maxim to be carried out, if we are always looking forward
into the Dark? There is little wisdom in the desperate
philosophy which teaches men "to eat and drink, for to-
morrow they die;" but surely there is reason in taking,
while we may, such moderate refreshment as may brace us
for the perils and labours that the dawning may bring.
Do you suppose that Teucer's galleys clove less swiftly
through the Egean, because their crews had feasted high
in Salamis on the eve of exile? I fancy those grim old
sea-dogs at their last home revels—cutting deeper into the
mighty chines, and dipping their grizzled beards into the
black wine with a keener zest, while the cheery voice,
clear and sonorous as if its owner had never known defeat
or disaster, rings out

> ———" O fortes pejoraque passi
> Mecum sæpe viri, nunc vino pellite curas :
> Cras ingens iterabimus æquor."

The torches flare and swirl in the wind that is rising
gustily; there is a dull sullen booming outside familiar
to the wanderers, for they have heard it ere this when
every sinew was strained to keep them clear of breakers
on their lee; they were met by dark lowering faces when
they sailed in through the harbour-mouth; the populace—

taught to call them traitors by the savage old childless
king—is now raving for their blood. What matters it
all? They catch their leader's eye as he stands up in the
midst, erect and dauntless, with the great gold crater in
his gripe, and they laugh out loud in defiance; remembering storms they have weathered and foes they have
tamed, and perils compared to which these are but child's-
play. Would their prospects have looked better, if they
had sat down with folded hands and covered heads, to
complain of mortals and immortals, and miserably to
make their moan? Truly I think not. Now—when
they cast off their moorings to-morrow—in despite of
envious Pallas, we need not fear to wish the exiles "good
speed."

CHAPTER VI.

GOLDEN DREAMS.

FIRST LOVE!

Do not they look and sound just as fresh as ever—those two pretty words? And yet, they have been harder worked than the tritest of school copies, by successive generations of romancists in prose and rhyme, from Anacreon and Sappho down to that more modern and practical enthusiast, who, in a simile that must come home to every maid and matron in Belgravia (about five P.M. daily), exclaims, "A first love is like the first cup of tea—all others like the second." The heresy were worse than Antinomian that would cavil at feelings allowed by common consent to be divinely delicious. Take warning by Tantalus; beware of misbehaviour at the celestial table; when nectar and ambrosia are set before you, accept them gratefully, without discussing too curiously their flavour. Perhaps it is best so; perhaps the children's plan is wisest—"Open your mouth and shut your eyes."

Why is it then that, at this moment, I feel inclined to be hypercritical and disparaging? Truly, there is no accounting for moods, any more than for tastes; the claret last night was undeniable, and the morning weather

(for a wonder) is perfect ; there is not a shadow of an excuse for evil tempers.   Can it be that the pet theme has
really been over-rated ; and will it turn out that, after all,
there's something quite as sweet in life as Love's young
dream ?

See—we have given the *sacerrima verba* every chance :
they stand in a line by themselves, at the head of the
chapter, producing a striking and rather pictorial effect.
Pictorial—I wish the word had not been written, for as-
sociation brings back the feeling with which we have
looked on some late acquisitions to our National Gallery,
procured at nearly their weight in gold.   " A good thing
in its way, but—hardly worth the money."   It would be
very difficult, I suppose, to convince our sisters that it is
advantageous for man or woman to go through a certain
amount of mild preparatory training, before either is
brought out for the last grand match against Time.   Shall
we suggest to Amoret the bride, that Fidelio's affections,
since they first gushed out from the remote fountain-head,
have rippled and murmured—not unmusically—through a
dozen *lovelets* at least, caressing on the way several fragrant
water-lilies and delicate lady-ferns, before they poured a
full undivided volume into the One deep channel, through
which (let us hope) they will flow on peacefully for evermore ?   And then, shall we hint that she ought rather to
rejoice thereat than chafe or complain ?   It were boldly—
it were rashly done.   However respectable our antecedents
—if we could bring testimonials to character signed by 10
responsible housewives (which I very much doubt if Sir
Galahad himself could have obtained)—the lady would
infallibly inscribe our name, foremost, on the Black List
of those dangerous and detrimental acquaintances who

were the bane of the Beloved's life, before she came—
another Pucelle—to the rescue; thenceforward we should
certainly "have our tea in a mug," whenever these fair
hands had to pour it.

Yet, Madonna, if you would deign to look at the subject
dispassionately, you could scarcely help perceiving that
the very guilelessness and simplicity which make a First
Love so charming and romantic, detract somewhat from
its actual value. It is a very pleasant and charitable
frame of mind, which "hopeth all things and believeth all
things;" but it involves a certain deficiency in discrimina-
tion, and, I think, in appreciative power. The Object may
possibly be superlative in beauty, goodness, or talent; but
what is our opinion worth, if we have had no practical experience of the other two degrees? Unless the paired
doves take flight at once to some uncolonized island in the
Pacific,

> "And there securely build, and there
> Securely hatch their young—"

each must stand comparison, in aftertime, with other birds,
tame and wild, whose plumage glistens with every gorgeous
variety of colour, whose notes sink and swell through all
the scales of harmony. Then it is the old story over and
over again. Madame Ste. Colombe does not care so much
for modest merit, and considers meekness rather a tame
and insipid virtue, since the keen black eyes of haughty,
handsome Count Aquila told her a flattering tale; sober
drab and fawn no longer seem a becoming apparel since
Prince Percinet (the Duchess's favourite lory) dazzled her
with his Court suit of crimson and gold. Her innocent
consort never dreams, of course, of repining; but he confesses to an intimate friend that cooing *does* sometimes

sound rather monotonous: he heard a few days ago, for
the first time, Lady Philomelle sing. Surely it were better
to endure loneliness a little longer—ay, even till "black
turns grey "—than to discover that we are unworthily or
unsuitably matched, when to change our mate would be a
double sin.   There are matrimonial mistakes euough,
Heaven knows, made as it is; but, if every oue were to
marry their first love, a decade of Judges more uutiring
thau Sir Cresswell would be insufficient to settle the differ-
ences of aspirants to dis-union.

This is the "wrong side of the stuff," of course; it
would be easy to quote thousands of opposite instances—
of the Anderson type—where no shadow of disconteut has
clouded a long life of happiness. Still, the dauger remains: you can no more ignore it than you can any other
disagreeable fact, or public nuisance; but it will probably
be lessened if oue or both of the contracting parties have
had practical experience enough to enable them to know
their own minds once for all. The wise old Stagyrite,
after discussing different sorts of courage, places high that
of Ἐμπειρία: shall we not, too, honour aud value most the
Love which has been matured and educated by a course of
preliminary and lighter experiments?

If we have wandered far, through many gardens—finding in each flowers fragrant and beautiful, but never a one
worthy to be placed in our breast—do we love her less,
when we choose her at last—our own Provence Rose?
Was it not well that we should review and admire other
fair pictures wrought by the Great Artist, before we
bought what we hold to be His masterpiece, at the price
of all our life's treasure? Had we not acquired some
cunning of the lapidary, by studying the properties of less

precious gems, could we value your pure perfections aright,
O Margarita, pearl of pearls?

(In spite of that last sentimental sentence, which, I
swear, was elaborated solely as a peace-offering to Them, I
feel a comfortable conviction of having left the prejudices
of every feminine reader in precisely the same state as I
found them when we broached the subject).

If you disagree entirely with these premises, you will
hardly allow that Miss Vavasour's frame of mind was either
correct or justifiable on this same August morning. It
would be difficult to conceive any human being more
thoroughly and perfectly happy. Yet it was not the bliss
of ignorance, nor even of unconscious innocence. In
some things the demoiselle was rather advanced for her
years: she could form opinions of her own, for instance,
and hold to them, pretty decidedly. Some of our maiden-
recruits contrive to acquire a tolerable knowledge of their
regiment and its proceedings, before they actually join:
they have probably several friends who have passed their
drill; and these are by no means loth to communicate any
intelligence likely to instruct or amuse the aspirant. So,
though Helen had not yet been presented, few of the *his-
toriettes* of the last two seasons (fitted for ears polite and
virginal), had failed to reach her, directly or circuitously.
In more than one of these Alan Wyverne's name had
figured prominently. Lady Mildred had not spoken unfairly or untruly when she characterized her daughter's
temperament as somewhat jealous and exacting; but the
jealousy was not retrospective. Helen decided, very wisely,
to bury the past, with its possible peccadilloes, and to
accept her present position frankly, without one *arrière
pensée.*

It seemed rather a pleasant position, too, as she sate in
the deep, cushioned recess of one of the oriel windows of
the picture gallery; the play of light through the painted
panes falling fitfully on the grand masses of her glossy
hair, and lending a brighter flush to her fair cheek than
even happiness could give it; her clasped hands resting on
her cousin's shoulder, as he half reclined on the black
bear-skin at her feet—(Alan was decidedly Oriental in his
choice of postures)—her head bent forward and low, so as
to lose not one of many murmured words. Would it have
been better if a suspicion had crossed her mind, just then,
that the voice she listened to was indebted possibly to
long practice in similar scenes, for the dangerous melody
of its monotone? I think not; there is no falser principle
than judging from results.

The line of demarcation between the cousin and the
lover is proverbially faint, so much so indeed, as sometimes
to become quite imaginary. There is one advantage about
this, certainly; the transition into the affianced state is
not so abrupt as to make either of the parties feel awkward
or shy; while, on the other hand, their transports are probably more moderate and rational. In the present case
there was not much danger of extravagance in this way.
Wyverne, as a rule, was the personification of tranquillity,
and Helen—though impulsive and quick-tempered enough
herself—held demonstrative damsels in very great scorn.
Still it would be difficult, if not impossible, to transcribe
their conversation that morning, up to a certain point.

Fortunately, one is not expected to do anything of the
kind. Where the story is meant to be melo-dramatic, it is
necessary sometimes to give a good strong scene of passion
and temptation, in which either guilt or innocence tri-

umphs tremendously; but the male writers of the present
day seem pretty well agreed that it is best to leave *domestic*
love passages (where everything is said and done under
parental sanction) quite alone. An odd authoress or so
does now and then attempt to give us a sort of expurgated
edition, which is about as much like the reality as the
midnight sun glimmering faintly over the North Cape
resembles that which blazes over Sahara. You will observe that even those dauntless and unscrupulous French
romanciers of the physiological school rather shirk these
scenes.

Perhaps occasionally a curious melancholy feeling mingles
with this our masculine reserve. It may be that Mnemosyné
(she can be stern enough, at times, you know) stands on
the threshold of the half-open door and warns us back
with uplifted finger; it may be that of all in the book, we
should have to draw hardest on our imagination for this
particular chapter. In either case it would not be a very
attractive one to have to begin. There is something dreary
in sitting down to an elaborate description of luxuries or
riches that have passed away from us long ago, or which
have hitherto eluded us altogether. I am not inclined to
laugh much at Mr Scrivener's enthusiasm (he writes the
"high-life" tales for the *Dustpan* and other penny periodi-
cals) when he dilates on the splendours of Lady Herme-
gild's boudoir, hung with mauve velvet and silver, or on the
glories of the Duke of Devorgoil's banquet, where everything is served on the purest gold profusely embossed
with diamonds. He lingers over the details with an extraordinary gusto, and goes into minutiæ which (if they
were not grossly incorrect) would imply an intimate personal acquaintance with the scenes he describes. Now,

Mr Scrivener's father is a very meritorious grocer in the Tottenham Court-road, and the most aristocratic assembly Jack ever attended was a party at Hackney, where (unfortunately for his prudence) he met his pretty little wife. But I know that he composes these gorgeous chapters in a close, stifling room, not much bigger or better furnished than that of Hogarth's poet, with the same wail of sickly children in his ears (the walls are like paper in those suburban lodgings) and with the notice lying on the mantelpiece that the acceptance comes due on Monday, which he must mortgage his brains to meet. I think the incongruity is too sad to be absurd.

Do you see the parallel? Velvet and gold are comfortable and costly, but they are not the most precious trifles that a man may lose or win; bills are very stubborn inconveniences, but there are debts yet harder to meet, on which we pay heavier usury.

Whether that pair in the picture-gallery made themselves in anywise ridiculous, either by word or deed, in the course of the morning, is a question between themselves and their consciences; for the only witnesses were the members of their ancestry on the walls, who looked down on the proceedings with the polite indifference of well-bred people who had seen a good deal of that sort of business in their time, and have found out that "this too is vanity." At the moment when we intrude on the *téte-à-téte*, its component parts were in a very decorous and rational condition; in fact, they had resolved themselves into a sort of committee of supply, and were discussing the financial affairs of the future. It was delightful to observe the perfect gravity and good faith with which they approached the subject; though it would have been diffi-

cult to decide which of tho two was most hopelessly and
absolutely ignorant of all matters pertaining to domestic
economy Wyverne was especially great on the point of
retrenchment as far as his own personal expenses were concerned.

" You have no idea how much I shall save by giving up
hunting," he was saying; " I don't care nearly so much
for it as I did, so it is hardly a sacrifice " (ho really *thought*
he was speaking the truth); " my present stud is too
small to be of much use, and I hate being mounted. So
that's settled. I shall have no difficulty in getting rid of
my horses; Vesey will give me 400 for Red Lancer any
day ; and Cuirassier ought to fetch three. Only fancy,
Helen, what one will be able to do with 700 sovereigns!
You must have a brougham to yourself, even if we stay at
the great house in town, and it will be useful in the
country, for I suppose people will want us to dine with
them sometimes. We must have our saddle-horses of
course—Maimouna carries you beautifully already—I shall
never let you give up riding, if only for the memory of
yesterday afternoon; and that will be all, besides the
ponies that Uncle Hubert gave you on your last birthday."

" But, dear Alan," his cousin objected, " it seems to
me, all those horses will cost more to keep than your
hunters do now; for, you know, you always stay somewhere throughout the season, where they get board and
lodging."

" Don't entangle yourself in calculations, child," Wyverne answered; " you haven't any idea how expensive
hunting from other people's houses is; sending on, costs a
fortune. I should like you to see my accounts for last

season " (he said this with intense gravity, just as if he
had kept them regularly) ; " I am certain I shall save 200
a-year at the lowest computation. Yes, we can do it
easily. I saw Harry Conway the other day (he married
that pretty Kate Carlyon two years ago) ; he began telling
me of his rectory in Hertfordshire, what a lovely garden
his wife had, and how all the country admired the Welsh
ponies she drove. Now, I know their income does not
touch 600 pounds. We can double that, at all events, O
cousin, cautious beyond your years ! "

The part of Dame Prudence was in reality so entirely
foreign to Miss Vavasour's nature and habits, that it
amused her very much to play it, so she still tried to look
solemn, but the laugh would not be dissembled in her
eyes.

" An Abbey is a more expensive residence than a rectory,
M. le Financier, even if the Lady Abbess should not be
enthusiastic about flower-gardens. Have you formed any
plans as to our life in the North ? I mean to make Mrs
Grant teach me housekeeping ; and I shall be *so* severe
about the weekly bills ! I can fancy the butchers and
bakers trembling when they bring up their little red books
to be settled."

" Certainly, *il faut vivre ;* I quite admit the necessity of
that. I have no doubt we shall do wonderfully well. I shall
slay a good number of creatures, finned, furred, and feathered,
and one does not get tired of game easily. We must not
have any one to stay with us, except in the shooting-
season ; though I believe the chief cost of guests is the
claret they drink ; fortunately there's a Red Sea of that in
the cellars. And now, my Helen, prepare to open your
great eyes very extensively ; I mean to annihilate your

scruples with my last idea in economy. When the present stock is exhausted (it's not large) the supply of Champagne at the Abbey will be cut off till I come into another inheritance."

He enunciated the words rather sententiously and solemnly, evidently feeling the confidence and self-satisfaction that might be pardonable in a Chancellor of the Exchequer who has thought of a new and productive tax that cannot possibly hurt or offend anybody, or in a calculator who has elaborated a scheme for materially reducing the national debt. This time Miss Vavasour's musical laugh was not repressed.

"Don't go any further, Alan; Prudence owns herself vanquished by that last tremendous retrenchment. I begin to think we shall manage perfectly; perhaps there is no danger of absolute penury. Whenever I find the larder is empty, and that there are no means of filling it, I shall bring in the Spur in the Dish with my own hands; you were born near enough the Border to know then that you and your lances must go out on the foray."

"That's right," Wyverne said; "they say nothing stimulates one to exertion like appreciation, and I've got an exertion before me this morning, in the shape of letter-writing, that I don't much fancy. It's a question of Bernard Haldane. (I can never call him and your father 'uncle' in the same breath, but he did marry my aunt, you know). He must be absurdly rich by this time; and, when I did not in the least want it, I believe I was to have been his heir. So I might still have been, they tell me, if I had been utterly and irretrievably ruined, and had come to him in the form of the pauper. But he never forgave the poor little salvage out of the wreck which

G

made me independent of his bounty. Very odd old man,
that, and intensely disagreeable, I own; but still I wish,
now, you two had met. I do believe you would have melted
the misanthrope, and a very trifling thaw in that quarter
would be of material advantage to us just at this juncture."

Miss Vavasour's haughty lip curled perceptibly; her
face did not care to conceal some aversion and disdain.

"I should certainly spare myself the annoyance of
writing that letter, if I were you, Alan. I don't think
mendicancy would suit you at any time, and it is rather
early to begin the trade. *I* should hardly succeed better,
even if I had the chance of trying. If I have any fascinations, I think I will keep them for some other subjects
than odd, disagreeable old men."

Wyverne was not in the least inclined to chafe at her
tone; in truth, admiration left no place for anger; it
would have been hard to quarrel with her, she looked so
handsome in her scorn. He knew, too, that her pride was
only half selfish, and that she would have dreaded humiliation for his sake, more than for her own. So he smiled
quite pleasantly, as he answered,

"O Queen, let your imperial mind be set at rest. Your
bond-servant had no intention of making obeisance to any
other tyrant. Do I look like one of 'the petitioners who
will ever pray?' (He certainly did *not* at that moment.)
I only meant to convey a piece of simple intelligence,
which perhaps Mr Haldane is entitled to in courtesy, and
leave him to think and act as he would. But I told you I
disliked doing even this; and I hesitated till I consulted
your mother on the point after breakfast. She decided at
once that I ought to do so. I own her look, as she said
it, would have puzzled me, if I had not given up long ago,

trying to decipher 'my lady's' countenance. I imagine
she expects not much will result. I'm sure *I* don't. But
if Plutus were only to part with a poor thousand, it would
help me to furnish two or three rooms prettily at the
Abbey for you and your friends. My pet, you will look
like Nell in the Curiosity Shop, in that dismal grey house,
with its faded old-fashioned furniture."

Helen was accusing herself already of having been unjust and unkind. Her conscience smote her yet more
keenly as her cousin spoke these last words. When she
laid her hand on his mouth to stop him, it was half meant
as a caress. Wyverne pressed the lithe white fingers
against his lips, and made them linger there not unwillingly; but his mood, usually so equable and gay, had become strangely variable since yesterday. The dark hour
came on suddenly now. His face seemed to gather anything but light from the bright loveliness on which he
gazed. Helen's hand was dropped almost abruptly, and
he went on muttering low to himself, as if unconscious of
her presence.

"Esau was wiser than I. He *sold* his birthright, at all
events: I gave mine away. God help us! Instead of
these miserable shifts and subterfuges, I ought at this moment to be talking about the fresh setting of my mother's
diamonds. I wonder who wore them at the last drawing-
room? I took my own ruin too lightly. I suppose that
is why it stands out so black and dismal, when I have
brought another down to share it. Ah me! If the struggle
and the remorse begin so early, what will the end be?"

She broke in quickly, her fingers trembling, as she
twined them in his, and her cheeks glowing with her passionate earnestness.

"Alan, how can you speak so? Do you want to make me feel more selfish than I do already? I might have known what it would come to when you proposed selling Red Lancer, and I ought to have resisted then. You would sacrifice all your own pursuits and pleasures to me and my fancies, and you take nothing in return except "— (the word-music could scarcely be heard here)—"except —my dear love. See, *I* do not fear or doubt for one in-stant. Am I to teach you courage—you that I have always heard quoted for daring since I was a little child?"

We have read in the *Magic Ring* how the draught mixed by Gerda the sorceress for Arinbiorn, before the great sea-king went forth to fight, doubled the strength of his arm and the sway of his battle-axe. Glamour, more potent yet, may be drawn from brilliant dark eyes, whose im-perial light is softened, not subdued, by tears that are des-tined never to fall. A tamer spirit than Wyverne's would have .leapt up, ready for any contest, under the influence of Helen's glance, when she finished speaking. Very scanty are the relics that abide with us of the old-time chivalry; but our dames and demoiselles still play their part as gallantly and gracefully as ever. "Even Sir Guy of the Dolorous Blast," when bound to the battle, will scarcely lack a maiden to brace on his armour.

Alan rose to his feet and leant over his cousin where she sate. He forgot to be ashamed of his own weakness; he felt so proud of his beautiful prize, as he wound his arm round her delicate waist and drew her close to his side, till the little head nestled on his shoulder and his lips touched her ears as they whispered,

"My own brave darling! you shall never have to revive me again. The dead past may bury its dead; my last moan is made; henceforward will we not hope, even against hope?"

In spite of his newly-born confidence, he scarcely repressed a start and a shiver, as, looking up during the happy silence that ensued, he seemed to be answered by the earnest melanchoy eyes of the last Baron Vavasour.

There are certain pictures, you know, whose gaze always follows you, however often you may change your position. This portrait was one of such. It ought to have been excepted from the other ancestors, when we spoke of the unconcern with which they regarded the proceedings of their descendants. It was a very remarkable face, as I have said before, and by far the most peculiar feature in it were those same eyes. Notwithstanding their soft beauty, there was something dark and dangerous about them, as if the devil that lurked in their languid depths *would* look out sometimes. They were just the eyes from which an Italian would dread the *jettatura*, seeming to threaten not only evil to others, but misfortune to their owner. In Fulke Vavasour's life certainly both promises were amply fulfilled. If those scornful lips could have spoken now, one might have guessed at the import of the words.

"No change since my time. Those old common-places about faith and hope and love are not worn out yet; but it amuses me to hear them again now and then—not too often. I could repeat them glibly enough myself once, and perhaps I believed in them a little. I am wiser now, and so will you be, *beau cousin*, before you have done. I had my romance, of course. You know how that was cut short one cold morning on Tower-hill; but you *don't* know where yours will end."

Some ideas like these shot across Wyverne's mind, but

he had no time to give them form or distinctness, even if he had wished to indulge in such an absurdity, for one of the doors of the gallery opened just then, and though the drawing aside of the heavy *portière* gave them a moment's grace, the cousins had scarcely time to resume an erect and decorous posture before their *tête-à-tête* was ended.

CHAPTER VII.

MATED, NOT MATCHED.

THE new comer was an elderly man, in a clerical dress. His figure, originally massive and powerful, had thickened and filled out of late years till little of fair proportion or activity remained. In his walk and general bearing there was the same lassitude and want of energy which spoilt his face. The features could never have been regularly handsome; they were too weakly moulded for *any* style of beauty; but their natural expression was evidently meant to be kindly and genial. This, too, had changed. There was a nervous, worried look about him, as of a man exposed to many vexations and annoyances. It was not grave enough to suggest any great sorrow. Geoffry Knowles's story is very soon told. He was three or four years the Squire's senior; but they had been great friends at college. Few of their old set were left when Geoffry went up to keep his "master's term;" so, unluckily, he was a good deal thrown on his own resources. His evil genius lured him one day to a certain water-party, where he met Laura Harding, the handsome, flashy daughter of an Oxford attorney in large and very sharp practice, who speedily entangled him irretrievably. If Hubert Vavasour had been in the way, it might have been prevented. His thoroughbred instincts would have revolted from the intense vulgarity of the whole family, and the great influence he possessed over his friend's facile mind would all have been exerted to free the latter from a connection which could only prove disastrous and unhappy. Geoffry Knowles himself, the most indolent and unobservant of men, saw from the first that the fair Laura's *entourage* was most objectional; and certain incongruities (to use a mild term) in the lady's own demeanour and dialect struck him now and then painfully, as they would have done any other man well-bred and well-born. But, though conscious of going down-hill, he was too idle to try to struggle back again; and when the moment for the final plunge came, he took it resignedly, if not contentedly, expecting no countenance from any of his friends, as he had not sought their counsel. Perhaps after all, retractation would have been worse than vain. The wily lawyer might have said with the Sultan,

> "Dwells in my court-yard a falcon unhooded,
> And what he once clutches he never lets go."

Though Knowles was of an impoverished family and rather an extravagant turn, Mr Harding knew he had powerful friends, first and foremost of whom was the Squire of Dene; so far he judged rightly. Hubert Vavasour not only disliked "hitting a man when he was down," but never would let him lie there without trying to help him up. So, in spite of the connection which he thoroughly disapproved, as soon as the rectory of Dene fell vacant, he did not hesitate to offer it to his ancient comrade: it was one of those great family livings that are almost as valuable as a fat priory or abbey might have been; and thenceforth its rector wanted no comforts that affluence could supply. When this event occurred the Squire had been married about three years: he took the step without consulting his wife, or in all probability Lady Mildrod would have interfered to some purpose. It was part of her creed never to waste either lamentations or reproaches on what was irrevocable; so she accepted the fact quite composedly, determining to judge for herself as to the feasibility of associating with the new-comer, and to act accordingly.

Neither the Squire's nor the rector's wife ever forgot the first evening they met. Truth to say, "my lady" had prepared herself for a certain amount of vulgarity; but the reality so far transcended her expectations, that the shock was actually too much for her. She could not repress a slight shiver and shrinking sometimes, as Mrs Knowles's shrill highly-pitched voice rattled in her ears, and her trained features did not always conceal wonder or aversion at certain words and gestures that grated horribly on her delicate sensibilities. The other's sharp eyes detected every one of these unflattering signs, and she never forgot them: though long years had passed and a reckoning-day had never come, the debt still remained, written out as legibly in her memory as Foscaro's in Loredano's tablets. That evening, when the visitors had taken their departure, the fair hostess leaned back wearily on her sofa and beckoned her husband to her side. When he came she laid her hand on his arm and looked up into his eyes rather plaintively, but not in the least reproachfully.

"Dear Hubert!" she said, "I fancy Mr Knowles very much, and I hope he will come here whenever he likes. He may bring his wife four times a year (when you have some of those constituency dinners, you know); but at

any other time or place, I absolutely decline to entertain
that fearful woman again!"

There was not a shade of anger, or even disdain, on the
placid face, but he must have been a bolder man than
Vavasour who would have argued the point with her then.
Hubert knew that the fiat just issued by those beautiful
lips, ever so little set, was irrevocable.

"She *is* an awful infliction!" he assented, gravely; "I
can't call you unjust, dear Mildred. Indeed, I almost
regret having brought her so near you. I must manage it
with Geoffry as best I can; I should not like to lose his
society. Poor fellow! I was very wroth when I first
heard of his derogation—but I can do nothing but pity
him now. If she affected us so disagreeably this evening,
think what it must be to have to live with her all the year
round! It is no use saying, 'He's used to it.' There are
some nuisances one never gets indifferent to."

Lady Mildred shrugged her round white shoulders
slightly, as though to intimate that Mr Knowles's domestic
Nemesis was essentially his concern; and so the matter
ended.

It was not long before that worried, nervous expression,
to which I have alluded, became the habitual one of poor
Geoffry's face. He never spoke of his troubles, even to
Hubert Vavasour; but they must have been heavy, and
almost incessant. His wife had captured him simply as a
measure of expediency: she would have married him just
as readily if he had been elderly and repulsive when she
first saw him; she very soon got tired of keeping up
affectionate appearances; indeed, that farce scarcely out-
lasted the honeymoon. The last phantasm of romance had
ceased to haunt the dreary fireside, years and years ago.

Laura's sharp tongue and acid face were enough to scare away a legion of such sensitive elves. As soon as she found that their income was far more than sufficient for their wants, she took severely to parsimony, and "screwed" to an extent scarcely credible. There never breathed a more liberal and open-handed man than Geoffry Knowles —it must have been a poor satisfaction to him to know that about 30 pounds per annum was saved by economy in beer alone, and that his servants'-hall was a by-word throughout the county. The wives of the squirearchy had been very kind and civil to her at first, and were not all inclined to follow the lead of the *grande dame* at Dene; but they couldn't stand her long, and one by one they fell off to a ceremonious distance, doling out their visits and invitations by measure and rule. This did not improve the lady's temper, which was exacting and suspicious to a degree: she never would allow that she ever lost a friend or failed to make one by her own fault; though she had a pleasant habit of abusing people savagely to their nearest neighbours, so that it was about ten to one that every syllable came round to them. They had one child—a son —who might have been some comfort to the Rector if his mother would have let him alone: but she asserted her exclusive right to the child even before he was christened, insisting on calling him by her own family's name—"Harding," (some one said, "it was to commemorate an incomplete victory over the aspirates"); and maintained her ascendancy over his mind by the simple process of abusing her husband to and before the boy, as soon as he was old enough to understand anything; it is needless to say that there was always more distrust than sympathy between father and son.

So, you see, Geoffry Knowles had a good deal to fight
against, and very little to fall back upon. His one consolation was, his neighbourhood to Dene: he clung fast to
this, and would not let it go, in spite of incessant sarcasms
levelled at his meanness of spirit for " always hanging
about a house where his wife was not thought good enough
to be invited: "—(she never missed one of those quarterly
dinners, though). It was inexpressibly refreshing to get
out of hearing of the shrill dissonant voice—ever querulous
when not wrathful, and to share

> "The delight of happy laughter,
> The delight of low replies,"

which one could always count on finding at Dene when its
mistress or her daughter were to the fore. Those visits
had the same effect on the unlucky Rector, in calming
and bracing his nerves, as change of air will work on an
invalid who moves up from the close dank valley to the
fresh mountain-side, where the breeze sweeps straight
from the sea over crag, and heather, and tarn. Lady
Mildred liked him—perhaps pitied him a little—in her
own cool way, and the Squire was always glad to see him;
so he came and went pretty much as he chose, till it
would have been hard to say to which family he really
most belonged. Helen was very fond of him: it would
have been strange had it been otherwise, for he had petted
her ever since he held her in his arms at the font, and indeed
had lavished on her all the father-love of a kindly nature,
which he was debarred from giving to his own child. As
her loveliness ripened from bud to blossom under their
eyes, no one could have said which was proudest of their
darling—the Rector or the Squire.

It rather spoils the romance of the thing—but, truth to

say, there were other and much more material links in the
chain that bound Geoffry Knowles so closely to Dene.
He had always been of a convivial turn, and from youth upwards, not averse or indifferent to the enjoyment of old
wine and fat venison: of late years he had become ultra-
canonical in his devotion to good cheer. I do not mean to
imply that he drank hard or carried *gourmandise* to excess;
but certainly not one of Vavasour's guests, whose name
was legion, savoured more keenly the precious vintages
that never ceased to flow from his cellars, or the master-
strokes of the great artist who deigned to superintend the
preparation of his banquets. Was it a despicable weakness? At all events, it was not an uncommon one. The
world has not grown weary of trying that somewhat
sensual anodyne, since Ulysses and his comrades revelled
on the island-shore till the going down of the sun—

δαινύμενοι κρέα τ' ἄσπετα καὶ μέθυ ἡδύ

a few hours after he crept out of the Cyclops' cave, leaving
the bones of six of his best and bravest behind; many
bond-slaves since Sindbad, as the jocund juice rose to
their brain, have forgotten for awhile that they carried a
burden more hideous and heavy than the horrible Old
Man of the Sea.

I have lingered much longer than I intended over the
antecedents of the Rector; but as one or two members of
his family play rather an important part in the story afterwards, there is some excuse for the interruption.

When Mr Knowles entered the picture-gallery, he was
evidently unaware that it held other occupants; he had advanced half way up its length, before Miss Vavasour's gay
dress, looking brighter in the strong sun-light, caught his

eyes; even then he had to resort to his glasses before he could make out who sat in the deep embrasure.

"This is a new whim, Helen," he said, as he turned towards them; "I never found you here in the morning before. Can you tell me where the Squire is? I want—"

He stopped abruptly, for he was near enough now for the fair face to tell its tale, and, short-sighted as he was, the Rector saw the state of things instantly. A few steps —very different from his usual slow, deliberate pace— brought him into the oriel; he stooped and kissed Helen on her forehead, and then griped Wyverne's hand hard, his lips moved twice before he could say unsteadily and huskily, "I am so very, very glad!"

It was a simple and hearty congratulation enough, but it was the first that the fair *fiancée* had had to encounter, and it threw her into considerable confusion, coming thus brusquely. To speak the truth, she "arose and fled away swiftly on her feet," covering her retreat with some indistinct murmur about going to find the Squire, and left her ally to bear the brunt of the battle alone. The Rector was not in the least vexed at her flight; he knew his pet too well to think that she could be ungracious; he only looked after her with a smile of pride and fondness as she glided away and disappeared through the curtained door, and then turned again to Alan.

"I have always dreamt of this," he said; "but so few of my good dreams come true that I scarcely hoped there would be an exception here. I am certain you will take all care of her; and how happy she will make you! And how long has this been going on? You have kept your secret well, I own, but I am so blind that it is very easy to keep me in the dark."

There was a faint accent of melancholy, and a half-reproach in the last few words which did not escape Wyverne's quick ear.

"My dear Rector, don't be unjust. What do you mean by suspecting us of keeping secrets from *you?* You won't give one time to tell you. We were all perfectly sober and sane till yesterday afternoon, when I lost my head riding in the Home Wood; and everybody has been following my lead ever since, for I ought to have been crushed on the spot instead of encouraged. You see I'm like other maniacs; they always know their companions are mad, and tell you so—don't they?"

"Imprudent, perhaps, but not insane," the other said, heartily; "and is 'my lady' as bad as the rest of you?"

"Well, not exactly; for, though she refused nothing, she was wise enough to stipulate that the time of our marriage should not be fixed till a year had passed. I believe Aunt Mildred likes me, but I don't think her partiality quite blinds her to my disadvantages."

It would have been hard to decide from Wyverne's face, whether he spoke in earnest or irony; but there was no mistaking the expression of the Rector's; disappointment was written there very legibly.

"You could hardly expect unreserved consent *there*," he said; "but it is a long delay before anything is actually fixed—too long, Alan, trust me. You don't mind my speaking frankly? Helen comes out next season, you know; and even if your engagement is announced, nothing will prevent half the 'eligibles' in London going wild about her. It will be fearfully tantalizing to 'my lady's' ambition, and I doubt if her good faith will last out the year. If that once fails, you will have a hard battle to fight and a dangerous one; none can say what a day may bring forth, and few of Lady Mildred's are wasted when she has determined to carry anything through. Surely you tried to shorten the probation-time?"

Wyverne bit his lip, frowning slightly.

"My triumph is great, I own, but really I don't require to be reminded that I am mortal. Of course there are risks and perils without end, but I have counted them already, Rector; don't trouble yourself to go through the list again. No, I did *not* remonstrate or resist, simply because I think it wiser to husband one's strength than to waste it. I might say to you as Oliver said to Sir Henry Lee—'Wearest thou so white a beard, and knowest thou not that to refuse surrendering an indefensible post, by the martial law deserves hanging?' My position, at the moment, was not quite so strong, numerically, as the Knight of Ditchley's, for he had *two* 'weak women' in his garrison, and, I fancy, I had only one brave girl. We can count on the Squire's goodwill to any extent, but he would be the merest reed to lean upon if matters went wrong. It is much the best plan to trust till you are forced to distrust; for it saves trouble, and comes to about the same thing in the end; pondering over your moves don't help you much when your adversary could give you a bishop or a castle. So for the present I believe in Aunt Mildred *coûte qui coûte*. You are right though—there will be a fair crop of rivals next spring; but I am vain enough to think that, with such a long start, I may hold my own past the post."

Alan threw back his head rather haughtily as he spoke these last words, and once again encountered the eyes of Fulke Vavasour. He turned quickly to his companion, before the latter could reply.

"An ominous neighbourhood to make love in, is it not? especially considering the resemblance. You have remarked it?"

Geoffry Knowles started visibly, and his countenance fell more than it had yet done.

"I wish you had not asked me. Yes, I have seen it coming out stronger every month for the last year; it was never there before. I have always avoided looking at that picture since I was forced to confess that the family likeness to Helen is far stronger than in her own brother's portrait that hangs there. If the Squire had only some excuse for putting it away! Such coincidences are common enough, of course, but I wish to God the features of the worst of her race had not been reproduced in our darling."

"Not the worst, I think," Wyverne answered, decidedly, "though he was wild and reckless enough in all conscience. It's an odd thing to say, but I've liked him better since I heard how and why he sold himself to Satan. I dare say you don't know that version of the story. Percie Ferrars, who is always hunting out strange family legends, told it me the other day. He found it in some book relating to the black art, written about 50 years after the Baron's death. It seems that he had always been meddling with magic, but he never actually came to terms with the fiend till the night of his arrest. He signed and sealed the contract within an hour after he entered his cell, on the condition that certain papers then at the Dene should be in his hands before the dawn; so he saved a woman's honour from being dragged through the mire of a public trial, and perhaps a delicate neck from the scaffold. This is how the horseman came alone at midnight, bearing the

Baron's signet-ring, when the arrest was not two hours old; and this is why the pursuivant who started before the prisoner was in the Tower, and never drew bridle on the way except to change his horses, found nothing but empty drawers and rifled caskets, with a mark here and there, they say, as if hot coals had been dropped on them. The author brings the case forward in a very matter-of-fact way, to show for what a miserably small consideration men will sometimes barter their souls, for he observes that Vavasour could not even obtain for himself safety of life or limb. Perhaps he did not try; he came of the wrong sort to stand chaffering over a bargain when he was in no position to make terms. I don't mean to deny that Fulke was very guilty; I don't mean to assert that a man has any right to sell his soul at all; but I am not prepared to admit the absurd smallness of the value received. The Baron himself, it appears, revealed the infernal contract to one man, his cousin and dearest friend. When the confidant, rather horror-stricken, asked " if he did not repent ? " he only answered—" What is done is well done " —and thenceforward would answer no question, declining to the last the consolations of religion or the visits of a priest. But every one knows, that at his trial and on Tower-hill he bore himself as coolly and bravely as if he had been a martyred bishop. Let him rest in peace if he may! If he erred, he suffered. For the sake of that last wild deed, unselfish at least, I will cast no stone on his grave."

His quiet features lighted up, and his eyes gleamed, just as they would do if he were reading some grand passage in prose or rhyme that chanced to move him strongly. No enthusiasm answered him from the other's face. The Rector evidently could not sympathize.

"It's a dark story," he said, "whichever way you look at it, and your version does not make me dislike that picture the less. But I'm not a fair judge. If I ever had any romance, it has been knocked out of me years ago. I won't argue the point. I'm only sorry that our talk has got into such a melancholy groove. It is my fault entirely. First I spoil your *tête-à-tête* by blundering in here, where I had no earthly business, and then I spoil your anticipations with my stupid doubts and forebodings. Just like me, isn't it?"

Wyverne's gay laugh broke in before the Rector's penitence could go further.

"Not at all like you," he answered cheerily; "and don't flatter yourself that either prophecy or warning will have the slightest effect. Ecclesiastes himself would fail if he tried to preach prudence to *us* just now. I told you we had all gone out of our sober minds up here. For my part I don't care how long the carnival lasts. We must keep the fasts in their order, of course; but, by St Benedict, we will not anticipate Lent by an hour."

Geoffry Knowles looked wistfully into the speaker's frank, fearless eyes, till his own brow began to clear, and a hearty genuine admiration shone out in his face.

"I do envy that hopeful geniality of yours, more than I can say, Alan. I have a dim recollection of having been able to 'take things easy,' once upon a time; but the talent slipped away from me, somehow, just when it would have served me best. It was acquired, not natural, with me, I suppose. I doubt if I could translate without blundering, now—*Dum spiro, spero.* I am glad, after all, that I caught you first, and got rid of my 'blue' fit before

I saw the Squire. He would not have taken it so well, perhaps, as you have done."

"I don't know about that," Alan said. "Uncle Hubert is pretty confident, and you would most likely have been carried away helplessly by the stream ; he put *me* to shame last night, I can tell you. You'll find him in his room by this time; and I can't stay here any longer. I've letters to write, and I mean to have Helen in the saddle directly after luncheon. I must make the best use of my chances now, for, unless the gods would

> ' Annihilate both Time and Space
> To make two lovers happy,'

(as the man in the play wanted them to do), and cut out the shooting season from the calendar, there would be no chance of keeping Dene clear of guests. They will be coming by troops in less than a fortnight. There is no such thing as a comfortable *causerie*, with keen eyes and quick ears all around you. *Ay de mi!* one will have to intrigue for interviews as if we were in Seville. I shouldn't wonder if we were driven to act the garden-scene in the *Barbière* some night. Even if I wanted to monopolize Helen, then (which I don't, for it's the worst possible taste), I know ' my lady' would not stand it. Well, thank you for all you have said—yes, *all*. I shall see you at luncheon?"

From the Squire's radiant face, when he came in with the Rector, it might be presumed that the latter comported himself during their interview entirely to his friend's satisfaction.

It was no vain boast of Wyverne's when he said that neither omen nor foreboding would affect his spirits materially that afternoon. Few people ever enjoyed a ride more thoroughly than the cousins did their very protracted one. They would not have made a bad picture, if any one could have sketched them during its slow progress. Alan on the Erl-King, a magnificent brown hunter of Vavasour's; Helen on the grey Arab, Maimouna, whom she mounted that day for the fourth time. The one so erect and knightly in his bearing; the other so admirably lithe and graceful—both so palpably *at home* in the saddle; even as they lounged carelessly along through the broad green glades, apparently lost to everything but their own low, earnest converse, at the first glance one could have recognized the seat and hand of the artist.

If one *must* be locomotive, when alone with the ladye of our love (not a desirable necessity, some will say), I doubt if we can be better than on horseback. A low pony carriage, with a *very* steady animal in the shafts, has its advantages; but I never yet saw the man who could accommodate himself and his limbs to one of these vehicles without looking absurdly out of his place; his bulk seems to increase by some extraordinary process as soon as he has taken his seat, till 10 stone loom as large as 14 would do under ordinary circumstances. The incongruity cannot always escape one's fair companion, and, if her sense of the ridiculous is once moved, our romance is ruined for the day: perhaps the best plan, on turning into a conveniently secluded road (always supposing that "moving on" is obligatory), would be, to get out and walk by her side, leaving the dame or demoiselle unrestricted scope for the expansion of her feelings and—her drapery. On the whole, I think one is most at ease *en chevauchant*. But then both steeds must be of a pleasant and sociable disposition—not pulling and tearing at the reins, till they work themselves into a white heat, whenever a level length of green-sward tempts one irresistibly to a stretching gallop; nor starting perversely aside at the very moment when, in the earnestness of discourse, your hand rests unconsciously (?) on your companion's pommel; but doing their five miles an hour steadily, with the long, even, springy gait that so few half-breds ever attain to,—alive, in fact, to the delicacy of the position and to their own responsibilities as sensible beasts of burden. Maimouna was a model in this respect: she could be fiery enough at times, and dangerous if her temper was roused; but she comported herself that afternoon with a courtesy and consideration for others worthy of the royal race from which she sprang—

> " Who could trace her lineage higher
> Than the Bourbon can aspire,
> Than the Ghibelline or Guelf,
> Or O'Brien's blood itself."

It was pretty to see her, champing the bit and tossing her small proud head playfully, or curving her full, rounded neck to court the caress of Helen's gauntlet; with something more than instinct looking all the while out of her great bright stag's-eyes, as if she understood everything that was going on and approved it thoroughly: indeed, she seemed not indisposed to get up a little mild flirtation on her own account, for ever and anon she would rub her soft cheek against the Erl-King's puissant shoulder, and withdraw it suddenly as he turned his head with a coy, *mutine* grace, till even that stately steed unbent somewhat from his dignity, and condescended, after a superb and sultanesque fashion, to respond to her cajoleries.

Altogether they made, as I have said, a very attractive picture, suggestive of the gay days when knights and paladins rode in the sweet summer-weather through the

forest-tracks of Lyonnesse and Brittany, each with his fair
paramour at his side, ready and willing to do battle for her
beauty to the death. Wyverne's proportions were far too
slight and slender to have filled the mighty harness of
Gareth or Geraint; but Helen might well have sate for
Iscult in her girlhood before the breath of sin passed over
the smooth brow—before the lovely proud face was trained
to dissemble—before King Mark's unwilling bride drank
the fatal philtre and subtler poison yet from her convoy's
eyes, as they sailed together over the Irish Sea.

Yes—no doubt

"It was merry in good greenwood,
When mavis and merle were singing;"

when silvered bridles and silvery laughs rang out with a
low, fitful music; when the dark dells, whenever a sunbeam
shot through, grew light with shimmer of gold and jewels,
or with sheen of miniver and brocade; when ever and
anon a bugle sounded—discreetly distant—not to recall
the lost or the laggards, but just to remind them that they
were supposed to be hunting the deer. Pity that almost
all these romances ended so drearily! We might learn a
lesson, if we would; but "we hear and do not forbear."
The modern knight's riding-suit is russet or grey—perhaps, at the richest, of sable velvet; a scarlet neck-ribbon
or the plumes of a tropical bird are the most gorgeous
elements in his companion's amazonian apparel; but I
fear the tone of their dress is about the only thing which
is really sobered and subdued. People will go on lingering till they lose their party, and looking till they lose
their hearts, and whispering till they lose their heads, to the
end of time; though all these years have not abated one
iota of the retribution allotted those who "love not wisely

but too well;" though many miserable men, since Tris-
tram, have dwined away under a wound that would never
heal, tended by a wife that they could never like, thirsting
for the caress of " white hands beyond the sea," and for a
whisper that they heard—never, or only in the death-pang ;
though many sinners, since Launcelot, have grovelled in
vain remorse on the gravestone of their last love or their
first and firmest friend.

Certainly none of these considerations could trouble
the cousins' pleasant ride; for every word that passed
between them was perfectly innocent and authorized;
they had, so to speak, been "blessed by the priest" before
they started. When Helen came down (rather late) to
dinner, her face was so changed and radiant with happiness
that it made "my lady's" for the rest of the evening unusually pensive and grave. Some such ideas shot across
her, as were in the cruel step-mother's mind, when she
stopped those who bore out the seeming corpse to its
burial, saying—

> "Drap the het lead on her breast,
>   And drap it on her chin;
> For mickle will a maiden do,
>   To her true love to win."

CHAPTER VIII.

CRŒSUS COMETH.

WE have been comfortable in our country-houses for centuries. Even in those rough-and-ready days—when the hall was strewn with rushes, and the blue wood-smoke hung over the heads of the banqueters like a canopy, and the great tawny hounds couched at their masters' feet, gnawing the bones as they fell from the bare oak tables, and the maids of Merry England recruited their roses with steaks and ale in the early morning—I believe the Anglo-Saxon squire had a right to be proud of his social privileges, and to contrast them favourably with the shortcomings of his Continental neighbours. But it looks as if we had only begun of late years thoroughly to appreciate these advantages; now—there is hardly a tale or a novel written, which does not sound a note or two of triumph on the subject. In truth, it is hardly possible to praise too highly this part of our social system. Nevertheless, in a few of these favoured mansions, there springs up something bitter from the midst of the fountain of delights which, to the minds of many of us, poisons the perfection of hospitality. Sometimes the officer in command is rather too exact and exacting about his morning-parade, insisting

upon his company being "all present and correct" within
a certain time after the warning gong has sounded.
Punctuality is an immense virtue, of course; but our frail
and peccant nature will not endure even virtues to be
forced upon it against the grain, without grumbling; and
there are men—sluggish if you will, but not wholly reprobate—who think that no amount of good shooting or good
cookery can compensate for the discomfort of having to
battle with a butler for the seisin of their grill, or being
forced to keep a footman at fork's length, while they hurry
over a succulent "bloater," should they wish to break their
fast at a heterodox and unsanctified hour.   There is some
sense in the objection, after all.   If you want to enforce
regularity with Spartan sternness, it is better to be consistent, and not tantalize one with contrasts, but recur to
the old black-broth and barley-bread form; choose your
system and stick to it: it never can answer to mix up
Doric simplicity with Ionian luxury.

So few things were done by line and measure at Dene
that it would have been strange if breakfast had formed the
solitary exception to the rule of—*Fais ce que voudras*.   The
general hour was perhaps "a liberal ten;" but if any
guest chanced to be seized with a fit of laziness, he could
indulge his indolent genius without fear of having to fast
in expiation.   At whatever hour he might appear, a separate breakfast equipage awaited him, with the letters of
that post laid out thereon, decently and in order, and the
servants seemed only too glad to anticipate his appetite.

The Squire himself was tolerably early in his habits, and
kept his times of starting very well in the shooting or
hunting season: he would never wait beyond a resonable
time for any one—making no distinction of persons—but

would start with those who were ready, leaving the laggards to follow when they would. There was a want of principle, perhaps, about the whole arrangement, but it answered admirably; even those who were left behind on such occasions never dreamt of being discontented or discomfited; indeed, it was not a very heavy penance to be condemned to spend a home-day at Dene with the feminine part of its garrison. There were few houses that people were so glad to come to, and so sorry to leave.

Wyverne was very capricious and uncertain as to the hours of his appearance, except when any sport by flood or field was in prospect: he was never a second behind time then. If the day chanced to be very tempting, it was even betting that he would be found sauntering about some terrace that caught the fresh morning sun, before the dew was off the flowers; but it would have been dangerous to lay odds about it; taking the average of the year, the balance was decidedly in favour of indolence.

When he came down on the sixth morning from that on which this story began, the Squire and Helen were lingering over their breakfast nearly finished, that Alan might not have to eat his in solitude. Nobody ever thought of apologizing for being late at Dene; so, after the pleasant morning-greetings were over, Wyverne sat down to his repast with his usual air of tranquil, appreciative enjoyment; he did not seem in any particular hurry to grapple with the pile of letters that lay beside his plate.

Have you ever observed the pretty flutter that pervades all the womanhood present when the post-bag is brought in—how eyes, bright enough already, begin to sparkle yet more vividly with impatient anticipation, and how little tremulous hands are stretched out to grasp as much of the contents as their owners can possibly claim? We of the sterner sex take the thing much more coolly—of course because we are so much graver and better and wiser than *they* are: when a man "plunges" at his letters, you may be quite sure he has a heavy book on an approaching race, or is a partner in some thriving concern, commercial or amatory; in such a contingency the speculator is naturally anxious to know if his venture is likely to prove remunerative. Where no such *irritamenta malorum* (or *bonorum*, in exceptional cases) exist, we are apt to accept what the post brings us with resignation rather than with gratitude, reflecting moodily, that all those documents must not only be read through, but answered—at what expense of time, money, or imagination, it is impossible at present to say.

Some years ago I heard of a female Phœnix—wise and fair, too, beyond her fellows—who actually wrote to a very intimate friend 10 consecutive letters, each containing, besides more confidential and interesting matter, all sorts of news and scandal, with the recording angel's comments annexed. They were model epistles, I believe—witty, but not *too* wicked; frank, without being too demonstrative; and to not one of the brilliant decade did the writer *expect an answer.* That was understood from first to last, for circumstances made silence, on one side, imperative. I hope her correspondent appreciated that rare creature, then: I am very sure he did, the other day, when he sat down to his writing-table with a weary sigh and the remark—that "of all fond things vainly imagined, a second post was the most condemnable." If charity covers a multitude of sins, surely such repeated acts of unselfish benevolence ought to cloak most of that poor Rosa's little faults and failings. Speaking quite disinterestedly (for I scarcely know her by sight), I think she deserves a statue —as a marvel of the Post-office—better than Rowland Hill: if I were bound to take a pilgrimage, I would pass by the shrine of Saint Ursula, and go a thousand miles beyond it, to the green Styrian hills where She withered and died—the only woman on record, who could persist, for three whole months, in amusing a silent correspondent without proximate hope of recompense.

Wyverne's letters were not very numerous that morning, nor did they appear to interest him much; for he took up one after the other, at intervals, and after just glancing at the contents put them aside, without interrupting a pleasant desultory conversation with his companions. At last only two remained unread.

The envelope of one was of thick blue-wove paper; the direction was in a large, strong, upright hand; the seal square, and solemnly accurate—such a seal as no man dare use unless he were in a position to set the world at defiance. If you or I, *amigo*, were to risk it, however numerous and unblemished our quarterings, we should lay ourselves open to all the penalties attendant on *lése-majesté*: the very crest was a menace—a mailed arm, with a mace in its gripe. If any possessor of that truculent coat-of-arms had put it on the outside of a love-letter, all passionate pleading must have been neutralized; the nymph to whom it was addressed would have fled away, swiftly, as Arethusa of light-footed memory, or a "homeless hare."

The other letter was of a widely different type; it bore no seal, but a scarlet monogram so elaborately involved as to be nearly illegible; after careful study of its intricacies, with a certain amount of luck, you might have made out the initials N. R. L. There was a *mignardise* about the

whole thing quite in keeping with the handwriting—
slender, sloping, and essentially feminine; at the same
time there was a good deal of *character* about it; without
much practice in graphiology, one guessed at once that
those lines had been traced by fingers long, lithe, and
lissome—fingers that either in love or hate would close
round yours—pliant and tenacious as the coils of a Java
serpent—fingers apt at weaving webs to entangle men's
senses and souls.

Alan took these letters up in the order in which we have
named them. The first was evidently very brief; as he
read it, an odd smile came on his lip, not altogether of
amusement, but rather bitter and constrained; just such a
smile as one might put on to mask a momentary discomfiture, if, in a contest of polite repartee, one had received a
home-thrust, without seeing exactly how to *riposter*. The
other envelope contained two full note-sheets, one of which
(of course) was crossed. Wyverne just glanced at the
first page and the last few lines, and then, putting it back
into its cover, laid it down with the rest; it was quite
natural that he should thus defer the perusal, for, however
well he might have known the handwriting, 10 minutes of
undivided attention could scarcely have carried him through
it. A very close observer might have detected just then a
slight darkening and contraction of his brows; but the
change lasted not five seconds, and then his face became
pleasant and tranquil as ever.

"Well, that is over, or nearly so," he said, drawing
rather a long breath. "Did anybody ever see such a day
for riding? I feel the Tartar humour on me, Helen—do
you sympathize? If so, we'll let our correspondence take
thought for the things of itself—*I* don't intend to put pen

to paper to-day—and go forth on a real pilgrimage, trusting to fate for luncheon. There's not an atom too much sun, and the breeze might have been made to order."

Perhaps the movement of Alan's arm, which pushed two or three of his letters off the table, was quite involuntary; and perhaps quite unintentionally, when he picked them up, he placed the *last* undermost: but the eyes of Lynceus were not keener-sighted than those dark languid orbs, held by many to be the crowning glory of Helen Vavasour's beauty. Neither the change in her cousin's face nor one detail of the apparent accident escaped her; and it is possible that she drew from them her own conclusions. Probably they were not very serious ones, and perhaps his careless tone contributed to reassure her; at any rate, nothing could be brighter than her face as she answered—

"I should enjoy it, of all things, Alan. On a day like this I believe Maimouna would tire before I should. I never knew what it was to feel *rested* while riding fast, till I mounted her. Don't be jealous if she begins to know me better than you; you never heard of my visits to the stable, under old Donald's escort, on purpose to pet her. You may order the horses as soon as you please. I must see mamma before we start; but would you like to bet that I am not ready first?"

Alan's reply was on his lips, when the door opened softly, and, gliding in with her usual quiet grace, Lady Mildred joined the party. It was rare indeed that the mistress of Dene favoured the world with her presence before noon. At intervals, upon state occasions, she condescended to preside at breakfast; but, as a rule, took her chocolate and its accessories in her own apartments, and got through the business of her day in solitude.

Her letters were always impounded, as soon as the letter-
bag was opened, by her own maid—a placid, resolute
person—a sort of cheap edition of her mistress—who had
held her place for many years, and was supposed to know
more of the secrets of the boudoir than any creature alive.
Women of Lady Mildred's calibre rarely change their
confidential servants.

"My lady" was seemingly in a charming humour that
morning; she greeted every one most affectionately, and
listened to the plan of the long ride, with a gentle approval, and even some show of interest.   But all the three
felt certain that she had good reason for her early appearance.   They were not kept long in suspense.

"I have had a letter from Max, this morning," Lady
Mildred remarked.   "Helen dear, he says all sorts of kind
things about you and Alan, but he reserves most of his
congratulations, as he hopes to see you so soon.   You
know he has been shooting with Lord Clydesdale, ·in
Perthshire, Hubert?   Before this news came, he had asked
him and Bertie Grenvil to come here for the early part of
September; but if you don't wish the engagement to
stand, you have only to let him know at once."

His astute helpmate could hardly refrain from smiling
at the queer embarrassed expression of the Squire's frank
face—she read his feelings so well!   Indeed poor Hubert
was the worst dissembler alive.   He looked wistfully at
his two confederates, but there was small chance of succour from that quarter.   Helen's glance met her mother's
for a second, and she bit her scarlet lip once, but remained
perfectly silent.   Alan was brushing away a stray crumb
or two from the velvet sleeve of his riding-coat, with a
provoking air of absolute unconcern.   Vavasour was so

intensely hospitable, that he would just as soon have thought of stabbing a guest in his sleep, as of grudging him entertainment; besides, there was no earthly reason why either of the names just mentioned should be distasteful to him, or to any one else present; if he felt any real objection, it was more like a presentiment impossible to put into words. Nevertheless there was an unusual gravity in his voice, as he replied—

"Rather an unnecessary question of Max's, dear Mildred. He ought to know, by this time, that his friends are quite as welcome here as my own. As it happens, we have ample room for those two guns during the *early* (the word was marked) part of September. So many anxious parents will be contending for the possession of Clydesdale, that he will scarcely waste his golden time here beyond a fortnight. Few men are fonder of being persecuted with the attentions of your sex than that very eligible Earl. I believe he thinks it is no use being *the parti* of England if you don't reap its advantages, before as well as after marriage. I dare say Bertie will stay longer; the mothers, at all events, don't hunt him. I hope he will, for there's no pleasanter boy in a house, and his detrimentalism wont hurt us here. Will you write at once and say that we shall be charmed to see them all?"

Those last words were spoken with rather an unnatural distinctness, it seemed as though it cost the Squire an effort to utter them, and he left the room almost immediately, muttering something about "people waiting for him in his study." After a few minutes more of insignificant conversation not worth recording, the cousins, too, went out to get ready for their ride. Lady Mildred

stayed her hand for a moment—she was crumbling bread
into cream, carefully, for the Maltese dog's luncheon—and
looked after them with a pensive expression on her face,
in which mingled a shade of pity. Just so much compassion may have softened, long ago, the rigid features of
some abbess on her tribunal, when, after pronouncing the
fatal *Vade in pace*, she saw an unhappy nun led out between the executioners, to expiate her broken vows.

Whatever might be Miss Vavasour's failings, dilatori-
ness in dressing was certainly not one of them; she would
have won her wager that morning; and yet it would have
puzzled the severest critic to have found a fault of omission
or commission in her costume, as she stood in the recess
of one of the windows of the great hall, waiting for the
horses and her cousin. He joined her almost immediately,
though, and Helen's eyes sparkled more brilliantly, as she
remarked a letter in his hand.

"I always quote you and Pauline," Wyverne said,
" when people keep their horses at the door for an hour by
Shrewsbury clock; but you have outdone yourselves to-
day. You deserve a small recompense—*la violà*. It must
be a satisfaction to a minor prophetess to find her predic-
tion perfectly realized. My beautiful Sibyl! I don't
grudge you your triumph, especially as I did not contradict you on the point. The oldest and ugliest of the
sisterhood never make a better guess at truth. Read *that*.
I shall give 'my lady' the sense of it; but I don't think
I shall show it her."

It was Bernard Haldane's answer, and it ran thus:

My dear Alan,—I thank you for your letter, because

I am sure it was courteously meant, and, I believe, disinterestedly too; though, as you are my nearest male relation, it might naturally be expected that I should do or promise something on an occasion like this. I wish you to understaud plainly, and once for all, that, in the event of your intended marriage taking place, you need anticipate no assistance whatever from me, present or future, before or after my death. I think it best to enter into no explanations and to give no reasons, but simply to state the fact of my having so determined. I have giving up congratulating people about anything; but, were it otherwise, I should reserve such formalities for some more auspicious occasion. Neither am I often astonished; but I had the honour of knowing Lady Mildred Vavasour slightly many years ago, and I own to being somewhat surprised at *her* sanctioning so romantically imprudent an engagement. I will not inflict any sermon upon you; it is only to their heirs that old men have a right to preach. It is unlikely that we shall meet or correspond often again. After what I have written, it seems absurd to say, "I wish you well." Nevertheless—it is so.

Believe me,
Very faithfully yours,
BERNARD HALDANE.

There was disappointment certainly on the beautiful face, but it sprung from a very different cause from that to which Wyverne naturally assigned it. Helen had expected the perusal of a more delicate handwriting. The quaint cynical letter did not interest her much under the circumstances; however, she read it through, and as she gave it

back, there was a smile on her proud lip partaking as much
of amusement as of disdain.

"Let us give credit where credit is due," she said. "I
believe it cost Mr Haldane some pains to compose that
answer, short as it is. If you ever speak to him about it,
will you say that we considered it very terse and straight-
forward, and rather epigrammatic? Don't show it to
mamma, though. I wonder when she knew Mr Haldane?
Is it not odd that she never alluded to it when his name has
been mentioned? Ah, there are the horses at last. Alan,
do you see Maimouna arching that beautiful neck of hers?
I am certain she is thinking of me. I defy the crossest of
uncles to spoil *my* ride to-day. Will he yours?"

Every shade of bitterness had passed away, and the sunniest side of Helen's nature—wayward and wilful at times,
but always frank and honest and affectionate—showed itself before she finished speaking.

Reader of mine, whether young or old—suppose yourself, I beseech you, to be standing, with none to witness
your weakness, by the side of the Oriana of the hour; let
the loveliest of dark eyes be gazing into yours, full of provocative promise, till their dangerous magnetism thrills
through brain and nerve and vein, and then—tax your
imagination or your memory for Alan Wyverne's answer.
You will write it out better than I, and it will be a charity
to the printer; for, were it correctly set down, it would be
so curiously *broken up* as to puzzle the cleverest compositor
of them all.

Alan and his cousin enjoyed their ride thoroughly, without one *arrière pensée*. Thus far there was not a shadow of
suspicion on one side, not the faintest consciousness of in-

tentional concealment on the other; nevertheless, there was already one subject on which they could not speak quite openly and freely. It was early, too early, to begin even a half-reserve. When such a sign appears in the " pure æther " so soon after the dawning of love, however light and small and white the cloudlet may be, the weather-wise foretell a misty noon and a stormy sunset.

CHAPTER IX.

THE LONG ODDS ARE LAID.

A MAN must be very peculiarly constituted—indeed, there must be something wrong about his organization—if he does not entertain a certain partiality for his female cousins, even to the third and fourth generation. But the same remark by no means applies to the brothers of those attractive kinswomen. Your male cousin either stands first and foremost on the list of your friends, or you are absolutely uninterested in his existence. There *are* instances of family feuds, of course, but these, now-a-days, are comparatively rare. The intercourse between Alan Wyverne and Max Vavasour had never gone deeper than common careless courtesy. It was not to be wondered at. Both were in the best society, but they lived in different sets, meeting often, but seldom coming in actual contact. Just so, they say, the regular passengers by the parallel lines of rail converging at London-bridge recognize familiar faces daily as they speed along side by side, though each may remain to the other "nameless, nameless evermore." Besides this, the tastes of the cousins were as dissimilar as their characters; for the mere fact of two men being extravagant, by no means establishes a real sympathy between them.

Alan's favourite pursuits you know already   Max was Lady Mildred reproduced, with the exception of her great talents, which he had not fully inherited; but he had the same cool, calculating brain, with whose combinations the well-disciplined heart never interfered. This, added to a perfect unscrupulousness of thought and action, many diplomatists besides Vavasour have found to be a very fair substitute for unerring prescience and profound sagacity. Both morally and physically he was wonderfully indolent, and, doing most things well, rarely attempted anything involving the slightest exertion. His shooting was remarkably good; but two or three hours of a battue about the time of the best *bouquets*, or a couple of turnip-fields swarming with birds, round which the stubbles had been driven for miles, were about the extent of his patience or endurance. As for going out for a real wild day after partridges, or walking a quaking bog after snipe, or waiting for ducks at " flight time," he would just as soon have thought of climbing the Schreckhorn. He rode gracefully, and his hand on a horse was perfection; but he had not hunted since he was 18, and his hacks, all thoroughbreds, with good action, were safe and quiet enough to have carried a Premier. He especially affected watching other men start for cover on one of those raw drizzling mornings which sometimes turn out well for hunting, but in every other point of view are absolutely detestable. It was quite a picture to see him return to his breakfast, and dally over it with a leisurely enjoyment, and settle himself afterwards into the easiest of lounging chairs, close to the library fire, with a pile of French novels within reach of his hand.   Occasionally, during the course of the morning, he would lay aside his book, to make some such reflective remark as—

"Pours still, doesn't it?   About this time Vesey's reins must be thoroughly soaked and slippery.   I wonder how he likes riding that pulling mare of his.   And I should think Count Casca has more mist on spectacles than he quite fancies.   It's a very strongly enclosed country, I believe, and the ditches are proverbially deep.   He must have 'left all to his vife' before this."

And then he would resume his reading, with a shrug of his shoulders, intimating as plainly as words could speak, intense self-congratulation, and contempt for those who were out in the weather.   Yet it was not nerve in which Max was deficient.   Twice already—he was scarcely 26— his life had been in mortal peril; once at Florence, where he had got into a bad gambling quarrel, and again in a fearful railway accident in England.   On both occasions he had shown a cool, careless courage, worthy of the boldest of the valiant men-at-arms whose large-limbed effigies lined the gallery at Dene.   In thews and stature and outward seeming he was but a degenerate descendant from that stalwart race, for he was scarcely taller than his sister, and had inherited his mother's smooth dark complexion and delicate proportions.   That same indolence, it must be owned, told both ways, and went far to neutralize, for evil as well as for good, the effect of the calculating powers we have referred to.   He had a certain obstinacy of will, and was troubled with few inconvenient scruples, but wanted initiative energy to entangle himself or others in any of those serious scrapes which are not to be settled by money. So far, Max Vavasour's page in the *Chronique Scandaleuse* was a blank.

The heir of Dene and his friends arrived so late, that they had barely time to dress for dinner. No private conference took place, apparently, between the mother and son that evening; but the latter joined the others very late in the smoking-room. It is scarcely to be presumed that the doffing of *la grande tenue* and the donning of an elaborately embroidered suit of purple velvet, would consume 45 minutes; so that half an hour remained unaccounted for, during which interval probably the boudoir was witness to a few important confidences.

Max was rather fond of his sister, after his own fashion, and never vexed or crossed her if he could help it; so, when they spoke of her engagement on the following morning, he not only forbore to reproach her with its imprudence, but expressed himself hopefully and kindly enough to satisfy Helen's modest expectations. She knew her brother too well to anticipate expansiveness or enthusiasm from *that* quarter. To Alan he was, naturally, much less cordial in his congratulations; indeed, it was only by courtesy that they could be called congratulations at all. Max had a soft, quiet way of saying unpleasant things— truths or the reverse—that some people rather liked, and others utterly abhorred. On the present occasion he did not scruple to confess frankly his opinion as to the undesirability of the match, to which the other listened with at least equal composure.

" I wish I had not gone to Scotland," Vavasour went on, reflectively. " I do believe I could have stopped it, if I had only been on the spot, or forewarned. I needn't say, I have no prejudices against you personally—nobody *has* any such weaknesses now-a-days "—(how very old the young face looked as he said it); " but it's a simple ques-

tion of political expediency. I may be very fond of
Switzerland or Belgium; but, as an ally, I should much
prefer France or Russia. The Squire has told you, of
course? Things are going hard with us just now. I
doubt if the smash can be staved off much longer. A *very*
great match might just have stood between us and ruin;
and Helen would have had the chance of it, I am certain.
You know that, as well as any one. There is something
peculiar about her style of beauty. I am not infatuated
about her because she is my sister; but I swear, there was
not a woman in London fit to be compared with her last
season, and I don't know that I ever saw one—except perhaps Nina Lenox in her best days. By the body of Bac-
chus! we might have had our choice of all the eligibles in
England!"

"Including Clydesdale, for instance,"—Wyverne remarked.

There was a smile on his lip, but no mirth in his eyes,
which fastened on his cousin's with a piercing earnestness
hard to encounter. Not a muscle of Max's face moved,
his pale cheek never flushed for an instant, and he returned the other's glance quite as steadily.

"Including Clydesdale,"—he answered, in his grave,
gentle tones. "Of course, that would have been the very
connection one would have liked. I should have tried to
make up the match, if you had not unfortunately come in
the way, and I should do so still if anything were to happen to you. Don't suppose I am going to have you
poisoned, or that I shall shoot you by accident, or ma-
chinate against you in any way whatever; but life is very
uncertain; and—my dear Alan,—you do ride remarkably
hard."

Wyverne laughed merrily, without the slightest affectation or bitterness. Perhaps he had never liked his companion better than at that moment.

"By heaven, Max," he said—contemplating the philosopher not without admiration—"you're about the coolest hand I know. I don't believe there's another man alive, who would speculate on the advantages contingent on his cousin's breaking his neck, to the face of the said unlucky relation. I've hardly the heart to disappoint you, but—I don't think I shall hunt much this season. I suppose you wouldn't allow Clydesdale to buy Red Lancer, if Vesey does not take him? Ah! I thought not. Seriously—I admit all your objections—and more; but I exhausted my penitence with 'my lady' and the Squire, who appreciated it better than you would do. What would you have? All are not born to be martyrs. I quite allow that I ought never to have tried to win Helen; but I'm not self-denying enough to give her up. I shall keep her, if I can."

"Of course you will," the other replied, resignedly. "Well, I have said my say, and now things must take their course. *I* am passive. I hope the event may be better than the prospect; but I shall give myself no trouble till the crash comes—nor then, if I can help it. *You* seem to get on rather better since you were ruined. By the by, there's no chance, I suppose, of that old ruffian Haldane's, dying and relenting? My lady told me about his letter—at least, as much as you chose to tell her."

Wyverne shook his head, but had not time to answer, for at that moment they joined the rest of the shooting-party who were at luncheon. Max had only come out just in time to have this talk with his cousin; but he remained

with them for a couple of hours in the afternoon, seemed
in capital spirits, and never shot better in his life.

I will try to sketch the scene, in the cedar drawing-
room at Dene, on the fourth evening after the arrival of
the fresh guests. They are the only addition, so far, to
the family party, though more are expected incontinently.

Helen Vavasour is at the piano, and close to her side, on
a low chair, placed so that his head almost touches her
shoulder, sits Alan Wyverne. He has behaved perfectly
to-day, never attempting to monopolize his *fiancée*, not even
securing a place near her when she came out to meet the
shooting-party at luncheon; apparently he thinks he has a
right to indemnify himself for a brief space now. It is
rather a brilliant piece she is playing, but not so difficult
as to interfere with a murmured conversation, evidently
very pleasant and interesting to both parties. The Squire
and the Rector are playing their everlasting piquet, which
has been going on for nearly a score of years, and is still
undecided. It is a very good match, and both are fair
players, though each is disposed privately to undervalue
his adversary's science, characterizing him as "the best
card-holder in Europe." The great difference is, that
Vavasour looks at a bad hand with a cheerful unconcern,
whereas Geoffry Knowles knits his brow and bites his lip
when luck is running against him, and has never learned
to dissemble his discontent or discomfiture. Lady Mildred is reclining on her own peculiar sofa, and, on a stool
close to her elbow, lounges Bertie Grenvil—better known
as 'The Cherub' in half the fast coteries of London, and
throughout the Household Brigade.

It is a very fair face to look upon, shaded by masses of
soft, sunny, silky hair, and lighted up by large, eloquent

eyes of the darkest blue. It would be almost faultless, were it not for the extreme effeminacy, which the delicately trained moustache fails to redeem. He is one of "my lady's" prime favourites: she has assisted him ere this with her countenance and counsel, when such help was sorely needed; for it is a wild, wicked little creature—reckless and enterprising as Richelieu in his page-hood—always gambling and love-making, in places where he has no earthly business to risk his money or his heart. With those smooth pink-and-white cheeks, and plaintive manner, and innocent ways of his, The Cherub has done more mischief already than a dozen years of perpetual penance will atone for. At this moment he is confiding to "my lady" the hopes and fears of his last *passion malheureuse*, suppressing carefully the name of the object—a very superfluous precaution, for Lady Mildred has guessed it long ago, and can afford to be amused—innocently. She knows, what Bertie does not wot of, that his pursuit will be absolutely *theoretical* and fruitless.

Very near them lounges Max Vavasour. He looks up, ever and anon, from that eternal *novelette*, and as his eye meets his mother's, a quick glance of intelligence passes between them. It is more than probable that he has been told off for "interior and picket duty" this evening; but the time for action has not yet come.

Only two of the party remain to be noticed. They are sitting together, rather remote from the rest, and somewhat in the shadow. We will take the younger man first, though his appearance is not exactly attractive.

His features, naturally coarse and exaggerated, bear evident traces of self-indulgence, if not of intemperance; that cruel sensual mouth would spoil a better face, and the effect of an unpleasantly sanguine complexion is rather heightened than relieved by crisp, strong reddish hair, coming low down on the heavy forehead, and framing the pendulous cheeks; his big, ungainly frame is far too full and fleshy for his years; one solitary sign of "race" shows itself in his hands, somewhat large, but perfectly shaped. Yet, if the possessor of all these personal disadvantages were to enter any London drawing-room side by side with Bertie Grenvil, and it were a question of being warmly welcomed, the odds would be heavily against the Guardsman. I wish an "alarum and flourish of trumpets" were available, to accompany the announcement of so august a name. That is no other than Raoul, tenth Earl of Clydesdale, Viscount Artornish, lord of a dozen minor baronies, and Premier *Parti* of England.

His income varies by tens of thousands, according to the price of divers minerals, but never falls short of the colossal. He owns broad lands and manors in nearly every county north of the Tyne; and, when he came of age four years ago, the Border-side blazed with as many bale-fires, as ever were lighted in old days to give warning that the lances of Liddesdale were out on the foray. Ever since he left college the match-makers of Great Britain have been hard on his trail; and his movements, as chronicled in the *Post*, are watched with a keener interest than attaches to the "progress" of any royal personage. He is so *terribly* wealthy that even the great city financiers speak of his resources with a certain awe; for, independently of his vast income, there are vague reports of accumulations, varying from a quarter to half a million. His father died when the present Earl was in his cradle.

There is nothing very remarkable, outwardly, about the

other man. Harding Knowles has rather a disappointing
face: you feel that it ought to have been handsome, and
yet that is about the last epithet you would apply to it.
The features individually are good, and there is plenty of
intellect about them, though the forehead is narrow; but
the general expression is disagreeable—something between
the cunning and the captious. There is a want of repose,
just now, about his whole demeanour—a sort of fidgety
consciousness of not being in his right place; he is always
changing his position restlessly, and his hands are never
still for a moment. He had been Clydesdale's "coach" at
Oxford for two or three terms, and had acquired a certain
hold on the latter's favour, chiefly by the exercise of a
brusque, rough flattery, which the Earl chose to mistake
for sincerity and plain-speaking.

No parasite can be perfect, unless he knows when to
talk and when to hold his tongue. Knowles had mastered
that part of the science thoroughly. On the present
occasion he saw that the silent humour possessed his
patron, and was careful not to interrupt the lordly meditations; only throwing in now and then a casual observation
requiring no particular answer. No one dreams of deep
drinking now-a-days in general society; but the Earl has
evidently taken quite as much claret as was good for him
—enough to make him obstinate and savage. That pair
at the piano seem to fascinate him strangely. He keeps
watching every movement of Wyverne's lips, and every
change in Helen's colour, as if he would guess the import
of their low earnest words. A far deeper feeling than
mere curiosity is evidently at work. It is well that the
half-closed fingers shade his eyes just now, for they are
not good to meet—hot and bloodshot, with a fierce longing

and wrathful envy. Not an iota of all this escaped Harding Knowles; but he allowed the bad brutal nature to seethe on sullenly, till he deemed it was time to work the safety-valve.

"A pretty picture," he said at last, with rather a contemptuous glance in the direction of the lovers—Clydesdale ground out a bitter blasphemy between his teeth; but the other went on as if he had heard nothing.—"Yes, a very pretty picture; and Sir Alan Wyverne deserves credit for his audacity. But I can't help feeling provoked at such a rare creature being so perfectly thrown away. If ever there was a woman who was born to live in state, she sits there; and they will have to be pensioners of the Squire's if they want anything beyond necessaries. It's a thousand pities."

"You mean she might have made a better match?" the other asked: he felt he must say something, but he seemed to speak unwillingly, and his voice, always harsh and guttural, sounded thicker and hoarser than usual.

"Yes, I am sure she might have made a better match: I *think* she might have made—the best in England."

Knowles spoke very slowly and deliberately, almost pausing between each of the last words. His keen steady gaze fastened on Clydesdale, till the Earl's fierce blue eyes sank under the scrutiny, and the flush on his cheek deepened to crimson.

"What the d—l's the use of talking about that now?" he grumbled out, "now that it's all over and settled?"

"Settled, but not all over. I'm not fond of betting as a rule; but I should like to take long odds—*very* long odds, mind, for Wyverne's dangerous when he is in earnest—that the engagement never comes off."

Lord Clydesdale paused quite a minute in reflection. There was a wicked crafty significance in the other's look that he could not understand.

"I don't know what you call long odds," he said at last, "but I'll lay *you* 5000 to 50 that it's not broken off within the year."

There are men, not peculiarly irascible or punctilious, who would have resented those words and the tone in which they were spoken as a direct personal insult; but Knowles was not sensitive when it was a question of his own advantage or advancement, and had sucked in avarice with his mother's milk.

"I'll book that bet," he answered, coolly. "I take all chances in. Sir Alan might die, you know, before the year is out; or Miss Vavasour might come to her senses."

So he wrote it down carefully on his ivory tablets, affixing the date and his initials. They both knew it—he was signing a bond, just as effectually as if it had been engrossed on parchment and regularly witnessed and sealed. But neither cared to look the other in the face now. In the basest natures there lingers often some faint useless remnant of shame. I fancy that Marcus rather shrank from meeting his patron's glance, when he went out from the Decemvir's presence to lay hands on Virginius's daughter.

While this conversation was going on, Max Vavasour had roused himself from his easy-chair, and strolled over towards the piano. It is probable that he had got his orders from "my lady's" eloquent eye. As he came near, Wyverne drew back slightly, with a scarcely perceptible movement of impatience, and Helen stopped playing.

K

They both guessed that her brother had not disturbed himself without a purpose.

"It's a great shame to interrupt you, Alan," Max said; "but one has certain duties towards one's guests, I believe; and you might help me very much, if you would be good-natured. You see, all this isn't much fun for Clydesdale; and I want to keep him in good humour, if I can— never mind why. He's mad after *écarté* just now, and he has heard that you are a celebrity at it. He asked me to-day if I thought you would mind playing with him? I would engage him myself with pleasure; but it would be no sport to either party. He knows, just as well as you do, how infamously I play."

Wyverne very seldom refused a reasonable request, and he was in no mood to be churlish.

"What must be, must be," he replied, with a sigh of resignation. "If the Great Earl is to be amused, and no other martyr is available, thy servant is ready, though not willing. I thought I had lost enough in my time at that game. It is hard to have to lose, now, such a pleasant seat as this. Tell him I'll come directly. I suppose he don't want to gamble? He has two to one the best of it, though, when he has made me stir from here. Helen, perhaps you would not mind singing just one or two songs? I am Spartan in my tastes so far: I like to be marshalled to my death with sweet music."

So the two sat down at the *écarté* table. Clydesdale betrayed an eagerness quite disproportionate to the occasion when Max Vavasour summoned him to the encounter. He suggested that the stakes should be a "pony" on the best of eleven games: to this Alan demurred.

"I have given up gambling now," he said; "but, even when I played for money, I never did so with women in the room. A pony is a nominal stake with you, of course: with me, it is different. You may have 10 on, if you like. I only play one rubber."

The other assented without another word, and the battle began. The Earl was far from a contemptible adversary; but he was palpably over-matched. Wyverne had held his own before this with the best and boldest of half the capitals in Europe. He played carelessly at first, for his thoughts were evidently elsewhere; but got interested as the game went on, and developed all the science he possessed: it carried him through one or two critical points against invariably indifferent cards. At last they were five games all, and were commencing "*la belle*." Max, Harding Knowles, and Bertie Grenvil (who never could keep away from a card-table, unless some extraordinary potent counter-excitement were present) had been watching the match from the beginning; the last having invested 11—10 on Wyverne—taken by Clydesdale eagerly. The cards ran evenly enough. By dint of sheer good play Alan scored three to his opponent's two. As he was taking up his hand in the next deal, Miss Vavasour came up softly behind him, and leant her arm on the high carved back of his chair. She felt sure that her cousin would win, and wanted to share even in that trivial triumph. I wonder how often in this world women have unconsciously balked the very success they were most anxious to secure? Alan held the king and the odd trick certain; but, if his life had depended on the issue, he could not have helped looking up into the glorious dark eyes to thank them for their sympathy. At that moment his adversary played first, and Wyverne followed suit, without marking. It was one of those fatal *coups* that Fortune never forgives. The next deal Clydesdale turned up the king, and won the *vole* easily.

Even Max Vavasour, who knew him well, and had seen him play for infinitely larger stakes, was astonished at the excitement that the Earl displayed; he dashed down the winning card with an energy which shook the table, and actually glared at his opponent with a savage air of exultation, utterly absurd and incomprehensible under the circumstances.

Alan leant back in his chair, regarding the victor's flushed cheek and quivering lips with an amused smile, not wholly devoid of sarcasm.

"On my honour, I envy you, Clydesdale," he said, quietly; "there's an immense amount of pleasure before you. Only conceive the luxury of being able to gratify such a passion for play as yours must be, without danger of ruin! I never was so interested about anything in my life as you were about that last hand; and bad cards for 10 years, at heavy stakes, would only get rid of some of your superfluous thousands."

The exultation faded from the Earl's face, and it began to lower sullenly. He felt that he had made himself ridiculous, and hated Wyverne intensely for having made it more apparent.

"You don't seem to understand that we were playing for love," he muttered. I had heard so much of your play, that I wanted to measure myself against it, and I was anxious to win. It appears that the great guns miss fire sometimes, like the rest of us."

"Of course they do," Wyverne answered, cheerfully.

"Not that I am the least better than the average. But we are all impostors from first to last."

The party broke up for the night almost immediately afterwards. Alan laughed to scorn all his fair cousin's penitential fears about "her having interrupted him just at the wrong moment." It is doubtful if he ever felt any self-reproach for his carelessness, till Bertie Grenvil looked up plaintively in his face, as the two were wending their way to the smoking-room.

"Alan, I *did* believe in your *écarté*," he said.

There was not much in the words, but the Cherub uttered them with the air of a man to whom so wonderfully few things are left to believe in, that the defalcation of one of those objects of faith is a very serious matter indeed.

Yet Wyverne was wrong, and did his adversary in some sort injustice, when he supposed that the spirit of the gambler accounted altogether for the latter's eagerness and excitement. Other and different feelings were working in Lord Clydesdale's heart when he sate down to play. One of those vague superstitious presentiments that men are ashamed to confess to their dearest friends, shot across him at the moment. He had said within himself—"It is my luck against his, not only now, but hereafter. If I win at this game, I shall beat him at others—at *all*." So you see, in the Earl's imagination much more was at issue than the nominal stakes ; and there was a double meaning in his words—"We were playing *for love*."

CHAPTER X.

" A SHINY NIGHT,

IN THE SEASON OF THE YEAR."

IT was the third evening after that one recorded in the last chapter; the party at Dene remained the same, though a large reinforcement was expected on the morrow. Only the younger Vavasour was absent; he had gone out to dine and sleep at the house of a county magnate, with whom a Russian friend of Max's was staying. Lady Mildred and her daughter had just left the drawing-room—it was close upon midnight—Wyverne followed them into the hall to provide them with their tapers, and had not yet succeeded in lighting Helen's—there was never such an obstinate piece of wax, or such an awkward πυρφόρος. It is possible he would have lingered yet longer over the operation, and some pleasant last words, but he suddenly caught sight of the Chief Butler standing in the deep doorway that led towards the offices. The emergency must have been very tremendous to induce that model of discretion to intrude himself on any colloquy whatever; he evidently did not intend to do so now; but an extraordinary intelligence and significance on the grave precise face, usually possessed by a polite vacuity, made Alan con-

clude his "good-nights" rather abruptly; he guessed that
he was wanted.

"What is it, Hales?" he said, as soon as he came within
speaking distance.

The butler's voice was mysteriously subdued as he replied—

"My master wishes to see you in his study immediately,
if you please, Sir Alan. Mr Somers is with him."

The said Somers was born and bred in Norfolk, but had
been head keeper at Dene for 15 years—a brave, honest,
simple-minded man, rather blunt and unceremonious with
his superiors, and apt to be surly with his equals and
subordinates; but not ill-conditioned or bad-hearted *au
fond*; a really sincere and well-meaning Christian, too,
though he would swear awfully at times. He had only
one aim and object in life—the rearing and preservation of
game; we should be lucky, some of us, if we carried out
our single idea as thoroughly well.

The Squire was looking rather grave and anxious, as his
nephew entered.

"Tell Sir Alan at once what you have been telling me,
Somers," he said. "There is no time to lose, if we mean
to act."

The keeper's hard, dark face, grew more ominous and
threatening, as he muttered—"Acting! I should hope
there's no doubt about *that*; there never was such a
chance." And then in his own curt, quaint way, he gave
Wyverne the sum of his intelligence.

It appeared that the neighbourhood had been infested
lately by a formidable poaching gang, chiefly organized
and directed by a certain "Lanky Jem;" their head
quarters were at Newmanham, and they had divided their

patronage pretty equally, so far, over all the manors in a
circle of miles around. They had done a good deal of
harm already; for they first appeared in the egging season,
and had netted a vast number of partridges and hares,
even before the first of September, since which day they
had been out somewhere every night. Of course it was
most important to arrest their depredations before they
could get at the pheasants. The gang had been seen more
than once at their work; but their numbers were too
formidable—they mustered quite a score—for a small
party to buckle with; and to track them home was impossible; they had carts always near, artfully concealed,
with really good trotters in the shafts; so, when they had
secured as much as they could carry, they were able to
insure their retreat, and dispose of their booty. In
Newmanham they took the precaution of changing their
quarters perpetually, which made it more difficult to catch
them "red-handed."

That very day, however, one of the lot, partly from revenge, partly on the certainty of a rich reward, had turned
traitor. Somers was in possession of exact information as
to time and place: about *catching* the poachers that night
there was no doubt whatever—*holding* them was another
question: for "Lanky Jem" had made no secret of his
intention to show fight if driven into a corner; indeed it
was supposed that he would not be averse to having a
brush, under favourable circumstances, with his natural
enemies, the guardians of the game.

"They terms him Lanky Jem," the head-keeper ex-
plained; "'cause he comes from Lankyshire. He's a ork-
ard customer in a row, they say, werry wenturesome and
werry wenomous; he's taught his gang what they calls

the 'rough-and-tumble game;' all's fair in that style, they says, and if they gets you down you may reckon on having their heel in your mouth before you can holler. I don't think that chap would have split, only he had words with Jem; he knocked two of his teeth out, and roughed him dreadful, by the looks on him. You'll see our man with the rest on 'em to-night, Sir Alan, and don't you go to hit him, he'll have a spotted handkercher half over his face, and won't be blacked like the others, that's how you'll know him. I've taken the liberty already of letting Sir Gilbert's folks know; we shall muster a score or there-abouts, and I don't see no fear about matching 'em. The moon won't be down these two hours, and they won't begin much afore that. They'll come back through Haldon-lane, and I thought of lining it, Sir Alan, and nipping down on 'em there, if it's agreeable to you; the banks are nicely steep, and they won't get out of *that* trap in a hurry "

The Squire could not help smiling at the quiet way in which the old keeper took his nephew's presence and personal aid for granted.

" You have not asked Sir Alan yet if he means to go out with you," he remarked.

" I should think not," Wyverne interposed. " Somers knows me too well to waste words in that way. What a piece of luck, to be sure! Haldon-lane is the very place for an ambush; if we manage well we ought to bag the whole batch of them. You shall be general, Somers—I see your baton's all ready—I'll do my best as second in command. I think I ought to let the other men know, Uncle Hubert? I shall be ready in 10 minutes, and so will they, I'll answer for them. If you've anything to do before we start, you had better see about it at once,

Somers. We'll all meet in the servants' hall in a quarter of an hour."

The keeper indulged in a short, grim laugh of satisfaction and approval.

"I like to hear you talk, Sir Alan," he said; "you always comes to the point and means business. Everything's ready when you are; but we needn't start for a good half-hour yet. My men are staunch enough, I reckon; but it's no good keeping 'em too long, sitting in the cold."

The Squire laid his hand kindly on his nephew's shoulder, and stood for a second or two looking into his face, with a hearty affection and pride.

"I can't tell you how glad I am you are here, Alan. Even if Max had been at home, I think I would have asked you to go out to-night. I am too old for this sort of thing now; but somebody must be there that I can trust thoroughly. There will be wild work before morning, I fear, and coolness may be needed as much as courage. There has been no bloodshed, for the game, in my time, that the village doctor could not staunch; and it would grieve me bitterly—*you* can guess why—if any one were dangerously hurt now. We have had no fray so serious as this promises to be. You will take care, Alan, will you not? I am very anxious about it; I half wish I were going out myself.

"I'll take every care, Uncle Hubert," the other answered, cheerily. "But I don't the least apprehend any grave accident; it isn't likely they will have guns with them, as they are out netting, and don't dream of being waylaid. · I must go and tell the others, and get ready. I shall see you before we start, and when we come back, perhaps, with our prisoners.

It was very characteristic of those two, that Vavasour never hesitated to expose his nephew to peril, nor of excusing himself for not going out to share it; while Wyverno accepted the position perfectly, simply, and naturally It was evidently a plain question of expediency; the idea that it was possible to shrink from mere personal danger never crossed either of their minds.

Lord Clydesdale and Bertie Grenvil decided at once on joining the expedition; though it must be confessed that the alacrity displayed by the former hardly amounted to enthusiasm: it had rather the appearance of making the best of a disagreeable necessity.

Alan had nearly finished his brief preparations when there came a knock at his door; when he opened it Lady Mildred's maid was on the threshold. "My lady" wished to speak to him particularly: she was in her boudoir, and would not detain him a moment.

There Wyverne found her. It struck him that her cheek was a shade paler than usual, but the effect of contrast, produced by her *peignoir* of deep purple, and her dark hair braided close round her small head, may have helped to deceive him. There was an accent of annoyance in her voice as she said—

"Alan, what is this I hear about your going out with the keepers? How can you be so rash? What on earth are those people paid for if it is not to take poachers? Surely they know their own business best, and can do it alone."

"Not on an occasion like this, Aunt Mildred: heads as well as hands are useful sometimes. Even as Venice used to send out a pacific civilian to watch the conduct of their generals, so am I deputed to-night to control the ardour of

the faithful Somers and his merrymen all. I hope to do
myself credit as a moderator."

" I wish you would be serious for once. Even if *you* must
go out, which I am certain there is no necessity for, there
can be no reason for those other two accompanying you.
Of course I don't suppose there is danger of life ; but it is
quite dreadful to think of that poor delicate Bertie *aux
prises* with some drunken ruffian ; and if Lord Clydesdale
were to meet even with a slight hurt or disfigurement, I
am sure he would detest Dene for ever and ever. Alan,
do try what you can do to stop it."

He laughed within himself as he muttered, under his
breath, " *Enfin, je te vois arriver ;* " but his manner was
quite easy and unsuspicious as he answered her—

" I'm not much afraid for the Cherub ; he can take good
care of himself anywhere. You all pet him so much that
you do injustice to his pluck. You never seem to remember that he is a soldier. He may have to guard his head
in sharp earnest one of these days. But you are quite
right about Clydesdale. I had much rather he stayed behind ; but I fear it would be useless to try to dissuade him
now. Aunt Mildred, you don't quite understand these
things. He *must* go. But you may sleep in peace. Not
a hair of that august head shall be harmed if *I* can help it.
You have read your *Maid of Perth ?* Well, your unworthy
nephew and other retainers of the house will do duty as a
body-guard, like Torquil and his eight sons. The word for
the night is, *Bas air son Eachin.* I only hope the parallel
won't quite be carried out. All the nine fell, you remember, and then—the young chief ran away. I must not
stay another second. Dear Aunt Mildred, give us your good
wishes. You may be easy, if you will only trust to me."

He kissed her hand before she was aware, and was gone before she could reply. When Alan came into the servants' hall he found the whole party mustered, with the exception of the Earl, who joined them almost immediately The latter had evidently bestowed some pains on his equipment. He wore rather an elaborate cap, with a black cock's feather in the band, white breeches, and boots coming above the knee; but the most remarkable feature was a broad belt of untanned leather, girding the shooting-coat of black velvet. From this was suspended a formidable revolver, balanced by a veritable *couteau-de-chasse*.

Wyverne scanned him from head to foot with a cool critical eye, and then took Clydesdale aside a little from the rest.

"It's a picturesque 'get up,'" he said; "a little too much in the style of the bold smuggler, but that's a matter of taste. May I ask what you intend to do with these?"

He touched the weapons with the point of his finger.

"Do with them? Use them, of course," the Earl replied, flushing angrily "I made my fellow load the revolver afresh while I was dressing. There's no fear of its missing fire."

The other laughed outright.

"Did you mean to let all those barrels off, and then go in and finish the wounded with that terrible hanger? I give you credit for the idea; but, my dear Clydesdale, we are not in Russia or the Tyrol, unluckily. A man's life is held of some account here, you know, and there's a d—l of a row if you massacre even a poacher. You must be content with the primeval club. See, there's a dozen to choose from. The Squire allows no other weapons. Ask him, if you like. Here he comes.

Vavasour, when appealed to, spoke so decisively on the subject, that the Earl had no option but to yield. He did so, chafing savagely, for he was unused to the faintest contradiction, and registered in his sullen heart another grievance against Alan Wyverne. After a few words of caution and encouragement addressed by the Squire to the whole party, they started. He griped his nephew's hand hard as the latter went out, and whispered one word— "Remember."

When they had gone a few hundred yards from the house, Wyverne fell back to the rear of the column and took Greuvil by the arm.

"Look here, Bertie," he said, gravely. "I'm rather sorry I didn't go out alone on this business. We shall meet a roughish lot in an hour's time. Now, don't be rash and run your head up against danger unnecessarily. I shall not be able to look after you; I've got a bigger baby in charge to-night. I should hate myself for ever if your beauty was spoiled."

The Cherub laughed carelessly and confidently. The burliest Paladin that ever wore a beard was not more utterly fearless than he. He could use those little hands of his (he was in the habit of exchanging gloves with his favourite partners) as neatly and prettily as he did everything else, and in sooth was no contemptible antagonist for a light-weight.

"Don't bother yourself about me, Alan," he answered. I'll look after my face, you may rely on it. I've been very diligent in my practice lately, and if I get hold of an extraordinarily small poacher, perhaps I may as-

tonish him with what The Pet calls the 'London Particular.'"

They met Sir Gilbert Nevil's men by the way, and when
they reached the place of ambush, numbered 22 stalwart
fighting men. The spot was admirably adapted for the
purpose; a narrow deep lane passed just there through
the crest of a small hill, and the brushwood on the steep
banks was sufficient to hide a larger party. The rest
nestled down there as comfortably as they could, while
Alan and the head-keeper climbed the ridge to look out
over the champaign lying beneath them. They had not
long to wait before two lights appeared on the plain below,
moving quickly within a foot or so of the ground, and
every now and then becoming stationary. They were
lanterns fastened round the necks of the steady pointers
quartering the stubbles.

The keeper gave vent to a suppressed groan, ending in
a growl.

"There they are, d—n' em," he muttered. "The very
beat I meant you to take to-morrow, Sir Alan. They
won't be long in filling that 'ere blasted bag of theirs. I
see five coveys on that forty-acre bit this arternoon. We'll
take our change out of 'em before we sleep, or my name
ain't Ben Somers."

Wyverne shook his head warningly.

"Your blood's hotter than mine, I do believe," he said,
"though you are old enough to be my father. But mind,
there is to be no unnecessary violence to-night. I've
passed my word to the Squire, and you ought to help me
to keep it. If they show fight, it's another matter, and
they may take the consequences."

"I'll pound it, they fight," the other grumbled; "it

comes more nateral to Jem than running, 'specially as
he'll find hisself in a middlin' tight trap. We may get
back to cover, sir, they'll not be long now; I reckon
they'll finish in that stubble close agin' the lane."

So they rejoined their companions. The ambush was
thus disposed. Eight men, including Somers, Wyverne,
and Lord Clydesdale, took post, four on either bank, at a
certain spot; six others, similarly divided, were left about
40 yards in the rear—Bertie Grenvil was with this lot—
the others concealed themselves at short intervals along
the vacant space; the signal was not to be given till the
poachers had got well into the space between the two
main bodies; that in advance was rather the strongest, as
it was expected the marauders would try to force their
way into the high road, where carts were sure to be waiting them. So, without a movement of tongue or finger,
they were to bide their time.

Unless one is gifted with exceptional nerves, that time of
suspense before action is very trying. To compare great
things with small, I heard one of the best and bravest of
all who went up to the Redan, confess, the other day, that
he never felt so uncomfortable as during those long
minutes when the men stood in their ranks waiting for the
last orders, and that it was an unspeakable relief when
the word was given for the stormers to advance.

Lord Clydesdale evidently liked his position less and
less every moment. "Cursedly cold, isn't it?" he muttered, at last, and in truth his teeth were chattering
audibly.

"Pocket-pistols are not interdicted, if other fire-arms
are," Wyverne whispered, good-humouredly. "Take a
pull at mine, and wrap my plaid round you; I really don't

want it, I'm better clothed for this work than you are, I fancy; I've been at it before."

The Earl took the plaid, and half drained the flask without a word of thanks; he was still brooding sulkily over the rebuff he fancied he had met with before starting; besides this, the world had spoilt him so long that self-sacrifice on the part of his fellow-men for the convenience of Lord Clydesdale, seemed to him the most natural condition of things imaginable; he accepted such tributes affably or morosely, according to his humour, but invariably as his proper due.

Alan interpreted his companion's feelings pretty correctly, and smiled contemptuously to himself in the darkness.

"You amiable aristocrat!" he muttered between his teeth; "if it were not for vexing Aunt Mildred, and for my promise to her, would I *not* let you look out for yourself this cold morning? I wonder if a thoroughly good thrashing would improve your temper; it were a good deed to allow the experiment to be tried. I do believe the most inveterate ruffian we shall meet has more natural courtesy than has fallen to your share."

But the momentary bitterness soon passed away. Alan —as is the wont of his kind—never felt so benevolent towards mankind in general as when the moment of danger approached, which was to bring him into conflict with certain units of the species. Surely that perfect physical fearlessness is an enviable, if not a very ennobling qualification; it enables you to charge a big fence, or a big adversary, with comparative comfort to yourself; in neither case, unfortunately, will it insure you against a bad fall; but unless quite disabled, you rise up and go on again, as cheerfully as Antæus, and are at all events spared any pains of anticipation. An interval of silence which seemed very long, ensued. Suddenly Wyverne laid a firm, steady grasp on Lord Clydesdale's arm.

"Take off that plaid," he said, in the lowest and quietest of whispers; "you'll be warm enough in five minutes. They are in the next stubble now."

The ear of the practised deer-stalker, accustomed to listen for the rattle of a hoof far up the corries, had already caught certain faint sounds imperceptible to his companions. Somers heard them, though, nearly as soon; they could just see him through the black darkness, stretching his brawny limbs, and twisting round his wrist the thong of his bludgeon.

The fall of footsteps came nearer and nearer, more and more distinct, as the poachers crossed the low fence one by one, and got on to the harder ground: they were evidently very numerous. They did not come on in detached straggling parties, but appeared to wait till all were in the lane, and then advanced in something like a regular column, in the centre of which four men carried, in two nets made for the purpose, the night's spoil; as this entirely consisted of birds, the weight was not overwhelming, though the result had been extraordinarily successful.

"Get on, two of ye, as soon as we top the hill," a deep, hoarse voice said, from the midst of the poachers; "and mind you see all clear."

The slightest touch of Wyverne's arm, and the discreetest chuckle, testified to Somers' intense appreciation of the impending "sell." The gang advanced with their habitually stealthy tread, but evidently quite unsuspiciously, till they were hemmed in by the divisions of the ambush. Then a whistle sounded shrill and ominous as Black Roderick's signal, and a dozen port-fires blazed out at once, casting a weird, lurid glare over the crowd of rugged blackened faces, working with various emotions of wonder, rage, and fear.

In the pause that ensued, while the assailed were still under the influence of the first surprise, and the assailants were waiting for orders, Wyverne's voice was heard, not raised by one inflection above its usual tone, and yet the most distant ear caught every syllable.

"Will you surrender at once? It is the best thing you can do."

The same voice answered which had spoken before—hoarse and thick with passion.

"Surrender be d—d! Here's the chance we've been wanting ever so long. Stick together, lads, and be smart with those bludgeons: there's enow of us to cut the —— keepers to rags."

Alan spoke again; and the curt, stern, incisive accents clove the still night-air like points of steel.

"Stand fast in the front: close up there in the rear. It is our own fault if a man gets through: we'll have all—or none."

He had only time for a hurried whisper—"Somers, whatever happens, look after Lord Clydesdale;" for Bertie and his men came on with a rush and a cheer. The port-fires were cast down and trampled out instantly, and so—darkly and sullenly—the *mêlée* began. It was likely to be an equal one; the poachers had the disadvantage of the surprise and the attack being against them, but they were slightly superior in numbers, and their bludgeons were of a more murderous character than those carried by the keepers, shod with iron for the most part, and heavily

leaded. For a minute or two the struggle went on in
silence, only broken by the dull sound of heavy blows, by
hard, quick breathings, and by an occasional curse or groan.
Lord Clydesdale had drawn slightly aside, and so, avoiding the first rush of the poachers, remained for awhile in-
active. Suddenly, as ill-luck would have it, he found himself face to face with the most formidable of all the gang.
"Lanky Jem" had forced his way to the front, partly
because safety lay in that direction, partly because he
fancied that there fought "the foemen worthiest of his
steel;" he had his wits perfectly about him, and was
viciously determined to do as much damage as possible,
whether he escaped or no. He saw the figure standing
apart from the rest, taking no part in the conflict, and
instantly guessed that he had to do with a personage of
some condition and importance: keepers are rarely cou-
templative or non-combatants at such a moment.

"Here's one of them —— swells!" he growled. "Come
on, d—n ye! I'll have *your* blood, if I swing for it."

Clydesdale was not exactly a coward; if any ordinary
social danger had presented itself, he would scarcely have
quailed before it. For instance, I believe he would have
faced a pistol at 15 paces with average composure. But
it so happened (he had not been at a public school) that
in all his life he had never seen a blow stricken in anger.
The aspect of his present adversary fairly appalled him.
Independently of the poacher's huge proportions and evidently great strength, there was a cool concentrated cruelty
about the bull-dog face—the white range of grinding teeth
showing in relief against the blackness of his sooty disguise—which made him a really terrible foe. The Earl
looked helplessly round, as though seeking for succour;

but all his party seemed to have already as much as they could do. He saw the grim giant preparing for a spring, and all presence of mind utterly deserted him; he drew hastily back without lifting his hands to defend himself; his heel caught in a projecting root, and he fell supine, with a loud, piteous cry. "Lanky Jem" was actually disconcerted by such absolute non-resistance; but the brutal instinct soon re-asserted itself, and he was rushing in to maim and mangle the fallen man, after his own savage fashion, when a fresh adversary stood in his path, bestriding Clydesdale where he lay.

Wyverne had been engaged with a big foundry-man, who chanced to come across him first; but even in the fierce grapple, where pluck and activity could scarcely hold their own against weight and brute strength, he had found time to glance repeatedly over his shoulder. He saw the Earl fall, and extricating himself from the opponent's gripe with an effort that sent the latter reeling back, he sprang lightly aside, just in time to intercept the Lancashire man from his prey. But the odds were fearfully against him now; for his original adversary had recovered himself, and made in quickly to help his comrade. Both struck at Alan savagely at the same instant. He caught one blow on his club, but was obliged to parry the other with his left arm: the head was saved, but the limb dropped to his side powerless. He ground his teeth hard, and threw all the strength that was left him into one bitter blow; it lighted on the temple of the man who had disabled him, and dropped him like a log in his tracks. But, before Wyverne could recover himself, the terrible Lancashire bludgeon came home on his brows, crushing in the low, stiff crown of his hat like paper, and beating him down, sick and dizzy, to his knee. He lifted his club mechanically, but it hardly broke the full sway of another murderous stroke, which stretched him on his face senseless. He looked as if he had remembered his promise to the last; for he fell right over Clydesdale, effectually shielding the latter with his own body.

Alan's life and this story had well nigh ended there and then. Such an abrupt termination might possibly have been to *his* advantage as well as to yours, reader of mine. But it was not so to be. Just as Jem was bracing his great muscles for one cool, finishing stroke on the back of Wyverne's unprotected skull, a lithe active form lighted on his shoulders, and slender, nervous fingers clutched his throat till they seemed to bury themselves in the flesh, and as he fell backward, gasping and half strangled, a voice, suppressed and vicious as a serpent's hiss, muttered in his ear three words in an unknown tongue—"*Basta, basta, carissimo!*"

The poacher's vast strength, however, soon enabled him to shake off his last assailant, and he was rising to his feet, more dangerous than ever, when a tremendous blow descended right across his face, gashing the forehead and crushing the bones of the nose in one fearful wound. The miserable wretch sunk down—all his limbs collapsing—without a groan or a struggle, and lay there half drowned in blood.

The old head keeper stooped for a moment to examine his ghastly handiwork, and then, lifting his head, remarked with a low fierce laugh—

"I gives you credit for that move, Master Bertie, it wur wery neatly done."

The poachers had been getting the worst of it all

through; they were so hemmed in in the narrow way that their numbers helped them but little; indeed, some in the centre of the crowd never struck a blow. Their leader's fall decided the fray at once; some voice cried out—"Don't hit us any more; we gives in:" and they threw down their bludgeons, as though by preconcerted signal.

So ended the most successful raid that had been heard of in that country for years; they talk of it still. Out of 26 men, only three escaped, and one of these was the informer. Neither was any one mortally or even dangerously hurt, though there were some hideous wounds on both sides; but, if you bar gunpowder, it takes a good deal to kill outright a real tough "shires-man." Even "Lanky Jem" recovered after awhile from Somers' swashing blow, though they were obliged to carry him back to Dene. The permanent disfigurement which ensued, made his repulsive countenance rather more picturesque in its ugliness, so that it was an improvement after all. He quitted those parts, though, as soon as he got out of gaol, and never returned.

Of all the wounded, perhaps Wyverne was the most seriously hurt; but, though his senses came back slowly, he was able to stagger home, leaning heavily on Bertie Grenvil's shoulder. You must imagine the satisfaction with which the Squire welcomed the conquerors and their captives.

> " Unwounded from the dreadful close,
> But breathless all, the Earl arose.

Even his overweening self-esteem could not prevent Clydesdale's feeling nervous and uncomfortable. He was conscious of having betrayed a very discreditable pusillanimity; and he could not guess how many might be in the secret

of his discomfiture. There was nothing in the mere fact
of his coming out of the fray scathless, for Grenvil had
not a scratch or a bruise; but it struck him as rather odd,
that nobody asked " if he were hurt in any way."   He was
so perturbed in spirit, as hardly to be able to display a
decent amount of solicitude about Wyverne's injuries, or to
sympathize, with a good grace, in the triumph of the rest
of the party.   There was one man, at all events, that he
could never look in the face again, without an unpleasant
feeling of inferiority and obligation.   Poor Alan!   He
meant well; but he did not make a very good night's
work of it, after all.   He got one or two hard blows, and
changed Clydesdale's previous dislike into a permanent
and inveterate hate.   Virtue is always its own reward, you
know.

Perhaps the Earl's *largesse* to every one concerned in
the capture would not have been so extravagantly liberal,
if he had guessed how thoroughly the old keeper appreciated the real state of affairs.   When Somers alluded to
the subject—which he did once a month for the rest of his
natural life—he generally concluded in these words:

" It wur the prettiest managed thing ever I see; but we
wery near got muddled at one time, all along of that there
helpless Lord."

CHAPTER XI.

DIAMONDS THAT CUT DIAMONDS.

HELEN VAVASOUR came of a race whose women, if tradition speaks truth, could always look, at need, on battle or broil without blenching; but it is probable she would hardly have slept so soundly that night, had she guessed at what was going on under the stars. She heard nothing of the preparations; the bustle was confined to those remote regions where a Servile War might have been carried on without the patricians wotting of it; the furlongs of passage and corridor in the vast old manoir swallowed up all ordinary sounds. Pauline would of course have enlightened her mistress, but Wyverne chanced to "head" her before she could "make her point." The quick-witted Parisian saw that he meant what he said, when he begged her not to open her lips on the subject, and kept silence through the night, though it was pain and grief to her. That sentimental *soubrette* kept for Alan the largest share of a simple hero-worship, and she lay awake for hours, listening and quaking, and interceding perpetually with her favourite Saint for the safeguard of her favourite Paladin. Judge if she indemnified herself for her reticence when she woke Miss Vavasour on the following morning!

She had got a perfect romance of the Forest ready, wherein Wyverne's exploits transcended those of Sir Bevis, and the physical proportions of his foes cast those of Colbrand or Ascapart into the shade.

Making all allowances for her handmaiden's vivid imagination, Helen came down to breakfast in a great turmoil of curiosity and anxiety. She had to wait for authentic particulars, till she got fevered with impatience. The Squire, quite determined in doing *his* share of the business thoroughly, had followed the prisoners, already, to the neighbouring town, where they were to answer their misdeeds before himself and other magistrates. Helen had no reason to believe that her mother was better informed than herself, and "my lady's" morning meditations were not lightly to be disturbed; no one else had shown any sign of life so far. At last Bertie Grenvil lounged into the breakfast-room. His appearance was somewhat reassuring; there was not a trace of conflict or even of weariness on the fair face; indeed, the Cherub was so used to turn night into day, that late hours and sleeplessness were rather his normal state. His answers to Helen's string of eager questions were rather unsatisfactory; much in the style of old Caspar's reminiscences about Blenheim :—

> " Why that I cannot tell," quoth he
> " But, 'twas a famous victory."

Perhaps there was no real reserve or affectation about it ; one's waking recollections of a midnight fray are apt to be strangely distorted and vague.

"I've seen Alan this morning," Bertie remarked, at length, casually. " He's wonderfully well, all things considered, and means to show at luncheon ; but I fear they've spoiled his shooting for some time; he won't be able to use that left arm for a fortnight."

Miss Vavasour's cheek lost its colour instantly, and her hand shook so that it could hardly set down the cup it held.

"You don't mean that Alan is seriously hurt?" she said. "And they never told me. I have never even sent to ask after him. It is *too* cruel." She rose quickly, and rang the bell, before Grenvil could anticipate her.

"What an idiot I am!" Bertie interjected, actually flushing with a real self-reproach. "I thought you had heard Alan had met with two or three hard blows, or I would not have mentioned it so abruptly. Don't be frightened; on my honour, they are nothing worse than bruises; he will tell you so himself in an hour's time."

Helen forced a smile, and recovered her composure immediately. But she did not seem comfortable till she had sent Pauline to bring a report of her cousin's state from his own lips. The *soubrette* had been kept in equal ignorance with her mistress as to Wyverne's hurts, and when she came back to repeat his cheerful message, her voice was trembling, and her bright black eyes were dim with tears.

The whole party—with the exception of the Squire—met at luncheon; for Max Vavasour returned in the course of the morning. The latter congratulated everybody very pleasantly on the success of the night's expedition; and, it is possible, congratulated himself quite as sincerely on having been out of the way; at all events, he affected no regret at having missed his share of peril and glory Alan Wyverne came in the last. With the aid of a scientific valet, he had contrived to dissemble very successfully the traces of the fray; the dark thick hair swept lower than usual over his brows, and almost concealed the spot where the first blow had fallen; the second had left no visible mark. He seemed in the best possible spirits, and his gay, pleasant laugh came as readily as ever, without an appearance of being forced or constrained; but his face was very pale, and his left arm hung helplessly in its sling.

The worst of Lord Clydesdale's enemies—already he had made not a few—might have been satisfied at the state of the Earl's feelings, as he sate there, brooding sullenly over the recollection of his own discomfiture, and watching the *empressement* which everybody seemed determined to manifest towards his unconscious rival. Miss Vavasour, as we have before said, was never "gushing" or demonstrative; but she considered it the most natural thing in the world that her cousin should be petted and tended under the circumstances. So she sate by his side, anticipating and ministering to his wants with the tact and tenderness that only a woman—and a loving one—can display, utterly ignoring the savage blue eyes that kept glaring at her from beneath their bushy brows. Clydesdale muttered curse after curse under his breath, and drained glass after glass of the strong brown sherry that stood close to his hand; the rich liquor seemed to be absorbed with no better effect, than a genial rain produces falling on a quicksand.

It was rather remarkable that no one seemed disposed to question *him* much about last night's adventure. Possibly Lady Mildred knew something of the truth—though not all—and had taken Max into confidence; for her maid might have been seen in close colloquy with one of the

keepers, early in the morning; and it is probable that
model of austere and dignified propriety would not so far
have derogated without good cause. However this might
be, her manner towards Alan Wyverne was kind and affectionate to a degree; when she spoke to Lord Clydesdale, a very close observer might have detected a certain
coolness in the perfect courtesy. "My lady" was only a
woman, after all; and the instincts of her sex, though
tamed and trained, would assert themselves sometimes.
She looked at the Earl as he sate there swelling with sulky
self-importance; ruddy, certainly—perhaps unpleasantly
so—but not "of a cheerful countenance;" then she looked
across at Wyverne, just as a bright, grateful smile lighted
up all his wan face, and thanked Helen for some trifling
act of kindness. The contrast was too much for Lady
Mildred; for once the cool diplomatist yielded to a real
frank impulse and forgot her cunning. When she rose
with the others, she crossed over to where Alan sate, and
leant over him, on pretence of settling his sling, till her
lips touched his hair. Even Helen, who was so near, did
not catch the whisper—

"Ah, so many thanks! Who can help loving you—
always braver and better than your word?"

Neither ever alluded to the events of that night again,
but they understood each other perfectly; and to the end
of his days, Wyverne considered his services over-paid.
In truth, it was no mean triumph to have made "my
lady," for more than a hundred seconds, thoroughly honest
and sincere.

That day brought a large influx of fresh guests to Dene;
but only four deserve especial mention, and perhaps these
might be reduced to three.

Grace Beauclerc was Alan's only sister. There was a
strong likeness between them, not only in features, but in
character. She had the same quiet thorough-bred face,
that no one ever called beautiful, but every one felt was
intensely loveable; the same slender, graceful proportions;
the same soft. winning manner; the same power of attract-
ing and retaining the affection of men and women. The
resemblance extended still further—to their fortunes.
Grace had not ruined herself, certainly—with the exception of a few fair speculators of whose daring The
Corner and Capel Court are conscious, they generally
leave that luxury to *us*—but she had gone as near the
wind as possible, by contracting the most imprudent of
alliances. How the Beauclercs lived, was a mystery to their
nearest and dearest friends. The crash had not come at
Wyverne Abbey when the marriage took place, and Alan
had then settled £400 a year on his sister; but this, added
to the interest of her own small fortune, and the pay of a
clerk of nine years' standing in the Foreign Office, hardly
carried their income beyond the hundreds. A cipher had
represented Algernon Beauclerc's own personal assets
long before he married. Yet they lived apparently in
great comfort, went out everywhere, gave occasionally the
nicest entertainments, at home, on a very tiny scale, that
you can conceive; and, it was said, were wonderfully little
in debt. It was a great social problem, in its way, and
one of those that it is not worth while puzzling oneself to
solve. But though Grace's husband had been very extravagant, and was still far from self-denying, he was weak
neither in mind nor principle; he loved his wife and his
children, after his fashion, far too well to involve himself
in any serious scrape; and contrived to utilize his amuse-

ments to a remarkable degree. He was passionately fond of whist, and had attained an exceptional excellence in that fascinating game. His plan was, to set aside a certain sum each year to risk on its chances: the profits went to the account of all sorts of *menus plaisirs*, in which Grace had more than her share; if the card-purse was emptied, nothing would induce him to play again till the time arrived for replenishing it. Algy Beauclerc hardly knew how to be angry, even with an incorrigibly careless or stupid partner, and the world in general found it impossible to quarrel with him. In appearance, he was a curious contrast to his wife—broad and burly, with a bluff, jovial face, half shrouded in a forest of blonde beard, and large, light, laughing eyes. Prince Percinet and Graciosa never got on better together than did that apparently ill-matched couple. The set in which they lived, though neither vicious nor reckless, was decidedly fast; looking at Grace's quiet, rather pensive face, one could not help fancying that she must have felt sometimes uncomfortably out of her element; but she had a singular power of adapting herself to circumstances without being deteriorated thereby. Presiding over one of those post-operatic *réunions*, where cigars, and even cigarettes, were not interdicted—or playing with her children, as she would do for hours of a morning—she always seemed perfectly and placidly happy.

Of a very different stamp were the other pair that remain to be noticed. Not only her intimate friends, and the men with whom she had flirted more or less seriously—they would have made a fair second-battalion to any regiment—but the whole of London, opened wondering eyes when handsome, daring Maud Dacres

married Mr Brabazon, a pillar of the Stock Exchange,
five-aud-twenty years her senior, after an acquaintance of
seven weeks beguu at Boulogue, where—for reasous, cogent
though temporary—her father was then residing.   It was
not that she was more unlikely than another to make a
money-match; but every one was surprised at her select-
iug that particular millionuaire.

Richard Brabazon was not only glaringly under-bred in
form, feature, mind, and manner, but he was popularly considered one of the most "aggravating" men alive.   He
had a knack of hittiug upon the topic most disagreeable to
his interlocutor or to the compauy in general, and of in-
troduciug the same at the most inappropriate moment,
always in a smooth, plausible way, which made it more irritating.   Eveu when he wished to be extraordinarily
civil, there was an evident affability and condesceusion
about him that very few could stand.   His slow, measured,
mincing way of speakiug—pronouncing a's like e's—affected one's ear like the hum of a mosquito; and his
plump, smug, smooth-shaven face was intensely provocative, inspiriug people, otherwise calm and pacific, with a
rabid desire to leap up and smite him on the cheek.   This
laudable and very general propeusity had never yet been
gratified; for Richard Brabazon was far too cunuing ever
to give a chauce away.   Many men would have given large
mouies for au opportunity of taking overt offence, but they
waited still in vain.

It was a marvel how his wife—high-spirited and quick-
tempered to a fault—coutrived to live with him, without
occasioually betraying annoyance or aversion.   It is probable that several bitter duels had in fact taken place;
but the antagonists kept their own secret and it was a

perfect neutrality now, though an armed one. The principle of non-interference was thoroughly established, and the contiguous powers did not even take the trouble to watch each other's frontier. Sometimes the spirit of aggravation would tempt Brabazon to launch a taunt or a sarcasm in the direction of his wife or her friends; but it was generally met by an imperial and absolute indifference —at rare intervals, by a retort, not the less biting because it was so very quietly put in. He *would* do it, though he knew he should get the worst of it, just as Thersites could not refrain from his gibe, though his shoulders were shaking already in anticipation of the practical retort of Ajax or Odysseus.

Lady Mildred was good-natured enough never to cross the plans or pleasures of her friends unless they interfered with hers; indeed, she would further them as far as was consistent with her own credit and convenience; but even in her benevolence some malice was mingled. She was rather glad to give Grenvil an opportunity of following out his love-dream, especially as she felt certain no harm could come of it; but, in mentioning to him the expected guests, she had purposely omitted the Brabazons.

Bertie had been indulging in an ante-prandial siesta, and only came down the great staircase as the others were filing past in to dinner; he was in time to see Maud Brabazon sweep by, more insolently beautiful, he thought, than ever. She just deigned to acknowledge his presence with the slightest bend of her delicate neck, and the sauciest of smiles. That wily Cherub could feign innocence right well when it served his wicked ends; but only one visible sign *really* remained to testify that he had once been guileless—perhaps it was a mere accident of complexion—he had not forgotten how to change colour. Lady Mildred watched the meeting. She saw Bertie's cheek flush—brightly as a girl's might do who hears the first love-whisper—and then grow pale almost to the lips. " My lady " laughed under her breath, in calm appreciative approbation, just as some scientific patron of the Arena may have laughed, when the net of the Retiarius glided over the shoulders of the doomed Secutor.

Any one interested in such psychological studies— and, to some people, a really well-managed flirtation is a very interesting and instructive spectacle—would have been much amused that evening watching the " passages " of Bertie's love. It was rather a one-sided affair, after all; for the Cherub was so hard hit as to forget his cunning of fence, and timidity for once was not in the least assumed. The lady was thoroughly at her ease, as women ever are who play that perilous game with their head instead of their heart.

Maud Brabazon was just on the shady side of 30; but such a pleasant shade it was! The sunniest year in the lives of her many rivals looked dull and tame by comparison. She was rather below the middle height, and rather fuller in her proportions, than was consistent with perfection of form; but no one was ever heard to hint that her figure could have been improved upon. Large bright brown eyes were matched by soft abundant hair of a darker shade; a slightly aquiline nose, a delicately chisselled *mutine* mouth, and the ripest of peach-complexions, made up a picture that every one found fascinating, many fatally so.

She was a very queen of coquetry, understanding and practising every one of its refinements. You always saw the most attractive elements of any company converging to the spot where she sate, like straws drawn in by an eddy. Where was the secret of her power? Men who had been led captive at her chariot-wheels asked themselves that question in after days, when freedom was partially regained, and got puzzled over it, as one does over the incidents of a very vivid dream. It was a fair face, certainly, but there were others more brilliant in their beauty, more winning in their loveliness. Her frank boldness of speech dazzled you at first with its natural, careless *verve*—she kept for special occasions the tender confidential tones that lingered in your ears through many sleepless night-watches—but several of her beaten rivals had really thrice her wit and cleverness, and, as conversationalists, could have distanced her easily. Maud Brabazon seemed to diffuse round her an atmosphere of temptation. Cold-blooded men, of austere morals and rigid propriety, felt irresistibly impelled to make love to her on the shortest acquaintance, not wildly or passionately, but in an airy, light-minded fashion, which left no remorse, hardly a regret, behind. It was strange that she had never yet got entangled in any of the toils she wove so deftly: for the bitterest of friends or foes had never dared to impute to her any darker crime than consummate coquetry. One who knew her well, when the subject was being discussed, thus expressed himself in the figurative language of the turf, of which he was a staunch supporter:

"Yes, she can win, when she's in front all the way. Wait till you see her collared; *they've never made her gallop yet.*"

Thereby intimating his opinion that the Subduer was

still in the future, by whom Maud's peace of mind was to be imperilled.

All things considered, it seemed likely that poetical justice was going to assert itself in the shape of merited retaliation impending over the Cherub's graceless head; a state of things so perfectly satisfactory that we may as well leave them there for the present.

Pressing affairs called Lord Clydesdale away from Dene on the following day. He had probably reasons of his own for cutting his visit short rather abruptly. He thought that whatever interests he might have at stake would be advanced fully as well in his absence, for the present. Somehow or another, before he went, Max Vavasour was made aware of the wager with Harding Knowles. On the occasion of a great robbery—

> "When the knowing ones, for once, stand in
> With some dark flyer meant at last to win—"

and the owners of one or two dangerous horses are put on, a "monkey to nothing," I believe they go through the form of registering it as a bet; so we may as well dignify the Earl's compact by that convenient name. It is more than likely that Clydesdale made the confession himself. He had little delicacy in such matters when he knew his man; and no Oriental despot could be more insolent in his cynicism. If he had thought he could do so safely, he would have offered money to her nearest relation to serve him in his pursuit of any woman he might fancy, without the faintest scruple or shame.

However the revelation was made, Max Vavasour never betrayed to Knowles his consciousness of the confederacy by word or sign; but he would look at the latter occasionally with a very peculiar expression in his cold dark eyes.

There was something of curiosity in that look, more of dislike and contempt. The wily schemer would accept readily
the aid of any instrument, however repulsive, that would
serve his purpose; but they never were stifled for one
moment—the instincts of patrician pride. Harding was no
favourite of Lady Mildred's; and her manner towards him
could not be said to be cordial now; but there certainly
was a shade more of courtesy and attention. She suggested
now and then that his name should be added to the dinner-
list, which she had never done before; and honoured him at
times with a fair share of her evening's conversation. There
was nothing strange in this. Knowles was evidently a
rising man; and "my lady" made a point of being at least
civil to such people, though she would just as soon have
thought of asking a real Gorilla to her house, as any living
celebrity—soldier, priest, lawyer, or literate—simply because
he chanced to be the lion of the day.

CHAPTER XII.

RUMOURS OF WARS.

HARDING KNOWLES had never been a hard-working man. Very little more reading would have turned a good Second in classics into an easy First, and this was so well known at Oxford that he might have had as many pupils as he liked during the year that he resided there after taking his degree. He would only take two or three—"just to have something to do in the morning," he said; and these were all of the Clydesdale stamp—men whose connection was worth a good deal, while their preparation cost no sort of head-work or anxiety. He had been called to the bar since then, but had never pretended to follow up the profession. There was not a trace of business about his chambers in the Temple ; no face of clerk or client ever looked out at the chrysanthemums through those pleasant windows, the sills of which were framed and buried in flowers. He could write a clever article, or a sharp sarcastic critique, when the fit seized him, and made a hundred or so every year thus in an easy desultory way : the Rector's allowance was liberal, so that Harding had more than enough to satisfy all his tastes, which were by no means extravagant ; in fact, he saved money. But he was avaricious to the heart's core, and could be painstaking and patient enough when the stake was really worth his while to win. He did not tarry long at Dene after Clydesdale's departure—long enough, though, to have another incentive to exertion in the latter's cause. Personal pique was added now to the mere greed of gain. The merest trifle brought this about, and you would hardly understand it without appreciating some anomalies in Knowles's character.

There never was a more thorough-going democrat. From his birth his sympathies and instincts had all taken the same direction, and these had been strengthened and embittered by his mother's evil training. He disliked the patrician order intensely; but their society seemed to have a strange fascination for him, judging from the pertinacity he displayed in endeavouring to gain and confirm a footing there. He would intrigue for certain invitations in the season as eagerly as a French deputy seeking the red ribbon of Honour. Yet he was always uncomfortable when his point was gained, and he found himself half way up the much-desired staircase. The mistress of the mansion greeted him probably with the self-same smile that she vouchsafed to nine-tenths of the five hundred guests who crowded her rooms; but Knowles would torment himself with the fancy that there was something compassionate or satirical in the fair dame's look, as if she penetrated a truth, of which he was himself conscious—that he had no business to be there. He felt that, if he got a fair start, he could talk better than the majority of the men round him; but he felt, too, that he had no chance against the most listless or languid of them all. They were on their own ground, and the intruder did not care to match himself against them there: his position was far too constrained, his footing too insecure. How he hated them, for the indolent *nonchalance* and serene indifference that he would have given five years of life to be able to assume! A wolfish ferocity would rise within him as he watched a beardless Coldstreamer dropping his words slowly, as if each were worth money and not lightly to be parted with, into the delicate ear of a haughty beauty from whom Knowles scarcely dared to hope for a recognizing bow. The innocent object of his wrath was probably only sacrificing himself to the necessities of the position, while his thoughts reverted with a tender longing to the smoking-room of his club, or anticipated the succulent chop that Pratt's was bound to provide for him before the dawning.

In all other respects Harding was as little sensitive as the most obstinate of pachyderms. He did not know what shame meant, and an implied insult that would have roused another savagely would scarcely attract his notice. You have seen one instance of this already. But he was nervously and morbidly alive to the minutest point affecting his position in society. After assisting at one of those assemblies of the *haute volée,* he would review in his memory every incident of the evening, and would be miserable for weeks afterwards if he thought he had made himself ridiculous by any awkwardness of manner or any incongruity of word or deed. If the choice had been forced upon him, he would have committed a forgery any day, sooner than a *gaucherie.*

I suppose everybody is sensitive somewhere, and it is only a question whether the shaft hits a joint in the harness, and so some go on for years, or for ever, without a scratch or a wound. Sometimes the weak point is found out very oddly and unexpectedly.

There is now living a man whom, till very lately, his friends used to quote as the ideal of impassibility. Even in his

youthful days, when he was "galloper" occasionally to
General Levin, war-worn veterans used to marvel at and
envy the sublime serenity with which he would receive a
point-blank volley of objurgation, double-shotted with the
hoarse expletives for which that irascible commander is world-
renowned.   I have seen him myself exposed to the "chaff"
of real artists in that line.   He only smiled in complacent
security, when "the archers bent their bows and made them
ready," and sate amidst the banter and the satire, unmoved
as is Ailsa Craig by the whistle of the sea-bird's wings.   It
was popularly supposed that no sorrow or shame which can
befall humanity would seriously disturb his equanimity, till
in an evil hour he plunged into print.   It was a modest little
book, relating to a Great War in which he had borne no ig-
noble part ; so mild in its comment and so meek in its suggestions, that the critics might have spared it from very pity.
But unluckily he fell early into the hands of one of the most
truculent of the tribe, and all the others followed suit, so
that poor Courtenay had rather a rough time of it.   They
questioned his facts and denied his inferences, accusing him
of ignorance and partiality in about equal degrees, and, what
was harder still to bear, they anatomized his little jokes
gravely, and made a mock at his pathetic passages, stigma-
tizing the first as "flippancy," the last as "fine writing."
Ever since that time, *le Beau Sabreur* has been subject to
fits of unutterable gloom and despondency.   Only last summer we were dining with him at the "Bellona."   The banquet
was faultless and the guests in the best possible form, so
that the prospects of the evening were convivial in the extreme.   It chanced that there was One present who had also
written a book or two, and had also been evil treated by the
reviewers.   A peculiarly savage onslaught had just appeared

in a weekly paper, imputing to the author in question every species of literary profligacy, from atheism down to deliberate immorality. The man who sat next to him opened fire upon the subject. It so happens that this much maligned individual—as a rule, quite the reverse of good-tempered—is stolidly impervious to critical praise or blame. This indifference is just as much a constitutional accident, of course, like exemption from nausea at sea, but one would think *he* must find it convenient at times. He joined in the laugh now quite naturally, and only tried to turn the subject because its effect on our host was evident. His kind, handsome face became overcast with a moody melancholy. The allusion to his friend's castigation brought back too vividly the recollection of his own. The cruel stripes were scarcely healed yet, and the flesh *would* quiver at the remote sound of the scourge.

Courtenay's fellow-sufferer would fain have cheered him. The first flask of " Dry " had just been opened (it was *una de multis, face nuptiali digna*—a wine, in truth, worthy to be consumed at the marriage-feasts of great and good men), he took the brimming beaker in his hand, before the bright beads died out of the glorious amber, and spoke thus, sententiously—

" O my friend, let us not despond overmuch ; rather let us imitate Socrates, the cheery sage, when he drained his last goblet. Do me right. Lo! I drink to the judge who hath condemned us—Τοῦτο τῷ καλῷ Κριτίᾳ."

Courtenay did drink—to do him justice, he will always do *that*—but his smile was the saddest thing I ever saw ; and it was three good hours before his spirits recovered their tone, or his great golden moustaches, which were drooping sympathetically, their martial curl.

If you realize Harding Knowles's excessive sensitiveness on certain points, you will understand how Alan Wyverne fell under his ban.

The cousins were starting for their afternoon's ride. Knowles had lunched at Dene, but was not to accompany them. He chanced to be standing on the steps when the horses came up, and Miss Vavasour came out alone. Something detained Alan in the hall for a minute, and when he appeared, Harding was in the act of assisting Helen to mount. Now that "mounting" is the simplest of all gymnastics, if you know how to do it, and if there exists between you and the fair Amazon a certain sympathy and good understanding; in default of these elements of concord, it is probable that the whole thing may come to grief. Harding was so nervously anxious to acquit himself creditably, that it was not likely he would succeed. He "lifted" at the wrong moment and too violently, not calculating on the elasticity of the demoiselle's spring, even though she was taken unawares. Nothing but great activity and presence of mind on Helen's part saved a dangerous fall. She said not one word as she settled herself anew in the saddle; but the culprit caught one glance from the depths of the brilliant eyes which stopped short his stammered apology. It was not exactly angry—worse a thousand times than that; but it stung him like the cut of a whip, and his cheek would flush when he thought of it years afterwards.

While Knowles was still in his confusion, he felt a light touch on his shoulder, and, turning, found Wyverne standing there. Nothing chafed Alan more than an exhibition of awkwardness such as he had just witnessed; besides this, he had never liked Harding, and was not inclined to make excuses for him now. The pleasantness had quite vanished

from his face ; and when he spoke, almost in a whisper, his
lip was curling haughtily and his brows were bent.

" *Fiat experimentum in corpore vili*," he said. " Your
classical reading might have taught you that much, at all
events. You want practice in mounting, decidedly ; but I
beg that you will select for your next lesson a fitter subject
than Miss Vavasour."

Knowles was ready enough of retort as a rule ; but this
time, before he could collect himself sufficiently to find an
answer Wyverne was in the saddle,

> " And lightly they rode away."

The animosity was not equally allotted, for Alan engrossed
far the bitterest share of it ; but thenceforward both the
cousins might fear the very worst from an enemy capable of
much stratagem, recoiling from no baseness, whose hatred,
if it were only for the coldness of its malignity, might not
safely be defied.

For some days after Knowles' departure everything went
on pleasantly at Dene ; and nothing occurred worthy of note
unless it were a slight passsage-of-arms between Bertie
Grenvil and Mr Brabazon. The latter was so rarely taken
at fault, that it deserves to be recorded.

The financier was perfectly aware of the flirtation in progress between his wife and the Cherub ; but he never disquieted himself about such trifles ; and it was simply his
" aggravating " instinct which impelled him one day, after
dinner, to select the topic which he guessed would be most
disagreeable to both. A certain Guardsman had just come
to great grief in money matters, and had been forced to be-
take himself in haste to some continental Adullam. He
was a favourite cousin of Maud's, a great friend of Grenvil's,

and in the same battalion. It was supposed that the Cherub was to a certain extent involved in his comrade's embarrassments, having backed the latter almost to the extent of his own small credit. On the present occasion, Mr Brabazon was good enough to volunteer a detailed account of the unlucky spendthrift's difficulties, which he professed to have received in a letter that morning, adding his own strictures and comments thereon. No one interrupted him, though Lady Mildred had the tact to give the departing signal before he had quite finished. Mr Brabazon felt that he had the best of the position, and determined to follow up his triumph. When the men were left alone, his plump, smooth face became more superciliously sanctimonious, till he looked like Tartuffe intensified.

"There is one subject I would not allude to," he said, "till *they* had left us. I have heard it hinted that Captain Pulteney's ruin was hastened by his disgraceful profligacy. It is said that he lavished thousands on a notorious person living under his name in a villa in St John's Wood. Mr Grenvil perhaps knows if my information is correct?"

Brabazon wished his words unsaid as Bertie's bright eyes fastened on his face, glittering with malicious mirth.

"Yes; I know something about it," he replied; "but I don't see that I'm called upon to reveal poor Dick's domestic secrets to uninterested parties. You don't hold any of his paper, I suppose? No—you're too prudent for that. Not quite 'prudent enough, though. I wouldn't say too much about St John's Wood, if I were you. You've heard the proverb about 'glass houses'? I believe there's a conservatory attached to that very nice villa in Mastic Road, to which you have the *entrée* at all hours. Have you got the latchkey in your pocket?"

If Richard Brabazon valued himself on one possession more than another, it was his immaculate respectability: in fact, an ostentatious piety was part of his stock-in-trade. For once, he was fairly disconcerted. His face grew white, and actually convulsed with rage and fear as he stammered out, quite forgetting his careful elocution—

"I don't pretend to understand you : but I see you wish to insult me."

"Wrong again, and twice over," the other answered, coolly. "I never insulted anybody since I was born. And you will understand me perfectly, if you will take the trouble to remember a very warm midnight last spring, when the cabman could not give you change for a sovereign, and you had to send him out his fare. You were in such a hurry to go in that you never saw the humblest of your servants, about fifteen yards off, lighting his cigar. I don't wonder at your impetuosity. I got a good look at the *soubrette* when she came out with the change ; and, if the mistress is as pretty as the maid, your taste is unimpeachable—whatever your morals may be."

The great drops gathered on Brabazon's forehead as he sate glaring speechlessly at his tormentor, who at that moment appeared intent on the selection of some olives, all the while humming audibly to himself, "The Young May Moon."

"It is an atrocious calumny," he gasped out, "or a horrible mistake. I wish to believe it is the last."

"You wish *us* to believe, you mean," the other retorted. "But I won't 'accept the composition' (that's the correct expression, isn't it?). There was no mistake about it. I saw you that night, just as plainly as I did the morning before, going into Exeter Hall to talk about converting the Pongo Islanders—only you were in your brougham *then*.

Quite right too. Never take your own carriage out on the war-trail: it only makes scandal, and costs you a night-horse. I always tried to beat so much economy into poor Dick Pulteney. If he would have listened to me, he might have lasted a month or two longer. I assure you I watched the whole thing with great interest. One doesn't see a *financier en bonne fortune* every day; and the habits of all animals are worth observing at certain seasons. A Frenchman wrote such a pretty treatise the other day about the 'Loves of the Moles!'"

Many men would have derived much refreshment from the spectacle presented just then by their ancient enemy. You cannot fancy a more pitiable picture of helpless exasperation, nor more complete abasement. Even with his usual crafty reserve, he would scarcely have held his own against the cool insolence of his opponent—thoroughly confident of his facts, and mercilessly determined to use them to the uttermost. If the Squire had been present, the skirmish would not have lasted so long; but he was presiding at a great agricultural dinner miles away. Max Vavasour, who sate in his father's place, was not disposed to interrupt any performance which amused him. Neither he nor any other man present felt the faintest sympathy with, or compassion for, the victim. Brabazon appreciated his position acutely. He was only reaping as he had sown; but some of those same crops are not pleasant to gather or garner. He rose suddenly, and muttering something about "not stay another instant to be insulted," made a precipitate retreat, leaving not a shred of dignity behind. Max Vavasour did rouse himself to say a few pacifying words of deprecation, but they did not arrest the fugitive, nor did the speaker seem to expect they would do so.

When the door closed, Wyverne looked at Bertie with an expression which was meant to be reproachful, but became, involuntarily, admiring.

"What a quiet, cruel little creature it is," he said. "Fancy his keeping that secret so long, and bringing it out so viciously just at the right time. Is it not a crowning mercy, though, that the Squire's 'agricultural' came off to-night? He would have stopped sport for once in his life. I wonder whether Brabazon is a 'bull' or a 'bear' on 'Change? Whichever he is, he was baited thoroughly well here; and, I think, deserved all the punishment he got. Cherub, I shall look upon you with more respect henceforth, having seen you appear as the Bold Avenger."

They soon began to talk of other things. A reputation fostered by years of caution, outward self-restraint, and conventional observances, had just been slain before their eyes; but those careless spirits made little moan over the dead, and seemed to think the obsequies not worth a funeral oration. Having once accepted his position, Brabazon, to do him justice, made the best of it. He made no attempt at retaliation, as he might easily have done, by removing himself and his belongings abruptly from Dene; indeed, during the remainder of a protracted visit there, he comported himself in a manner void of offence to man or woman. The Squire, who knew him well, remarked the change, and congratulated himself and others thereupon; but they never told him of the somewhat summary process by which the result had been achieved. It was simple enough, after all. Some horses will never run kindly till you take your whip up to them in earnest.

Though Sir Alan Wyverne had no property left worth speaking of, he still had "affairs" of one sort or another to attend to, from time to time, and of late it had become still more necessary that these be kept in order. Before very long, he too was obliged to go up to town on business. He was only to be absent three or four days; but he seemed strangely reluctant to leave Dene. In good truth, there was not the slightest reason for any gloomy presentiment; but Helen remembered in after years, that during the last hours they spent together then, her cousin made none of those gay allusions to their future that he was so fond of indulging in; and that though his words and manner were kind and loving as ever, there was something sad and subdued in their tenderness. So far as Alan knew, it was a simple case of business which called him away; more than once afterwards he thought it would have been better if he had died that night, with the music of Helen's whisper in his ears, the print of her ripe scarlet lips on his cheek, the pressure of her lithe twining fingers still lingering round his own.

Many men, before and since, have thought the same. It is, perhaps, the most reasonable of all the repinings that are more futile than the vainest of regrets. Two life-times would not unravel some tangles of sorrow and sin, that are cut asunder, quite simply, by one sheer sudden stroke of Azräel's sword. Be sure, the purpose of God's awful messenger is often benevolent, though his aspect is seldom benign. The legend of ancient days bears a sad significance still. His arm is "swift to smite and never to spare;" black as night is the plumage of his vast shadowy wings; his lineaments are somewhat stern in their severe serenity; but in all the hierarchy of Heaven—the Rabbins say—is found no more perfect beauty than in the face of the Angel of Death.

CHAPTER XIII.

THE FIRST SHELL.

So Wyverne went on his way—not rejoicing; and Helen
would have been left "sighing her lane," if she had been at
all given to that romantic pastime. But they were not a
sentimental pair; and did not even think it necessary to
bind themselves under an oath to correspond by every
possible post—a compact which is far more agreeably feasible
in theory than in practice However, a long letter from
Alan made his cousin very happy on the third day after his
departure. It was a perfect epistle in its way—at least, it
thoroughly satisfied the fair recipient; to be sure, it was her
first experience in that line. Two lines—evidently written
after the rest—said that his return must be deferred four-
and-twenty hours. Helen did not hear again from her
cousin; but on the morning of the day on which he was expected, the post brought two strange letters to Dene which
changed the aspect of things materially. One was addressed
to Lady Mildred, the other to her daughter. Both were
written in the same delicate feminine hand, and the contents
of both were essentially the same, though they varied slightly
in phrase. "My lady's" communication may serve as a
sample :—

"When Alan Wyverne returns, it might be well to ask him three simple questions :—What was the business that detained him in town ? Who was his companion for two hours yesterday in the Botanical Gardens (which they had entirely to themselves) ? Where he spent the whole of this afternoon ? I would give the answers myself, but I know him well, and I am sure he will not refuse to satisfy your natural curiosity. As my name will never be known, I need not disguise my motive in writing thus. I care nothing about serving you, or saving your daughter ; I simply wish to serve my own revenge. I loved him dearly once, or I should not hate him so heartily now. If Alan Wyverne chooses to betray so soon the girl to whom he has plighted faith, I do not see why *one* of his old loves should engross *all* the treachery."

Helen's letter was to the same purport ; but at greater length, and more considerately and gently expressed, as though some compassion was mingled in the writer's bitterness.

I should very much like to know the *fiancée* who would receive such a communication as this with perfect equanimity—supposing, of course, that her heart went with the promise of her hand. Miss Vavasour believed in her cousin to a great extent, and her nature was too frank and generous to foster suspicion ; but she was not such a paragon of trustfulness. She was thoroughly miserable during the whole of the day. There was very little comfort to be got out of her mother (it was decided that the subject should not be mentioned, at present, to the Squire) ; " my lady " said very little, but evidently thought that matters looked dark. When she said—" Don't let us make ourselves unhappy till you have spoken to Alan ; I am certain he can explain everything "—

it was irritatingly apparent that she really took quite an opposite view of the probabilities, and was only trying to pacify Helen's first excitement, as a nurse might humour the fancies of a fever patient.   Nevertheless, the *demoiselle* bore up bravely; not one of the party at Dene guessed that anything had occurred to ruffle her; and there were sharp eyes of all colours amongst them.

Mrs Fernley was there—the most seductive of "grass-widows"—whose husband had held for years some great post high up in the Himalayas, only giving sign of his existence by the regular transmission of large monies, wherewith to sustain the splendour of his consort's establishment. There, too, was Agatha Drummond—whose name it is treason to introduce thus episodically, for she deserves a story to herself, and has nothing whatever to do with the present one—a beauty of the grand old Frankish type, with rich fair hair, haughty aquiline features, clear, bold blue eyes, and long elastic limbs—such as one's fancy assigns to those who shared the bed of Merovingian kings. She passed most of her waking hours in riding, waltzing, or flirting; seldom or ever read anything, and talked, notwithstanding, passingly well; but for daring, energy, and power of supporting fatigue in her three favourite pursuits, you might have backed her safely against any woman of her age in England. Both were very fond of Helen, and would have sympathized with her sincerely had they seen cause; but their glances were not the less keenly inquisitive; and, under the circumstances, she deserved some credit for keeping her griefs so entirely to herself.

I have heard grave, reverend men, with consciences probably as clear and correct as their banking-books, confess that they never returned home, after a brief absence during which no letters had been forwarded, without a certain vague apprehension, which did not entirely subside till they had met their family and glanced over their correspondence. I will not affirm that some feeling of the sort did not cross Wyverne's as he drove up the long dark avenue to Dene. He arrived so late that almost every one had gone up to dress, so he was not surprised at not finding Helen downstairs; it is possible that he was slightly disappointed at not encountering her somewhere—by chance, of course—in gallery or corridor. When they met, just before dinner, Alan did fancy that there was something constrained in his cousin's welcome, and unusually grave in his aunt's greeting; but he had no suspicion that anything was seriously amiss, till Helen whispered, as she passed him on leaving the dining-room—" Come to the library as soon as you can. I am going there now." You may guess if he kept her waiting long.

Miss Vavasour was sitting in an arm-chair near the fire, her head was bent low, leaning on her hand; even in the uncertain light you might see the slender fingers working and trembling; there was a listless despondency in her whole bearing, so different from its usual proud elasticity, that a sharp conviction of something having gone fearfully wrong, shot through Wyverne's heart, like the thrust of a dagger. His lips had not touched even her forehead yet, but he did not now attempt to caress; he only laid his hand gently on her shoulder—so light a touch need not have made her shiver—and whispered—

" What has vexed you, my own ? "

For all answer, she gave him the letter, that she held ready

He read it through by the light of the shaded lamp that stood near. Helen watched his face all the while with a

fearful, feverish anxiety; it betrayed not the slightest shade
of confusion or shame, but it grew very grave and sad, and,
at last, darkened, almost sternly. When he came to the
end he was still silent, and seemed to muse for a few
seconds. But she could bear suspense no longer. Yet there
was no anger in the sweet voice, it was only plaintive and
pleading—

"Ah, Alan, do speak to me. Won't you say it is all
untrue?"

Wyverne roused himself from his reverie instantly; he
drew nearer to his cousin's side, and took her little trembling hand in his own, looking down into her face—lovelier
than ever in its pale, troubled beauty—with an intense love
and pity in his eyes.

"The blow was cruelly meant, and craftily dealt," he
said; "but they shall not part us yet, if you are brave
enough to believe me thoroughly, and implicitly, this once.
I will never ask you to do so again. Yes, the facts are
true—don't draw your hand back—I would not hold it
another second if I could not say the inferences are as false
as the father of lies could make them. A dozen words
answer all the questions. I was with Nina Lenox, in the
Gardens; and yesterday afternoon I stayed in town on *her*
business, not on my own. There is the truth. The lie is—
the insinuation that I had any other interest at stake than
serving a rash unhappy woman in her hard need. That unfortunate is doomed to be fatal, it seems, even to her friends
—she has right few left now to ruin. Darling, try to believe that neither she nor the world have ever had the right
to call *me* by any other name."

Mrs Rawdon Lenox was one of the celebrities of that
time. Her face and figure carried all before them, when

she first came out; and even in the first season they set her up as a sort of standard of beauty with which others could only be compared in degrees of inferiority. She married early, and very unhappily. Her husband was a coarse, rough-tempered man, and tried from the first to tyrannize over his wayward impetuous wife—who had been spoilt from childhood upwards—just as he was wont to do over the tenants of his broad acres, and his countless dependents. Of course it did not answer. Years had passed since then, each one giving more excuse to Nina Lenox for her wild ways and reckless disregard of the proprieties; but—not excuse enough. Men fell in love with her perpetually; but they did not come scathless out of the fire, like the admirers of Maud Brabazon. The taint and smirch of the furnace-blast remained; well if there were not angry scars, too, rankling and refusing to be healed. Mothers and mothers-in-law shook their heads ominously at the mention of Nina's name; the first, tracing the ruin of their son—moral or financial— the last, the domestic discomfort of their daughter, to those fatal lansquenet-parties and still more perilous morning tête-à-têtes.

Was it not hard to believe that a man, still short of his prime, and notoriously epicurean in his philosophy, could be in the secret of the sorceress without having drunk of her cup? That he could serve her as a friend, in sincerity and innocence, without ever having descended to be her accomplice? Yet this amount of faith or credulity—call it which you will—Wyverne did not scruple to ask from Helen, then.

It may not be denied that her heart seemed to contract, for an instant, painfully, when her lover's lips pronounced so familiarly that terrible name. But it shook off distrust

before it could fasten there.   She rose up, with her hand in
Alan's, and nestled close to his breast, and looked up earnestly and lovingly into his eyes.

"My own—my own still," she murmured, "I do believe
you thoroughly, now, even if you tell me not another word.
But do be kind and prudent, and don't try me again soon, it
is so very hard to bear."

"If I had only guessed——"

That sentence was never finished, for reasons good and
sufficient; such delicious impediments to speech are unfortunately rather rare.   The kiss of forgiveness was sweeter
in its lingering fondness, than that which sealed the affiancement under the oak-trees of the Home Wood.

"Sit here, child," Wyverne said, at last.   "You shall
hear all, now."

He sank down on a cushion at her feet, and so made his
confession.   Not a disagreeable penance, either, when absolution is secured beforehand, and a delicate hand wanders at
times, with caressing encouragement, over the penitent's
brow and hair.

It is quite unnecessary to give the explanation at length.
Mrs Lenox had involved herself in all sorts of scrapes, of
which money-embarrassments were the least serious.   Things
had come to a dangerous crisis.   She had been foolish enough
to borrow money of a man whose character ought to have
deterred her, and then to offend him mortally.   The creditor
was base enough to threaten to use the weapons he possessed, in the shape of letters and other documents, compromising
Nina fearfully.   She heard that Wyverne was in town, and
wrote to him to help her in her great distress.   She preferred trusting him to others on whom she had a real claim,
because she knew him thoroughly; and if there was no love-

link between them, neither was there any remorse or reproach. She was heart-sick of intrigue, for the moment, and
would try what a kind honest friend could do. It was true.
Their intimacy had been always innocent. These things are
not to be accounted for ; perhaps Alan never cared to offer
sacrifice at an altar on which incense from all kingdoms of
the earth was burned. Mr Lenox's temper had become of
late so brutally savage, that Nina felt actual physical fear at
the idea of his hearing of her embarrassments. This was the
reason why she had met Wyverne clandestinely in the Botanical Gardens. Her husband was absent the whole of the
next day ; so she had received him at home. It was a difficult and delicate business ; but Alan carried it through.
He got the money first—not a very large sum—found out
the creditor with some trouble, and satisfied him, gaining
possession of every dangerous document. It was a stormy
interview at first ; but Wyverne was not easily withstood
when thoroughly in earnest ; and his quiet, contemptuous
firmness fairly broke the other down. You many fancy
Nina's gratitude: indeed, up to a certain point, Alan had
congratulated himself on having wrought a work of mercy
and charity without damage to any one. You have seen how
he was undeceived. He did not dissemble from Helen his
self-reproach at having been foolish enough to meddle in the
matter at all.

"Some one must be sacrificed at such times," he said ;
"but, my darling, it were better that all the *intrigantes* in
London should go to the wall, than that you should have an
hour's disquiet. Trust me, I'll see to this for the future.
I am sure Mrs Lenox would not be a nice friend for you ;
and it is better to cut off the connection before you can be
brought in contact. One can afford to be frank when one

has done a person a real service. I'll write her a few lines—
you can correct them, if you like—to say that this affair has
been made the subject of anonymous letters; and that I
cannot, for *your* sake, risk more misconstruction; so that
our acquaintance must be of the slightest henceforward."

So peace was happily restored. We need not go into a
minute description of the "rejoicings" that ensued. One
thought only puzzled and troubled Alan exceedingly.

"I can't conceive who can have written that letter," he
said, "or got it written. The hand of course proves nothing,
nor the motive implied, which is simply not worth noticing.
It is just as likely the work of a man's malevolence as of a
woman's. Helen, I own frankly I would rather it were the
first than the last. But I thought I had not made an enemy
persevering enough to watch all my movements, or cruel
enough to deal that blow in the dark."

It was evident that the shock to his genial system of be-
lief in the world in general affected him far more than the
foiled intent of personal injury

When Lady Mildred saw her daughter's face, as the latter
re-entered the drawing-room alone, she guessed at once the
issue of the conference, and knew that it would be useless
now to cavil at an explanation which must have been absolutely satisfactory She was not in the least disappointed;
indeed, the most she had expected from this first shock to
Helen's confidence was a slight loosening of the foundations.
From the first moment of reading the anonymous letter, she
detected fraud and misrepresentation; and argued that the
Truth would this time prevail. So, when Alan had audience
of her in her boudoir late that evening, he found no difficulty
in making his cause good. "My lady" did just refer to
something she had said on a former occasion, and quite coin-

cided in Wyverne's idea, that this was one of the dangerous
acquaintances that it was imperative on him to give up: indeed, she was very explicit and decided on this point. Otherwise, she was everything that was kind and conciliatory;
and really said less about the imprudence in meddling with
such an affair at all, than could have been expected from the
most indulgent of aunts or mothers. Just before he left the
boudoir, Alan read the letter through that "my lady" had
given him—he had scarcely glanced at it before. When he
gave it back his face had perceptibly lightened, though his
lip was curling scornfully.

"I'm so glad you showed me that pleasant letter, Aunt
Mildred," he said. "My mind is quite easy now as to the
sex of the informer. No woman, I dare swear, to whom I
ever spoke words of more than common courtesy could have
written such words as those. Perhaps I may find out his
name some day, and thank him for the trouble he has
taken."

Lady Mildred did not feel exactly comfortable just then.
She would have preferred the whole transaction being now
left in as much obscurity as possible. She knew how determined and obstinate the speaker could be when he had real
cause to be unforgiving. She knew that he was capable of
exacting the reckoning to the uttermost farthing, though the
settlement was ever so long delayed. On the whole, however, she was satisfied with the aspect of affairs as they remained. She had good reason to be so. Doubt and distrust
may seem to vanish; but they generally leave behind them a
slow, subtle, poisonous influence, that the purest and strongest faith may not defy. Of all diseases, those are the most
dangerous which linger in the system when the cure is pronounced to be perfect.

I knew a man well who passed through the Crimean war untouched by steel or shot, though he was ever in the front of the battle. Even the terrible trench-work did not seem to affect him. He would come in, wet but not weary, sleep in his damp tent contentedly, and rise up in his might rejoicing. When, quite at the end of the war, he was attacked by the fever, no one felt any serious alarm. We supposed that Kenneth McAlpine could shake off any ordinary sickness as easily as Samson did the Philistines' gyves. In truth, he did appear to recover very speedily; and, when he returned to England, seemed in his usual health again. But soon he began to waste and pine away without any symptoms of active disease. None of the doctors could reach the seat of the evil, or even define its cause. It took some time to sap that colossal strength fairly away; but month by month the doom came out more plainly on his face, and the end has come at last. Poor Kenneth's grave will be as green as the rest of them, next spring, when the grass begins to grow.

Standing by the sepulchre of Faith, or Love, or Hope—if we dared look back—we might find it hard to remember when and where the first seeds of decay were sown, though we do not forget one pang of the last miserable days that preceded the sharp death-agony.

CHAPTER XIV

THE LETTERS OF BELLEROPHON.

WYVERNE's valedictory note to Mrs Lenox, though kindly and courteous, was brief and decisive enough to satisfy Helen perfectly. The answer came in due course; there was no anger or even vexation in its tone, but rather a sad humility —not at all what might have been expected from the proud, passionate, reckless *lionne*, who kept her sauciest smile for her bitterest foe, and scarcely ever indulged the dearest of her friends with a sigh. A perpetual warfare was waged between that beautiful Free Companion and all regular powers; though often worsted, and forced, for the moment, to give ground, she had never yet lost heart or shown sign of submission; the poor little Amazonian target was sorely dinted, and its gay blazonry nearly effaced, but the dauntless motto was still legible as ever—*L'Empire c'est la guerre.*

So for awhile there was peace at Dene, and yet, not perfect peace. Miss Vavasour's state of mind was by no means satisfactory; though it seemed, at the time, to recover perfectly from the sharp shock, it really never regained its healthy elastic tone. Miserable misgivings, that could hardly be called suspicions, would haunt her, though she tried hard not to listen to their irritating whispers, and always hated

herself bitterly afterwards for her weakness. She felt how
unwise it would be to show herself jealous or exacting, yet
she could hardly bear Alan to be out of her sight, and when
he was away, had no rest, even in her dreams. Her unknown correspondent, in a nice cynical letter, congratulated
Helen on her good-nature and long-suffering, and hinted that
Mrs Lenox had been heard to express her entire approval of
Alan's choice—" it would be very inconvenient, if there were
bounds to the future Lady Wyverne's credulity." She did
not dare to confess to her cousin that she had read such a
letter through, and so only took her mother into the secret.
Lady Mildred testified a proper indignation at the spiteful-
ness and baseness of the writer, but showed plainly enough
that her own mind was by no means easy on the subject.
All that day, and all that week, Miss Vavasour's temper was
more than uncertain, and though no actual tempest broke,
there was electricity enough in the atmosphere to have furnished a dozen storms. "My lady" had always indulged her
daughter, but she took to humouring and petting her now,
almost ostentatiously; the compassionate motive was so very
evident, that instead of soothing the high-spirited demoiselle,
it chafed her, at times, inexpressibly.

The change did not escape Alan Wyverne. He felt a
desolate conviction that things were going wrong every way,
but he was perfectly helpless, simply because there was nothing tangible to grapple with; he did not wish to call up
evil spirits, merely to have the satisfaction of laying them.
Helen's penitence after any display of waywardness or
wickedness of temper was so charming, and the amends she
contrived to make so very delicious, that her cousin found it
the easiest thing imaginable to forgive; indeed, he would not
have disliked that occasional petulance, if he had not guessed

at the hidden cause. The only one of the party who failed to realize that anything had gone [amiss, was the Squire; and perhaps even his gay genial nature would scarcely have enabled him to close his eyes to the altered state of things, if he had watched them narrowly ; but, having once given his adhesion frankly and freely, he troubled himself little more about the course of the love-affair, relying upon Alan's falling back on him as a reserve, if there occurred serious difficulty or obstacle. The troubles threatening his house were quite enough to engross poor Hubert's attention just then.

A few weeks after the events recorded in that last chapter, Wyverne came down late, as was his wont. His letters were in their usual place on the breakfast table ; on the top of the pile lay one, face downwards, showing with exasperating distinctness the fatal scarlet monogram.

Seldom in the course of his life had Alan been so intensely provoked. He felt angry with Nina Lenox for her folly and pertinacity—angry with the person unknown, whose stupidity or malice had put the dangerous document so obtrusively forward—angry, just a very little, with Helen, for betraying, by her heightened colour and nervous manner, that she had already detected the obnoxious letter—angrier than all with "my lady," whose quiet bright eyes seemed to rest on him, *judicially*, not caring to dissemble her suspicion of his guilt. It is always unwise, of course, to act on impulse, and of all impulses, anger is supposed to be the most irrational. Such folly was the more inexcusable in Wyverne, because his power of self-command was quite exceptional : it only enabled him, now, to preserve a perfect outward composure ; he acted just as stupidly and *viciously* as if he had given way to a burst of passion. In the first five seconds he had fully determined to burn that letter, unread—a most sage resolve

certainly—the only pity was, that he could not bring himself
to execute his purpose there and then, or at all events confide
his intention to the parties most interested therein.   But
you must understand that Alan—with all his chivalrous devotion to womankind—held orthodox notions (so *we* should
say) as to the limits of their powers, and by no means favoured any undue usurpation of the Old Dominion; he held,
for instance, that the contents of the post-bag, unless volun-
tarily confided, should be kept as sacred from feminine
curiosity as the secrets of the Rosicrucians.   In the present
case, he could hardly blame Helen for betraying consciousness
of a fact that had been, so to speak, "flashed" before her eyes;
but he felt somehow as if she ought to have ignored it.   He
would not make the smallest concession.   I have told you
how obstinate and unrelenting the frank, kindly nature could
at times become: the shadow of a great disaster was closing
round him fast, and his heart was hardened now, even as the
heart was hardened of that unhappy king, predestined to be
a world's wonder, whom the torments of nine plagues only
confirmed in his fell purpose—" not to let Israel go."

He pushed all the letters aside with an impatient movement
of his arm, and thrust them into the pocket of his shooting-
jacket before he left the table, without opening one of them.
All through breakfast he persisted in talking carelessly on
indifferent subjects, in spite of the evident discomfort and
nervousness of his cousin, and the reticence of "my lady;"
eventually he had to fall back on the Squire, who, ignorant
of this fresh cause of discord as he had been of the former
one, was open to any fair offer in the way of conversation.

An hour or so later, as Wyverne was going down to his
uncle's room (they were to shoot some small outlying covers)
he met Helen in the picture-gallery.

" I suppose you are aware that a letter came for me this morning from Mrs Lenox ? " he said.

There was no particular reason why Miss Vavasour should feel guilty, and blush painfully, nevertheless she did both, as she answered him,

" Yes, Alan, I could not help seeing it, you know, and—"

He interrupted her, somewhat impatiently.

" Of course you could not help it, child. You were bound to remark it, where it lay. I suppose it was so forcordained by Fate, or some more commonplace power. I know it worried you; but, indeed, it vexed me quite as much. I have no idea what she wrote about, for I burnt the letter half an hour ago, without breaking the seal."

Helen did not answer at once, and when she looked up, for the first time in their lives her cousin read uncertainty in her eyes. His own face grew dark and stern.

" Ah, Helen, it cannot have come to this, yet—that you doubt me when I state a simple fact."

Her cheek had paled within the last few seconds, but it crimsoned now from very shame.

" No, no, Alan," she said impetuously, " I don't doubt you. I never do, when I am myself; but sometimes I feel so changed—so wicked—"

Wyverne would not let her go on; but the kiss which closed her lips carried scarcely more of caress than did his voice, as he answered what she meant to say,

" My own, I guess it all. It is a hard battle when such as you and I have to fight against principalities and powers. I feel we are not cool and crafty enough to hold our own. God knows how it will all end—and when. The sooner, perhaps, the better for you. But if they would only let *you* alone, darling ! It has been my fault from the first, and I

O

ought to have all the trouble and pain.   But indeed, now, I
have done my best.   I burnt the letter unread, and I have
written six lines to tell Mrs Lenox so.   Now, we won't speak
of it any more just now.   There can be no repetition of *this*
annoyance, at all events.   Will you tell Aunt Mildred what
I have done ?   *I* had better not enter into the subject with
her, that's certain."

Wyverne's perfect sincerity carried all before it, for the
moment; when he left her, Helen felt happier than she had
done for days.   Even had it been otherwise, of course she
would have made the best of it to her mother.   It is the
woman's way, you know—at least till, with middle age,
wisdom has waxed and passionate affection has waned—if in
anywise maltreated by her lover, she will make her moan
loudly enough to *him*, but she will tax her little ingenuity to
the utmost, to palliate that same offence to her nearest and
dearest friend.

It was well that Helen's spirits were high, when she went
to her audience in the boudoir; certes she reaped small encouragement there.   Lady Mildred was by no means disposed to be enthusiastic or unreserved in her trustfulness,
and, indeed, hinted her doubts and fears and general disap-
probation, much more plainly than she had hitherto done.
She believed Alan *now*, of course, but she could not help
thinking that the relations between him and Mrs Lenox must
have been far more intimate than she had had any idea of.   It
would have been much more satisfactory, if he could have
opened the letter and shown it to Helen.   So he had written
to say what he had done ?   That was right, at all events.
(What made " my lady " smile so meaningly just then ?)
But every day made her more fearful about the future.

"I ought to have been firmer at first, darling," she murmured.

The look of self-reproach was a study, and the penitential sigh rightly executed to a breath.

"It is not that I doubt Alan's meaning fairly; indeed, I believe he does his best; but when a man has lived that wild life, old connections are very difficult to shake off; sometimes it is years before he is quite free. You don't understand these things; but I do, my Helen, and I know how you would suffer. You are not cold-blooded enough to be patient or prudent. Even now, see how unhappy you have been at times lately. I was very weak and very wrong."

It is not worth while recording Helen's indignant disclaimer and eager profession of faith, especially as neither in anywise disturbed or affected the person to whom they were addressed. "My lady" kissed the fair enthusiast with intense fondness, but not in the least sympathetically or impulsively, and went on with her scruples and regrets and future intentions as if no interruption had occurred. There ensued a certain amount of desultory discussion, warm only on one side, it is needless to say. Lady Mildred did not actually bring maternal authority to the front, but she was *very* firm. At last it came to this. "My lady" was understood to have taken up a fresh position, and now to disapprove actively; but she consented to take no offensive step, nor even to mention the changed state of her feelings to the Squire or Alan Wyverne, till some fresh infraction of the existing treaty should justify her in doing so. Then, the crisis was to be sharp and decisive. This was all Helen could gain after much pleading, and perhaps it was as much

as could be expected. The Absent, who are always in the
wrong, don't often come off so well.

The instant her daughter left her, Lady Mildred rang for
her own maid, and said a dozen words to the attentive Abi-
gail; though they were alone in the boudoir, she whispered
them. All outward-bound letters at Dene were placed in a
certain box, which was kept locked till they were transferred
to the post-bag. The confidential *cameriste* carried on her
watch-chain several keys, one of which fitted the letter-box
with curious exactness. It was not often used; but in the
dusk of the evening a small slight figure, with a footfall soft
and light as the velvet tread of a cheetah, might have been
seen (if she had not chosen her time so well) flitting through
the great hall, and tarrying for a few seconds in that special
corner.

That day there were two letters burnt at Dene, both with
their seals unbroken.

Though all was not bitter in her recollections of the last
twenty-four hours—those few minutes in the picture-gallery
told heavily on the right side—Miss Vavasour's state of
mind, when she woke on the following morning, was none of
the pleasantest or calmest. Her mother's overt opposition
did not dismay or discourage her much; for, after the grateful excitement of the first interview had passed away, she
had entertained in spite of herself certain misgivings as to
the duration, if not the genuineness, of " my lady's " favour,
or even neutrality. But the demoiselle could not deny to
herself—though she had denied it to her mother—that the
latter had spoken truly with regard to her own present unhappiness, and wisely as to the perils of the future. Helen's
heart, brave as it was, sank within her as she thought of what
it would be if she were destined to experience for years the

wearing alternations of hope and fear, pleasure and pain, that
had been her portion only for a few weeks.   Sho did believe
in her cousin's good faith *almost* implicitly (there was a
qualification now), but she did not feel sure that he would
always resist temptations; and, even with her slight knowledge of the world, she guessed that such might beset his
path dangerously often.   New enemies to her peace might
arise any day ; and Nina Lenox's pertinacity showed plainly
enough how loth Alan's old friends were to let him go free.
Could *she* wonder at their wishing to keep him at all risks,
so as at least to hear the sound of his voice sometimes—she,
who could never listen to it, when softened to a whisper,
without a shiver and a tingle in her veins ?

" Nina ! "

As she uttered that word aloud, and fancied how he might
have spoken it, and might speak it again, black drops of bitterness welled up in the girl's heart, poisoning all its frank
and generous nature : she set her little white teeth hard, and
clenched her slender fingers involuntarily, with a wicked
vengeful passion.   If wishes could kill, I fear Nina Lenox
would have been found next morning dead and cold.   Helen
had seen her fancied rival once—at the great archery meeting of the Midland shires—and even her inexperience had
appreciated the fascinations of that dark dangerous beauty.
She remembered, right well, how one man after another drew
near the low seat on which Mrs Lenox leant back, almost reclining, and how the lady never deigned to disturb her
queenly languor by an unnecessary look or word, till one of
her especial friends came up ; she remembered how the pale
statuesque face brightened and softened then ; how the rosy
lips bestirred themselves to murmur quick and low ; and how
from under the long heavy eyelashes glances stole out, that

Helen felt were eloquent, though she could not quite read their meaning. She remembered watching all this, standing close by, and how the thought had crossed her heart, How pleasant it might be to hold such power.

Do you suppose that, because Miss Vavasour did perhaps more than justice to the charms of the woman she had lately learned to hate, she was unconscious of her own, or modestly disposed to undervalue them? It was not so. Helen was perfectly aware that she herself was rarely lovely and unusually fascinating. If she had been cool enough to reason dispassionately, she would probably have acknowledged that comparison might safely be defied. Both flowers were passing fair; but on the one lingered still the dewy bloom and scented freshness of the morning; the other, though delicate in hue and full of fragrance still, bore tokens on her petals, crisped here and there and slightly faded, of storm-showers and a fiery noon; nor, at her best, could she ever have matched her rival in brilliancy of beauty.

But, supposing that Miss Vavasour had over-estimated herself and under-estimated her enemy to such a point as to imagine any comparison absurd, do you imagine it would have lightened one whit her trouble, or softened her bitterness of heart? I think not.

Feminine jealousy is not to be judged by the standard of ordinary ethics: you must measure it by the "Lesbian rule," if at all, and will probably, even so, be wrong in your result. Not only is its field more vast, its phases more varied, but it differs surely in many essentials from the same passion in our sex. Don't be alarmed: I have no intention of writing an essay on so tremendous a subject. The pen of Libyan steel, that the old chroniclers talk about, would be worn down before it was exhausted. Take one distinction as an example. I suppose it is because we have more of conceit, pure and simple; but, when we once thoroughly establish the fact that the man preferred before us is really and truly one inferior in every way, it helps materially to soften the disappointment. Comfortable self-complacency disposes us to be charitable, compassionate, and forgiving; we try (not unsuccessfully) to think that the bad taste displayed by the Object is rather her misfortune than her fault; nor do we nourish enduring malice even to him who bears away the bride. Remember the story of Sir Gawaine. When the huge black-browed carle would have reft from him his dame by force, he bound himself to do battle to the death; but when the lady had once made her choice, the Knight of the Golden Tongue thought no more of strife, but rode on his way, resigned if not rejoicing. With our sisters it is not so. Let a woman realize ever so completely the inferiority of her rival, — moral, physical, and social,—it will not remove one of her suspicious fears, nor dull the sting of discomfiture when it comes, nor teach forgetfulness of the bitter injury in after-days.

When wild Kate Goring created universal scandal and some surprise by eloping with that hirsute riding-master, Cecil Hamersley was intensely disgusted at first, but did not nurse his griefs or his wrath long: when the unlucky couple came to the grief which was inevitable, Kate's jilted lover pitied them from the bottom of his great honest heart, and seemed to think it the most natural thing in the world that he should help them to the utmost of his power. It was entirely through Cecil that Mr Martingale was enabled to start in the horse-dealing business, which he has conducted with average honesty and fair success ever since.

Take a converse example. Ivor Montresor, for the last

year or more, has been laying his homage at the feet of Lady
Blanche Pendragon, and it has been accepted, not ungra-
ciously; at the end of last season it was understood that it
was nearly a settled thing. But the wooer has not displayed
intense eagerness since in pressing on the preliminaries.
There is a certain Annie Fern, whose duty it is to braid the
somewhat scanty gold of Lady Blanche's tresses—the most
captivating little witch imaginable, with the most provoking
of smiles, that contrasts charmingly with her long, pensive,
dark-grey Lancashire eyes. She is prettier a thousand-fold,
and pleasanter, and really better educated, than the tall,
frigid, indolent descendant of King Uther whom she has
the honour to serve; but that is no excuse, of course,
for Ivor's infatuation. A dreadful whisper has got abroad
of late, that he admires the maid above the mistress. Lady
Blanche is supposed to be not unconscious of all this; but,
if she guessed it, she would not deign to notice it in any
way, or even to discharge her fatally attractive handmaid.
Let us hope that the vagrant knight will be recalled to
a sense of his duty, and, remembering that he is a suitor
nearly accepted, " act as such." However it may turn out,
let us hope, for Annie's sake (she has been absolutely innocent of intriguing throughout), that it will never happen to
her " to be brought low even to the ground, and her honour
laid in the dust; "—in such a case, I know *who* will be the
first to set the heel of her slender brodequin on the poor
child's neck, and keep it there too.

No; that conscious superiority does not help them at all.
As it is now, so it was in the ancient days. Did it much
avail Calypso, that in her realm there was wealth of earth's
fairest fruits and flowers, while in Ithaca it was barren all—
that ages passed over her own divine beauty, leaving no

furrow on her brow, no line of silver in her hair, while with every year the colour faded from the cheek, and the fire died out of the eyes of her mortal rival—if her guest still persisted in repining? Be sure she never felt more wretched and helpless than when, wreathing her swan's neck haughtily, she spoke those words of scorn:

Οὐ μέν θην κείνης γε χερείων εὔχομαι εἶναι,
Οὐ δέμας, οὐδὲ φυήν, ἐπεὶ οὔ πως οὐδὲ ἔοικεν
Θνητὰς ἀθανάτῃσι δέμας καὶ εἶδος ἐρίζειν.

O gentle Goddess! would your kindly heart have been most pained or pleased, if you could have guessed how ample was the final retribution? You never knew how often— wearied by petty public broils, worried by Penelope's shrill shrewish tongue, overborne by the staid platitudes of the prim respectable Telemachus—your ancient lover strode over bleak rocks and gusty sandhills, till his feet were dipped in the seething foam, and he stood straining his eyes seaward, and drinking in the wind that he fancied blew from Ogygia,— the island to which no prow of mortal ever found the backward track. You never knew how often his thoughts rushed back, with a desperate longing and vain regret, to the great cave shrouded by the vine heavy with clusters of eternal grapes, deep in the greenwood where the wild birds loved to roost, girdled by the meadows thick with violets—where cedar and frankincense burned brightly on the hearth, making the air heavy with fragrance — where the wine, that whoso drank became immortal, mantled ever in unstinted goblets—where you bent over your golden shuttle singing a low sweet song—where your dark divine eyes never wearied in their welcome.

I have always thought that, of all men alive or dead, of all characters in fact or fiction, Odysseus, in his declining years, must have been the most intensely bored.　But then, you know, though passing wise in his generation, he was wholly a pagan and half a barbarian.　Far be it from me to insinuate that any Christian and civilized Wanderer. when once reinstated in his domestic comforts, ever wastes a regret on a lost love beyond the sea.

CHAPTER XV

PAVIA.

IT is said that when a man is struck blind by lightning he never forgets afterwards the minutest object on which his eyes rested when the searing flash shot across them. Even so, when the crash of the great misfortune is over, and we wake from dull heavy insensibility to find the light gone out of our life for ever, we remember with unnatural distinctness the most trivial incidents of the last hour of sunshine; we actually seem to see them over again sometimes, as we grope our way, hopelessly and helplessly, through the darkness that will endure till it is changed into night; for it may be, that from our spirit's eyes the blinding veil will never be lifted, till they unclose in the dawn of the Resurrection.

Both the cousins had good cause to treasure in their memories every word and gesture that passed between them on one particular evening; for it was the last—the very last—of pure unalloyed happiness that either of them ever knew. Years afterwards, Wyverne could have told you to a shade the colour of the ribbons on Helen's dress, the fashion of the bracelets on each of her wrists, the scent of the flowers she wore. She, too, remembered right well his attitude when they parted; she could have set her foot on the very square of marble on which his was planted; she could recall the exact intonation of his gentle voice, as he bade her farewell on the lowest step of the great staircase, for he was to start very early the next morning. She remembered, too, how that night she lingered before a tall pier-glass, passing her hands indolently through her magnificent hair, while the light fell capriciously on the dark shining masses, rejoicing in the contemplation of her surpassing loveliness; she remembered how she smiled at her image in saucy triumph, as the thought rose in her heart—that Nina Lenox's mirror held no picture like this.

Ah, Helen, better it were the glass had been broken then; it may show you, in after years, a face disdainful of its own marvellous beauty, or tranquil in its superb indifference, according to your varying mood; but a happy one—never any more.

The Squire had to go to town for a few days, and Alan, who had also business there, accompanied him. They were to be back for Christmas-day—the last in that week. Wyverne got through his affairs quicker than he had anticipated, so he determined to return a day sooner without waiting for his uncle. His evil genius was close to his shoulder even here; for, if Hubert Vavasour had been present, it is just possible, though not probable, that things might have gone differently.

Alan started by an early train, so that he arrived at Dene soon after midday. Perhaps it was fancy, but he thought that the face of the chief butler wore rather a curious and troubled expression; if it were possible for that sublimely vacuous countenance to betray any human emotion, something like a compassionate interest seemed to ruffle its serenity. The letters of expected visitors were always placed on a particular table in the great hall. Again—on the top of the pile waiting for Alan—lay one in the well-known handwriting of Nina Lenox. This time it was placed naturally, with the seal downwards.

The first, the very first imprecation that had ever crossed Wyverne's lips in connection with womankind, passed them audibly, when his eye lighted on the fatal envelope. He knew right well that it held the death-warrant of his love; but even now the curse was not levelled at the authoress of his trouble, but at his own evil fortune. As he took up the letters, he asked, half mechanically, where his aunt and cousin were. The answer was ominous:

"My lady was exceedingly unwell and confined to her room. Miss Vavasour was somewhere in the Pleasance, but she wished to be sent for as soon as Sir Alan arrived." He had written the night before, to say he was coming.

Wyverne walked on into the library without another word. For the moment he felt stupid and helpless, like a man just waking after an overdose of narcotics. He sat down, and began turning the letter over and over as if he were trying to guess at its contents. From its thickness it was evidently a long one—two or three note-sheets at least. A very few minutes, however, brought back his self-composure entirely, and he knew what he had to do. It was clear the letter could not be burnt unopened, this time. He drew his breath hard once, and set his teeth savagely; then he tore the envelope and began to read deliberately.

Alan once said, when he happened to be discussing feminine ethics,—"I can conceive women affecting one with any amount of pain or pleasure; but I don't think anything they could do would ever *surprise* me." Rash words those—per-

haps they deserved confutation; at any rate the speaker was
thoroughly astounded now. He knew that no look or syllable
had ever passed between himself and Nina Lenox that could
be tortured into serious love-making; yet this letter of hers
was precisely such as might have been written by a passionate, sinful woman, to the man for whom she had sacrificed
enough, to make her desertion almost a second crime. There
was nothing of romance in it—nothing that the most indulgent judge could construe into Platonic affection—it was
miserably *practical* from end to end. No woman alive,
reading such words addressed to her husband or her lover,
could have doubted, for a second, what his relations with the
writer had been, even if they were ended now. Griselda
herself would have risen in revolt. It is needless to give
even the heads of that delectable epistle. Mrs Lenox acknowledged that she wrote in despite of Alan's repeated
prohibition; but—*c'était plus fort qu'elle*, and all the rest
of it. One point she especially insisted on. However *he*
might scorn her, surely he would not give *others* the right to
do so? He would burn the letter, she knew he would,
without speaking of it, far less showing it, to any human
being; she suffered enough, without having her miserable
weakness betrayed for the amusement of Miss Vavasour.

Every line that Alan read increased his bewilderment
Was it possible that dissipation, and trouble, and intrigue
had told at last on the busy brain, so that it had utterly
given way? Such things had been; there was certainly
something strange and unnatural in the character of the
writing, sometimes hurried till the words ran into each
other, sometimes laboured and constrained as if penned by a
hand that hesitated and faltered. He knew that Nina was
rash beyond rashness, and would indulge her sudden caprices

at any cost, without reckoning the sin or even the shame, but he could not believe in such a wild *velleité* as this.

" She must be mad."

Wyverne spoke those words aloud; they were answered by a sigh, or rather a quick catching of the breath, close to his shoulder; he started to his feet, and stood face to face with Helen Vavasour, who had entered unobserved while he sat in his deep reverie.

Helen was still in her walking-dress; a fall of lace slightly shaded her brow and cheeks, but it could not dissemble the bright feverish flush that made the white pallor of all the lower part of the face more painfully apparent; the pupils of her great eyes were contracted, and they glittered with the strange *serpentine* light which is one of the evidences of poison by belladonna; but neither cheeks nor eyes bore trace of a tear. She had schooled herself to speak quite deliberately and calmly; the effect was apparent, not only in the careful accentuation of each syllable, but in her voice— neither harsh nor hollow, yet utterly changed.

" Mad, Alan? Yes, we have all been mad. It is time that this should come to an end. You think so, too, I am sure."

Wyverne had known, from the first moment that he saw the letter, how it would fare with him; but the bitter irritation which had hardened his heart on a former occasion was not there now; he could not even be angry with those who had brought him to this pass; all other feelings were swallowed up in an intense, half-unselfish sorrow.

" Dear child, it *is* more than time that you should be set free from me and my miserable fortunes. We will drift away alone henceforth, as we ought always to have done. It was simply a sin, ever to have risked dragging you down

with the wreck; it must founder soon. Ah, remember, I
said so once, and you—never mind that—I'll make what
amends I can; but I have done fearful harm already. Three
months more of this would wear you out in mind and body;
even now they will tell in your life like years. We must
part now. Darling, try to forget, and to forgive, too—for
you have much to forgive."

He stopped for a moment, but went on quickly, answering
the wild, haggard question of her startled eyes; she had
understood those last words wrongly.

"No—not that;" he struck the letter he still held,
impatiently, with a finger of the other hand. "I told you
once I would never ask you to believe me again as you did
then. I don't ask you to act as if you believed now. But,
Helen, you will know one day before you die whether I
have been sinned against or sinning in this thing; I feel
sure of it, or—I should doubt the justice of God."

The soft, sad voice quite broke down the calmness it had
cost Helen so much to assume; she could not listen longer
and broke in with all her own impetuosity—

"Ah, Alan! don't ask it; it is not right of you. You
know I *must* believe whatever you tell me, and I dare not—
do you hear—I dare not, now. It is too late. I have promised—" and she stopped, shivering.

Wyverne's look was keen and searching; but it was not
at *her* that his brows were bent. He took the little trembling
hand in his own, and tried to quiet the leaping pulses, and
his tones were more soothing than ever.

"I know it all, darling; I know how bravely you have tried
to keep your faith with me; I shall thank you for it to my
life's end, not the less because neither you nor I were strong
enough to fight against fate, and—Aunt Mildred. I cannot

blame her: if I could, *you* should not hear me. She was right to make you promise before you came here. It was unconditionally, of course?"

The girl's cheek flushed painfully.

"There was a condition," she murmured under her breath; "but I hardly dare. Yes; I dare say anything—to you. Mamma sent for me when that letter came, or I should never have heard of it. She did not say how *she* knew. You cannot think how determined she is. I *was* angry at first; but when I saw how hard she was, I was frightened; and, Alan, indeed, indeed I did all I could to soften her. At last she said that she would not insist on my giving you up, if—if you would show me that letter. Ah, Alan—what have *I* done?"

He had dropped her hand before she ended, and stood looking at her with an expression that she had never dreamt could dwell in his eyes—repellant to the last degree, too cold and contemptuous for anger. It softened, though, in a second or two at the sight of Helen's distress.

"Did you doubt what my answer would be? I am very sure your mother never doubted: she knew me better."

No answer; but she bowed her beautiful head till it could rest on his arm; a stormy sob or two made her slender frame quiver down to the feet; and then, with a rush like that of Undine's unlocked well, the pent-up tears came. The passion-gust soon passed away; and her cousin kept silence till Helen was calm again: then he spoke very gently and gravely.

"Do forgive me; I did not mean to be harsh. You—only gave your message, I know; but it was like a stab to hear your lips utter it. Child, look up at me, and listen. I need not tell you I am speaking God's truth—you feel it. You

P

know what I have done to stop these accursed letters. I believe the writer to be mad; but that will not help us. I think I would stand by and see her burned at the stake, as better women have been before her, if by that sacrifice I could keep your love. But—if I knew, that by this one act I could make you my very own, so that nothing but the grave could part us—I would not show you a line of her letter. It may be that there are higher duties which justify the betrayal of an unhappy woman when her very confidence is a sin. I dare say I am wrong in my notions of honour, as well as in other things; but, such as they are, I'll stand by them to the death, and—to what I think must be harder to bear than death. I don't hesitate, because I have no choice. I know that I am casting, this moment, my life's happiness away: Helen—see—my hand does not tremble."

He tossed the letter as he spoke into the wood fire blazing beside them; it dropped between two huge red logs, and, just flashing up for a second, mingled with the heap of ashes.

Now, Wyverne's conduct will appear to many absurdly Quixotic, and some will think it deserves a harsher name than folly. I decline to argue either point. It seems to me —when one states fairly at the beginning of a story, "that it has no Hero"—the writer is by no means called upon to identify himself with the sentiments of his principal character, much less to defend them. I have not intended to hold up Alan Wyverne either as a model or a warning. He stands here just for what he is worth—a man not particularly wise or virtuous or immaculate, but frank and affectionate by nature, with firmness enough to enable him to act consistently according to the light given him. Whether that light was a false one or no, is a question that each particular reader may settle *à son gré*. Purely on the grounds of probability, I would suggest that others have sacrificed quite as much for scruples quite as visionary. Putting aside the legions of lives that have been thrown away on doubtful points of social professional honour, have not staid and grave men submitted to the extremes of penury, peril, and persecution, because they would not give up some favourite theory involving no question of moral right or wrong? The *Peine forte et dure* could scarcely have been an agreeable process; yet a Jesuit chose to endure it, and died under the iron press, rather than plead before what he held to be an incompetent tribunal. You constantly say of such cases, "One can't help respecting the man, to a certain extent." Now, I don't ask you to respect Alan Wyverne: it is enough, if you admit that his folly was not without parallels.

Among those who could blame or despise him, Helen Vavasour was not numbered: she never felt more proud of her lover than at that moment when his own act had parted them irrevocably. She was not of the "weeping-willow" order, you know: the tears still hanging on her eyelashes were the first she had shed since childhood in serious sorrow. Quick and impetuous enough in temper, she was so unaccustomed to indulge in any violent demonstration of feeling, that she felt somewhat ashamed of having yielded to it now. But the brief outbreak did her good; it lightened her brain and brought back elasticity to her nerves. There is nothing like a storm for clearing the atmosphere. Nevertheless, the haughty, bold spirit was for the moment thoroughly beaten down. There was something in her accent piteous beyond the power of words to describe, as she whispered half to herself,

"Yes, we must part; but is too, too hard."

" Hardest of all," he said, " to part on a pretext like this.
There is either madness, or magic, or black treachery against
me, I swear. Some day we shall know. But, darling, sooner
or later it must have come. I have felt that for weeks past,
though I tried hard to delude myself. I must say good-bye
to Dene in an hour. When shall I see the dear old house
again? I am so sorry for Uncle Hubert, too. If he had
been here—no, perhaps it is best so—there would have been
more wounded, and we could never have won the day."

" Don't go yet; ah, not yet "—the sweet voice pleaded—
all its dangerous melody had stolen back to it now, and lithe
fingers twined themselves round Alan's, as though they
would never set him free.

But Wyverne was aware that the self-control which had
carried him through so far, was nearly exhausted. He had
to think for *both*, you see ; and it was the more trying,
because the part of Moderator was so utterly new to him ;
nevertheless, he played it honestly and bravely.

" I dare not stay. I *must* see Uncle Hubert before I
sleep; and it is only barely possible, if I leave Dene in half
an hour. Listen, my Helen : I am not saying good-bye to
you, though I say it to our past. I lose my wife ; but I do
not intend to lose my cousin. I will see you again as soon
as I can do so safely. A great black wall is built up now
between the future and all that we two have said and done :
I will never try to pass it again by thought or word. You
will forget all this. Hush, dear. You think it impossible at
this moment, but *I* know better. You will play a grand part
in the world one of these days, and perhaps you may want a
friend—a real friend. Then you shall think of me. I will
help you with heart and hand as long as life lasts ; and I will

do so in all truth and honour—as I hope to meet my dead mother, and Gracie, and you, in heaven."

She did not answer him in words. The interview lasted about a hundred seconds longer, but I do not feel called upon to chronicle the last details. Writers, as well as narrators, have a right to certain reserves.

Alan Wyverne was away from Dene before the half-hour was out; but he left a sealed note behind him for his aunt. "My lady" was waiting the issue somewhat anxiously; it is needless to say, her health was the merest pretext. She read the note through calmly enough; but when she opened her escritoire to lock it up safely, her hands shook like aspen-leaves, and she drank off eagerly the strongest dose of "red lavender" that had passed her lips for many a day.

Does not that decisive interview seem absurdly abrupt and brief? It is true that I have purposely omitted many insignificant words and gestures; but if all these had been chronicled, it would still have been disappointingly matter-of-fact and meagre.

Nevertheless—believe it—to build up a life's happiness is a work of time and labour, aided by great good fortune: to ruin and shatter it utterly is a question of a short half-hour, even where no ill luck intervenes. It took months of toil to build the good ship Hesperus, though her timbers were seasoned and ready to hand; it took hours of trouble to launch her when thoroughly equipped for sea; but it took only a few minutes of wave-and-wind-play to shiver her into splinters when her keel crushed down on the reef of Norman's Woe.

CHAPTER XVI.

MISANTHROPOS.

On the morning after the most disastrous of all his bad nights at hazard, Charles Fox was found by a friend who called, in fear and trembling, to offer assistance or condolence, lying on his sofa in lazy luxury, deep in an eclogue of Virgil. The magnificent indifference was probably not assumed, for there was little tinsel about that large honest nature, and he was not the man to indulge in private theatricals. Since I read that anecdote, I have always wondered that the successes achieved by the great Opposition leader were not more lasting and complete. Among the triumphs of mind over matter, that power, of thoroughly abstracting the thoughts from recent grief or trouble, seems to stand first and foremost. Such sublime stoicism implies a strength of character and of will, that separates its possessor at once from his fellows : sooner or later, He must rule, and they must obey.

Alan Wyverne was not so rarely gifted. The bustle of the hurried journey from Dene to the railroad, and the uncertainty about catching the train, helped him at first; but when all that was over, and he was fairly on his way to town, he was forced to *think*, whether he would or no.

Anything was better than brooding over the past; he tried desperately to force his thoughts into the immediate future — to imagine what he should say to his uncle, and how the Squire would take the heavy tidings. The effort was worse than vain. The strong stream laughed at the puny attempts to stem it, sweeping all such obstacles away, as it rushed down its appointed channel. All the plans he had talked over with Helen, even to the smallest details of their proposed domestic economy, came back one by one; he remembered every word of their last playful argument, when he tried to persuade her that certain luxuries for her boudoir at Wyverne Abbey were necessities not to be dispensed with: he remembered how they had speculated as to the disposal of the money, if his solitary bet on the next Derby, 1000 to 10 about a rising favourite—should by any chance come off right; how they had weighed gravely the advantages of three months of winter in Italy against the pleasures of an adventurous expedition whose turning-point should be the Lebanon. What did it matter now who won or lost? Was it only yesterday that he had an interest in all these things? Yesterday — between him and that word there seemed already a gulf of years. Yesterday, he had felt so proud in anticipating the triumphs of his beautiful bride; now, he could only think of her certain success with a heavy sinking of the heart, or a hot fierce jealousy; for she was all his own treasure then; one night had made her the World's again. That miserable journey scarcely lasted four hours; but when it ended, Wyverne was as much morally changed as he might have been physically by a long wasting sickness.

Does it seem strange that a man who up to this time had met all reverses with a careless gaiety that was almost provoking, should go down so helplessly now before a blow that would scarcely stagger many of our acquaintance? A great deal, in such cases, depends on the antecedents. Human nature, however elastic and enduring, will only stand a certain amount of "beating." When Captain Lyndon is in good luck and good funds, he accepts the loss of a hundred or two with dignified equanimity, if not with chirping cheerfulness; but supposing the bad night comes at the end of a long evil "vein" — when financial prospects are gloomier than the yellow fog outside—when the face of his banker is set against him, as it were a millstone—when that reckless soldier

> "Would liever mell with the fiends of hell,
> Than with Craig's-Court and its band?"

O, my friend! I marvel not that a muttered imprecation shot out from under your moustache last night when the Queen of Hearts showed her comely face—your adversaries having the deal at three.

Now Alan Wyverne had been playing for his last stake, so far as he knew: he had put it down with some diffidence and hesitation, and it had followed the rest into the gulf, leaving him without a chance of winning back his losses. Under the circumstances some depression, surely, was not wholly despicable. Remember, he was not so young as he had been: though still on the better side of middle age, he had in many ways anticipated his prime, and had not much left to look forward to.

> "Qu'on est bien dans un grenier
> Quand on a vingt ans!"

So sings Béranger, well, if not wisely. But—add another score of years or so—what will the lodger say of his quarters? Those seven flights of stairs are dark and steep; the bread is hard and tasteless; the wine painfully sour and thin; the fuel runs short, and it is bitter cold, for Lisette is no longer there to hang her cloak over the crazy casement, laughing at the whistle of the baffled wind.

Wyverne saw his uncle that night. The Squire was equally provoked and grieved; the intelligence took him completely by surprise, for he had never guessed that anything was going wrong; he would not allow at first that the engagement was irrevocably broken off, and wished to try what he could do to re-cement it; but Alan was so hopelessly firm on the point that Hubert was forced to yield. He believed in his nephew implicitly, and acquitted him of blame from first to last; but he was completely puzzled by Mrs Lenox's strange conduct; he only dropped the subject when he saw how evidently it pained Alan to pursue it.

" I shall not write, even to reproach her," the latter said. " I am too heart-sick of her and her caprices. I suppose she will explain herself if we ever meet, and I have patience to listen."

When they parted, the Squire clasped Wyverne's hand hard, looking wistfully into his face.

" I—I did my best, boy," he said huskily.

The old genial light came back for an instant, only an instant, into the other's weary eyes, and he returned the gripe right cordially.

" Do you think I don't know that ? " he answered; " or that I shall ever forget it ? We all did our best; but Aunt Mildred has her way, after all. Take care of Helen; she will need it. And if you would write soon to tell me the truth about her, it would be so very kind."

The next morning Alan started for the North, alone. If

the Christmas-tide was dreary at Wyverne Abbey, it was not a "merry" one at Dene. The Squire did not seek to disguise his discontent, though he said little on the subject of the broken engagement, either to his wife or Helen. There was a gloomy reserve in his manner towards the former, that showed that he more than suspected her of unfair play; to the latter he was unusually gentle aud considerate. Miss Vavasour bore up bravely. No one looking at the girl's pale proud face would have dreamt of the dull, heavy pain coiled rouud her heart, like the serpent round Don Roderic in the tomb. She accepted her father's caresses gratefully, and her mother's with placid indifference. No words of recrimination had passed between those two; but there is an instinct of distrust as well as of love or fear; the last few days had slaiu sympathy outright, and even the tough seusibility of the cool diplomatist was not always unmoved as she realized the utter estraugement. So even "my lady," though the game was wou, did not feel iu vein for the festivities of the season. Her conscience had loug ceased to trouble her wheu it was a question of expedieucy; she compassionated the sorrows of her misguided daughter about as much as a great surgeon does the sufferings of a patient who has just passed under his knife; but she was not quite philosopher enough wholly to disbelieve in Retribution. Her dreams of a brilliant future for Helen were sometimes disturbed by a vision of sad, earnest eyes, pleading only that truth might be met by truth—she had answered their appeal so well!

It was an odd sort of life that Wyverne led at the Abbey. He took to shooting over his broad manors with a dogged determination that rejoiced the hearts of his keepers and teuants and every one interested in the preservation of his game. He went out always early in the morning, and never returned till darkness set in; then he slept for a couple of hours, dined late, and sat smoking and musing far into the night. But it did him good in every way; the strong exercise and the keen north-country air stirred up the iron in his blood, and braced his nerves as well as his sinews. I believe that permanent melancholy implies a morbid condition, not only of the mind but the body. I believe—be it understood that this is only a theory, so far—that a man will not *mope* in the Queen's Bench, though he may hate himself occasionally, and find the position irksome, if he sticks to cold water and rackets. The genial hopefulness which had resisted so many rude shocks, was dead in Alan for ever and aye; but it was not in his nature to become sullen or saturnine; he rejoiced simply and sincerely when his uncle's letter brought good news of Helen; he was not selfish enough to quarrel with his lost love because her wreath was not always ostentatiously twined of the willow. Some men are never satisfied unless they leave more than half the misery behind them.

Wyverne had been at the Abbey about a month, when he got a letter which surprised him not a little. Mr Haldane wrote, to beg his nephew to visit him, for a single night, and pressed it on the ground that his health was failing.

Castle Daere was situated far up in the hills, thirty miles or so from the Abbey. They had nicknamed it "Castle Dangerous" through the country-side, for the roads all round it were so infamous as to be sometimes impassable. Very few, of late years, had found it worth their while to encounter such perils. It was a huge dreary pile—a tall grey keep in the centre, dating back to the time of the Danes—round this long low ranges of more modern buildings were grouped, all in the same pale gaunt granite. The trees clustering about the castle in clumps, and thickly studded over the bleak park, hardly took away from the bare desolate effect; some of them were vast in the trunk and broad in the top, but it seemed as if the bitter north wind had checked their growth, though it could not waste their strength. You shivered involuntarily when you looked at the house from the outside; the contrast was the more striking when you entered. The whole of the interior was almost oppressively light and warm; great fires blazed in huge grates in the most unexpected corners, and bright lamps burned in the remotest nooks of passage, and hall, and corridor. A Belgravian establishment might have been maintained for a whole season at the cost of the coals and oil consumed in Dacre Castle; but such was the whim of its eccentric and autocratic master.

Alan Wyverne arrived very late, and did not see his uncle till they met at dinner. Mr Haldane must always have been small and slight of frame; he was thin now to emaciation; there was not a particle of colour in the face or the delicate hands; the articulations in the last were so strongly marked as almost to spoil the perfection of their shape. His features might have been handsome once, and not disagreeable in their expression, but evil tempers and physical suffering had left ruinous traces there; the thin lips had forgotten how to smile, though they were meaning enough when they curled sardonically; he had a curious way of perpetually drawing himself together, as if struck with a sudden chill.

He was just the sort of man you would have set down as a great judge of pictures and collector of curiosities. So it was. The whole house was overflowing with the choicest productions of nature and art, gathered from every quarter

of the known world. A long gallery was completely filled
with the rarest specimens of china that the last three centuries could display. Some of our connoisseurs would have
sold their souls for the plundering of that one chamber.

The dinner was simply perfection. You might have
feasted for a whole season at half the best houses in London,
and have missed the artistic effects which awaited you in
that lonely castle of the far North. The wines of every sort
were things to dream of. Mr Haldane drank nothing but
Burgundy Even Alan Wyverne, accustomed as he was to
witness deep wassail, felt wonder approaching to fear, as he
saw his host drain glass after glass of the strong rich liquor
without betraying a sign of its influence, either by the
faintest flush on his thin parchment cheek, or a change of
inflection in his low monotonous voice. It seemed as if he
were trying to infuse some warmth into his veins, in defiance
of the curse laid upon him—to remain frozen and statuelike
for ever.

While dinner lasted, the conversation went languishing on,
never coming to a full stop, but never in the least animated.
It was evident that the thoughts of both often wandered far
away from the subject they were talking of. At last they
drew their great arm-chairs up to the fire, one on each side
of the horse-shoe table, with a perfect barricade of glass between them in the shape of decanters and claret-jugs. For
the first ten minutes after they were left alone the host kept
silence, leaning forward and spreading his hands over the
fierce fire ; they were so thin and white that the light seemed
to pass through them as it does through transparent china.
He raised his head suddenly and glanced aside at his companion, who was evidently musing, with an expression half
inquisitive, half satirical, in his keen grey eyes.

"So everything is at an end between you and Helen Vavasour. I am very glad of it, and not in the least surprised."

It is never pleasant to have one's reveries abruptly broken ;
the nerves are *agacés*, if nothing worse. Besides this, both
words and manner grated on Alan's sensibilities disagreeably.
He did not fancy those thin cynical lips pronouncing that
name with such scant ceremony ; so his tone was anything
but conciliatory.

"Thank you. I don't seem to care much about being
congratulated, or condoled with, either ; and I cannot conceive what interest the subject can have for you. You
ignored it pretty decisively some months ago. Perhaps you
will be good enough to do so now."

The look on his face, that had been simply listless before,
grew hard and defiant while he was speaking. If Bernard
Haldane was inclined to take offence, he certainly controlled
his temper wonderfully. He filled a great glass to the brim
with Chambertin, held it for a minute against the blaze, letting the light filter through the gorgeous purple, and drained
it slowly before he replied—

"I am not surprised at your engagement being broken off,
because I know right well with whom you had to deal. I
am glad, because I have always taken an interest in you,
Alan. You don't believe it ; but it is true, nevertheless ;
and I do so still. I would sooner see a man I cared for
dead than married to Mildred Vavasour's daughter."

Wyverne's anger ceased as soon as he saw that the old
man had some reason, real or fancied, for his strange conduct ; but he spoke coldly still.

"Strong words, sir. I suppose you have strong provocation to justify them ?"

Bernard Haldane drew a folded letter from his breast-pock   , and put it into the other's hand, silently. The paper was yellow with age, the ink faint and faded; but Alan knew the handwriting instantly. His astonishment deepened as he read on. Was it possible that his cool, calculating, diplomatic aunt could have penned such words as these—words in which passion seemed to live and vibrate still, untamed by passage through thirty years?

Mr Haldane drained two glasses in rapid succession while the letter was reading. There was no thickness or hesitation in his voice when he spoke again, but it was hard and hoarse, as if his throat were dust-dry in spite of all the Burgundy.

"That is her last letter—the last of forty or more. I have them all still, and I think I know them all by heart. You may laugh out if you like; I shall not be angry. She wrote once more—not a letter, only a note—to break all off without a word of remorse for herself or pity for me. A fresh fancy or a better match came across her, so she turned me adrift like a dog she was tired of. She would have given me a dog's death, too, if she could, I dare say; for, till she was married, she never felt safe. Do you wonder now, or blame me, for what I have said and done or *not* done?"

Six weeks ago such a story as this would have won hearty sympathy from Alan Wyverne; but he had suffered too lately himself to be moved by a tale of wrong thirty years old. He could not forget Bernard Haldane's answer to his own letter, and the idea would haunt him that in some way or other it had materially affected his matrimonial prospects.

"I neither wonder nor blame," he said, wearily. "If any one is right in visiting the sins of the mothers on the children, I suppose you were. Certainly, "my lady" has a good deal to answer for. I understand her look now when I mentioned your name. Yes, I *do* wonder at one thing. I don't understand why you married my father's sister."

The old man glanced darkly at the speaker from under his strong grey eyebrows.

"I hope my poor wife never knew the lie I uttered at the altar; or, if she did, that she forgave me before she died. But God knew it, and punished it. Alan—you are my nearest heir."

After those significant words there was silence for some minutes, only broken by a faint tinkle and gurgle, as the host filled his glass repeatedly, and his guest followed the example in more moderate fashion. At last Mr Haldane spoke again.

"Alan, I wonder what would be your line if you came into this inheritance? Do you know, it is larger than the one you threw away?"

A few weeks ago, when Wyverne's fortunes were bound up with Helen Vavasour's, such a speech as that would have sent a hot thrill of hope through all his being: he heard it now with an indifference which was not in the least assumed.

"It would be a hazardous experiment," he answered, carelessly. "They say there is a great pleasure in hoarding, when you have more money than you know what to do with. I never tried it; perhaps I should take to avarice for a change. But I might take to playing again; it's just as likely as not; and then everything would go, if my present luck lasted—the pictures, and the gems, and the china, and the mosaics. It would be a thousand pities, too; I don't believe there's such another collection in England."

Bernard Haldane seemed determined that night not to be provoked by anything that his nephew could do or say. He was so accustomed to be surrounded by helpless dependents, bowing themselves without remonstrance or resistance before his tyrannical temper, that he had got weary of obsequiousness. Alan's haughty *nonchalance*, though it evidently proceeded from dislike or displeasure, rather refreshed the old cynic than otherwise.

"You are honest, at all events," he muttered; "it's no use trying to bribe you into forgetting injuries; if you *will* bear malice,—there's an end of it. We won't speak of inheritances: they put unpleasant thoughts into a man's head, whose health is breaking faster every day."

Once more a shiver ran through the speaker's emaciated frame, as it cowered and shrunk together; and once more the thin white hands spread themselves eagerly to the blaze. After a pause he rose, evidently to go, and there was something actually approaching to cordiality in his manner.

"It is hardly fair to ask you to stay on in this dreary place; but it would please me very much if you would spare me a few days. They tell me the covers are full of game, and you can have a hundred beaters at half an hour's notice. You will be nearly as much alone here as at the Abbey, for I never appear till dinner-time, and I go to bed very early, as you see. The Burgundy is a good sleeping-draught, but it must be humoured. You will stay over to-morrow, at least? I am glad of that. Perhaps you would like to see the keeper? Give any orders you please, not only about this, but about anything you may fancy: I *can* answer for their being promptly obeyed. Good-night."

His step, as he left the room, was slow and feeble, but not the slightest uncertainty or unsteadiness of gait gave token of the deep incessant draughts of fiery liquor that would long ago have dizzied any ordinary brain. Every family of

Q

ancient name, besides its statesmen and soldiers, preserves
the moist memory of some bacchanalian Titan, whose exploits
are inscribed on bowl, or tankard, or beaker.   We may not
doubt that there were giants in those days ; but the prowess
of the mightiest of all those stalwart squires would have
been hardly tried if he had "drunk fair" that night with
the little, wan, withered hypochondriac.

CHAPTER XVII.

A WISE MAN IN THE EAST.

Day succeeded day, and Alan Wyverne still lingered at Dacre Castle. He could hardly have told you what kept him there. The shooting certainly was a great attraction, for, though the season closed in the first week of his stay, there were snipe and wild-fowl enough to have found work for half a dozen guns; but it was not the only one. The truth was, that a sort of liking had sprung up between the cynical host and his quiet guest. No amount of deep drinking could warm Bernard Haldane into an approach to conviviality; but his morose, moody temper decidedly softened during the few hours that he spent each evening in Alan's society. There was no sympathy perhaps, strictly speaking, between these two, but there was a certain affinity of suffering. The same soft white hand had stricken them both sorely, though one wound was yet green, and the other had been rankling more than a score of years. After that first night, neither made the faintest allusion to the subject; but ever and anon, when they were talking about pictures or other things in which both took an interest, the conversation would drop suddenly, and a silence would ensue as if by mutual consent; then, each felt conscious that his companion's thoughts were wandering in the same direction as his own, and with equal bitterness. After a few minutes you might have seen each break from his reverie, with the same half-angry impatience, as if despising himself for the weakness of such idle musing, knowing all the while that the return of the dreaming-fit was as much a certainty and a question of hours as the rising of the morrow's sun.

Wyverne's visit would probably have been still further prolonged, if an invitation had not come one morning, suiting his present humour so exactly, that he accepted it without a moment's hesitation. An old comrade of Alan's was on the point of starting in his yacht for a roving cruise round the shores of Greece and Syria, with an intention of penetrating as far as the hunting-grounds that lie westward of the lower spurs of the Caucasus; indeed, there was a charming indefiniteness about the whole thing; the limits of their wanderings and the time of their return were to depend entirely on circumstances and the fancy of the travellers. Raymond Graham had heard of his friend's late disappointment, though he made no allusion to it in his letter, only enlarging on the sporting prospects of the expedition and the attractions of a very pleasant party. He thought it would be just the proposal to tempt Wyverne, and he guessed right.

None of the new-fashioned remedies beat some of the old ones, after all. Change of climate and change of scene enable the sufferer to make a stand against sickness of mind or body just as effectually as they did four thousand years ago.

Hot blinding tears stream down Dido's stricken face as she steals on board her galley in the harbour of Tyre; for nights she will not close her heavy eyes, lest a dead man should stand by her couch pointing to the gash of Pygmalion s dagger; the boldest of her true friends and lcal vassals dares not trouble with a word of comfort that great hopeless sorrow. But see, the headlands of Cyprus are yet blue in the leeward distance, and the rich blood had begun to colour the pale cheek again; when the dark lashes lift, men see that the divine light is not quenched in the glorious eyes; nay, the sweet lips do not dissemble a faint, sad smile as she hears Bitias boasting loud of the bride he will win before sun-down. Of a truth, I think the fair Queen's dreams will cease to be spectre-haunted before her prow touches ground in the sands of Bagradas.

They are more definite now as to the seasons of donning and doffing their weeds, and will not set their tresses free a day too soon; but, O Benedict, my friend, are you sanguine enough to believe that so long a voyage would be needed, to replace despairing grief by decorous woe, in the desolate bosom of your widow, or mine?

Remember, we have been speaking of creatures, many of whom must find a certain pleasure in a mild languid melancholy "They would not, if they could, be gay." Wyverne's temperament, though it contained womanlike elements of gentleness and tenderness, was essentially masculine. He was, indeed, stouter of heart and stronger in will than most of the rough-and-ready Stryver sort, who cannot argue without blustering or advise without bullying; who, neither in love nor war, ever lay aside the speaking trumpet. The battle of life had gone hard against him of late; but he did not therefore conclude that there was nothing left worth living for. The example just then before his eyes was not without a significant warning. Alan felt that absence from England would suit him best for a while: but he had no idea of banishing himself indefinitely. The proposed expedition would have tempted him at any period of his life, and he looked forward to it now with a real interest and an honest determination to make the best of everything.

Bernard Haldane did not attempt to alter his nephew's purpose; indeed, he approved of it thoroughly; but he sat much later than usual on the last evening, and seemed loth to say good-bye.

"If I am alive when you return, you will come here, I hope," he said, at last. "If I am gone, I am sure, you will, for good reasons. Your programme promises well—so well that it would be a pity not to carry it out thoroughly. Don't let money stop you. Where you have to deal with semi-barbarians, it's often a mere question between silver and steel; the first saves an infinity of trouble, and, I think, it's the most moral argument of the two. So take my advice and bribe Sheikhs and chiefs to any extent. I have written to-day to my bankers, to give you unlimited credit there. Now, don't annoy me by making objections. You know perfectly well that *I* sacrifice nothing. If I did, my generosity would still begin very late—too late, I fear. It would be the falsest delicacy if you were to refuse; for, though we have been almost strangers hitherto, through my fault, Alan —you *are* my nephew, after all."

He laid his hand gently, almost timidly, on Wyverne's as he finished speaking, and the thin white fingers quivered with his nervous eagerness, though they remained always deadly cold.

It must be a very mortifying and humiliating time when an old man, who has started in life with exceptional advantages of intellect and fortune, is compelled to admit the probability of the whole thing having been a mistake from first to last; unless there is some grievous sin to be acknowledged

and repented of, I think it would be more satisfactory to go
blundering on unconsciously to the end. To such a frame
of mind Mr Haldane had been coming gradually for days
past. He quite realized the fact that, in default of a son, he
would have chosen Wyverne out of all England as the heir
to his broad lands and great possessions. He knew enough
of Alau's character to feel sure that no more than common
kindness in earlier days would have been needed to win his
affection and keep it; but he had held him at arm's length
with the rest till it was too late to do anything better than
change dislike into indifference. For thirty years he had sat
alone, " nursing his wrath to keep it warm," fancying that he
could make the many suffer for the crime of one. He had
succeeded perhaps in discomfiting a few miserable dependents, and in disappointing or disgusting a few relatives and
friends; but he had never ruffled a rose-leaf in the couch
of the fair " enemy who did him that dishonour." Who had
been the real sufferer, after all ? The unhappy misanthrope
almost gnashed his teeth as he answered the question, and
acknowledged the childish impotence of his rancour. If he
had only had the courage at first to look his wrongs and
griefs fairly in the face, they might have been easily kept at
bay; it was too late to strive for the mastery when they had
become a part of his morbid being. He saw all this clearly
enough now. The old, old story,—theory perfected, when to
work it out is physically impossible—the alchemist just
grasping the Great Arcanum, without a stiver left to buy
powder for the crucible or coal for the furnace.

Nevertheless, that inveterate habit of looking at things
au noir rather misled Bernard Haldane as to the state of
Wyverne's feelings. It would be too much to say that he
had begun to conceive a real affection for his uncle; but he

was not insensible to the change in the latter's demeanour. He felt that the old man was trying, after his fashion, to make some amends for the past, and rather reproached himself for not having met such advances more cordially. Day by day the wall built up between them had been crumbling, and this last act of generosity made the breach quite practicable. An orthodox hero would, of course, have taken the "pale and haughty" line, and have rejected the golden olive-branch, preferring sublime independence to late obligation. Alan was much more practical and prosaic in his ideas; he accepted without hesitation, and did not scruple to express his gratitude warmly, though not demonstratively. It is needless to say that he did not intend to work the *carte blanche* unreasonably hard. So those two parted, in all amity. Bernard Haldane knew that he would be alone again on the morrow, and that in all probability he saw his nephew's face for the last time; but he drank less and slept better that night than he had done for years.

Wyverne wrote to tell Hubert Vavasour of his plans as soon as they were fixed. He got a very characteristic answer, full of kind wishes and prophecies of great success to the expedition. In truth, the Squire rather envied any one who at that juncture could get well clear of England, home, and beauty. He spoke cheerfully about Helen, but his hopes for her seemed about the brightest of his domestic prospects. Evidently he thought that the crash could not be much longer averted, and that the close of the current year would find wrack and ruin at Dene. None the less, from the bottom of his honest heart, he wished his nephew good-speed.

A fortnight later strong healthy excitement tingled in Alan's veins, as he stood on a wet sloping deck, his arm coiled through the weather-rigging, and looked ahead, through spray driving thick and blindly, over a turmoil of black foam-flecked water, betting with himself as to when the next sea would come tumbling in-board. The *Goshawk* was a stout schooner, measuring two hundred liberal tons; there was no handier or honester craft in all the Royal squadron; but she had to do all she knew that afternoon, fighting her way foot by foot and tack by tack against a boisterous south-wester, with Cape Finisterre frowning on her lee. We have not to follow in the track of the outward-bound; our business is, now, with the girls they have left behind them.

CHAPTER XVIII.

A STAR IN THE WEST.

THE season opened early, and promised brilliantly. There was an unusually good entry of "maidens;" but among these one held easily, from the first, an undisputed pre-eminence. They would have made a favourite even of a *protégée* of Lady Mildred Vavasour's; you may guess what *prestige* attached to her only daughter. In truth, the demoiselle could have won upon her merits; before that first drawing-room when, it was said, Royal eyes lighted upon her kindly and admiringly, the triumph was secured. Such a success had not been achieved within the memory of the oldest inhabitant of White's. Hardly any one had heard of her brief engagement, and those who did know, only looked upon it as a childish, *cousinly* folly, entailing no serious consequences. Certainly, there was nothing in Helen's demeanour suggestive of regret or repining. Most people would have laughed incredulously, if they had been told that the superb head, which carried itself so imperially, had ever been bowed down hopelessly and helplessly, or that the lustre of the glorious eyes had ever been drowned in miserably unavailing tears. She seemed generally in good spirits, but they were not equable; her humour was cruelly capricious, and it was impossible to calculate upon her temper; she would be dangerously captivating one evening, and the next morning absolutely inaccessible. They very soon found out that she would sometimes be moved to serious anger on absurdly slight pretexts, or—none at all.

To speak the truth, Miss Vavasour was by no means insensible to the admiration she commanded, and appreciated homage thoroughly. It was very pleasant to keep the best men in town *en faction* near the Statue, looking eagerly for her appearance in Rotten-row; and to know, at a ball, that her rivals were waiting with blank tablets, till her own was filled up to the cotillon. She was strictly impartial at first, and the sharpest eyes could not detect the shadow of a pre-ference; she made it a rule not to indulge the best of her partners with more than his one regular turn. There was sur-prise, if not scandal, throughout Babylon, when Bertie Gren-vil engrossed her almost entirely on a certain evening. The Cherub was not disposed to undervalue his advantages of any sort; so he never confided to the world that he had received in the morning a long letter from Alan Wyverne, and had discussed it with Helen, line by line.

Almost all our old acquaintances are in town. Max Vavasour has returned from Northern Italy, where some mysterious attraction had detained him since last November, and signalizes himself by an exemplary attention to his domestic duties; he sacrifices readily all the early part of his evenings whenever "my lady" requires his attendance, and breaks his morning sleep, without a murmur, to chaperon his sister in her rides. Such virtue deserves to be rewarded; and it is possible that Max sees the glitter of a rich compensa-tion not far off in futurity. There is Maud Brabazon, you see —more perilously provocative than ever; her coquetry seems

to have blossomed with the spring flowers; she is still dis-
porting herself mischievously with Bertie Grenvil's facile affections, who has not gained a foot of ground since we left
them at Dene. The Cherub begins to acknowledge that he
is getting very much the worst of it; but finds, apparently,
a certain satisfaction in the maltreatment, and submits to
cruelty and caprice with an uncomplaining docility worthy
of a better fate and a better cause. Harding Knowles, too,
has opened the campaign with unusual prodigality and
splendour; he rides the neatest of hacks, is profusely hospitable in luncheons at his chambers and suburban dinners,
and speaks—always with bated breath and in the strictest
tête-à-tête—familiarly of "Clydesdale." He is to be seen at
all Lady Mildred's parties, who treats him with marked consideration; but he keeps clear of her daughter, for the
recollection of that discomfiture at Dene still rankles
bitterly.

Before long diffidence and despondency showed themselves
in the circle of Miss Vavasour's assiduous admirers; the
Detrimentals drew back in fear and trembling, and even the
best of the Eligibles stood aloof for a season, watching how
things would go. The Great Earl had come to the front,
evidently in serious earnest.

Such reserve is, surely, most just and natural. Shall we
be ruder than the lower animals, who by their example
teach us a proper respect of persons?

See — a company of beautiful bright-eyed antelopes are
drinking at their favourite pool, deep in the green heart of the
jungle; the leopards have tracked them, and steal nearer
and nearer, till a few seconds more will bring the prey within clutch of their spring: suddenly the ravenous beasts
cease to trail themselves forward, crouching lower and lower

till their muzzles seem buried in the ground : there they lie, rigid and motionless, showing no sign of life, even by a quiver of the listening ear: tho sounds close by are significant enough to *them*, though the poor little antelopes hear nothing—a soft, heavy footfall—a deep breath drawn long and savagely — a smothered rustle, as though some huge body were forcing stealthy passage through the tangled jungle-grass: the leopards know, right well, that the King of the Forest is at hand, and, famished as they are, will not betray their presence even by a growl, till their Seigneur shall have chosen his victim and satiated his appetite. Could the most patient and discreet of courtiers or parasites act more decorously ?

The simile is not altogether inapposite, I fancy, nor very new either: nevertheless, O fairest reader! I *do* pray you to pardon the truculence of that carnivorous comparison.

Clydesdale did not seek to dissemble his admiration ; indeed, he seemed desirous to *afficher* it as much as possible, for he knew that it was the surest way of keeping the ground clear, and that was precisely what he wanted. If it had been possible, he would have liked, when he was calling in Guelph-crescent, to have left some visible token of his presence outside, to warn off the vulgar and profane, even as the Scythian chiefs used to plant their spear at the door of the tent wherein dwelt the favourite of the hour. From the moment that he heard, with a fierce throb of exultation, of the breaking off of Helen's engagement, the Earl had made up his resolve, and never doubted as to the event. Alan's departure made him still more confident; he felt that the last barrier had been taken away: he had nothing to do now but to sit still and win. He was doggedly obstinate in his attentions, yet by no means demonstrative ; he seldom tried

to secure more than two of Miss Vavasour's waltzes in an
evening, but these were the only ones in which he deigned
to exhibit himself; when she was dancing with any one else
he would stand watching her swift, graceful movements with
a critical complacency on his broad sensual face that was
enough to aggravate even an indifferent spectator—the conscious pride of proprietorship was so very evident. With
just that same expression, the chief of a great stable watches
the Oaks favourite as she sweeps past him, leading the string
of two-years-olds—so easily—with her long sweeping stride.
Lord Clydesdale was always sparing of his conversational
treasures, if he possessed any; nor did he lavish them even
on the woman whom he delighted to honour. His eyes
ought to have been more expressive, for they had a good
deal of duty to do; his pertinacious gaze scarcely left
Helen's face when he was in her presence, and he seemed
to consider this homage quite sufficiently expressive, without
translating it verbally. Riding by her rein in Rotten-row,
lounging in Lady Mildred's drawing-room for hours of an
afternoon,—the moody suitor was always the same silent,
sulky, self-satisfied statue of Plutus. If the real truth had
been known, I believe he would have preferred doing all the
wooing by proxy.

No amount of coldness on Miss Vavasour's part would
have checked the Earl in his obstinate determination to win
her; but it must be confessed that he did not meet with
much discouragement.

If a purely conventional marriage had been proposed to
Helen some months ago, she would probably have rejected
it with much indignation and scorn; but things were altered
now. Women, as well as men, turn readily to ambition—
never so readily as when love has just been rudely thwarted

—and the demoiselle, though proud as Lucifer, was not too proud to be ambitious. The little she had seen of her admirer had not impressed her very favourably; but no active dislike was working the other way. She knew how eagerly matrons and maidens had striven and schemed to attain the Clydesdale coronet—it was, in truth, better worth wearing than some Grand Ducal crowns—there was a certain triumph in the consciousness that she had only to stretch out her little hand to place it on her brows.

"There's nothing like competition," they say; the maxim holds good in other things besides commerce and Civil Service examinations. I believe that there is hardly any folly, short of sin—let us be generous, and make that possible exception—to which a woman may not be tempted, if she is once thoroughly imbued with the spirit of rivalry. There is no end to the absurdities they will commit, when this emulous devil possesses them. I have seen a most excellent young person, ordinarily a model of demure propriety, attempt to vault over high timber and come thereat to grief absolutely unutterable, sooner than be beaten by a companion better versed in gymnastics, who had just performed the feat safely and gracefully amidst general applause. I have known a fair dame—maturer, it is true, in attractions than in years —utterly ignore her habitual prudence, and compromise herself gravely by waltzing thrice almost consecutively with the same partner, simply because she alone could induce that languid hussar to break an anti-terpsichorean pledge which he had entered into for no earthly reason but laziness; yet, on her purity of principle and honesty of intention I would peril the residue of my life, or—what is more to the purpose—of my patrimony.

The Apple may be crude or withered, and scarcely worth

the plucking; but if the fatal legend be once visible on its rind, you will see divine eyes glitter with something more than eagerness; and even chaste, cold Pallas may not repress a jealous pang when the prize is laid in Aphrodite's rosy palm.

If it had been a question of keeping faith with Alan Wyverne, Miss Vavasour would not have wasted one thought or one regret on the present triumph or the splendid future; but knowing that they were separated for ever and ever, she was inclined to try if "the pomps and vanities of this wicked world" could not make some amends for what she had lost. She would not suppose it possible that a new affection could ever replace the passionate love that had been crushed and thwarted, but which would not die. There was her great mistake. It is in our early years that we ought to be patient; but we never recognize this till we are old: we hope while we are young, but we will not wait. So Helen accepted Clydesdale's saturnine devotion, on the whole rather graciously; her haughty, wayward temper, which would break out at times, rather attracted than repelled him.

It soon began to be noised abroad that the Great Fish was firmly hooked, if not landed. Certain astute chaperons acknowledged, with a sigh, that it was time to desist from a futile pursuit, and to seek humbler and more available victims. Dudley Delamere, the Earl's heir-presumptive, who had nourished wild hopes of succession, on the strength of his cousin's notorious habits of self-indulgence, came down to the Foreign Office two mornings running, with whiskers uncurled, thereby intimating prostration and despair as plainly as if he had rent his perfect garments, or scattered ashes on his comely head.

"I won't fight any longer," he said, plaintively; "the luck's too dead against me. Throw up the spouge; the Begum has won it fairly."

Those profligates were wont thus irreverently to designate a certain elderly Indian widow—very stout, good-humoured, and dark-complexioned, with rather more thousands in the funds than she had years on her head—who, for the last two seasons, had manifested an unrequited attachment to the ungrateful but not unconscious Delamere. It must have been the attraction of contraries that made her bow down so helplessly before that slim, golden-haired irresistible. He rather avoided her than otherwise; made a merit of coming to her artistic dinners, and treated her, when they met, with cruelly cold courtesy; but the impassioned Eurasion still kept hoping and worshipping on; pursuing the reluctant Adonis with pertinacious blandishments, with broad benevolent smiles that terrified him inexpressibly, and with glances out of her great black eyes that sent a shiver through his sensitive organization. Patient fidelity was rewarded at last. When Dudley had once made up his mind to the dire necessity, he accepted the position in a manly and Christian-like spirit, and sacrificed himself for the benefit of his country and his creditors, with a calm chivalrous bravery worthy of Regulus or—Smith O'Brien. They say it is a very comfortable *ménage*, on the whole; certainly, the Begum's smiles are more oppressively radiant than ever, and I should think she had gained about two stone in weight, since the day that crowned her constancy as it deserved.

Nevertheless, though Lord Clydesdale's attentions were so marked, and his intentions so evident, the season ended without his coming to the point of a formal proposal. It would be rather hard to define his reasons for the delay.

u

Possibly, holding the game in his hand, he chose to dally
over his triumph, and play it out to the last card. Possibly,
too, when a man's bachelor-life comprises every element of
comfort and luxury, he lingers with a fond reluctance over
its close. Besides this, the Earl appreciated the advantages
of his position thoroughly ; it pleased him to be the centre-
point at which the machinations of mothers and the fascinations of marriageable virgins were levelled ; he had observed
of late—not without regret—a manifest slackening in these
assiduities, and, vain as he was, he felt that it would be rather
unsafe to rely on his personal attractions for securing such
pleasant homage, after his future was once decided irrevocably. Absolutely unalloyed selfishness will make even the
dullest of intellects calculating and crafty. But Clydesdale did not vacillate in his set purpose for an instant.
His last words, both to Lady Mildred and her daughter,
before he left town for Scotland, were perfectly significant and
satisfactory

   " My lady " had shown herself throughout worthy of her
fame as a consummate tactician. The cunning mediciner
was always at hand to give aid if aid was required, but she
was far too wise to interfere with Nature, when it was working favourably. She guessed aright as to the state of her
daughter's feelings ; she could understand how bitter memories
were perpetually conflicting with ambitious hopes in the poor
child's troubled breast ; but she knew that a certain order and
harmony must inevitably succeed, ere long, the chaos and
discord ; so she waited for the event in quiet confidence,
without irritating Helen by consolation, or advice, or surmises. With Clydesdale Lady Mildred was equally cautious
and reserved ; she was always charmed to receive him, of
course, and ready to accept his attendance ; but her bitterest

enemy could not have accused her of betraying any undue eagerness to attract or to monopolize it. The accomplished dissembler could afford to despise affectation; when the Earl's marked attentions showed that he was thoroughly in earnest, she did not pretend unconsciousness, but accepted them with a composed courtesy, as if such homage was only her daughter's due. She bore herself somewhat like a monarch of olden days, receiving the fealty of a mighty vassal—evidently gratified by the tribute, yet by no means overpowered by the honour. She did not attempt to conceal her approval, but she would not derogate from her position one step; she was ready to conciliate, not to concede. The suitor soon understood that his position did not entitle him to follow his own fashion of wooing, or to dictate his own terms; he could not claim a single privilege that had not been granted from time immemorial to such as were worthy to aspire to a Vavasour of Dene. Do not suppose that "my lady's" demeanour ever expressed this too plainly; dignified stiffness or majestic condescension were utterly out of her line; her manner never lost the gentle caressing languor which made it so charming. The tacit way in which the understanding was established showed the perfection of the art. The engine would not have been complete if soft quilted velvet had not masked the steel springs so thoroughly.

Lady Mildred was not in the least vexed or disappointed when Clydesdale left town without bringing matters actually to a crisis. She knew right well it was the simplest question of time. When the Earl spoke, rather eagerly, about meeting the Vavasours again very soon, she only replied "that she hoped they might do so; but that her own summer arrangements were scarcely fixed yet. They would

R 2

be at Dene in the autumn, certainly, and would be very happy to see him, if he could spare them a week in the shooting season."

Her coolness quite disconcerted Clydesdale; he bit his lip, and looked for a moment as if he were going to be angry; but he checked himself in time, only giving "my lady" a look before he went, that, if she had been at all disquieted, would have set her mind effectually at rest.

It is rather an humiliating confession to make about one's Prima Donna—but I am afraid Helen was really more disconcerted than her mother at the abeyance in which affairs just then remained. It is not certain if she had made up her mind to accept Lord Clydesdale at once; but it *is* certain that she would have liked to have had the option of refusing him. In truth there were other disagreeable incidents, besides a passing mortification of vanity. Miss Vavasour's marvellous beauty had not in anywise palled upon public admiration; men gathered round her, wherever she appeared, just as eagerly as at the beginning of the season, and the candidates for inscription on her card were numerous and emulous as ever; but there was a marked reserve and reticence in their homage. When a damsel is once assigned, by general consent, to a high and puissant seignior, even though no contract shall have been signed, a certain wall of observance is built up around her that few care seriously to transgress, except those incorrigible reprobates who make a mock at all social and conventional obligations, and never see a fence without wanting to "lark" over it. Perhaps it *is* rather aggravating to be obliged to conform to all the constraints of affiancement without having so far reaped its solid advantages.

I am well aware that poor Helen's market-value as a

heroine will have gone down about fifty per cent. in this chapter. But what would you have? The ancient answer to the question—"What does Woman most care for?—holds good still. We can solve the riddle, now, without the Fairy's help, affirming boldly that it is—Power.

CHAPTER XIX.

HOW WOLVES AND FOXES DIE.

ONE of our characters need trouble us no more. The summer passed, and autumn came on quickly; but Bernard Haldane never saw the leaves change. Life had been flickering within him, fitfully, for some time past; it went out suddenly at last; the mortal sickness did not endure through forty-eight hours. He betrayed no fear or impatience when he heard that his end was approaching rapidly; only muttering under his breath—"There is time enough for all I have to do." He paid no sort of attention to the remonstrances of the physician, but caused himself to be carried at once into his library, where he remained locked in for nearly two hours, with a servant whom he could trust thoroughly. Paper after paper was examined and burnt—a packet of yellow faded letters, first of all; and Mr Haldane retained throughout a perfect intelligence and self-possession. He leant back in his chair when all was done, and closed his eyes with a sigh of satisfaction, but roused himself from the stupor that was creeping over him, to write, with great difficulty, a few lines to Alan Wyverne; the signature was scarcely legible, and as he was trying to direct the envelope, his head fell forward heavily on the table. When they got him back to his room, he was almost too weak to speak, though he rallied somewhat after taking strong restoratives.

The rector of the parish—a meek, single-minded, conscientious man—thought it his duty to offer what comfort and succour he could, though he feared the case was nearly desperate. What doubts, and misgivings, and repinings entered into the system of Bernard Haldane's dark cynical philosophy, God only can tell; he never tried to make a proselyte. As regards any communion with the Church, or outward observance of her ceremonies, he might have been the veriest of infidels; but he had never shown himself her overt antagonist. He listened now to all that the priest had to say, quite patiently and courteously, but with an indifference painfully evident. When asked, "if he repented?" he answered, "Yes, of many things." Then came the question, "Are you in peace and charity with all the world?" No word of reply passed the firm white lips, but they curled with a terribly bitter smile; and the skeleton hand that lay on the coverlet was clenched, as though the long filbert nails would pierce its palm.

The good rector felt utterly disheartened; he had not nerve enough to cope with that intractable penitent; it would have been a simple mockery to speak of a Sacrament then; so he did the best he could—praying long and fervently, even against hope, for the troubled soul that was so near its rest. The sick man lay quite still, watching the movements of the priest, at first with mere curiosity, soon with a growing interest; at last it seemed as if his eyes would fain have thanked the kindly intercessor; but they waxed dimmer every moment, till the heavy lids closed slowly and wearily, not to be lifted again.

The physician standing by bent down his ear to the lips

that still kept moving. He caught one word—" Mildred "
—and some other syllables absolutely unintelligible. The
frown on the brow and the contraction of the features, just
then, surely did not come from pain. So—murmuring a
farewell, that savoured, I fear, rather of ban than blessing—
died Bernard Haldane—more tranquilly and serenely than
saints and martyrs have died, who bore uncomplainingly all
the burden and heat, and shrank from no self-sacrifice that
could benefit their kind.

The bitter face changed and softened strangely, they say,
before the corpse was cold, till it settled into intense sadness,
and 10 years seemed taken from the dead man's age.
That grave, pensive expression perhaps was a natural one,
before the keen morbid sensibility was so cruelly warped
and withered. It may be that he *did* repent heartily at last,
though he could not forgive; thinking of the poverty all
round him that he had never stretched a hand to help, of the
honest affection that he may have barred out when he shut
himself up in his arid misanthropy. If he did once thoroughly
realize this, and his utter impotence to make any amends, be
sure the latest pang of his life was the sharpest of all.
That is the worst of all philosophy—Epicurean or Stoic,
seductive or repellant; it *will* often fail just at the critical
time of trial. The tough, self-reliant character, that meets
misfortune savagely and defiantly like a personal foe, holds
its own well for a while; but, if there be not Faith enough
to teach humble, hopeful endurance, I think it fares best in
the end with the hearts that are only—broken.

Mr Haldane's will was very brief, though perfectly explicit and formal. Every one who had ever suffered from
his temper or caprices found themselves overpaid beyond
their wildest expectations. These legacies excepted, he left

all that he possessed, without fetter or condition, to his
nephew.

There was great exultation among the many who knew
and loved Alan Wyverne well, when they heard of his goodly
heritage. Bertie Grenvil, on guard at the Palace on the
Sunday when the news came to town, called his intimates
around him to rejoice over the "pieces of silver" that his
friend had found, and presided at a repast such as Brillat-
Savarin might have ordered if he had served in the Household
Brigade. Algy Beauclerc lost heavily at the club that night,
for he was tied, after the Mezentian fashion, to a partner
who never played the right card even by accident; but he
laughed a great honest laugh, and told the incorrigible
sinner, when the penance was over, that "he would make a
very fair player in time, if he would only sit still and take
pains." The Squire appeared at dinner radiant and triumph-
ant, as if there were no such things as mortgages or Jews
on this side of eternity. Lady Mildred looked delighted
and vaguely sympathetic, as if she would have liked to con-
gratulate *some one* on the spot, but did not quite see her
way. Helen Vavasour's cheek flushed for an instant and
then grew very pale ; her lip trembled painfully, as she whispered to herself, "Too late—ah me! too late!"

The *Goshawk* was lying off Beyrout when "the good news
from home" came out. Wyverne received them with a
placidity approaching to indifference, which exasperated his
companions intensely ; but he left the party immediately,
and returned alone by the next steamer. When he landed in
England, he went straight to Castle Dacre. The first paper
that he opened was Bernard Haldane's letter. It ran thus :

"MY DEAR ALAN,—I wish I could have seen you once

more, though I have little to say besides farewell. Think
as kindly of me as you can ; but don't try to persuade
yourself, or others, that you are sorry I am gone. I leave
no chief mourner. If a dog howls here to-night, it will be
because the moon is full. It is but common justice that we
should reap as we have sown; nevertheless, these last
hours are rather dreary. I have left everything undone
that I ought to have done for thirty years and more, but I
have tried to make amends—at least to you. You are young
enough to enjoy this second inheritance thoroughly, and
wiser than when you lost your own. I will not attach to
my bequest even the shadow of an implied condition ; yet
I pray you to keep the old house and its contents together
as long as you can. You said yourself it would be a pity
to part them. I would leave you my blessing if I dared ;
but it would be a sorry jest, and might turn out badly. I
do wish you all the good luck that can be found in this
mismanaged world. I wish it—even if you persuade her
mother to allow Helen Vavasour to share your altered
fortunes. I am too tired to write more. It has been a
long, rough journey, and I ought to sleep soundly. Good-
night.

" Yours, in all kindness,

"BERNARD HALDANE."

It would be absurd to say that Wyverne felt deep sorrow
for his uncle's death ; but an intense pity welled up in his
honest heart as he read that strange letter, and fancied the
lonely old man tasking the last of his strength to trace the
weak wavering lines ; in truth, the characters seemed still
more hazy and indistinct, when he laid the paper down.

By my faith—it is somewhat early in the day to become

funereal. Let us pass over two or three months and change the *venue* entirely.

It is a soft grey December morning, with a good steady breeze, cool but not chilly. The Grace-Dieu hounds are about to draw Rylstone Gorse for the first time this season. It is a favourite fixture, and no wonder—sufficiently central to let the best men in of two neighbouring packs, yet sufficiently remote from town and rail to keep the profane and uninitiate away. There is a brook, too, in the bottom, over which the fox is sure to go, not very wide, but deep enough to hold a regiment, which always weeds the field charmingly. The meet is in a big pasture hard by: while the ten minutes' law allotted by immemorial courtesy to distant comers is expiring, it may be worth while to mark a few of the "notables."

There, leaning over the low carriage-door, and doing the honours of the meet to Lady Mildred, stands the Duke of Camelot. There is nothing of *morgue* or reserve in the character or demeanour of that mighty noble, but his manner is, in despite of himself, somewhat superb and stately. Wherever he appears, there is diffused around an ambrosial atmosphere savouring of the *ancien régime.* Nature never meant him for a warrior or statesman. His mission through life has been to *poser* before the world, unconsciously, as a perfect type of his order; you see it in every movement of the long taper limbs, in the carriage of the patrician head, in the peculiar sweep and curl of the ample grey whisker, in every line of the clear-cut prominent features, in the smile which—intended to be genial and benevolent—is simply condescending and benign. What his mental capacities may be, it is impossible to say; he has never tried them. But in his own country he hath great honour; the peasantry

believe him to be omniscient and omnipotent, if not omni-
present. Were the fancy to seize him to rebel against the
powers that be, I fancy the stalwart yeomen would muster
strong round the ancient banner, in defiance of the claims of
Stuart or Guelph. Nevertheless, the Duke is, on the whole,
a very good-natured and convivial potentate ; when no
state-party is in question, he loves to gather round him pleasant people who suit each other and suit him, without regard
to their pride of place or order of precedence. He brings,
in one way or another, more than 20 guests to the meet
to-day, including, besides the family from Dene, the
Brabazons and Lord Clydesdale.

The Master has just fallen to the rear, after a brief
conference with the huntsman. He sits there, you see, with
a listless indifference on his dark handsome face, as if henceforth he had no earthly interest in the proceedings ; but in
reality he is watching everything and everybody with keen,
inevitable eyes. Lord Roncesvaux is a cold, stern man, born
with tact and talent enough to have made him great in his
generation, if he had not devoted both exclusively, together
with half his fortune, to the one favourite pursuit. He
speaks seldom in society—never in the senate ; but if a
thrusting rider gets a step too forward at the gorse, or presses
on his hounds to-day, you will hear that well-shaped mouth
open very much to the purpose.

A little to the left, with a clear space round him, is
Clydesdale, looking hot and savage, even this early hour.
The horse would be quiet enough if the rider would only let
his mouth alone ; but the Earl has a knack of bullying his
dependents, equine as well as human ; so "Santiago's"
temper is getting fast exasperated, and his broad brown
chest is already flecked with foam.

Do you mark that lithe erect figure, on the wicked-looking bay mare, moving from one group to another in the foreground? Everybody seems glad to see him, and he has a jest or a smile ready for each successive greeting. That is Major Cosmo Considine, who began life as a Guardsman, and has served since in more Irregular corps than he now chooses to remember. The habitual expression of the face is gay and pleasant enough, but sometimes the features look strangely haggard and worn, as if the past was trying to tell its tale; and the thin lips, under cover of the huge blonde moustache, will set, as though in anger or pain. Redoubtable in battle—dangerous, they say, in a boudoir—he is especially hard to beat when hounds are running straight and fast; no matter how big the fencing may be, if it is a real good thing, Satanella's lean eager head will be seen creeping to the front; and once there, like her master on certain other occasions, she is "not to be denied."

Major Considine married a wife, wealthy and fair, some three years ago, and has ever since been purposing, gravely but vaguely, to become steady and respectable. The pious intentions have not been carried out with uniform success. The weak mind of his unhappy spouse is supposed to oscillate almost daily between furious jealousy and helpless adoration; but the silver tongue of the incorrigible Bohemian is still seductive as when, in spite of relatives' advice and warning, it won him his bride; about 20 minutes' persuasion always reduces her to the dreamy, devotional phase, in which she remains till the next offence awakes her. To do Cosmo justice, his aberrations are much more harmless than the world gives him credit for; nor does he often seek now to illustrate his theories practically.

There is Nick Gunstone, the great stock-breeder and

steeple-chaser, expatiating to a knot of true believers on the
merits of a long, low, raking five-year-old, with whom he
expects to pull off a good thing before next April. The
young one looks wild and scared and fretful, and evidently
knows little of his business yet; but his rider has nerve
enough for both, and a hand as light as a woman's, though
his muscles are like steel. When the hounds are well away
you will see the pair sailing along in front, quite at their
ease: a "crumpler" or so is a moral certainty; but Nick
Gunstone is all wire and whalebone, and seems to rebound
harmlessly from the earth, if he hits it ever so hard; he
believes religiously that "nothing steadies a young one like a
heavy fall," on which principle he generally sends them at the
strongest part of the fence, and the stiffest bit of the timber.
He is in rather a bad humour to-day, for objections have
just been made and sustained to his receiving the aristocratic
"allowance" in future; and Mr Gunstone's sensitive soul
chafes indignantly at the injustice—of course on account of
the diminution of his dignity, not in the least because of the
addition to his weight!

The Amazonian division muster in great force, displaying
every variety of head-gear, coquettish and business-like.
There is one of the number—far in the background, with a
solitary attendant—that even a stranger would single out
instantly, but with an instinctive feeling that his glance
ought not to rest there long. To be sure, her horse is well
worth looking at; for if shape and "manners" go for any-.
thing, Don Juan must be a very cheap three hundred guineas'
worth. But the rider's appearance is still more remarkable.
It would be rather difficult to define exactly why. There is
nothing particularly eccentric or "fast" in her demeanour,
so far as one can judge while she is in repose; her equip-

ment and appointments, though faultless in every respect, are perfectly quiet and unobtrusive; only a very stern critic would remark that the miraculous habit fits her superb bust a shade *too* well. You see a frank fearless face, at times perhaps a trifle too mutinously defiant; a broad, brent, white forehead; clear, bold blue eyes, flashing often in merriment, seldom in anger; and thick coils of soft gold-brown hair, braided tightly under the compact riding-hat. It is not exactly a pretty picture, though its piquancy might be attractive to such as admire that peculiar style.

The solitary horseman who never leaves her side is Mr Lacy, the professional artist, who has reduced riding over fences to a science. In consideration of large monies, perfect mounts, and unlimited claret and cigars, he consents to act as mentor and pioneer to the reckless *Reine des Ribaudes:* the office is no sinecure, and the wages are conscientiously earned. There is a look of grave anxiety on his pale intellectual face to-day, such as may well become a brave man who estimates aright the importance and perils of a task set before him, and prepares to encounter them without reluctance or fear. Of a truth, in a country like this, where, as a stranger, she rides "for her own hand," and means going, it is no child's-play to *chaperon* Pelagia.

One other personage remains to be noticed—I venture to hope you are not tired of him yet—Alan Wyverne; looking thinner and browner than when we saw him last, but in very fair plight notwithstanding, who has just come down into the Shires, with a larger stud than he ever owned in the old days. He had no idea of the Vavasours being in the neighbourhood, or perhaps even Rylstone Gorse would not have tempted him to ride the score of miles that lay between the fixture and his hunting quarters. He has got over the

meeting with his uncle most successfully; how cordial it was
on both sides, you may easily imagine.   But he has so many
friends to greet, and congratulations to answer, that he has
not found time, yet, to approach the carriage in which Lady
Mildred is reclining.   Alan has nothing in his stable, so far,
that he likes so well as his ancient favourite; he rides him
first-horse to-day.   In truth, Red Lancer is a very model of
a fast weight-carrier; you cannot say whether blood or bone
predominates in the superb shape and clean powerful limbs,
and all his admirers allow "that he is looking fitter than
ever."   He is apt to indulge in certain violent eccentricities
in the first five minutes after he is mounted, but he has
settled down now, and bears himself with a quiet, stately
dignity; nevertheless, there is a resolute look about his
head, implying obstinacy to be ruled only by a stronger will.

   The ten-minutes' law has more than expired, and, at an
imperceptible signal from the Master, the pack moves on
slowly towards the gorse.   We will not wait to witness the
certain find, but get forward a mile or two, to a point that
the fox is almost sure to pass; being invisible we can do no
harm, even if we do cross his line.

   Did you ever see a more truculent fence than that on
your right, which stretches along continuously for 1200
yards or more, on the Rylstone side of the road on which
we are standing?   The double rails, both sloping out-
wards, are much higher and wider apart than usual, and
the charge of a squadron would hardly break the new tough
oak timber; to go in and out is impossible, for there is a
deep ditch in the middle fringed by meagre, stunted quick-
set; and on the landing side there is actually another trench
vast enough to swallow up horse and rider, if by any chance
they got so far.   The only outlet is through double gates,

with a bridge of treacherous planks between them. There was malice prepense in the mind that contrived that fearful barrier. The owner of the farm is a morose, hard-fisted Scotch presbyterian, who regards all sport as a snare and device of the Evil One, and acts according to his narrow light, viciously. When he came into the country a year ago, he was afraid to warn the hounds off his land, but went to a considerable expense to stop them, as he thought, quite as effectually. The pleasant innovation of wiring the fences was unknown in those days (soon, I suppose, they will strew calthrops along the headlands, and conceal spring-guns cunningly, to explode if you hit the binders); but David Macausland did his worst after the fashion of the period; and so sat down behind his entrenchment with the grim satisfaction of a consummate engineer, waiting for the enemy to come on.

You know the occupants of that low phaeton that sweeps round the corner so smoothly and rapidly, pulling up within 100 yards of us? Miss Vavasour's ponies are too fiery to be trusted in a crowd, so she has listened to Maud Brabazon's suggestion that they should take their chance of seeing something of the run, instead of going to the meet—yielding the more readily because her own fancy, to-day, inclines to comparative solitude. There they are, left entirely to their own devices, with only a small elderly groom to keep them out of mischief.

The fair adventuresses have not to wait: before they have been posted five minutes, a symphony and crash of hound-music comes cheerily down the wind, and a dark speck, developing itself into shape and colour as it approaches, steals swiftly down the fifty-acre pasture. Fortunately they are not forward enough to do any harm; even the restless

s

ponies stand still, as if by instinct, while a big dog-fox crosses the road, quite unconscious of the bright eyes that are following him; he whisks the white tag of his brush knowingly, just as he clears the fence, evidently thinking it will prove a "stopper," at least to his human foes. Two minutes more, and the pack sweeps compactly over the crest of the rising ground; a little in the rear, on either flank, come the real front-rankers—the ambitious spirits who, wherever they go, will assert their pride of place; the very flower of science and courage; the best and boldest of England's *Hippodamastæ*. Do you think the whole world could show you such another sight as this?

There is Cosmo Considine, sending Satanella along as if he had another spare neck at home, in case of accidents, and as if she had 10 companions in the stable (instead of a brace) to replace her if she comes to grief. There is Lord Roncesvaux, riding as jealous as any of them, though he would scorn to confess such a weakness; there is a fierce light now in his broad black eyes, though the listlessness has scarcely left his face. There is Nick Gunstone, holding his own gallantly, discreet enough to give "the swells" a widish berth. And there, in the van of the battle, flutters the bright-blue habit, and gleams the soft golden hair.

"How very fortunate!" Helen Vavasour cried. "We are just in the right place; they must cross the road, and we shall see all the fencing."

Mrs Brabazon was more experienced than her companion, and, indeed, had been no mean performer over a country in her day. She shook her pretty head negatively, as she answered—

"I am afraid not, dear, unless there is an unusual amount of chivalry out to-day. I have been looking at that place, and I believe it is simply impracticable. They must get round it somehow, and the hounds will leave them here."

The old groom, standing at the ponies' heads, touched his hat, in assent and approval.

"You're quite right, my lady," he said. "There's no man in these parts as would try that fence; no more there didn't ought to. It's hard on a thirty-foot fly, let alone the drop; and it's a broken neck or back if you falls short, or hits a rail."

The *impasse* is evidently well known, and the leaders of the field appear to be very much of the speaker's opinion; for instead of following the hounds down the middle of the pasture, they begin to diverge on either side, the huntsman setting the example. Will Darrell takes fences as they come, very cheerfully, in an ordinary way; but a great general has no business to risk his life like a reckless subaltern; and the idea of being laid up with a broken limb so early in the season is simply intolerable. With Lord Roncesvaux's servants duty stands first of all; they know that no credit won by mere hard riding would excuse a fault of rashness, or soften the implacable Master's anger. Cosmo Considine acknowledges the necessity of a compromise, growling out an imprecation in some strange outlandish tongue; and Pelagia's pilot, after a hurried word exchanged with the Major, for whom he has a great respect and esteem, follows him to the right, utterly disregarding the remonstrances of his impetuous charge. Even Nick Gunstone thinks that this will be rather too strong an illustration of his favourite theory, and reserves the young one's steadying lesson for a more convenient season.

A few sceptics determine to judge for themselves, and ride right down to the fence; but one glance satisfies them, and

they gallop along it in both directions, rather losing ground
by their obstinacy than otherwise. Amongst these is Lord
Clydesdale. Perhaps the Earl is aware of the proximity of
the pony-carriage; at any rate he thinks it necessary to make
a demonstration; so he takes a short circuit and pretends to
charge the fence, with much bluster and flurry. Santiago
behaves with a charity and courtesy very amiable, considering
the provocation he has undergone, and tries to save his master's honour by taking on himself the odium of a decisive
refusal. But the sham is too glaring to deceive the veriest
novice; Maud Brabazon's smile is marvellously meaning,
and Miss Vavasour's curling lip does not dissemble its scorn.

Half a minute later Maud happened to be looking in an
opposite direction; an exclamation from the groom, and a
low cry, almost like a moan, from her companion, made her
turn quickly. Helen had dropped the reins; her hands
were clasped tightly as they lay on the bearskin-rug, and her
great eyes gleamed bright and wild with eagerness and terror; they were riveted on a solitary horseman, who came
down at the fence straight and fast.

Alan Wyverne had been baulked at the brook by some
one's crossing him, and the pace was so tremendous that even
Red Lancer's turn of speed had not yet quite enabled him
to make up lost ground. It so happened, that he had ridden
along that double on his way to the meet, and though he
fully appreciated the peril, he had then decided that it was
just within his favourite's powers, and consequently ought
to be tried.

Truly, at that moment, the pair would have made a superb
picture. Alan was sitting quite still, rather far back in the
saddle; his hands level and low on the withers, with hold
enough on Red Lancer's mouth to stop a swerve, but giving

the head free and fair play; his lips slightly compressed, but
not a sign of trepidation or doubt on his quiet face. The
brave old horse was, in his way, quite as admirable; like his
master, he had determined to get as far over the fence as
pluck and sinew would send them; so on he came, with his
small ears pointing forward dagger-wise, momentarily increasing his speed, but measuring every stride, and judging his
distance, so as to take off at the proper spot to a line.

They were within 30 yards of the rails now, and still
Helen Vavasour gazed on—steadfast and statue-like—without a quiver of lip or a droop of eyelash. Maud Brabazon's
nerves were better than most women's, but they failed her
then. She felt a wild desire to spring up and wave Alan
back; but a cold faint shudder came over her, and she could
only close her eyes in helpless terror.

There came a rush of hoofs sounding on elastic turf—a
fierce snort as Red Lancer rose to the spring—and then a
dull smothered crash, as of a huge body's falling.

Maud felt her companion sink back by her side, trembling
violently: then she heard a hoarse exclamation from the
groom of wonderment and applause; then Wyverne's clear
voice speaking to his horse encouragingly, and then—she
opened her eyes just in time to see the further road-fence
taken in the neatest possible style.

There had been no fall after all. Red Lancer's hind hoofs
broke away the outer bank of the ditch, and he "knuckled"
fearfully on landing; but a strong practised hand recovered
him just in time to save his credit and his knees.

Negotiations were entered into soon afterwards with Mr
Macausland, and powerful arguments brought to bear upon
his cupidity; the austere Presbyterian compromised with
the unrighteous Mammon, so far as to suppress the obnoxious

middle ditch and render the fence barely practicable. But
they point out the spot still, as a proof of the space that a
perfect hunter can cover, with the aid of high courage and
strong hind-quarters, if he is ridden straight and fairly.
That elderly groom, who is saturnine and sceptical by nature,
prone to undervalue and discredit the exploits of others, when
one of his fellows speaks of a big leap, always quells and
quenches the narrator utterly, by playing his trump-card of
the great Rylstone double.

It is almost an invariable rule—if a man by exceptional
luck or pluck "sets" the field, the hounds are sure to throw
up their heads within a couple of furlongs. Fortune, as if
tired of persecuting Alan Wyverne, gives him a rare turn
to-day.

There was a scent, such as one meets about twice in a season. The field, spread out like a fan, begins to converge
again, and the front rank are riding like men possessed, to
make up their lost ground. All in vain—nothing without
wings would catch the "flying bitches" now, as they stream
over the broad level pastures without check or stay, drinking
in the hot trail through wide up-turned nostrils, mute as
death in their savage thirst for blood. It was a trivial
triumph, no doubt, hardly worthy of a highly rational being;
but the hunting instinct is one of the strongest in our imperfect nature, after all: I believe that it falls to the lot of
very few to enjoy such intense, simple happiness as Wyverne
experienced for about 18 minutes, as he swept on alone,
on the flank of the racing pack, rejoicing in Red Lancer's
unfaltering strength. Such a tremendous burst must necessarily be brief. As Alan crashes through the rail of a great
"oxer," an excited agriculturist screams—"He's close afore
you." Close—the hounds know that better than you can

tell them. Look how the veterans are straining to the
front. Suddenly, as they stream along a thick bullfinch, old
Bonnibelle wheels short round and glides through the fence
like a ghost; her comrades follow as best they may; there is
a snap—a crash of tongues—and a savage worry. Alan
Wyverne, too, turns in his tracks; and driving Red Lancer
madly through the blackthorn, clears himself from the falling
horse, just in time to rush in to the rescue, and—with the
aid of a friendly carter, who uses whip and voice lustily—to
save from sharp wrangling teeth rather a mutilated trophy.

Now, is not that worth living for? Wyverne could answer
the question very satisfactorily, as he loosens Red Lancer's
girth and turns his head to the wind, pulling his small ears,
and stroking his lofty crest caressingly. Nearly five minutes
have passed, and the hounds are beginning to wander about
in a desultory, half-satisfied way, as is their wont after a kill,
before Lord Roncesvaux, and the huntsman, and three or
four more celebrities, put in a discomfited appearance.

It speaks ill for our chivalry that we should have left the
pony-carriage to itself all this time; but that "cracker" over
the grass was too strong a temptation; we were bound to
see the end of it.

Mrs Brabazon was the first to speak, breathing quick and
nervously.

"Oh, Helen, was not that magnificent? But were you
ever so frightened?"

The wild look had passed out of the girl's eyes, yet they
were still strangely dreamy and vague.

"It was very fearful," she said; "but I ought not to have
been frightened. There is no one like *him*—no one half so
cool and brave. I have known that for so many years!"

Maud's keen glance rested on the speaker's face for a

second or two. What she read there did not seem greatly to
please her.

" I think we had better be turning homewards," she said,
gravely : "I feel tired already, and I am sure we shall see
nothing more to-day."

From Miss Vavasour's flushing cheek, and the impatient
way in which she gathered up the reins and turned her
ponies, it was easy to guess that she did not wish her thoughts
to be too closely scanned just then. But before they had
driven 300 yards, she was musing again. At last her lips
moved involuntarily. Maud Brabazon's quick ear caught a
low, piteous whisper—" I don't think he even saw me "—and
then a weary, helpless sigh. In just such a sigh may have
been breathed the dying despair of that unhappy Scottish
maiden, who pined so long for the coming of her lover from
beyond the sea, and whose worn-out heart broke when he
rode in under the archway, without marking the wave of her
kerchief, or looking up at her window.

It was a very silent drive homewards. One of those two
had good right to be pensive. Last night, Lord Clydesdale,
utterly vanquished and intoxicated by her beauty, spoke out
right plainly. The day of grace that Helen claimed for reflection is half gone already, and the irrevocable answer must
be given to-morrow.

Shall we say—as they said in olden times to criminals
called upon to plead—" So God send you good deliver-
ance ? " Truly it was a kindly, courteous formula enough ;
but I fancy it carried little meaning to the minds of the
judge or jury, and little comfort to the heavy heart of the
attainted traitor.

Throughout the country side that night men seemed unable
to talk long about anything, without recurring to the morn-

ing's run and the feat which had made it so singularly re-markable. Even Clydesdale did not venture to dissent or show discontent when Wyverne's nerve and judgment were praised up to the skies; he only swelled sulkily, and indulged under his breath in a whole string of his favourite curses, registering another involuntary offence against the name he hated so bitterly. Red Lancer came in for his full share of the glory; they discussed his points and perfections one by one, till you might have drawn his portrait without ever having seen him. He was as famous now as that mighty war-horse of whom the quaint old ballad sings—

> " So grete he was, of back so brode,
> So wight and warily he trode,
> On earth was not his peer ;
> Ne horse in land that was so tall ;
> The knight him clepèd ' Lancivall,'
> But lords at board and grooms in stall
> Clepèd him—' Grand Destrere.' "

In the servants'-hall at Beauprè Lodge, the witness of the feat thus expressed himself, an honest admiration lighting up for once his hard, rough-hewn face—

"It's very lucky I ain't a young 'oman of fortun'" (signs of unanimous adhesion from his audience, especially from the feminine division). "Ah, you may laugh. If I was, I'd follow Sir Alan right over the world, without his asking of me, if it was only for the pleasure of blacking his boots."

After this, who will say that "derring-do" is not still held in honour, or that hero-worship has vanished out of the land ?

CHAPTER XX.

QUAM DEUS VULT PERDERE.

THE noon of night is past, and Helen Vavasour is alone in her chamber, without a thought of sleep. In truth, the damsel is exceeding fair to look upon—though it is a picture over which we dare not linger—as she leans back, half reclining, on the low couch near the hearth; a loose dressing-robe of blue cachemire faced with quilted white satin draping her figure gracefully, without concealing its grand outlines; her slender feet, in dainty velvet slippers broidered with seed-pearl, crossed with an unstudied coquetry that displays the arched instep ravishingly; a torrent of shining dark hair falling over neck and shoulder; a thin line of pearly teeth showing through the scarlet lips that are slightly parted; the light of burning embers reflected in her deep eyes, that seem trying to read the secrets of the Future in the red recesses and the fitful flames.

She had been musing thus for many minutes, when a quick step came across the corridor; there was a gentle tap at the door, and it opened to admit Mrs Brabazon.

"I thought I should find you up," she said. "I'm strangely wakeful to-night, Helen, and very much disposed to talk. Do you mind my staying here till you or I feel more sleepy "

Miss Vavasour assented eagerly; indeed, she was rather glad of an excuse for breaking off her " maiden meditation ;" so she established her visitor in the most luxurious chair she could find, not without a caress of welcome.

Nevertheless, in spite of their conversational inclinations, neither seemed in a particular hurry to make a start; and, for some minutes, there was rather an embarrassed silence. At length Mrs Brabazon looked up and spoke suddenly.

" Helen, what answer do you mean to give to the Great Earl to-morrow? Don't open your eyes wonderingly; I drew my own conclusions from what I saw last night. Besides, Lady Mildred is perfectly well informed; though she has not said a word to you, she has spoken to me about it, and asked me to help the good cause with my counsel and advice, if I could find time and occasion. Shall I begin ? "

She spoke lightly; but the grave anxiety on her face belied her tone. Miss Vavasour's thoughts had been devoted so exclusively to one subject, that its abrupt introduction now did not startle her at all. Her smile was cold and somewhat disdainful, as she replied—

" Thank you very much. But it is hardly worth while to go through all the advantages of the alliance; I have had a full and complete catalogue of them already. They chose Max for an ambassador, and I assure you he discharged his duties quite conscientiously, and did not spare me a single detail; he was nearly eloquent sometimes; and I never saw him so near enthusiasm as when he described the Clydesdale diamonds. He made me understand, too, very plainly, that the fortunes of our family depend a good deal upon me. Did you know that we are absolutely ruined, and have hardly a right, now, to call Dene ours ? "

Ah, woe and dishonour ! Is it Helen's voice that is speaking ? Have 12 months changed the frank, impulsive girl into a calculating, worldly woman, a pupil that her own mother might be proud of ? For all the emotion or interest she betrays, she might be a princess, wooed by proxy, to be the bride of a king whom she has never seen.

Some such thoughts as these rushed across Maud Brabazon's mind as she listened ; great fear and pity rose up in her kind heart, till her eyes could scarcely refrain from tears.

" I had heard something of this," she said, sadly ; " though I did not know things were so desperate. There are 100 arguments that would urge you to say—Yes, and only two or three to make you say—No. It is absolutely the most brilliant match in England. You will have the most perfect establishment that ever was dreamt of, and we shall all envy you intensely ; it has been contemplated for you, and you have expected the proposal yourself for months ; I know all that. Yesterday—I should not have thought it probable you could hesitate ; to-day—I do beg and pray you to pause. I think you will be in great danger if you marry the Earl. Have you deceived yourself into believing that you love him ? "

" I don't deceive myself ; and I have never deceived him. He is ready and willing to take what I can give, and expects no more, I am certain. I do not love Lord Clydesdale ; and I am not even sure that we shall suit each other. But he is anxious to make the trial, and I—am content. I know that I shall try honestly to do my duty as his wife, if he will let me. That is all. Time works wonders, they say; it may do something for us both."

Still the same slow, distinct utterance; the same formal, constrained manner; as if she were repeating a lesson thoroughly learnt by rote. Maud Brabazon was only confirmed in her purpose to persevere to the uttermost in her warning.

" I have no right to advise," she said; " and moral preaching comes with an ill grace, I dare say, from my foolish lips. But indeed—indeed—1 only speak because I like you sincerely, and I would save you if I could. One may deceive oneself about the past as well as the future. Are you sure that you can forget? Are you sure that an old love has not the mastery still? Helen, if I were your mother I would not trust you."

The girl's cheek flushed brightly—less in confusion than in anger.

" You need have no false delicacy, Maud. If you mean that I shall never love any one as I have loved Alan, if you mean that I still care for him more than for any living creature, you are quite right. But it is all over between us, for ever and ever. We shall always be cousins henceforth—no more; he said so himself. If a word could make us all we once were, I don't think I would speak it; I am sure *he* never would. But, my dear, it does surprise me beyond everything, to hear *you* arguing on the romantic side. You never could have worshipped Mr Brabazon, before or after marriage; and yet you amuse yourself better than any one I know."

Miss Vavasour's quick temper—always impatient of contradiction—was in the ascendant just then, or she would scarcely have uttered that last taunt. She bitterly repented it when she saw the other cower under the blow, bowing her head into her clasped hands, humbly and sorrowfully.

When Maud looked up, not one of the many who had admired and loved her radiant face would have recognized it in its pale resolve.

"You only spoke the truth, Helen. Don't be penitent; but listen as patiently as you can. At least, my example shall not encourage you in running into danger. I will tell you a secret that I meant to carry to my grave. You incur a greater risk than ever I did; see how it has fared with me. It is quite true that I did not love my husband when I accepted him; but I had never known even a serious fancy for any one else. I imagined I was hardened enough to be safe in making a conventional marriage. And so — so it went on well enough for some years; but my falsehood was punished at last. They say it is sharp pain when frozen blood begins to circulate; ah, Helen — trust me—it is worse still, when one's heart wakes up. I cannot tell you how it came about with me. He never tried to make me flirt, like the rest of them; but when he spoke to me his voice always changed and softened. He never tried to monopolize me, but wherever I went, he was sure to be; and, some nights, when I was more wild and mischievous than usual, I could see wonder and pity in his great melancholy eyes: they began to haunt me, those eyes; and I began to miss him and feel disappointed and lonely, if an evening passed without our meeting. But I never betrayed myself, till one night Geoffrey told me, suddenly, that he was to sail in four days for the coast of Africa. I could not help trembling all over, and I knew that my face was growing white and cold; I looked up in his—just for one second

—and I read his secret, and confessed mine. He had mercy on my weakness — God reward him for it! — he only asked for a flower that I wore, when I would have given him my life or my soul; for I was wicked and mad that night. It was so like him: I know he would never tempt me: he would save me from going wrong if it cost him his heart's blood. Fevers and horrors of all sorts beset them on that coast: I might read Geoffrey's death in the next *Gazette,* and yet — his lips have not touched my hand. You say I amuse myself. Do you know, that I must have light, and society, and excitement, or I should go mad? I dare not sit at home and think for an hour. I have to feed my miserable vanity, to keep my conscience quiet. I am pure in act and deed, and no one can whisper away my honour; but in thought I am viler than many outcasts — treacherous, and sinning every day, not only against my marriage vow, but against *him.* I often wish I were dead, but I am not fit to die."

She had fallen forward as she spoke, and lay prone with her head buried in Helen's lap—a wreck of womanhood in her abasement and self-contempt. The wind, that had been rising gustily for hours past, swelled into fury just then, driving the sleet against the casements like showers of small-shot, and howling savagely through the cedars, as though in mockery of the stricken heart's wail. Maud Brabazon shivered and lifted up her wild scared face—

"Do you hear *that?*" she said. "I never sleep when a gale is blowing. The other night Bertie Grenvil was pleading his very best; I answered at random, and I daresay I laughed nervously; he fancied it was because his words had confused me. I was only thinking—what the weather might be on the Western coast, for a gust like that last was sweeping by. Ah, Helen, darling! do listen and be warned in time: if you don't see your danger, pause and reflect, if only for my sake. Have I made my miserable confession in vain?"

Miss Vavasour's expression was set and steadfast as ever, though tears swam in her eyes: she leant down and clasped her soft white arms round Maud Brabazon's neck, and pressed a pitiful tender kiss on the poor humbled head.

"Not in vain, dearest!" she whispered; "I shall always love and trust you henceforth, because I know you thoroughly. But I cannot go back. It is too late now, even if I would. I hope I shall be able to do my duty; at least, I need not fear the peril of ever loving again. I must accept Lord Clydesdale to-morrow."

Maud drew quickly out of the close embrace, and threw herself back, burying her face in her hands once more; when she uncovered it, it was possessed by nothing but a blank white despair.

"The punishment is coming!" she said; "I can do harm enough, but I can do no good, if I try ever so hard—that is clear. I will help you always to the uttermost of my power; but we will never speak of this again."

She rose directly afterwards, and after the exchange of a long caress—somewhat mechanical on one side—quitted the room with a vague, uncertain step. So; Helen's very last chance was cast away, and she was left to the enjoyment of her prospects and her dreams.

The decisive interview came off on the following morning. There was not a pretence of romance throughout. Lord Clydesdale manifested a proper amount of eagerness and *empressement*; Helen was perfectly cool and imperial; nevertheless, the suitor seemed more than satisfied. The negotiation was laid in due form before the Squire and Lady Mildred in the course of the day. To do the Earl justice, he had never been niggardly or captious in finance, and his liberality now was almost ostentatiously magnificent. By some means or other he had been made thoroughly aware of the state of affairs at Dene. Besides superb proposals of dower and pin-money, he offered to advance, at absurdly moderate interest, enough to clear off all the encumbrances on the Vavasour property; and the whole of the sum was to be settled on younger children—in default of these, to be solely at Helen's disposal.

The poor Squire, though not taken by surprise, was fairly overwhelmed. The temptation of comparatively freeing the dear old house and domain would have proved nearly irresistible even to a stronger mind and will; still, he felt far from comfortable. He did try to salve his unquiet conscience by requiring an interview with his daughter, and seeking therein to arrive at the real state of her heart. It was an honest offer of self-sacrifice, but really a very safe one. Helen did not betray the faintest regret or constraint; so Hubert Vavasour resigned himself, not unwillingly, to the timely rescue. I have not patience to linger over Lady Mildred's intense, undemonstrative triumph.

It was settled that the marriage should take place early in the spring. All the preliminaries went on swiftly and smoothly, as golden wheels will run when thoroughly adjusted and oiled. Miss Vavasour behaved admirably: she accepted numberless congratulations, gratefully and gracefully; in her intercourse with her *fiancé*, she evinced no prudery or undue reserve, but nevertheless contrived to repress the Earl's enthusiasm within very endurable limits.

Only one scene occurred, before the wedding, which is worth

T

recording : it was rather a characteristic one.   Perhaps you
have forgotten that, in the second chapter of this eventful
history, there was mentioned the name of one Schmidt, a
mighty iron-founder of Newmanham, who had bought up all
the mortgages on Dene ?   His intention had been evident
from the first ; and just about the time of the last affiancement, his lawyers gave notice that he meant to call in the
money or foreclose without mercy.

Now the Squire, though he naturally exulted, as a Gentile
and a landed proprietor, in the discomfiture of the Hebrew
capitalist, would have allowed things to be arranged quietly,
in the regular professional way.   But this Lord Clydesdale,
when consulted on the subject, would by no means suffer.
He begged that the meeting of the lawyers might take place
at Dene; and that, if it were possible, Ephraim Schmidt
should be induced to attend in person ; the paying off of the
mortgages was not to be previously hinted at in any way.
The whims of great men must be sometimes humoured, even
by the law: and this was not such a very unreasonable
one after all.

"I wouldn't miss seeing the Jew's face if it cost another
thousand!" the Earl said, with a fierce laugh : so it was settled that he was to be present at the interview.

Mr Schmidt and his solicitor arrived punctually at the appointed hour; there was no fear of the former's absenting
himself on so important an occasion.   "Nothing like looking
after things yourself" was one of his favourite maxims, enforced with a wink of intense sagacity.   He was absolutely
ignorant of legal formalities, but not the less convinced that
such could not be properly carried out without his own
superintendence.

The financier's appearance was quite a study.   He had for

some time past affected rather a rural style of attire, and his costume now was the Newmanham ideal of a flourishing country squire. He chose, with ostentatious humility, the most modest of his equipages to take him to Dene; but he mounted it like a triumphal car. Truly there was great joy in Israel on that eventful morning, for all his family knew the errand on which their sire and lord was bent, and exulted, as is their wont, unctuously.

Ephraim Schmidt was a short bulky man, somewhat under fifty; his heavy, sensual features betrayed at once his origin and the habits of high living to which he was notoriously prone. His companion was a striking contrast. There was rather a foreign look about Morris Davidson's keen handsome face, and those intensely brilliant black eyes are scarcely naturalized yet on this side of the Channel—but the Semitic stamp was barely perceptible. His manner was very quiet and courteous, but never cringing, nor was there anything obsequious about his ready smile. He was choice in his raiment, but it was always subdued in its tone, and he wore no jewels beyond a signet key-ring, and one pearl of great price at his neck. He was the type of a class that has been developed only within the last half-century—the *petit-maître* order of legalists—whose demeanour, like that of the Louis Quinze Abbé's, is a perpetual contradiction of their staid profession, but who nevertheless know their business thoroughly, and follow it up with unscrupulous obstinacy. When Mr Davidson senior died (who had long been Ephraim Schmidt's confidential solicitor), men marvelled that the cautious capitalist could entrust his affairs to such young and inexperienced hands; in truth, he had at first many doubts and misgivings, but these soon vanished as he began to appreciate Morris's cool, pitiless nature, and iron nerves. The wolf-cub's coat

was sleek and soft enough, and he never showed his teeth
unnecessarily; but his fangs were sharper, and his gripe more
fatally tenacious, than even his gaunt old sire's.

So, through the clear frosty morning, the two Jews drove
jocundly along, beguiling the way with pleasant anticipations
of the business before them.   The lawyer had heard of Lord
Clydesdale's engagement to Miss Vavasour, and thought it
just possible that under the circumstances some compromise
might be attempted.   But to this view of the case his patron
would in nowise incline, and he discreetly forbore to press
it.   They passed through the double towers flanking the
huge iron gates; and the broad undulating park stretched
out before them, clumps of lofty timber studding the smooth
turf, while grey turrets and pinnacles just showed in the
distance through the leafless trees.   The Hebrew's heart
swelled, almost painfully, with pride and joy.   He had been
wandering for many a year—not unhappily or unprofitably,
it is true—through the commercial Desert, and now, he
looked upon the fair Land of Promise, only waiting for him
to arise and take possession, when he had once cast out the
Amorite.   When they drove up to the great portico, he was
actually perspiring with satisfaction, in spite of the cold.
He grasped his companion's arm, and whispered, hoarsely—

"Mind, Morris, they'll ask for time: but we won't give
them a day!—not a day."

The chief butler received the visitors in the hall, and
ushered them himself to the library.   Ephraim Schmidt, in
the midst of his unholy triumph, could not help being impressed by the grave dignity of that august functionary.   He
began to think if it would not be possible, by proffer of large
monies, to tempt him to desert his master's fallen fortunes,
and to abide in the house that he became so well.   A pleas-

ant, idle dream! Solomon made the Afreets and Genii his slaves; but, if the Great King had been revived in the plenitude of his power, he would never have tempted that seneschal to serve him, while a Gentile survived on the land.

The family solicitor of the Vavasours was sitting before a table overspread with bulky papers, with his clerk close by his side. He was thin, and white-haired, with a round withered face, pleasant withal, like a succulent Ribstone pippin; his manner was very gentle, and almost timid, but no lawyer alive could boast that he had ever got the best of a negotiation in which Mr Faulkner was concerned. He greeted the capitalist very courteously, and Mr Davidson very coldly, for—he had seen *him* before. There was one other occupant of the library—a tall man, lounging in the embrasure of a distant window, who never turned his head when the new-comers entered: it seemed as though the bleak winter landscape outside had superior attractions. Ephraim Schmidt hardly noticed him; but Davidson felt a disagreeable thrill of apprehension as he recognized the figure of Lord Clydesdale. It is needless to enumerate the verifications and comparisons of many voluminous documents that had perforce to be gone through. The mortgagee got very impatient before they were ended.

"Yes, yes," he kept repeating, nervously, "it is all correct; but come to the point—to the point."

Mr Faulkner was perfectly imperturbable, neither hurrying himself in the least, nor making any unnecessary delay.

"I believe everything is quite correct," he said, at last. "Now, Mr Davidson, may I ask you what your client's intentions are? Is there any possibility of a compromise?"

"I fear, none whatever," was the quiet answer. "We have given ample notice, and the equity of redemption cannot be extended. My client is anxious to invest in land, and we could hardly find a more eligible opening than foreclosure here would afford us."

"Exactly so," the old lawyer retorted. "I only asked the question, because I was instructed to come to an explicit understanding. It does not much matter; for—we are prepared to pay off every farthing."

The small thin hand seemed weighty and puissant as an athlete's, as he laid it on a steel-bound coffer beside him, with a significant gesture of security too tranquil to be defiant.

Cool and crafty as he was, Davidson was fairly taken unawares. He recoiled in blank amazement. Ephraim Schmidt started from his chair like a maniac, his eyes protruding wildly, and his face purple-black with rage.

"Pay off everything?" he shrieked. I don't believe it: it's a lie—a swindle. Not have Dene? I'll have it, in spite of you all?" The churned foam flew from his bulbous lips, as from the jaws of a baited boar.

The silent spectator in the window turned round, then, and stood contemplating the group, not striving to repress a harsh, scornful laugh. That filled up the measure of the unhappy Israelite's frenzy. He made a sort of blind plunge forward, shaking off the warning fingers with which Davidson sought to detain him.

"D—n you, let me go," he howled out. "Who is that man? What does he do here? I *will* know."

The person addressed strode on slowly till he came close to the speaker, and looked him in the face, still with the same cruel laugh on his own.

"I'll answer you," he said. "I was christened Raoul Delamere, but they call me Lord Clydesdale now; and I hope to marry Mr Vavasour's only daughter. I am here—

because I am infidel enough to enjoy seeing a Jew taken on the hip. I wouldn't have missed this—to clear off the biggest of your mortgages. So you fancied you were going to reign at Dene? Not if you had had another hundred thousand at your back. If we only have warning, the old blood can hold its own, and beat the best of you yet. Mr Faulkner, don't you think you had better pay him, and let him go?"

The change of tone in those last words, from brutal disdain to studied courtesy, was the very climax of insult. It was an unworthy triumph, no doubt, but a very complete one. The Earl remained as much master of the position as ever was Front de Bœuf. The Jew was utterly annihilated. To have come there with the power of life and death in his hand, and now to be treated as an ordinary tradesman presenting a Christmas bill! He staggered back step by step, and sunk into a chair, dropping his head, and groaning heavily. Davidson had recovered himself by this time. The elder lawyer only sat silent, and scandalized, lifting his eyebrows in mute testimony against such unprofessional proceedings.

"We can hardly conclude such important business to-day," Morris said. "My client's excitement is a sufficient excuse. We know your intentions now, Mr Faulkner, and there is ample time to settle everything. I will call upon you at any time or place you like to name."

So, after a few more words, it was settled.

Ephraim Schmidt went out, like a man in a dream, from the house that he had hoped to call his own; only moaning under his breath, like a vanquished Shylock—"Let us go home, let us go home." The chief butler (who had been aware of the state of affairs throughout) dealt him the last blow in the hall, by inquiring with exquisite courtesy, 'If he would take any luncheon before he went?'" The miserable Hebrew quivered all over, as a victim at the stake might shrink under the last ingenuity of torture. Truly, the meanest of the many debtors who had sued him in vain for mercy, need not have envied the usurer then.

O dark-eyed Miriam, and auburn-haired Deborah! lay aside your golden harps, or other instruments of music that your soul delights in: no song of gladness shall be raised in your tents to-night; it is for the daughters of the uncircum-cised to triumph.

When the Squire heard an account of the morning's proceedings, he by no means shared in Clydesdale's satisfaction, and rather failed to appreciate the point of the jest. Hubert's thoroughbred instincts revolted against the idea of even a Jew usurer's having been grossly insulted under his roof, when the man only came to ask for his own; besides this, he understood the feeling that had been at work in the Earl's breast, and despised him accordingly. The difference in social position was too overwhelming to make the match a fair one; but in other respects the antagonists were about on a par. It was just this—a phase of purse-pride vanquished by another and a more potential one. Such a victory brings little honour. The transformed rod of the lawgiver swallowed up the meaner serpents; but it was only a venomous reptile, after all.

Wyverne felt neither wrath nor despair when the news of Helen's engagement came: he had quite made up his mind that she would marry soon; but he was sad and pensive. He did not change his opinions easily, and he had formed a very strong one about Clydesdale's character: he thought the Earl was as little likely as any man alive to rule a high-spirited mate wisely and well. Nevertheless, Alan indited an epistle that even Lady Mildred could not help admiring: it was guarded, but not in the least formal or constrained; kind and sincerely affectionate, without a tinge of reproach, or a single allusion that could give pain. He saw "my lady" twice, Helen once, before the latter's marriage, and was equally successful with his verbal congratulations. Of course the interviews were not *tête-à-têtes:* all parties concerned took good care of that. Wyverne and his aunt displayed admirable tact and *sang froid;* but the demoiselle cast both into the shade: her manner was far more natural, and her composure less studied. Truly, the training of the *Grande Dame* progressed rapidly, and the results promised to be fearfully complete.

Alan did intimate an intention of being present at the wedding; but I fear he was scarcely ingenuous there. At all events, urgent private affairs took him abroad two days before the ceremony, no one knew exactly where; and it was three weeks before he appeared on the surface of society again.

Io, Hymenæe! Scatter flowers, or other missile oblations, profusely, you nubile virgins. O choir of appointed youths! roll out, I beseech you, the Epithalamium roundly: let not the fault be imputed to you, if it sounds like a requiem.

So, we bid farewell to Helen Vavasour's maiden history— not without heaviness of heart. Henceforth it befits us to stand aside, with doffed beaver and bated breath, as the Countess of Clydesdale passes by.

CHAPTER XXI.

MAGNA EST VERITAS.

FIFTEEN or sixteen months are come and gone, and the faces of people and things are but little changed. Yes, one of our dramatic personages is a good deal altered for the worse—Alan Wyverne. He became sadder and wiser in this wise.

I forgot to tell you that the delicate state of Mrs Rawdon Lenox's health, and of her affairs, had made a lengthened Continental tour very desirable. She remained abroad nearly two years, and did not return to England till the summer immediately following the Clydesdale marriage. It was late in the autumn when she and Alan met. If the latter had been forewarned of the *rencontre*, it is probable he would have avoided it by declining the invitation to Guestholme Priory; but when he found himself actually under the same roof with the "Dark Ladye" (so some friend or enemy had re-christened her), he felt a certain satisfaction in the idea of clearing up a mystery that had never ceased to perplex and torment him. Their first greeting was rather cold and constrained on both sides; but things could not remain on this footing long. Nina had no fancy for an armed neutrality with an ancient ally, and always brought the question of war or peace to an issue with the least possible delay.

When Alan came into the drawing-room after dinner, Mrs Lenox's look was a sufficient summons, even without the significant movement of the fan, which she managed like a Madrilena. He sat down by her side, his pulse quickening a little with expectation; but curiosity was the sole excitement. For awhile they talked about their travels and other indifferent subjects. The lady got tired of that child's-play first, and broke ground boldly.

"I suppose the interdict is taken off now?" she said. "Will you believe, that I am really sorry that there is no longer a cause for your avoiding me? Will you believe, that no one regretted it, and felt for you more than I did, when I heard your engagement was broken off? Do tell me, that neither I nor my unfortunate affairs had anything to do with it. I have been worrying myself ever since with the fancy, that your great kindness to me may have cost you very dear."

Wyverne was gifted with coolness and self-control quite exceptional, but both as nearly as possible broke down at that moment. He certainly deserved infinite credit for answering, after a minute's silence, so calmly,

"Then it would be a satisfaction to you to know this? Have you any doubts on the subject?"

"Well, I suppose I ought not to have any," Nina said, frankly. "The engagement lasted for months after those wretched anonymous things were written, and I am sure I did all I could to set matters straight. My letter was everything that is meek and quiet and proper, was it not? And it was honest truth, too, every word of it."

"Your letter? Yes, of course—the letter you wrote in answer to mine; but the other—the other?"

He spoke absently and almost at random, like a man half awake.

"What on earth are you talking about?" Mrs Lenox said, with manifest impatience. "What other letter? Did you suppose me capable of writing one other line beside that necessary reply? What have you suspected? I *will* know. Alan, I believed you more generous. You have a right to think lightly of me, and to say hard things, but not —not to insult me so cruelly."

There were tears in the low, tremulous voice, but none in the deep dark eyes that had dilated at first wonderingly, and were now so sad in their passionate reproach that Wyverne did not dare to meet them. He knew that Nina was capable of much that was wild and wicked, but that very recklessness made dissimulation with her simply impossible. If she had been pure and cold as St Agnes, Alan would not have felt more certain of the truth and sincerity of her meaning and words. The fraud, that he had vaguely suspected at the time, stood out black and distinct enough now. He hated himself so intensely that for the moment all other feelings were swallowed up in self-contempt,—even to the craving for vengeance on the conspirators who had juggled him, which ever afterwards haunted him like an evil spirit. Wyverne had always cherished, you know, a simple generous faith in the dignity of womanhood; if his chivalry had carried him one step further—if, in despite of the evidence of his senses, he had refused to believe in womanhood's utter debasement—it would have been perhaps the very folly of romance; but he might have defied the forger. He took the wisest course now, by telling Nina the whole truth, as briefly and considerately as possible.

" You see, I did you fearful wrong," he said. "Though I have paid for it heavily already, and shall suffer to my life's end, that is no reason why you should forgive me. I don't even ask you to do so."

Mrs Lenox was, indeed, bitterly incensed. A perfectly immaculate matron might have laughed such a conspiracy against her fair fame to scorn: Nina could not afford to be maligned unjustly. Nevertheless all her indignation was levelled at the unknown framer of the fraud; not a whit rested on Alan. She had been used to see people commit themselves in every conceivable way, and make the wildest sacrifices, for her sake; but she had learnt to appreciate these follies at their proper worth. Strong selfish desire and the hope of an evil reward were at the bottom of them all. Truly, when a man ruins himself simply to gratify his ruling passion, the lover deserves little more credit than the gambler. But the present case was widely different. She had not a shadow of a claim on Alan's service or forbearance Though he seemed to see no merit in a simple act of duty she knew right well what it had cost him to destroy the supposed evidence of her shame; and now—instead of ex pecting thanks—he was reproaching himself for having mis judged her while believing his own eyes. As she thought on these things, Nina's hard battered heart grew fresh and young again. Not a single unholy element mingled in the tenderness of her gratitude; but, if time and place had not forbidden, she would scarcely have confined her demonstra tions to a covert pressure of Wyverne's hand.

" Forgive you ? " she said, piteously. "It drives me wild to hear you speak so. I would give up every friend I have in the world to keep *you*. The best of them would not have done half as much for me. And we can never be friends—really. My unhappy name has dragged you down like a millstone; don't attempt to deceive yourself; you must hate the sound of it now and always. Ah, do try to believe me. I would submit to any pain or penance or shame, and not think it hard measure, if I could only give you back what you have lost through me."

In despite of his exasperation, the sweet voice fell soothingly on Alan's ear. A man need not greatly glorify himself for having simply acted up to his notions of right and honour; nevertheless, appreciation in the proper quarter must be gratifying to all except the *very* superior natures. Many are left among us still who "do good by stealth," but the habit of "blushing to find it known" is antiquated to a degree.

So, as he listened, Wyverne's mood softened; and he began quite naturally to play the part of consoler, trying to prove to Nina that she had been an innocent instrument throughout, and that if the conspirators had been foiled in this instance, they would surely have found some other engine to work out the same result.

"But it was such base, cruel treachery," she said, trembling with passion. "Will you not try to trace it, for my sake, if not for your own? You must have some suspicions. If I were a man, and could act and move freely, I should never sleep soundly till I was revenged."

Wyverne answered very slowly, and, as he spoke, his face hardened and darkened till it might have been carved in granite.

"You may spare the spur; there is no fear of my sleeping over it. I'm not made of wax or snow, to be moulded like this into a puppet for their profit or pleasure, and I owe you a vengeance besides. Yes, I have suspicions; I'll make them certainties, if I live. Your never having got my note, telling you of my burning the first of tho two letters, gives me a clue. They may double as they like, they won't escape, if I once fairly strike the trail. Now, we will never speak of this again till—I give you *the name*."

The change of Alan's character dated from that night; most of his friends noticed it before long. He was never morose or sullen, but always moody, and absent, and pre-occupied; without exactly avoiding society, he found himself alone, unwontedly often, and solitude did him far more harm than good. To speak the truth, his credit as a pleasant companion began sensibly to decline. A Fixed Idea, even if it be as rosy as Hope, interferes sadly with a man's social merits; if it chance to be sombre or menacing in hue, the influence is simply fatal to conviviality.

But autumn and winter passed, and it was spring again, before Wyverne could set his foot on more solid ground than vague surmises. He felt certain that Lady Mildred had countenanced, if not directed, the plot—the note having mis-carried from Dene was strong evidence—but he was equally sure that her delicate hands were clear of the soil of actual fraud. Who had been the working instrument? For a moment his thoughts turned to Max Vavasour, but he soon rejected this idea, remembering that the latter was not in England that Christmas-tide; besides which, he could not fancy his cousin superintending the practical details of a vulgar forgery; he would far sooner have suspected Clydes-dale, but there was not the faintest reason, so far, to connect the Earl with foul play. So he went groping on, for months, in the twilight without advancing a step, growing more gloomy and discontented every day.　It was a curious chance that put him on the right scent at last.

An Inn of Court is not exactly the spot one would select for setting "a trap to catch a sunbeam;" a wholesome amount of light and air is about as much as one can expect to find in such places; heavy, grave decorum pervades them very fittingly; but it may be doubted if any quarter of a populous city, respectable in its outward seeming, has a right to be so depressingly dull and dingy, as is the Inn of Gray; the spiders of all sorts, who lurk thereabouts, had best not keep the flies long in their webs, or the victims would scarce be worth devouring.

Some such thoughts as these were in Wyverne's mind as he wandered through the grim quadrangle, one cold evening towards the end of March, looking for "Humphrey and Gliddon's" chambers.　The firm had an evil name; men said, that if it was difficult to find out their den, it was twice as hard to escape from it without loss of plumage.　Alan's temper had certainly changed for the worse, but his good nature stood by him still; so when a comrade wrote from the country, to beg him to act as proxy in a delicate money transaction with the aforesaid attorneys, he assented very willingly, and was rather glad to have something to employ his afternoon.　He had just come up from his hunting quarters, where the dry, dusty ground rode like asphalte, and scent was a recollection of the far past.

After some trouble he lighted on the right staircase.　Raw and murky as the outer atmosphere might be, it was pure æther compared to that of the low-browed office into which the visitor first entered; at any hour or season of the year, you could fancy that room maintaining a good, steady condensed dusk of its own, in which fog, and smoke, and dust, had about equal shares. Two clerks sat there, writing busily. The one nearest the door—a thickset, sullen man, past middle age—looked up as Alan came in, and stretching out a grimy hand, said, in a dull, mechanical voice,

" Your card, sir, if you please—Sir Alan Wyverne wishes to see Mr Humphrey."

It was evidently the formula of reception in that ominous ante-chamber.

The other clerk had not lifted his head when the door opened ; but he started violently when he heard the name, so as nearly to upset the inkstand in which he chanced to be dipping his pen, and turned round, with a sort of terror on his haggard, ruined face. It might have been a very handsome face once, but the wrinkled, flaccid flesh had fallen away round the hollow temples and from under the heavy eyes ; the complexion was unhealthy, pale, and sodden ; the features pinched and drawn, to deformity ; the lines on the forehead were like trenches, and the abundant dark hair was, not sprinkled, but streaked and patched, irregularly, with grey.

But, at the first glance, Wyverne recognized the face of a very old friend; he recognized it the more easily because, when he saw it last, it wore almost the same wild, scared look—on the memorable Derby day when " Cloanthus " swept past the stand, scarcely extended, the two leading favourites struggling vainly to reach his quarters.

All his self-command was needed to enable him to suppress the exclamation that sprang to his lips; but he rarely made a mistake when it was a question of tact or delicacy. He followed his conductor into the next room silently ; it chanced to be vacant at that moment ; then Alan laid his hand on the clerk's shoulder, as he stood with averted eyes, shaking like an aspen, and said, in tones carefully lowered—

" My God! Hugh Crichton—you here ? "

" Hush," the other answered, in a lower whisper still ; " that's not my name now. You wouldn't spoil my last chance if you could help it? If you want to see me, wait five minutes after you leave this place, and I'll come to you in the square."

" I'll wait, if it's an hour," Wyverne said, and so passed into the inner room without another word. His business was soon done ; even Humphrey and Gliddon could find no pretext for detaining clients who came with money in their hand. Alan did not exchange a glance with either of the occupants of the clerk's-room as he went out ; he breathed more freely when he was in the chill March air again. As he walked up and down the opposite side of the square, which was nearly deserted, his thoughts were very pitiful and sad.

Hardly a year passes without the appearance of one or more comets in society ; none of these have sparkled more briefly and brilliantly than Hugh Crichton. Everybody liked, and many admired him, but the world had hardly begun to appreciate his rare and versatile talents, when he shot down into the outer darkness. He had friends who would have helped him if they could, but all trace of him was lost and none could say for certain whether he lived or no.

Wyverne had not waited many minutes, when a bent shrunken figure came creeping slowly, almost stealthily towards him, keeping well in the shadow of the buildings In another moment, Alan was grasping both his ancient comrade's hands, with a cordial, honest gripe, that migh have put heart and hope into the veriest castaway.

" Dear old Hugh! how glad I am to light on you again though you are so fearfully changed. Why, they said you had died abroad."

" No such luck," the other answered, with a dreary laugh.
" I did go abroad, and stayed there till I was nearly starved ;
then I came back. London's the best hiding-place, after
all ; and if you have hands and brain, you can always earn
enough to buy bread, spirits, and tobacco. I've been in this
place more than a year ; I get a pound a week ; and I think
of " striking " soon, for an advance of five shillings. They
won't lose me if they can help it ; I save them a clerk, at
least ; old Gliddon never asked me another question after he
saw me write a dozen lines. My work is all in-doors, that's
one comfort ; they haven't asked me to serve a writ yet ; my
senior—you saw him—the man with a strong cross of the
bull about his head—does all that business, and likes it.
But the firm don't trust me much, and they would be more
unpleasant still, if they knew 'Henry Carstairs' was a false
name. No one has much interest now in hunting me down ;
it's old friends' faces I've always been afraid of meeting. But
I did think that none of our lot would ever set foot in that
den, and I had got to fancy myself safe. You didn't come
on your own affairs, Alan, I know. I had an extra grog the
night I heard you had fallen in for Castle Dacre. I rather
think I am glad to see you, after all."

He jerked out the sentences in a nervous, abrupt way,
perpetually glancing round, as if he were afraid of being
watched ; he was so manifestly ill-at-ease that Wyverne had
not the heart to keep him there ; besides, it was cruelty to
expose the emaciated frame, so thinly clad, a minute longer
than was necessary, to the keen evening air.

" Why, Hugh, of course you're glad to see me," Alan said,
forcing himself to speak cheerily ; " the idea of doubting about
it ! But it's too cold to stand chattering here. I'm staying
at the Clarendon : you'll come at seven, sharp, won't you ?

We'll dine in my rooms, quite alone, and have a long talk about old days, and new ones, too. I'll have thought of something better for you by that time, than this infernal quill-driving."

Hugh Crichton hesitated visibly for a few seconds, and appeared to make up his mind, with a sudden effort, to something not altogether agreeable.

"Thank you ; you're very good, Alan. Yes, I'll come, the more because I've something on my mind that I ought to tell you ; but I should never have had the pluck to look you up, if you had not found me. I hope your character at the Clarendon can stand a shock ; it will be compromised when they hear such a scarecrow ask for your rooms. I can't stay a moment longer, but I'll be punctual."

He crept away with the same weak, stealthy step, and his head seemed bent down lower than when he came.

Nevertheless, when, at the appointed hour, the guest sat down opposite his host, the contrast was not so very striking. The office-drudge was scarcely recognizable ; he seemed to freshen and brighten up wonderfully, in an atmosphere that had once been congenial. Even so, those bundles of dried twigs that Eastern travellers bring home, and enthusiasts call "Roses of Sharon" (such Roses!) expand under the influence of warmth and moisture, so as to put forth the feeble semblance of a flower. The black suit was terribly threadbare, and hung loosely round the shrunken limbs, but it adapted itself to the wearer's form, with the easy, careless grace for which Hugh Crichton's dress had always been remarkable ; his necktie was still artistic in its simplicity, and the hair swept over his brow with the old classic wave ; his demeanour bore no trace of a sojourn in Alsatia, and a subtle refinement of manner and gesture clung naturally to the wreck of a gallant gentleman. Some plants, you know—

not the meanest nor the least fragrant—flourish more kindly in the crevices of a ruin than in the richest loam.

It was a pleasant dinner, on the whole, though not a very lively one ; for Alan had too much tact to force conviviality. Crichton ate sparingly, but drank deep; he did not gulp down his liquor, though, greedily, but rather savoured it with a slow enjoyment, suffering his palato to appreciate every shade of the flavour ; the long, satisfied sigh that he could not repress as he set down empty the first beaker of dry champagne, spoke volumes.

They drew up to the fire when the table was cleared, and they were left alone. Wyverne rose suddenly, and leant over towards his companion with a velvet cigar-case in his hand, that he had just taken from the mantelpiece.

"You must tell me your story of the last few years," he said ; but put that case in your pocket before you begin. There are some regalias in it of the calibre you used to fancy, and—a couple of hundreds, in notes, to go on with. You dear, silly old Hugh ! don't shake your head and look scrupulous. Why, I won thrice as much of you at *écarté* in the week before that miserable Derby, and you never asked for your revenge. You should have it now if either you or I were in cue for play. Seriously—I want you to feel at ease before you begin to talk ; I want you to feel that your troubles are over, and that you never need go near that awful *guet-à-pens* again. I've got a permanent arrangement in my head, that will suit you, I hope, and set you right for ever and a day. Hugh, you know if our positions were reversed, I should ask you for help just as frankly as I expect you will take it from me."

Crichton shivered all over, worse than he had done out in the cold March evening.

"Put the case down," he said, hoarsely. "It will be time enough to talk about that and your good intentions half-an-hour hence. I'll tell you what I have been doing, if you care to hear."

Now though the story interested Wyverne sincerely, it would be simple cruelty to inflict it on you; with very slight variations, it might have applied to half the *viveurs* that have been ruined during the last 100 years. Still, not many men could have listened unmoved to such a tale, issuing from the lips of an ancient friend. When he had come to a certain point in his story, the speaker paused abruptly.

"Poor Hugh!" Alan said. "How you must have suffered. Take breath now; I'm certain your throat wants moistening, and the claret has been waiting on you this quarter of an hour. It's my turn to speak; I'm impatient to tell you my plan. The agent at Castle Dacre is so wonderfully old and rheumatic, that it makes one believe in miracles when he climbs on the back of his pony. I would give anything to have a decent excuse for pensioning him off. I shall never live there much, and the property is so large, that it ought to be properly looked after. If you don't mind taking care of a very dreary old house, there's £800 a year, and unlimited lights and coals (they used to burn about 10 tons a week, I believe), and all the snipe and fowl you like to shoot, waiting for you. I shall be the obliged party if you'll take it; for it will ease my conscience, which at present is greatly troubled. The work is not hard, and you've head enough for anything."

Not pleasure or gratitude, but rather vexation and confusion showed themselves in Crichton's face.

"Can't you have patience?" he muttered, irritably. "Didn't I ask you to wait till you had heard all? There's more, and worse, to tell; though I don't know, yet, how much harm was done."

He went on to say that about the time when things were at the worst with him, he had stumbled upon Harding Knowles; they had been contemporaries at Oxford, and rather intimate. Harding did not appear to rejoice much at the encounter; though he must have guessed at the first glance the strait to which his old acquaintance was reduced, he made no offer of prompt assistance, but asked for Crichton's address, expressing vague hopes of being able to do something for him; Hugh gave it with great reluctance, and only under a solemn promise of secresy. He did not the least expect that Knowles would remember him, and was greatly surprised when the latter called some five or six weeks afterwards. Harding's tone was much more cordial than it had been at their first meeting; he seemed really sorry at having failed so far in finding anything that would suit Crichton, and actually pressed him to borrow £10—or more if it was required—to meet present emergencies. An instinctive suspicion almost made Hugh refuse the loan; he felt as if he would rather be indebted to any man alive than to the person who offered it; but he was so fearfully " hard up " that he had not the courage to decline. Knowles came again and again, with no ostensible object except cheering his friend's solitude, and each time was ready to open his purse. "We must get you something before long, and then you can repay me," he would say. Crichton availed himself of these offers more than once, moderately; he began to think that he had done his benefactor great injustice, and looked for his visits eagerly; indeed, few *causeurs*, when he chose to exert himself, could talk more brilliantly and pleasantly than Knowles.

One evening the conversation turned, apparently by chance, to old memories of college days.

"That was the best managed thing we ever brought off," Harding said, at last, "when we made Alick Drummond carry on a regular correspondence with a foreign lady of the highest rank, who was madly in love with him. How did we christen the Countess? I forget. But I remember the letters you wrote for her; the delicate feminine character was the most perfect thing I ever saw. Have you lost that talent of imitating handwriting? It must have been a natural gift; I never saw it equalled."

"Write down a sentence or two," Hugh replied; "I'll show you if I have lost the knack."

He copied them out on two similar sheets of paper, and gave the three to Knowles after confusing them under the table: the latter actually started, and the admiration that he displayed was quite sincere: the *fac similes*, indeed, were so miraculously like the original, that it was next to impossible to distinguish them.

"I can guess what is coming," Alan whispered softly, seeing the speaker pause. "Go on straight and quick to the end, for God's love, and keep nothing back. Don't look at me."

The white working lips had no need to say more: the other saw the whole truth directly. He clenched his hand with a savage curse, but Alan's sad deprecating eyes checked the passionate outbreak of remorse and anger. Sullenly and reluctantly—like a spirit forced by the exorcist to reveal the secrets of his prison-house—Hugh Crichton went through all the miserable details.

Knowles had represented himself as being on such very

intimate terms with Wyverne, as fully to justify him in attempting a practical joke.

"Alan's the best fellow in the world," he said, airily, "but he believes that it is impossible to take him in about womankind. There's the finest possible chance just now, and it can be managed so easily, if you will only help me."

Hugh's natural delicacy and sense of honour, dulled and weakened by drink and degradation, had life enough left to revolt suspiciously. But the other brought to bear pretexts and arguments, specious enough to have deluded a stronger intellect and quieted a keener conscience: he particularly insisted on the point that the lady's character could bear being compromised, and that the secret would never go beyond Alan and himself. Hugh had to contend, besides, against a sense of heavy obligation, and the selfish fear of offending the only friend that was left to back him. Of course, eventually he consented. The next morning Harding brought a specimen of the handwriting—a long and perfectly insignificant note, with the signature torn off—(he was a great collector of autographs) : he was also provided with paper and envelopes, both marked with a cipher, which he took pains to conceal. Crichton could not be sure of the initials, but he caught a glimpse of their colour—a brilliant scarlet. The tone of the fictitious letter, though the expressions were guardedly vague, seemed strangely earnest for a mere mystification ; certainly an intimate acquaintance was implied between the writer and the person to whom it was addressed. The copyist was more than half dissatisfied ; he grumbled a good many objections while employed on his task, and was very glad when it was over. The signature was simply "N.," an initial which occurred more than once

in the specimen note, so that it was easy to reproduce a
very peculiar wavy flourish. The imitation was a masterpiece, and Knowles was profuse of thanks and praises.

He did not allude to the matter more than once during
the next few weeks, and then only to remark, in a careless
casual way, that the plot was going on swimmingly. This
struck Crichton as rather odd; neither the pleasure of
Knowles's society nor the comparative luxuries which liberal
advances supplied, could keep him from feeling very uncomfortable at times. One morning, late in December, a note
came, begging him to dine with Harding that night in the
Temple; the writer was "going into the country almost
immediately."

It was a very succulent repast, and poor Hugh, as was his
wont, drank largely: nevertheless, when, late in the evening,
Knowles asked him to repeat his caligraphic feat, and showed
the draft of a letter, it became evident, even to his clouded
brain, that something more than "merry mischief" was intended. At first he refused flatly and rudely Indeed, any
rational being, unless very far gone in drink or self-delusion,
must have suspected foul play. Not only was the tone of
the letter passionate to a degree, but it contained allusions
of real grave import; and one name was actually mentioned
—Helen Vavasour's. Knowles was playing his grand *coup*,
and necessarily had to risk something. He was not at all
disconcerted at the resistance he encountered; he had a
plausible explanation ready to meet every objection. " He
was going down to Dene the next day, on purpose to enjoy
the *dénouement;* it would be such a pity to spoil it now.
Miss Vavasour was a cousin who had known Alan from her
infancy; she would appreciate the trick as well as any one;
but, of course, she was never to know of it. This was the

very last time he would ask his friend's help." So the
tempter went on, alternately ridiculing and cajoling Hugh's
scruples, all the while drenching him with strong liquor: at
length he prevailed.

Crichton was one of those men whose hand and eye, often
to their own detriment, will keep steady when their brain
is whirling. He executed his task with a mechanical perfection, though he was scarcely aware of the meaning of each
sentence as he wrote it down. Knowles took possession
of the letter as soon as it was done, and locked it up carefully.

The revel became an orgie: the last thing that Hugh
remembered distinctly was—marking a devilish satisfaction
on his companion's crafty face, that made his own blood boil.
After that everything was chaos. He had a vague recollection of having tried to get back the letter—of high words
and a serious quarrel—even of a blow exchanged; but the
impressions were like those left by a painful nightmare.
He woke from a long heavy stupor, such as undrugged liquor
could scarcely produce, and found himself on a door-step in
his own street, without a notion of how he had got there,
subject to the attentions of a benevolent policeman, who
would not allow him to enjoy, undisturbed, "a lodging upon
the cold ground." The next day came a curt contemptuous
note from Harding Knowles, to say "that he was glad to
have been of some assistance to an old friend, and that he
should never expect repayment of his advances; but that
nothing would induce him to risk a repetition of the painful
scene of last night." They had never met since. Crichton
was constantly haunted with the idea of having been an
accessory to some base villany; and would have communi-
cated his suspicions, long ago, to Wyverne, if it had not been

for the false pride which made him keep aloof from all ancient acquaintance, as if he had been plague-stricken.

Alan sat perfectly quiet and silent, till the other had finished, only betraying emotion by a convulsive twisting of the fingers that shaded his eyes. All at once he broke out into a harsh bitter laugh.

"You thought it was a practical joke? So it was—a very practical one, and right well played out. Do you know what it cost me? The hope and happiness of my life—that's all. Why, if I were to drain that lying hound's blood, drop by drop, he would be in my debt still!"

Then his head sank on his crossed arms, and he began to murmur to himself—so piteously—

"Ah, my Helen! my lost Helen!"

The beaten-down, degraded look possessed the castaway's face stronger than ever.

"Didn't I ask you to wait till I had told you all?" he muttered. "I knew how it would be; that was why I hesitated to accept your invitation to-day. Let me go now; I cannot comfort you nor help you either. You meant kindly though, old friend, and I thank you all the same. Good-bye."

Alan lifted his head quickly. His eyes were not angry—only inexpressibly sad.

"Sit down, Hugh," he said, "and don't be hasty. You might give one a moment's breathing-time after a blow like that. I haven't spirits enough for argument, much less for quarrelling. I know well if you had been in your sober senses, and had thought it would really harm me, no earthly bribe would have tempted you to pen one line. You *can* help me very much; and I will trust you so far, from the bottom of my heart; as for comfort—I must trust to God.

I hold to every word of my offers. I am so very glad I
made them before I heard all this; for I can ask you to
serve me now without your suspecting a bribe."

Length of misery tames stoicism as it crushes better feelings: a spirit nearly broken yields easily to weakness that
would shame hearts inexperienced in sorrow. The pride of
manhood could not check the big drops that wetted Crichton's
hollow cheeks before Wyverne had finished speaking.

They talked long and seriously that night. Alan did not
trust by halves; he forced himself to go into every detail
that it was necessary the other should know, though some
words and names seemed to burn his lips in passing. Before
they parted their plan was fully arranged. Hugh was
to resign his clerkship at once, so as to devote himself
exclusively to completing the chain of proofs that would
criminate at least the main movers in the plot. Alan clung
persistently to the idea that Clydesdale had a good deal
to do with it.

It is needless to say that the amateur detective worked
with all his heart, and soul, and strength. His temperance
was worthy of an anchorite; and, when he kept his senses
about him, Crichton could be as patient and keen-scented as
the most practised of legal blood-hounds. Before a week
was over, he had collected evidence, conclusive and consecutive enough to have convinced any Court of Honour, though
perhaps it would not have secured a verdict from those free
and enlightened Britons who will make a point of acquitting
any murderer that does not chance to be caught " red-
handed." Truly ours is a noble Constitution, and the Trial
by Jury is one of its fairest pillars; but I have heard a
paragon Judge speak blasphemy thereanent. If the Twelve
were allowed the French latitude of finding "extenuating

circumstances," I believe the coolest on the Bench would
go distranght, in helpless wrath and contempt.

Wyverne knew the shop that Mrs Lenox patronized for
papeterie. They ascertained there that a man answering
exactly to the description of Knowles had called, one day in
that autumn, and had asked for a packet of her envelopes
and note-paper, stating that he was commissioned to take
them down into the country, and producing one of the lady's
cards as a credential. The stationer particularly remembered
it from the fact of the purchase having been paid for on the
spot. Trifling as the amount was—only a few shillings—it
was a curious infraction of Nina's commercial system, which
was, as a rule, consistently Pennsylvanian. Crichton had
certainly contracted no new friendships during his office-
servitude, but he had made a few acquaintances at some of
the haunts frequented nightly by revellers of the clerkly guild.
He worked one of these engines of information very effectually. Harding had more than once given him a cheque to
a small amount, which he had got cashed through one of the
subordinates of the bank, whom he had chanced to fraternize
with at the "Cat and Compasses," or some such reputable
hostel. At the expense of much persuasion, and a timely
advance to the official, whose convivial habits were getting
him into difficulties, Hugh was in a position to prove that
Knowles had paid in to his account, early in the January
following that eventful Christmas, a cheque for £5000, signed
by Lord Clydesdale. The money remained standing to his
credit for some time, but had since been drawn out for investment. The dates of the composition of the fictitious
letters corresponded exactly with the times at which Alan
had received them.

Altogether, the case seemed tolerably clear, and a net of

proof was drawn round Harding Knowles that it would
puzzle even his craft to escape from.

I do not enter into the question whether the influences of
high Civilization are sanctifying, or the reverse; but on
some grounds, it surely ought to improve our Christianity,
if it were only for the obstacles standing in the path of
certain pagan propensities. One would think that even an
infidel might see the folly of letting the sun go down on
futile wrath. In truth, now-a-days, the prosecution of a
purely personal and private vengeance is not alone immoral
in itself, but exceedingly difficult to carry out. You cannot
go forth and smite your enemy under the fifth rib, whereso-
ever you may meet, after the simple antique fashion. You
must lure him across the Channel before you can even
proceed after the formula of the polite *duello*—supposing
always that the adversary had not infringed the criminal
code.

Alan Wyverne's nature was not sublime enough to admit
a thought of forgiveness, now. Since he held the instruments
of retaliation in his hand, he had never faltered for one
moment in his vindictive purpose; but—how best to complete it?—was a problem over which he brooded gloomily
for hours, without touching the solution.

CHAPTER XXII.

AN OLD SCORE PAID.

It is needless to explain, that on Harding Knowles
Wyverne's anger was chiefly concentrated.   Clydesdale
came in for his share ; but, so far, it was difficult to establish
the extent of the Earl's connection with the plot.   When the
Divine warning, " Vengeance is Mine," has once been ignored,
very few men are so cold-blooded as to exclude entirely
from their plan of retribution the old simple method of
exacting it with their own right hand.   As Alan sat thinking, a vision would rise before him, dangerously attractive :
he saw a waste of sand-hills stretching for leagues along the
coast of France ; so remote from road or dwelling, that a
shot would never be heard unless it were by a stray fishing-
boat out at sea ; so seldom traversed, that the body of a
murdered man might lie there for days undiscovered, unless
the gathering birds told tales ; he saw the form of his enemy
standing up in relief against the clear morning-light, within
a dozen paces of the muzzle of his pistol.   I fear it was more
the impracticability of the idea than its sinfulness, which
made Alan decide that it ought to be relinquished.   Sometimes it needs no great casuistry to enable even the best-
natured of us to give, in our own minds, a verdict of Justifi-

able Homicide. But upon calm consideration, it was about a million to one against Harding's being induced to risk himself in a duel, which he might guess would be to the death, where the chances would be heavily against him. As a rule, forgers don't fight.

There were great difficulties, too, about a public exposure —so great that Alan never really entertained the idea for a moment. He would just as soon have thought of publishing a scurrilous libel about those whom he loved best, as of allowing their names to be paraded for the world's amusement and criticism.

While he was still in doubt and perplexity, he chanced to meet one morning a famous physician, with whom he was rather intimate, though he had never employed him professionally. Dr Eglinton was a general favourite; many people, besides his patients, liked to hear his full cheery tones, and to see his quaint pleasant face, with the *fin sourire* that pointed his inexhaustible anecdotes; he was the most inveterate gossip that ever steered quite clear of ill-nature.

" You're not looking in such rude health as one would expect at the end of the hunting season," the Doctor said, " but I suppose there's nothing in my way this morning." I wish I could say as much for an old friend of yours, whom I have just left at the Burlington. It's the Rector of Dene. By the by, it would be a great charity if you would call on him to-day: he seems lonely and out of spirits—indeed, the nature of his disease is depressing. I know he's very fond of you, and you might do him more good than my physic can. I fear it is a hopeless case—a heart-complaint of some standing — though the symptoms have only become acute and aggravated within the last two years. Do you know if he has had any great domestic troubles or worries of late ?　He was not communicative, and I did not dare to press him.　Nothing can be so bad for him as anything of the sort; and any heavy or sudden shock might be instantly fatal."

It was not only surprise and pain, but sharp self-reproach too, that made Wyverne turn so pale.　Revenge is essentially selfish, even when it will reason at all; he had actually forgotten his kind old friend's existence while pondering how to punish his son.　He knew right well what had been the great trouble that had weighed on Gilbert Knowles's heart for the last two years.　The Rector was of course unable to intercede or avert the catastrophe; but when he heard of the final rupture of Helen's engagement, he bowed his head despairingly, and had never raised it since.　I told you how he loved her, and how sincerely he liked Alan.　On their union rested the last of his hopes; when that was crushed, he felt he should never have strength or spirits enough to nourish another.

No wonder Wyverne's reply was strangely embarrassed and inconsequent :

"I don't know—yes—perhaps there may have been some trouble on his mind.　The dear old Rector; I wish I had heard of this before.　Of course I'll go to him; but not to-day—it's impossible to-day　Good-bye: I shall see you again very soon.　I shall want to hear about your patient."

His manner, usually *posé* to a degree, was so abrupt just then, that it set the Doctor musing as he walked away.

"There's something wrong there," he muttered, half aloud (it was a way he had); "I wish I knew what it was; he's well worth curing.　He's not half the man he was when he was ruined.　None of us are, for that matter: I suppose there's something bracing in the air of poverty.　I did hear something about a cousinly attachment, but it cant't be that : Wyverne is made of too sterling stuff to pine away because an *amourette* goes wrong: besides, he's always with Lady Clydesdale now, they say. What *don't* they say, if one had only time to listen," &c., &c.

The good physician had a little subdued element of cynicism in his nature, which he only indulged when soliloquizing, or over the one cigar that professional decorum winked at, when the long day's toil was done.

" Not to-day." No ; Alan felt that it would be impossible to meet the father, till the interview with the son was over. He went back to his rooms, and sat there thinking for a full hour. Then he took some papers from a locked casket, and went straight to the Temple.

Knowles's servant chanced to be out, so he came himself to open the door of his chambers. He was prosperous and careful, you know, and could meet the commercial world boldly, abroad or at home ; but the most timorous of insolvents never felt so disagreeable a thrill at the apparition of the sternest of creditors, as shot through Harding's nerves when he saw on the threshold, the calm courteous face of the man whom he disliked and feared beyond all living. There was something in that face—though a careless observer would have detected no ruffle in its serenity —that stopped the other in his greeting, and in the act of offering his hand. Not a word passed between the two, till Knowles had followed his visitor into the innermost of the two sitting-rooms, closing the doors carefully behind them. Then Wyverne spoke—

" An old friend of mine has given me a commission to do. I had better get through that before coming to my own business. You advanced several sums to Hugh Crichton at different times, lately; will you be good enough to say, if that list of them is right?"

There could not be a more striking proof of how completely Knowles's nerves were unstrung, than the fact that he looked at the paper without having a notion as to the correctness of the items, and without the faintest interest in the question. He answered quite at random, speaking quick and confusedly—

"Yes, they are quite right; but it doesn't in the least matter. I never expected——"

"Pardon me," Alan interrupted, "it does matter very much—*to us*. Perhaps since you have become a capitalist, you can afford to be careless of such trifles. Hugh Crichton does not think it a trifle to owe money to you. Here is the exact sum, as far as he can remember it. It is your own fault if you have cheated yourself. I will not trouble you for a receipt. I dare say you did not expect to be paid, still less by my hand. That is settled. Now I will talk about my own affairs."

Though he spoke so quietly, there was a subtle contempt in his tone, that made every word fall like a lash. Again and again, Harding tried to meet the steady look of the cold, grave eyes, and failed each time signally. He tried bluster, thus early in the interview, in sheer despair.

"I can't guess at your object, but your manner is not to be mistaken. It is evident you come here with the deliberate purpose of insulting me. I'm afraid I must disappoint you, Sir Alan. I decline to enter into your own affairs at all, and I consider our conversation ended here."

The other laughed scornfully, and his accent became harder and more *trenchant* than ever.

"Bah!—you lose your head! There are two gross errors

in that last speech. I don't come to insult, because, to
insult a person, you must presume he has some title to self-
respect. I utterly deny your right to such a thing. And
you will listen as long as I choose to speak ; you may be sure
I shall not use an unnecessary word. I come here to make
certain accusations and to impose certain conditions—or
penalties, if you like. It's not worth while picking expressions."

Harding sat down, actually gnashing his teeth in impotent
rage, leaning his elbows on his knees, and resting his chin
on his clenched hands.

" Go on, then," he snarled, " and be quick about it."

" I accuse you," Alan answered, steadily, " of having
played the part of a common spy ; of having composed, if
you did not write, two anonymous letters to Lady Mildred
and her daughter ; afterwards, of having maligned a woman
whom you never spoke to, by causing her handwriting to be
forged ; of having made a dear friend of mine, a gentleman
of birth and breeding, unwittingly your accomplice, when he
was brought so low that the Tempter himself might have
spared him ; of having done me, and perhaps my cousin, a
mortal injury, when neither of us had ever hurt you by word
or deed. I accuse you of having done all this for hire, for
the specific sum of £5000, paid you by Lord Clydesdale
within a month after your villany was consummated. You
need not trouble yourself to contradict one syllable of this,
unless you choose to lie for the pleasure of lying. I have
the written proofs here."

Knowles's head went down lower and lower while
Wyverne was speaking ; when he raised his face, it was
fantastically convulsed and horribly livid, like one of those
that we see in the illustrations to the *Inferno*, besetting the

path of the travellers through the penal Circles. He was
too anxious to escape from his torture, to protract it by a
single vain denial; but he would not throw one chance of
palliation away.

"It was not a bribe," he gasped out, "it was a regular
bet. Look, I can show it you."

He drew his tablets out and tore them open with a shaking hand; and after finding the page with great difficulty,
pointed it out to Wyverne.

The latter just glanced at the entry, and cast down the
book with a gesture of crushing contempt.

"Five thousand to fifty," he said; "I've been long
enough on the turf to construe those odds. The veriest
robber in the ring would not have dared to show your
"regular bet." Now answer me one question—How far
was Clydesdale cognizant of your plot?"

"He has never heard one word of it, up to this moment," the other answered, eagerly. "I swear it. You
may make any inquiries you like. I *can* defy you there.
But some one else did know of it, and approved it too;
that was——"

Wyverne's tone changed savagely as he broke in—

" *Will* you confine yourself to answering the questions
you are asked? I don't want any confessions volunteered.
I attach no real importance to them, after all; but it
grates on one, to hear people maligned unnecessarily.
Now, I'll tell you what I mean to do about it. I thought
at first of inducing you to cross the Channel, and giving
you a chance for your life against mine there; but I gave
that up, because—I knew you wouldn't come. Then I
thought—a brutal, last resource—of beating you into a
cripple—here. I gave that up, because I never could

thrash a dog that lay down at the first cut, writhing and howling; I know so well that would have been your line. Do you want to say anything?"

A sudden change in Harding's countenance made Alan pause. You may have seen how utterly deficient he was both in moral and physical courage; but the last faint embers of manhood smouldered into sullen flame under the accumulation of insult. He had risen to his feet with a dark devilish malice on his face, and made a step towards a table near him.

Wyverne's keen gaze read his purpose thoroughly, but never wavered in its freezing contempt.

" Ah, that's the drawer where you keep your revolver," he said. "If you drive a rat into a corner, he *will* turn sometimes. I don't believe you would have nerve to shoot; but I mean to run no risks. I came prepared after I gave up the bastinado. There's something heavier than wood in this malacca. I'll break your wrist if you attempt to touch the lock. That's better; sit down again and listen. Then—I thought of bringing the matter before a committee of every club you belong to, suppressing all the names but my own. I could have done it; my credit's good for so much, if I choose to use it. I only gave up that idea three hours ago. It was when I heard of the Rector's being so seriously ill. The fathers suffer for the sins of the children often enough; but I have not the heart to give *yours* his death-blow. You will appreciate the weakness thoroughly, I don't doubt. On one condition I shall keep your treachery a secret from all, except those immediately concerned; that condition is—that you never show yourself in any company where, by the remotest chance, you could meet either Lady Clydesdale, Mrs Lenox, any of the Dene family, or myself. I'll do my duty to society so far, at all events. Do you accept or refuse?"

"I have no choice," the other muttered, hoarsely and sullenly; " you have me in a vice, you know that."

"Then it is so understood," Wyverne went on. " You needn't waste breath in promising or swearing. You'll keep your quarantine, I feel sure. If not——" (it was a very significant pause). "After all, my forbearance only hangs on your poor father's life, and I fear that is a slender thread indeed."

The mention of Gilbert Knowles's name seemed to have no effect whatever upon his son; he did not even appear grateful for its mute intercession between him and public shame: but Alan's tone softened insensibly as he uttered it. When he spoke again, after a minute's silence, his tone was rather sad than scornful.

"If you wanted money so much, why, in God's name, did you not come to me? I would have sold my last chance of a reversion, and have begged or borrowed from every friend I had, sooner than have let Clydesdale outbid me. The plunge was taken, when you could once think of such infamy: you might as well have sold yourself to me. Those miserable thousands must have been your only motive, for you had no reason, that I know of, to dislike me."

For the first time since the interview began, Harding Knowles looked the speaker straight in the eyes: his face was still white as a corpse's, but its expression was scarcely human in its intense malignity.

"You're wrong," he said, between his teeth: " the money wasn't the only motive. Not dislike you! Curse you!— I've hated you from the first moment that we met. Do you fancy I thank you for your forbearance now? I'd poison you if I could, or murder you where you stand, if I dared. I hated your languid ways, and your quiet manner, and your soft speech, and your cool courtesy—hated them all. You never spoke naturally but once—on the hall-steps of Dene. Do you suppose I've forgotten that, or the look in your cousin's eyes? I tell you, I hated you both. I felt you despised and laughed at me all the while, and you had no right to do so—then. It is different—different—now."

His brain, usually so calculating and crafty, for the moment was utterly distraught; he could not even command his voice, which rose almost into a shriek while he was speaking, and in the last words sank abruptly into a hollow groan. It was a terrible and piteous sight. But you have heard how implacable at certain seasons Alan Wyverne could be; neither the agony of the passion, nor the misery of the humiliation, moved his compassion in the least: he watched the outbreak and the relapse, with a smile of serene satisfaction that had been strange to his face for some time past.

"So you really disliked my manner?" he said, in his own slow, pensive way. "I remember, years ago, an ancient Duchesse of the Faubourg telling me it had a savour of the *Vieille Cour*. I was intensely flattered then, for I was very young. I am not sure that I ought not to be more gratified now. I think I am. The instincts of hate are truer than those of love. Mde. de Latrêaumont was as kind as a mother to me, and might have been deceived. I have no more to say. You know the conditions: if you transgress them by a hair's-breadth, you will hear of it—not from me."

He left the room without another word. It is doubtful if Knowles heard that last taunt, or knew that his visitor was gone. He had buried his face again in his hands; and so, for minutes, sat motionless. All at once he started up, went to the outer "oak," and dropped the bolt which made his servant's pass-key useless, and then returned to his old seat, still apparently half stunned and stupefied.

Do you think the forger and traitor escaped easily? It may be so; but remember the exaggerated importance that Harding attached to his social position and advancement. I believe that many, whose earthly ruin has just been completed, have felt less miserable, and hopeless, and spirit-broken, than the man who sate there, far into the twilight, staring at the fire with haggard eyes, that never saw the red coals turn grey.

It is true, that when Nina Lenox heard from Alan a ré-sumé of the day's proceedings, she decided at once that the retribution was wholly inadequate and unsatisfactory. But one need not multiply instances to prove the truism—if women are exacting in love, they are thrice as exacting in revenge. I cannot remember where I read the old romaunt, of the knight who came just in time to save his lady from the burning, by vanquishing her traducer in the lists. The story is commonplace and trite to a degree. I only re-member the one incident that made it remarkable. The conqueror stood with his foot on the neck of the enemy; his chivalrous heart melted towards the vanquished, who, after all, had done his devoir gallantly in an evil cause. He would have suffered him to rise and live; but he chanced to glance inquiringly towards the pale woman at the stake, and, says the chronicler, " by the bending of her brows and the blink of her eyes he wist that she bade him

—'not spare!'" So the good knight sighed heavily, and turning his sword-point once more to the neck of the fallen man, drove the keen steel through mail and flesh and bone.

Ah, my friend! may it never be your lot or mine, to lie prone at the mercy of a woman whom we have wronged past hope of forgiveness; be sure, that eyes and brows will speak as plainly as they did a thousand years agone, and their murderous message will be much the same.

CHAPTER XXIII.

DIPLOMACY AT A DISCOUNT.

IT would be rather difficult to define Wyverne's feelings after his interview with Knowles. I fear that the utter humiliation of his enemy failed entirely to satisfy him; but, on the whole, I think he scarcely regretted not having pushed reprisals to extremities. At least there was this advantage; he could sit with the Rector, now, for hours, and strive to cheer the poor invalid, with a quiet conscience; he could never have borne to come into his presence with the deliberate purpose at his heart of bringing public shame on Gilbert's son.

At the beginning of the following week, Alan heard that the Squire and Lady Mildred were in town for a couple of days, on their way home from Devonshire. He knew the hour at which he was certain to find " my lady " alone, and timed his visit accordingly. Now, though the family breach had been closed up long ago, and though Wyverne was with Lady Clydesdale perpetually, apparently on the most cousinly terms of intimacy, it somehow happened that he met his aunt very seldom. Still, it was the most natural thing that he should call, under the circumstances, and " my lady " was in no wise disconcerted when his name was announced. The greeting, on both sides, was as affectionate as it had ever been in the old times; it would have been impossible to say why, from the first, Lady Mildred felt a nervous presentiment of impending danger, unless it was—it might have been pure fancy—that Alan's manner did seem unusually grave. So she was not surprised when he said,

"Would you mind putting off your drive for half an hour? I will not keep you longer; but I have one or two things that I wish very much to say to you."

"I'll give you the whole afternoon, if you wish it, Alan," she said, in the softest of her silky tones; "it is no great sacrifice; I shall be glad of an excuse for escaping the cold wind. Will you ring, and tell them I shall not want the carriage, and that I am not at home to anybody?"

So once again—this time without a witness—the trial of fence between those two began; it was strange, but all the prestige of previous victories could not make "my lady" feel confident, now.

Alan broke ground boldly, without wasting time in "parades."

"Aunt Mildred, if some things that I have to refer to should be painful to you, try and realize what they must be to me; you will see, then, that only necessity could make me speak. Do you remember, when those wretched anonymous letters first came to Dene, I told you I would find out their author, and thank him? I did both, last week. More than this, I have seen and spoken with the man who wrote those letters, which we all supposed came from Mrs Rawdon Lenox. You never had a doubt on the subject, of course, Aunt Mildred? I thought you would be surprised; you will be still more so when you hear the forger's name—Harding Knowles."

"My lady" really *did* suffer from headaches sometimes —with that busy, restless brain it was no wonder—and she always had near her the strongest smelling-salts that could be procured; but she did not know what fainting meant, so she was absolutely terrified, when the room seemed to go round, and Wyverne's voice sounded distant and strange, as if it came through a long speaking-tube; the sensation passed off in a few seconds, but while it lasted she could only feel, blindly and helplessly, for the jewelled vinaigrette which lay within a few inches of her elbow. Wyverne's eyes had never left her face for a moment; he caught up the bottle quickly and put it, open, into her hand without a word.

"It—it is—nothing," Lady Mildred gasped (the salts must have been *very* pungent). "I have not been well for days; the surprise quite overcame me. But oh, Alan, are you quite—quite sure? I don't like Harding Knowles much; but it would be too cruel to accuse him of such horrors, unless you have certain proofs."

"Make yourself easy on that score," Alan said, with his quiet smile; "no injustice has been done. I will give you all the proofs you care to see, directly. While you recover yourself, Aunt Mildred, let me tell you a short story. Years ago, when we were cruising about the Orkneys, they showed us a certain cliff that stood up a thousand feet clear out of the North Sea, and told us what happened there. A father and his son, sea-fowlers, were hanging on the same rope, the father undermost. Suddenly they found that the strands were parting one by one, frayed on a sharp edge of rock. The rope might possibly carry one to the top—not two. Then quoth the sire, "Your mother must not starve—cut away, *below*." As he said, so was it done, and the parricide got up safely. Do you see my meaning? You say you don't like Harding Knowles? I can well believe it; but if you cared for him next to your own children, I should still quote the stout Orkneyman's words—"cut away below." Now, if you will look at these papers, you will see how clear the evidence is on which I rely."

There was silence for some minutes, while "my lady" pretended to read attentively; in real truth, she could not fix her attention to a line. All her thoughts were concentrated on the one doubt—"How much does he know?" The suspense became unendurable; it was better to hear the worst at once. Suddenly she looked up and spoke.

"Is it possible? Can you believe that Clydesdale was mixed up with such a plot as this?"

"No," Wyverne answered, frankly. "I confess I did suspect him at first; but I don't believe, now, that he was privy to any of the details. I think, after securing his agent's services, he left him *carte-blanche* to act as he would. He is quite welcome to that shade of difference in the dishonour. Well—are those proofs satisfactory? If not, I may tell you that I saw Harding Knowles four days ago, and that he confesses everything."

The peculiar intonation of the last two words made Lady Mildred, once more, feel faint with fear. She had never encountered such a danger as this. But her wonderfully trained organ did not fail her, even in her extreme strait; though tiny drops of dew stood on her pale forehead, though her heart throbbed suffocatingly, her accent was still measured and full of subdued music.

" Did he implicate any one ? "

It was the very desperation of the sword-player, who,
finding his science baffled, comes to close quarters, with
shortened blade.   Alan did indulge vindictiveness so far,
as to pause for a full minute before answering, regarding
his companion all the while intently.   But, though he
could be pitiless towards his own sex at times, he never
could bear to see a woman in pain, even if she had injured
him mortally ; that minute—a fearfully long one to "my
lady "—exhausted his revenge.

" He *would* have done so," he replied, "but I stopped
him before a name could pass his lips.   I am very glad I
did.   It don't follow that I should have believed him.
But it is better as it is.   Don't you think so, Aunt Mildred ? "

The revulsion of feeling tried her almost more severely
than the previous apprehension had done.   At that moment "my lady" was thoroughly and naturally grateful.
Wyverne saw that she was simply incapable of a reply
just then.   He was considerate enough to give her breathing space, while he went into several details with which
you are already acquainted, and mentioned the conditions
he had imposed upon Knowles, which the latter had sub-
scribed to.

Lady Mildred listened and approved, mechanically.
Her temperament had been for years so well regulated
that unwonted emotion really exhausted her.   Her bright
dark eyes looked dull and heavy, and languor, for once,
was not feigned.

" There is another question," Alan went on; "it is
rather an important one to me, and, I think, my chief
reason for coming here to-day was to ask your opinion,

and your help, if you choose to give it. What is to be done about Helen? You know, when a man has been in Norfolk Island for several years, and it comes out that some one else has committed the forgery, they always grant him a free pardon. That is the government plan; but it don't suit me. Besides, Helen has forgiven me long ago, I believe, and we are perfectly good friends now. For that very reason I cannot throw the chance away of clearing myself in her eyes. There are limits to self-denial and self-sacrifice. Yet it is delicate ground to approach, especially for me. As far as I am concerned—'let conjugal love continue;' it would scarcely promote a mutual good understanding, if Helen were told of the part her lord and master played in the drama, and of the liberal odds that he laid so early in their acquaintance. Yet it would be hard to keep his name out of the story altogether: mere personal dislike would never account for Knowles' elaborate frauds. Aunt Mildred, I tell you fairly, I am not equal to the diplomatic difficulty; but I think *you* are. Shall I leave it in your hands entirely? If you will only satisfy Helen that I have satisfied *you*—if you will make her believe implicitly that I have been blameless throughout in thought, and word, and deed, and that black treachery has been used against us both—on my honour and faith I will never enter on the subject, even if she wished to do so, unless Helen or I were dying. She shall send me one line only to say—'I believe'—and then, we will bury the sorrow and the shame as soon as you will. I think none of us will care to move the gravestone."

For a moment or two "my lady" was hardly sure if she heard aright. She knew that it was impossible to overestimate the danger to which Wyverne had alluded.

Y

Helen's temper had grown more and more wilful and determined since her marriage; it was hard to say, to what rash words or deeds resentment and remorse might lead her. She knew Alan, too, well; but she scarcely believed him capable of such a sacrifice as this. And could he be serious in choosing *her* as his delegate? She gazed up in his face, half expecting to find a covert mockery there; but its expression was grave, almost to sternness.

"Do you really mean it?" she faltered. "It is so good, so generous of you. And will you trust me thoroughly?"

"Yes, Aunt Mildred, I will trust you—*again*."

A thousand complaints and revilings would not have carried so keen a reproach as that which was breathed in those few sad, quiet words. Lady Mildred shrank as she felt them come home. Involuntarily she looked up once more; it was a fatal error. She encountered the full light of the clear, keen eyes—resistless in the power of their single-hearted chivalrous truth. In another second her head had gone down on Wyverne's shoulder, as he sate close to her couch, and she was sobbing out something incoherent about "forgiveness."

Now, I do not suppose that the annals of intellectual duelling can chronicle a more complete defeat than this. It is with the greatest pain and reluctance that I record it. What avails it to be a model *diplomate*, to sit for half a lifetime at the feet of Machiavel, to attain impassibility and insensibility—equal to a Faquir's as a rule—if womanhood, pure and simple, is to assert itself in such an absurdly sudden and incongruous way? It is pleasant to reflect, that this human nature of ours is hardly more consistent in evil than in good. There are doubts if even the arch-cynicism of Talleyrand carried him through to the very last. I once before ventured to draw a comparison between him and "my lady"—that was when I *did* believe in her.

Wyverne was intensely surprised, rather puzzled what to do or say, and decidedly gratified. Though he had suspected her from the first, he had never nourished any bitter animosity against Lady Mildred. He had a sort of idea that she was only acting up to her principles—such as they were—which were very much what popular opinion assigns to the ideal Jesuit. Quite naturally and easily, he began to soothe her now.

"Dear Aunt Mildred, I hardly know what I have to forgive" (this was profoundly true); "but here, in my ignorance, I bestow plenary absolution. I fear I have worried you, when you were really not well. I won't tease you with a word more. Mind, I leave everything in your hands, with perfect confidence."

Lady Mildred had fallen back on her sofa again, pressing her handkerchief against her eyes, though no tears were flowing.

"If I had only known you better—and sooner," she murmured.

I dare say she meant every word sincerely when she said it; nevertheless, as a historian, I incline to believe that no insight into Alan's character would have altered "my lady's" line of policy at any previous moment. Perhaps some such idea crossed Wyverne's mind, for there certainly was a slight smile on his lip, as he rose to take an affectionate farewell. The few parting words are not worth recording.

Alan was more than discontented, whenever he thought over these things, calmly and dispassionately, in after days. Twice he had looked his enemies in the face, and on both occasions had doubtless borne off the honours of the day; but it was an unsubstantial victory at best, and a triumph scarcely more profitable than that of the Imperial trifler, who mustered his legions to battle, and brought back as trophies shells from the seashore. The recollection was not poisonous enough to destroy the good elements of his character, but it darkened and embittered his nature, permanently.

The fact is, when a man has been thoroughly duped and deluded, and has suffered irreparably from the fraud, it is not easily forgotten, unless retaliation has been fully commensurate with the injury. I am not advocating a principle, but simply stating a general fact. With a great misfortune it is different. We say—"Let us fall into His hand, not into the hand of man." So, at least, is consolation more easily sought for, and found.

Remember Esau—as he was before he sold his birthright —as he is when, in fear and trembling, Jacob looks upon his face again. That score of years has changed the cheery, careless hunter of deer into the stern, resolute leader of robber-tribes—ruling his wild vassals with an iron sceptre —no longer "seeking for his meat from God," but grasping plunder, where he may find it, with the strong hand, by dint of bow and spear—truly, a fitting sire from whose loins twelve Dukes of Edom should spring—not wholly exempt from kind, generous impulses, as that meeting between Penuel and Succoth proves—but as little like his former self as a devil is like an angel. If the eyes of the blind old patriarch, who loved his reckless first-born so well, had been opened as he lay a-dying, he could scarcely have told if " this were his very son Esau, or no."

CHAPTER XXIV

SEMI-AMBUSTUS EVASIT.

ARE you curious to know how, all this while, it fared with the Great Earl and his beautiful bride? If the truth is to be told, I fear the answer must be unsatisfactory. No one, well acquainted with the contracting parties, believed that the marriage would be a *very* happy one; but they hoped it would turn out as well as the generality of conventional alliances. It was not so. Alan Wyverne was right enough in thinking that Clydesdale was most unfitted to the task of managing a haughty, wilful wife; but even he never supposed that dissension would arise so quickly, and rankle so constantly. There had been few overt or actual disputes, but a spirit of bitter antagonism was ever at work, which sooner or later was certain to have an evil ending.

It would be unfair to infer that the fault was all on the Earl's side. It was his manner and demeanour that told most against him; he had been so accustomed to adulation from both sexes, that he could not understand why his wife should not accept his dictatorial and overbearing ways, as patiently as his other dependents: so even his kindnesses were spoilt by the way in which they were offered, or

rather enforced.   But—at all events, in the early days of
their married life—he was really anxious that not a wish
or whim of Helen's should remain ungratified, and spared
neither trouble nor money to insure this.

The fair Countess was certainly not free from blame.
She had said to Maud Brabazon—"I will try honestly to
be a good wife, if he will let me."   Now, her most partial
friend could hardly assert, that she had fairly acted up
to this good resolve.   Perhaps it would have been too
much to expect that she should entertain a high respect or
a devoted affection for her consort; but she might have
masked indifference more considerately, or, at least, have
dissembled disdain.   Her hasty, impetuous nature seemed
utterly changed; she never by any chance lost her temper
now, at any provocation, especially when such came from
her husband.   It would have been much better if she *had*
done so, occasionally: nothing chafes a character like
Clydesdale's so bitterly, as that imperial *nonchalance*, which
seems to waver between contempt and pity   Besides, her
notions of conjugal obedience were rather peculiar.   The
Earl was, at first, perpetually interfering with her arrangements, by suggestions for or against, which sounded unpleasantly like orders; if these chanced to square with
Helen's inclination, or if the question was simply indifferent to her, she acted upon them, without claiming any
credit for so doing; if otherwise—she disregarded and dis-
obeyed them with a serene determination, and seemed to
think, "having changed her mind since she saw him,"
quite a sufficient apology to her exasperated Seigneur.

An incident very characteristic of this had, somehow,
got abroad.

Lady Clydesdale was about to accompany her husband

to a tremendous State dinner, the host being one of the greatest personages in this realm, next to royalty—no other than the Duke of Camelot. When she came down, ready to start, one would have thought it impossible to have found a fault in her toilette. But the Earl chose to consider himself an authority on feminine attire, and chanced to be in a particularly captious humour that evening: the ground colour of Helen's dress—a dark Mazarine blue—did not please him at all, though really nothing could match better with her *parure* of sapphires and diamonds. She listened to his comments and strictures without contradicting them, apparently not thinking the subject worth discussion: her silent indifference irritated Clydesdale excessively. At last he said—

"Helen, I positively insist on your taking off that dress; there will be time enough if you go up immediately. Do you hear me?"

For an instant she seemed to hesitate; then she rose, with an odd smile on her proud lip—"Yes, there will be time enough," she said, and so left the room.

But minutes succeeded minutes, till it was evident that the conventional "grace" must even now be exceeded, and still no re-appearance of Helen. The Earl could control his feverish impatience no longer, and went up himself, to hurry her. He opened the door hastily, and fairly started back, in wrath and astonishment, at the sight he saw.

The Countess was attired very much as Maud Brabazon found her when she paid the midnight visit that you may remember. Perhaps her dressing-robe was a shade more gorgeous, but there was no mistaking its character. There she sat, buried in the depths of a luxurious *causeuse*, her little feet crossed on the fender (it was early spring and

the nights were cold); all the massy coils of cunningly
wrought plaits and tresses freed from artistic thraldom, a
half-cut *novelette* in her hand,—altogether, the prettiest
picture of indolent comfort, but not exactly the "form" of
a great lady expected at a ducal banquet.

The furious blood flushed Clydesdale's face to dark
crimson.

"What—what does this mean?" he stammered. His
voice was not a pleasant one at any time, and rage did not
mellow its tone. The superb eyes vouchsafed one careless
side-glance, a gleam of scornful amusement lighting up
their languor.

"The next time you give your orders," she replied, "you
had better be more explicit: you commanded me to take
off that blue dress, but you said nothing about putting
on another. Perhaps my second choice might not have
pleased you either. Besides, one is not called upon to
dress twice, even for a State dinner. You can easily make
a good excuse for me: if the Duke is very angry, I will
make my peace with him myself. I'm sure he will not bear
malice long."

Now, putting predilection and prejudice aside, which do
you think was most in the wrong? The Earl was unreasonable and tyrannical, first; but under the circumstances, I do think he "did well to be angry." He was *so*
angry—that he was actually afraid to trust himself longer
in the room, and hurried down-stairs, growling out some of
his choicest anathemas (not *directed*, it must be owned);
as has been hinted before, Clydesdale kept at least one Recording angel in full employment. The spectacle of marital
wrath did not seem greatly to appal the wilful Countess.
She heard the door of the outer chamber close violently,

without starting at the crash, and settled herself comfortably to her book again, as if no interruption had occurred.

About this time the Earl began to be haunted by a certain dim suspicion: at first it seemed too monstrously absurd to be entertained seriously for a moment; but soon it grew into form and substance, and became terribly distinct and life-like—the possibility of his wife's despising him. When he had once admitted the probability, the mischief was done: he brooded over the idea with a gloomy pertinacity, till a blind, dull animosity took the place of love and trust. He swore to himself that, at whatever cost, he would regain and keep the supremacy: unfortunately he had never had it yet; and it would have been easier for him to twist a bar of cold steel with his bare hands, than to mould the will of Countess Helen. Every day he lost instead of gaining ground, only embittering the spirit of resistance, and widening a breach which could never be repaired. As if all this were not enough, before the year was out, another and darker element of discord rose up in the Earl's moody heart—though he scarcely confessed it even to himself—a fierce, irrational jealousy of Alan Wyverne.

No one who had chanced to witness the parting of the cousins in the library at Dene, would have allowed the possibility of a free unreserved intimacy, troubled, as it would seem, neither by repining nor misgiving, being established between them within two years. Though Alan spoke hopefully at the time, it may be doubted if he believed in his own words. Yet such contradictions and anomalies happen so often, that we ought to be tired of wondering. They moved in the same set, both in town and country, and were necessarily thrown much together.

Wyverne soon managed to persuade himself that there was not the slightest reason why he should purposely avoid his fascinating cousin. As for Helen, I fear she did not discuss the question with her conscience at all. So, gradually and insensibly they fell into the old pleasant confidential ways—such as used to prevail before that fatal afternoon when Wyverne's self-control failed him, and he " spake unadvisedly with his lips " under the oak boughs of the Holme Wood.

Perhaps there might have been a certain amount of self-delusion ; but I fancy that for a long time there was not a thought of harm on either side. As far as Alan was concerned, I do believe that his affection for Helen was as pure and honest and single-hearted as it is possible for a sinful man to entertain.

Nevertheless, the change in the usual demeanour of the cousins, when they chanced to be together, was too marked to escape observation. Her best friends could not deny that marriage had altered Lady Clydesdale very much for the worse : her manner in general society was decidedly cold, and there was often weariness in her great eyes, when they were not disdainful or defiant. The first sound of Alan's voice seemed to act like a spell in bringing the Helen Vavasour of old days, with all the charming impulses and petulance of her maidenhood. Ever since his interview with Nina Lenox, Wyverne had been constantly moody and pre-occupied ; but the dark cloud was always lifted before he had been five minutes in his cousin's presence ; the frank, careless gaiety which once made him such a fascinating companion returned quite naturally, and he could join in the talk or enter into the project of the hour with as much interest as ever. It *was* remark-

able, certainly—so much so that the Earl might perhaps
have been justified in not altogether approving of the state
of things, especially as he could not be expected to appreciate Alan's feelings, simply because a chivalrous and unselfish affection was something quite beyond his mental grasp.

Notwithstanding all this, I repeat that his jealousy was
irrational. He was sulky and uneasy in Wyverne's presence, and disliked seeing him with Helen, not because he
actually mistrusted either, but because he hated the man
from the bottom of his heart. He did not believe in the
possibility of his haughty wife's ever straying, even in
thought or word, from the path of duty ; but she was the
chief of his possessions, and it exasperated him, that his
enemy should derive profit or pleasure from her society
In despite of an inordinate self-esteem, Clydesdale could
not shake off the disagreeable idea, that, wherever they
had met, so far Alan had got the better of him. He
fancied he could detect a calm contemptuous superiority
in the latter's tone (it was purely imaginary), which irritated him to the last degree. Added to all this—and it
was far the strongest motive of all—was the consciousness
of having done Alan a deadly wrong, in intention, if not
in fact. It was true that he knew nothing of Harding
Knowles's treachery. He had carefully abstained from
asking a question, either before or after the result; but he
knew that he had bought an unscrupulous agent, on a
tacit understanding that a full equivalent should be given
for the money; and he could guess how thoroughly the
contract had been carried out. In one word, the Earl
wished Wyverne dead, simply because he could not comfortably look him in the face. Rely on it, that poison-bag
lies at the root of many fangs that bite most sharply.

Nevertheless, Lord Clydesdale abstained from confiding his antipathies even to his wife. Deficient as he was in tact, he felt that a battle would probably ensue, to which all other disseusions would have been child's play. He had no solid grounds to go upon, and he did not see his way clearly to a satisfactory result. So, in spite of his frowns and sulkiness, matters went on smoothly enough up to the time of the disclosures recorded in the last chapter.

It is probable that Lady Mildred discharged her embassage faithfully, albeit discreetly. The subject was never mentioned between them; but Helen's manner towards her cousin perceptibly softened, though she felt a strange constraint occasionally that she could hardly have accounted for. The truth was—if she had indulged in self-examination, at this conjuncture she ought to have begun to mistrust herself. It was dangerous to brood over Alan's wrongs now, when it was too late to make him any substantial amends.

But the world would not long "let well alone." Before the season was far advanced, *cancans* were rife; and Lady Clydesdale's name was more than lightly spoken of: glances, when levelled at her, became curious and significant, instead of simply admiring. Of course, the parties most intimately interested are the last to hear of such things; but Wyverne did begin to suspect the truth, not so much from any hints or inuendoes, as from a certain reticence and reserve among his intimates at the clubs and elsewhere. One evening, Maud Brabazon took heart of grace, and told him all she had heard, after her own frank fashion.

Not even during the hours which followed the miserable

parting in the library at Dene, had Alan felt so utterly
hopeless and spirit-broken as he did that night, as he sate
alone, thinking over the situation, and trying with every
energy of his honest heart to determine what he ought to
do. Men have grown grey and wrinkled under briefer
and lighter pain. It did seem hard: when he was conscious of innocence of intention—when he had so lately,
at such costly self-sacrifice, abstained from personally jus-
tifying himself in Helen's eyes, sooner than compromise
her husband—when he had just found out that he had
been juggled out of his life's hope through no fault or
negligence of his own—he was called upon to resign the
shadow of happiness that was left him still, merely because
the world chose to be scandalous, and not to give him
credit for common honesty. But, after his thoughts had
wandered for hours in darkness and in doubt, the light broke
clear. Half-measures were worse than useless. To remain in England and to maintain a comparative estrange-
ment—to meet Helen only at appointed times and seasons
—to set a watch upon his lips whenever he chanced to be
in her society—was utterly impracticable. Like other
and braver and wiser men, he owned that he had no altern-
ative—he was bound to fly. Weak and fallible as he was
in many respects, Wyverne's character contained this one
element of greatness—when he had once made up his
mind, it was easier to move a mountain than to change his
resolve.

He never went near Clydesdale House for three days,
and in that space all his arrangements were made, irrevocably. Early in the year Alan had purchased a magnificent schooner; she was fitting out at Ryde, and nearly
completed; he had purposed to make a summer cruise in

the Mediterranean, it was only turning the *Odalisque* to a more practical purpose, now. Two of his friends had organized a hunting expedition on a large scale, first through the interior of Southern Africa, then on to the Himalayas and the best of the "big game" districts of India. Of course they were delighted to have Wyverne as a comrade, especially when he placed his yacht at their service; the *Odalisque*, both in size and strength, was perfectly equal to any ocean voyage. Their absence from England was to last at least three years. Alan felt a certain relief when it was all settled; nevertheless his heart was cold and heavy as lead, as he walked towards Clydesdale House to break the tidings. He found Helen alone; indeed, the Earl was out of town for the whole of the day, and was not to return till late in the evening. She could not understand what had kept her cousin away for the three days—of course she had wanted him particularly for all sorts of things—and she was inclined to be mildly reproachful on the subject. Wyverne listened for awhile, though every word brought a fresh throb of pain, simply because he had not courage to begin to undeceive her.

At last he spoke, you may guess how gently and considerately, yet keeping nothing back, and not disguising the reasons for his departure. He had felt sure, all along, that Helen would be bitterly grieved at his determination, and would strive to oppose it; but he was not prepared for the passionate outbreak which ensued.

The Countess's cheek had changed backwards and forwards, from rose-red to pale, a dozen times while her cousin was speaking, and on the beautiful brow there were signs, that a child might have read, of a coming storm; but she did not interrupt him till he had quite said his say; then she started to her feet; a sudden movement—swift, and lithe, and graceful as a Bayadère's spring—brought her close to Alan's chair; she was kneeling at his side, with her slender hands locked round his arm, gazing up into his face, before he could remonstrate by gesture or word.

"You shall not go. I don't care what they say—friends or enemies—you shall not go. Alan, I will do anything, and suffer anything, and go anywhere; but I will not lose *you*. With all your courage, will you fail me when I am ready to brave them? You cannot mean to be so cruel. Ah, say—say you will stay with me."

Alas! if her speech was rash, her eyes were rasher still; never, in the days when to love was no sin, had they spoken half so plainly

Wyverne's breath came thick and fast, for his heart contracted painfully, as if an iron hand had grasped it. It was all over with self-delusion now; the flimsy web vanished before the fatal eloquence of that glance, as a gauze veil shrivels before a strong straight jet of flame.

Now—though this pen of mine has done scant justice to Helen's marvellous fascinations—let any man, in the prime of life, endowed with average passions and not exceptional principle, place himself in Alan's position, and try to appreciate its peril. Truly, I think, it would be hard measure, if human nature were called upon twice in a lifetime, to surmount such a temptation, and survive it. Yet he only hesitated while that choking sensation lasted. He raised Helen from where she knelt, and replaced her on the seat she had left, with an exertion of strength, subdued and gentle, but perfectly irresistible; when he spoke, his voice sounded unnaturally stern and cold.

"If I had doubted at all about my absence being right and necessary, I should not doubt now. Child—you are not fit to be trusted. How dare you speak, at your age and in your station, of setting society at defiance, and trampling on conventionalities? You have duties to perform, and a great name to guard; have you forgotten all this, Countess Helen?"

On the last words there was certainly an inflexion of sarcasm. The bitter pain gnawing at his heart made him for the moment selfish and cruel. Perhaps it was as well, the hardness of his tone roused her pride, so that she could answer with comparative calmness.

"God help me! I have forgotten nothing—my miserable marriage least of all. Alan, what is the use of keeping up the deception? We need not lie to each other, if we are to part so soon. I never pretended to love Lord Clydesdale; but I think I could have done my duty, if he would have let me. How can you guess what I have to endure? I may be in fault too; but it has come to this—it is not indifference or dislike, now, but literally loathing. Do you know how careful he is not to wound my self-respect? Only yesterday, he left in my dressing-room, where I could not help seeing it, a letter—ah, such a letter—from some *lorette* whom he protects. It was a delicate way of showing that he was displeased with me. And I have a dreadful misgiving that I shall become afraid of him—physically afraid, some day—I am not that yet—and then it will be all over with me. I feel safe—I can't tell why—when you are near; and you are going to leave me alone, quite alone."

Now, to prevent mistakes hereafter, let me say explicitly that I do not defend Lady Clydesdale's conduct throughout.

I don't know that any woman is justified, on any provocation, in speaking of her husband in such a strain, to her own brother, much less to her cousin, supposing that a warmer sentiment than the ties of kindred is manifestly out of the question. Still, if you like to be lenient, you might remember that a passionate, wilful character like Helen's requires strong and wise guidance while it is being formed; certainly her moral training had not been looked after so carefully as her accomplishments; the mother considered her duty done when she had selected a competent governess; so perhaps, after all, the Countess had as much religion and principle as could be expected in Lady Mildred Vavasour's daughter.

It was a proof of the danger of such confidences, that Wyverne's blood boiled furiously as he listened, and all his good resolves were swallowed up for the moment in a savage desire to take Clydesdale by the throat; but with a mighty effort he recovered self-control, before Helen could follow up her advantage.

"I did guess something," he said, "though not half the truth. I ought to preach to you about 'submission,' I suppose, and all the rest; but I don't know how to do it, and I'm not in the humour to find excuses for your husband just now. Yet I am more than ever certain that I can do no good by staying here. I should only make your burden heavier; you will be safer when I am gone. Of all things, you must avoid giving a chance to the scandalmongers. Child, only be patient and prudent, and we shall see better days. Remember, I am not going to be absent for ever. Three years or so will soon pass. We shall all be older and steadier when I come back, and the world

z

will have forgotten one of us long before that. Say you will try."

Dissimulation is sometimes braver than sincerity. Perhaps Alan got large credit in heaven for the brave effort by which he forced himself to speak half hopefully, and to put on that sad shadow of a smile.

In a book of this length, one can only record the salient points of conversations and situations; your imagination must fill up the intervals, reader of mine, if you think it worth the trouble to exercise it. It is enough to say, that gentle steadfastness of purpose carried the day, as it generally does, against passionate recklessness, and Helen perforce became reasonable at last. Though the cousins talked long and earnestly after this, the rest of the interview would hardly keep your interest awake. Such farewells, if they are correctly set down, savour drearily of vain repetitions, and are apt to be strangely incoherent towards their close.

"If you are in any great trouble or difficulty, promise me that you will send for Gracie; she will help you, I know, fearlessly and faithfully, to the utmost of her power."

That was almost the very last of Wyverne's injunctions and warnings. If at the moment of parting his lips met Helen's, instead of only touching her forehead, as he intended, I hope it was not imputed to him as a deadly sin; the sharp suffering of those few hours might well plead in extenuation; and, be sure, He who "judges not after man's judgment," weighs *everything* when He poises the scale.

I never felt inclined to make a "hero" of Alan till now. I begin to think that he almost deserves the dignity.

You must recollect that he was not an ascetic, nor an eminent Christian, nor even a rigid moralist, but a man essentially "of the world, worldly." If the Tempter had selected as his instrument any other woman of equal or inferior fascinations, I very much doubt if Wyverne's constancy and continence would have emerged scatheless from the ordeal. But here, it was a question of honour rather than of virtue. When his second intimacy with Helen began to be a confirmed fact, he had signed a sort of special compact with himself, and he felt that it would be as foul treachery to break it, as to make away with money left in his charge, or to forfeit his plighted word. I do not say that this made his conduct more admirable; I simply define his motives.

Alan went down to the North the next day to wind up his home business, and he never saw Lady Clydesdale alone before he sailed. But he went forth on his pilgrimage an unhappy, haunted man. Wherever he went those eyes of Helen's followed him, telling their fatal secret over and over again, driving him wild with alternate reproaches and seductions. He saw them while couching among the sand-banks of an African stream watching for the wallowing of the river-horse; at his post in the jungle ravine, when rattling stones and crashing bushes gave notice of the approach of tiger or elk or bear; oftenest of all, when, after a hard day's hunting, he lay amongst his comrades sound asleep, looking up at the brilliant southern stars. His one comfort was the thought, "Thank God, I *could* ask Gracie to take care of her."

Alan was expiating the miserable error of fancying that his love was dead, because he had chosen formally to sign its death-warrant. The experiment has been tried for cycles of ages—sometimes after a more practical fashion—and it has failed oftener than it has succeeded.

Think on that old true story of Herod and his favourite wife. Lo! after a hundred delays and reprieves the final edict has gone forth; the sharp axe-edge has fallen on the slender neck of the Lily of Edom; surely the tortured heart of the unhappy jealous tyrant shall find peace at last. Is it so? Months and months have passed away; there is high revel in Hebron, for a great victory has just been won; the blood-red wine of Sidon flows lavishly, flushing the cheeks and lighting up the eyes of the "men of war;" and the Great Tetrarch drinks deepest of all, the cup-bearer can scarcely fill fast enough, though his hand never stints nor stays. So far, all is well; the lights and the turmoil and the crowd may keep even spectres aloof; but feasts, like other mortal things, must end, and Herod staggers off to his chamber alone. Another hour or so, and there rings through hall and corridor an awful cry, making the rude Idumean guards start and shiver at their posts—fierce and savage in its despair, but tremulous with unutterable agony, like the howl of some terrible wild beast writhing in the death-pang—

"Mariamne! Mariamne!"

Does that sound like peace? The dead beauty asserts her empire once again; she has her murderer at her mercy now, more pitiably enslaved than ever.

Ah, woe is me! We may slay the body, if we have the power, but we may never baffle the Ghost.

CHAPTER XXV

VER UBI LONGUM, TEPIDASQUE PRÆBET
JUPITER BRUMAS.

AT first it really did appear as if, in expatriating himself for a season, Wyverne had acted wisely and well.

The purveyors of scandal, wholesale and retail, were utterly routed and disconcerted. The romance was a promising one, but it had not had time to develop itself into form and substance. As things stood, it was impossible to found any fresh supposition on Alan's prolonged absence, especially as no one ventured to hint at any quarrel or misunderstanding to account for his abrupt departure. Some were too angry to conceal their discomfiture. One veteran gossip, in particular, went about, saying in an injured, querulous way, that "he wondered what Wyverne would do next. He shouldn't be surprised to hear of his making a pilgrimage to Mecca, having turned Turk for a change." It was a great sport to hear Bertie Grenvil, at the club, "drawing" the old *cancanier*, condoling with him gravely, and encouraging him with hopes "of having something *really* to talk about before the season was over." Indeed it seemed by no means improbable that the Cherub, in person, would furnish the materials; for, having convinced himself by repeated experiments that Maud Bra-

bazon either had no heart at all, or that it was absolutely
impregnable, he had taken out lately a sort of roving commission, and was cruising about all sorts of waters, with
the red signal of "no quarter" hoisted permanently

Lord Clydesdale rejoiced intensely, after his saturnine
fashion, at Wyverne's departure. It put him into such
good humour that for days he forgot to be captious, or
overbearing, and actually made some clumsy overtures towards a reconciliation with his wife. It must be confessed, he met with scant encouragement in that quarter.
Helen was in no mood to "forgive and forget" just then.
There are women whom you may tyrannize over one week,
and cajole the next, amiable enough to accept both positions with equanimity; but the haughty Countess was not
of these Griseldas. Her temper was embittered rather
than softened by her great sorrow and loneliness; for the
void that Alan had left behind him was wider and darker
than ever she had reckoned on. Of course she tried the
old counter-irritation plan (nine out of ten do), seeking
for excitement wherever it could be found. The result
was not particularly satisfactory, but the habits of dissipation and recklessness strengthened their hold hourly She
had a legion of caprices, and indulged them all, without
pausing to consider the question of right or wrong, much
less of consequences. Before the season closed, Helen
was virtually enrolled in the fastest of the thorough-bred
sets, and might have disputed her evil pre-eminence with
the most famous *lionne* of the day.

Naturally the scandal-mongers began to open—first
their eyes, and then their mouths again. Every morning
brought some fresh story, generally founded at least on
fact, with Lady Clydesdale for its heroine. They made

wild work with her name before long, but so far no one could attach to it the shame of any one definite *liaison*. A circle of courtiers followed her wherever she went, but not one of these—jealously as they watched for the faintest indication of a decided preference—could have told who stood first in the favour of their wilful, capricious sovereign. Sometimes one would flatter himself, for a moment, that he really had gained ground, and made an abiding impression; but, before he could realize his happiness, the weary, absent look would return to the beautiful eyes, and the unhappy adorer had only to fall back to the dead level of his fellows, in wrath and discomfiture.

No one the least interested in Helen could see how things were going, without serious alarm. Lady Mildred, Max Vavasour, and Maud Brabazon, each in their turn, attempted remonstrance. The Countess met her mother's warning apathetically, her brother's contemptuously, her friend's affectionately—with perfect impartiality disregarding them all.

It was more than doubtful if Clydesdale could have done any good by interfering. He certainly did not try the experiment. From first to last he never stretched out a finger to arrest his fair wife on her road to Avernus. He allowed her to go where she would—very often alone —only, indeed, escorting her when it suited his own plans or purposes. Whether he was base enough to be actually careless about her temptations, or whether he resolutely shut his eyes to the possibility of her coming to harm, it would be hard to say. Nevertheless, from time to time, Helen had to endure furious outbreaks of his temper; and with each of these, that strange thrill of physical fear grew stronger and stronger. But jealousy had nothing

whatever to do with rousing the storms, which usually burst
forth on some absurdly frivolous provocation.   The fact
was, when the Earl was sulky or wroth, ho chose to vent
his brutal humour on the victim nearest to his hand that
was likely to feel the blows most acutely.   He saw that
such scenes *hurt* his wife in some way, though he did not
guess at her real feelings; and it pleased him to think
that there was a vulnerable point in her armour of pride
and indifference.   He would have rejoiced yet more if he
had detected the effort which it cost her sometimes—not
to tremble while she vanquished his savage eyes with the
cold disdain of her own.

The domestic picture is not pleasant enough to tempt
us to linger over it.   Perhaps, after all, it would have
been better—it could scarcely have been worse—if Alan
had stayed on, and braved it out; but this is only arguing
from consequences.

For a long time there were no certain tidings of the
hunting-party: a vague report got abroad of an encounter
with lions in which some Englishman had been terribly
hurt, but it was not even known whether it was Wyverne
or one of his companions.   So months became years, and
Alan's place in the world was nearly filled up; a few of
his old friends, from time to time, "wondered how he was
getting on,"—that was all.   Yet he was not entirely forgotten.   Every morning and evening, in her simple orisons,
Grace Beauclerc joined his name to those of her husband
and her children; and another woman—you know her well
—seldom dared to pray, because she felt it would be a
mockery to kneel with a guilty longing and repining at
her heart.

It was the fourth winter after Wyverne's departure;

the last intelligence of the party dated from some months back; it reported them all alive and well, in the northern provinces of India; there were wonderful accounts of their sport, but no word as to any intention of returning.

The Clydesdales were at Naples. Helen's health, which had begun to fail rapidly of late, was pretext enough for a change of climate; but it is more than doubtful if her husband would have taken this into consideration, if other inducements had not drawn him southwards.

The Earl's home was certainly not a happy one; but even modern society does not admit domestic discomfort as an excuse for outraging the common proprieties of life the most profligate of his companions agreed, that he might at least have taken the trouble to mask his infidelities more carefully; they could not understand such utter disregard of the trite monachal maxim—*Si non casté cauté tamen.* Personally, one would have thought, Lord Clydesdale was not attractive; but a great Seigneur rarely has far to go when he seeks "consolations:" there are always victims ready to be sacrificed, no matter how repulsive the Idol may be; for interest and vanity, and a dozen other *irritamenta malorum*, work still as potently as ever. It so chanced that the siren of the hour had selected South Italy for her winter quarters, so that the Earl's sudden consideration for his wife was easily accounted for.

Naples was crowded that year; every country in Europe was nobly represented there; so that it really was no mean triumph when the popular voice, without an audible dissentient, assigned the royalty of beauty to Lady Clydesdale. Rash and wilful in every other respect, it was not likely that Helen would be prudent about her own health; indeed, if she would only have taken common precautions, her state was not precarious enough to forbid her mixing in society as usual.

If you could only have ignored certain dangerous symptoms, you would have said she was lovelier than when you saw her last: her superb eyes seemed larger than ever; softer, too, in their languor, more intense in their brilliancy; the rose-tint on her cheek was fainter, perhaps, but more exquisitely delicate and transparent now; and her figure had not lost, so far, one rounded outline of its magnificent mould.

She had a perfectly fabulous success: before she had been in Naples a fortnight they raved about her, not only in her own circle, but in all others beside. It was literally a popular *furore:* the laziest *lazzarone* would start from his afternoon sleep to gaze after her with a muttered oath of admiration, when "la bellissima Contessa" drove by. She had adorers of all sorts of nations, and was worshipped in more languages than she could speak or understand.

At last, one man singled himself out from the crowd— like the favourite "going through his horses"—and, for awhile, seemed to carry on the running alone. That was the Duca di Gravina. Perhaps Europe could not have produced a more formidable enemy, when a woman's honour was to be assailed. The Duke was not 30 yet, and he had won long ago an evil renown, and deserved it thoroughly. Few could look at his face without being attracted by its delicate classical beauty; the dark earnest eyes, trained to counterfeit any emotion—never to betray one—strengthened the spell, and an indescribable fascination of manner generally completed it. There was not a vestige of heart or conscience to interfere with his combinations; to say that he had no principle does not express the truth at all: the Boar of Caprew himself was not more coolly cynical and cruel. Nevertheless, these last pleasant attributes lay far below the surface; and a very fair seductive surface it was.

The Duke was more thoroughly in earnest now than he had ever been in his life; and people seemed to think there could be but one result—the most natural and reasonable one, according to the facile code of Southern morality. Lord Clydesdale persisted in ignoring the whole affair; and no one cared to take the trouble of enlightening him against his will. It looked as if he had exhausted his jealousy and suspicions on Alan Wyverne, and had none to waste on the rest of the world. One could not help thinking of the old fable, of the stag who always fed with his blind eye towards the sea, suspecting danger only from the land-quarter. It was an ingenious plan enough; but the sea is wide and hunters are wily: they came in a boat, you remember, and shot the poor horned Monops to death with many arrows.

Di Gravina was almost as daring and successful at play as in intrigue; in both he was well served by a half-intuitive sagacity which suggested the right moment for risking a grand *coup*. He began to think that such a crisis was now near at hand. One afternoon Lady Clydesdale and several more of her set went up to Capo di Monte to lounge about in the gardens and drink the fresh sea-breeze. The party broke up into detachments very soon, and the Duke found it easy to bring about a comfortably confidential *tête-à-tête*. Helen was in a dangerous frame of mind that day. She had gone through a stormy scene with her husband in the morning, whose temper had broken out as usual without rhyme or reason. The velvet softness of the Italian's tone and manner contrasted strangely with the Earl's harsh voice and violent gestures. At first it simply *rested* her to sit still and listen; but gradually the fascination possessed her till her pulse began to quicken, though her outward languor remained undisturbed. Not a particle of passion, much less of love, so far, was at work in her heart; but in the desperation of weariness she felt tempted to try a more practical experiment in the way of excitement than she had ever yet ventured on. Di Gravina saw his advantage and pressed it mercilessly. For some minutes the Countess had ceased to answer him; she sat, with eyes half closed, just the dawning of a dreamy smile on her beautiful lips, like one who yields not unwillingly to the subjugation of a mesmerizer's riveted glance and waving hands.

At last she looked up suddenly, evidently with her purpose set. How her lips or her eyes would have answered can never be known, for at that instant she became aware of the presence of a third person, who had approached unheard while they were talking so earnestly.

The new comer leant against the trunk of a palm-tree, contemplating the pair with a quaint expression of mingled curiosity and sadness. His face was sun-burnt to a black bronze, and almost buried in a huge bushy beard; but the disguise was not complete. Helen sprang to her feet impulsively as of old, with a low, happy cry, and in another second she had clasped her hands round Alan Wyverne's arm, with just breath enough left to gasp out a few fond incoherent syllables of welcome.

The Italian did not quite comprehend the situation at first; but he saw instantly that he had lost the game. A smothered blasphemy worthy of the coarsest *facchino* (and

they swear hard in those parts, remember) escaped from
his delicate, chiselled lips. For a moment his scowling
eyes belied their training, and all the soft beauty vanished
from his face, malign as a baffled devil's. Nevertheless,
he was his own silky self again, before Helen recovered
from her emotion sufficiently to make her excuses, and to
present "her cousin." To do the Duke justice, he behaved
admirably.

"It is a most happy meeting," he said. "Will the
Countess permit the *stranger* to offer his felicitations and
—to retire? She must have so much to say to the cousin
who has so suddenly returned."

There was not an inflection of sarcasm in his voice; but
he turned once as he went, and his glance crossed Wyverne's. These two understood each other thoroughly.

The pen of the readiest writer would fail in recording
the long incoherent conversation which ensued. Helen
had so much to ask and so much to tell that she never
could get through a connected sentence or allow Alan to
finish one. She was so simply and naturally happy that
he had not the heart to check or reprove her. Even
Stoicism has its limits and intervals of weakness, and
Alan was a poor philosopher with all his good intentions
"given in."

Certain members of her party came to reclaim Lady
Clydesdale, before half their say was said. (Would they
have intervened so soon, if the Duca di Gravina had remained master of the position?) So Alan had to content
himself with accompanying his cousin to her own door.
On the whole, he thought it better not to risk meeting
the Earl that night; he did not feel quite cool and collected
enough for the encounter.

Let me remark casually that there was nothing extra-ordinary in the opportune apparition. The *Odalisque* had anchored in the bay late on the previous night. Wyverne met an old acquaintance immediately on landing, who told him at once that the Clydesdales were in Naples. He could not resist the temptation of calling, and the servants directed him naturally to the place where he was sure to find Helen. Nevertheless I own that the situation savours of the *coup de théâtre*. I don't see why one should not indulge in a slight touch of melodrama now and then; but there are men alive who can testify that such an inter-vention, coming exactly at the critical moment, is an actu-ally accomplished fact.

No words can do justice to Lord Clydesdale's intense exasperation, when he heard that his enemy had returned, sound in life and limb. He could not for very shame for-bid his wife to receive him just yet, but his whole nature was transformed; the careless, negligent husband became sud-denly a suspicious, tyrannical jailor. Besides this, another foe lay in wait for Wyverne. The Duca di Gravina made no secret of his discomfiture or of his lust for revenge. This last enmity came round to Helen's ears, and she confessed her apprehension frankly to her cousin. He only laughed carelessly and confidently.

"I've seen a good deal of the feline tribe in these three years," he said, "and I begin to understand them. That leopard is too handsome to be very vicious. Nevertheless, I think it's as well you've given up *domesticating* him."

There was no bravado in his tone; he had only one honest purpose—to reassure Helen. The event proved the correctness of his judgment. The Duke had been "out" more than once; but it was only when he was compelled to pay with his body for some one of his iniquities. He loved life and its luxuries too well to risk the first without absolute necessity. Exaggerated reports of Wyverne's prowess in the Far East had got abroad; and the crafty voluptuary thoroughly appreciated valour's better part, when a formidable foe was to be confronted.

But the ground under their feet was nothing else than a Solfaterra, and the volcanic elements could not remain quiet long. Early one morning, Wyverne got a hurried message from his cousin, asking him to meet her immediately in the garden of the Villa Reale. As he approached the spot where she was sitting, he was struck painfully by the listless exhaustion of her attitude. When she looked up, as he came to her side, a cold thrill of terror shot through Alan's frame. He saw the truth at last—a truth that Helen had striven so carefully to conceal, that it was no wonder her cousin had failed to realize it. Her cheeks were perfectly colourless, and seemed to have grown all at once strangely thin and hollow; the dark circles under her eyes made them unnaturally bright and large, and a wild haggard look possessed and transformed her face. The signs were terribly plain to read—not of death immediately imminent, but of slow, sure decay.

Alan's courage and self-control were well-nigh exhausted before he had listened to half of what she had to tell. It appeared that on the previous evening there had been an outbreak of Lord Clydesdale's temper, incomparably more violent than any which had yet occurred. For the first time he had brought Wyverne's name into the quarrel—upbraiding, and accusing, and threatening his wife by turns, till he worked himself to a pitch of brutal frenzy that did not quite confine itself to words. He swore that the intimacy should be broken off at any cost, and signified his determination to start with Helen for England within 48 hours. This was the last thing she remembered; for just then she fainted. When she recovered she was alone with her maid, and had not seen her husband since.

"Ah, Alan! will you not save me?" she pleaded, piteously "There is no one else to help me—no one. And I *am* afraid now—really afraid: I have good reason. Do you see *this?*"

She drew back her loose sleeve: on the soft white flesh there was the livid print of a brutal grasp—marks such as were left on poor Mary of Scotland's arm by Lindsay's iron glove.

A groan of horror and wrath burst from Wyverne's white lips, and he shook from head to foot like a reed. A few minutes of such intense suffering might atone for more than one venial sin. He knew well enough what Helen meant, as her eyes looked over the bay, and rested with a feverish longing eagerness on the spot where the *Odalisque* lay at anchor, the tall taper masts cutting the sky-line. He knew that he had only to speak the word, and that she would follow to the world's end. He knew that her health was failing under tyranny and ill-treatment; while gentle nursing—such as he could tend her with—might still arrest the Destroyer. He knew how much excuse even society would find in this special case for the criminals. No wonder that he hesitated, muttering under his breath—

"God help me! It is trying me *too* hard."

There was silence only for a few seconds. During that brief space Alan's brain was whirling, but the images on his mind were clear. He remembered how he swore to himself to guard Helen from harm or temptation, faithfully and unselfishly; he thought of the End—possibly very near—and of the dishonour that would cling to his darling even in her grave; last of all rose Hubert Vavasour's face, when he should hear that the man whom he loved as his own son had brought his daughter to shame. That turned the scale, and it never wavered afterwards. When Wyverne spoke his voice was firm, though intensely sad.

"It is too late to wish that the fever or the lion had not spared me. If I had guessed what my return would cost, I would have stayed away till we both grew old. I did hope that we had grown steadier and wiser, and that people would have left us alone, and allowed us to be quietly happy. But I did not go through the pain of parting three years ago, to come back and ruin all. I stood firm then, and so I will—to the last. You will never call me cold or cruel; I feel that. You know how I suffer now while I am speaking; yet I say once more, we are better apart. Dear child, I am powerless to help you, unless it were in a way that I dare not think of. But you shall not be left to Clydesdale's tender mercies defenceless. I'll speak to Randolph to-day. He starts for England immediately, and he shall not lose sight of you till you reach it. He knows enough of your husband not to be surprised at being asked to watch over you. You may trust him as thoroughly as you could trust me. His heart is as soft as a woman's, and his nerves are steel: I've seen them tried, often and hardly. Write to Dene, and go there straight from Dover. Clydesdale will have come to his senses before that, and will scarcely object. Remember, I shall follow by the next steamer, and not sleep on the road; so that I shall be in England almost before you. Then we will see what is best to be done,

2 A

I swear that you shall have rest and peace at any cost. This worry is killing you. Darling, do bear up bravely. just for a little while; and be prudent and take care of yourself. It breaks my heart to see you looking so wan and worn."

His voice shook, and his lip quivered, and his eyes were very dim.

Helen's head had sunk lower and lower while her cousin was speaking: she felt no anger, only utter weariness and despair; she had listened with a mechanical attention, hardly realizing the meaning of all the words, and she answered helplessly and vaguely,—

"Thank you, dear Alan, I dare say you are right. I am sure you mean to be kind; and I know you suffer when I suffer. It is foolish to be frightened when there is no real danger; but I am not strong now, so there is some excuse. Lord Clydesdale is probably ashamed of himself by this time, and I shall have nothing to fear for some days—not even annoyance. Still, if it suits Colonel Randolph to go so soon, I shall be glad to feel there is one friend near me. You are sure you are coming straight to England? And you *will* come to Dene? Even if I am not there, I hope you will. I must not stay longer than to say good-bye; perhaps I have been watched and followed already. I don't know why I ventured here, or sent for you: I knew it could do no good; but I felt so weak and unhappy. Now—say good-bye, kindly, Alan?"

Though Wyverne knew it was wrong and unwise to detain her, a vague presentiment that it might be long before they met again, made him linger before uttering the farewell. While he paused a heavy foot crunched on the gravel behind them, and a hoarse, thick voice, close by, muttered something like a curse. The Earl stood there

gazing at the cousins, his face flushed with passion, and a
savage glare iu his pale blue eyes. He essayed to speak
with calmness and dignity; but the effort was absurdly
apparent and vaiu.

"Lady Clydesdale, I am excessively surprised and displeased at finding you here, especially after what passed
last night. I request that you will returu home instantly.
You have more than enough to do in making your preparations, and there are some necessary visits that you
must pay. We start by to-morrow's steamer. I will follow you in a few minutes."

The assumption of marital authority was a miserable
failure. Neither of the supposed delinquents seemed at
all awed or discomfited by the Earl's sudden apparition,
or by his set speech. Helen rose to depart, silently, without vouchsafing a glance to her exasperated lord; Alan
accompanied her a few steps, to whisper a few words of
farewell, and to exchange a long pressure of hands; then
he came back, aud waited quietly to be spoken to.

Clydesdale's manner was arrogant and domineering to a
degree; but he was evidently ill at ease; he kept lashing
the gravel, augrily and nervously, with his caue, and his
eyes wandered everywhere except where they were likely
to encounter Wyverne's.

"I don't mean to have any discussion," he said; "and I
choose to give no reasous. You will understand that I
decidedly disapprove of your intimacy with Lady Clydesdale; I shall uot allow her to meet you, on any pretence,
at any future period; and I beg that you will not attempt
to visit her. I mean to be master of my own house, and
of my own wife. You will take this warning, or—you will
take the consequences!"

For once in his life—he reproached himself bitterly, afterwards, for the weakness—Alan fairly lost his temper. When he replied, his tone was, if anything, more galling than the other's, because its insolence was more subtle and refined.

"You might have spared threats," he said; "they would scarcely have answered, even if I had known you less thoroughly than I happen to do. You may frighten women—especially if they are weak and ill—but men, as a rule, don't faint. Consequences! What do you mean? I fancy I have gauged your valour tolerably well; it is superb up to a certain point—when personal risk comes in. If you had stayed on here, perhaps you *would* have hired a knife. You might have laid some ruffian 5000 piastres to 50, for instance, that I should not be found dead within a week—those are your favourite odds, I believe— that's about the extent of what one has to fear from your vengeance. I am not prepared to say how far a husband's dictation ought to extend, who does not take the trouble to conceal his intrigues abroad, and treats his wife brutally at home; and I'm not going to argue the point either. You certainly have a right to close your doors against me, or any one else. I shall not attempt to see my cousin while she remains in your house, or under your authority; her father had better decide how long that ought to last. I am no more inclined for discussion than you are; neither do I threaten. I simply give you fair warning. You had better put some constraint on your temper when your wife has to bear it; she has friends enough left to call you to an account, and make you pay it too. Max Vavasour will do his duty, I believe. If he don't—by G—d—I'll do mine!"

He turned on his heel with the last word, and walked away very slowly; but he was out of earshot before the Earl could collect himself enough to speak intelligibly. If he had received a blow between the eyes, delivered straight from the shoulder by a practised arm, he would hardly have been more staggered. He had been so accustomed, from childhood, to deference and adulation, that a direct, unmistakable personal insult literally confounded him; for a brief space he felt thoroughly uncomfortable and humiliated; even his favourite curses came with an effort, and failed to act as anodynes. But he remembered every word that had passed, and acted accordingly.

From that day forth, Clydesdale hated both his wife and Wyverne more bitterly than ever; but he entirely changed his tactics for the present. The idea of a public *esclandre* and separation did not suit him at all. His manner towards Helen on their journey homewards was kinder and more considerate than it had ever been; he even condescended to express penitence for his late violence, and went so far as to promise amendment. He encouraged her wish to go straight to Dene, and only stipulated that he should accompany her there. The Countess was neither satisfied nor convinced; but she was weary, and wanted rest, and so acquiesced listlessly and passively.

On the very first opportunity after his arrival at Dene, the Earl sought an interview with Lady Mildred. It was easy to make his case good; he lied, of course, liberally; he confessed his failings, with certain reserves, and professed great contrition; he only insisted on one point— the necessity of keeping Wyverne at a distance, at least for a time. " My lady " was equally anxious to avoid any public scandal, and she was not disposed to look too closely

into the facts.   Helen did not choose to make a confidante
of her mother, so there was little fear of her contradicting
anything.   When Alan reached England and wrote to his
uncle, he found the ground mined under his feet.   The
Squire believed in his nephew thoroughly, but he was not
strong-minded enough to take any decidedly offensive step,
and under the circumstances, inclined to temporize.   He
talked about " faults on both sides," spoke of a reconciliation being certainly effected, and ended, by begging Alan
not in anywise to interfere with it.

Wyverne felt sick and hopeless ; he knew how much to
believe of all this ; but he had only one course open to
him now—to avoid meeting the Clydesdales as carefully
as possible.   He hardly showed at all in town that spring,
and encountered Helen very seldom, then only for a few
minutes, when there was no opportunity for a confidence,
even if either had had the heart to attempt such a thing.
He spent all the summer and early autumn in Scotland.

Let me say now—for *your* comfort—my patient reader,
that the End is very near.

CHAPTER XXVI.

IMPLORA PACE.

THAT same year was drawing to its close, in a damp dreary December—one of those "green Yules" which greedy sextons are supposed to pray for, and which all the rest of the world utterly abhor. Alan Wyverne was at the Abbey, with Crichton for his only companion, who had come over from Castle Dacre to join a large shooting-party which was to assemble on the morrow. He had travelled far that day; and he sat more than half-asleep, before the huge wood-fire, waiting for dinner and for Hugh, who had not finished dressing yet. He was dozing so soundly, that he never heard the great entrance-bell clang; but he rose to his feet with a start, as Algy Beauclerc came in. From that moment, Wyverne never heard a door open suddenly, without shuddering.

There was no mistaking the bearer of evil tidings: he had evidently ridden far and fast; he was drenched and travel-stained from heel to head; his bushy beard was sodden and matted with the driving rain; and his bluff, honest face looked haggard and weary.

Alan spoke first.

"Where do you come from? Some one is dying or dead, I know. Who is it?"

The other answered, as if it cost him an effort to speak, clearing his throat huskily:

"I have ridden here from Clydesholme. You must come back with me directly: Helen is dying. I don't know if I have done right in fetching you, but I had no heart to refuse her; and Gracie said I might come. We must have fresh horses, and strong ones, and some one who knows the country: I can never find my way back through such a night as this; the waters were high in two places when I came through, and they are rising every hour. Don't lose a minute in getting ready."

Wyverne turned and walked to the bell without a word; he staggered more than once before he reached it: then he sate down, burying his head in his hands, and never lifted it till the servant entered. His face, when he uncovered it, was ghastly pale, and he was shivering; but he gave his orders quite distinctly and calmly.

"Don't talk now, Algy," he said; "you shall tell me all when we are on our way. I shall be ready before the horses are. Eat and drink meanwhile, if you can: you must need it now, and you will need it more before morning."

In less than a quarter of an hour Wyverne returned, fully accoutred for the journey; while he was dressing he had made arrangements with Hugh Crichton about telegraphing to put off the shooting party: his faculties seemed clear as ever; he literally forgot nothing. But Beauclerc was not deceived by the unnatural composure.

"For God's sake, take something to keep your strength up," he said. "It's a long five-and-twenty miles, and the road and the weather are fearful. You'll never stand it if you start fasting."

Alan looked at him vacantly, with a miserable attempt at a smile.

"I don't think I could eat anything just now," he answered; "and water suits me best to-night."

He filled a huge goblet and drained it thirstily; the horses were announced at that moment. Beauclerc remembered afterwards how carefully his companion looked at girth and bit before they mounted: all his thoughts and energies were concentrated on one point—how to reach Clydesholme as soon as possible—he would not risk the chance of an accident that might delay them for a moment. Two grooms followed them, to insure a spare horse in case of a break-down; and so they rode out into the wild weather on their dismal errand. It was a terrible journey, and not without danger; the road was so steep and stony in places, that few men even in broad daylight would have cared to ride over it at that furious pace; and twice the horses were off their feet in black rushing water. Strong and tough as he was, Beauclerc was almost too exhausted to keep his saddle before they reached Clydesholme. Nevertheless, he found breath and time to give his companion all the details it was requisite he should know.

It appeared that the Earl had brought his wife to Clydesholme, about a fortnight back, on the pretext of making preparations for a large party, which was to assemble there immediately after Christmas. During the whole of their stay they had been perfectly alone. Her health had been breaking faster every day; while, from some inexplicable cause, his temper had grown more consistently tyrannical and savage in proportion to Helen's increasing weakness and physical inability to make even a show of resistance. On the previous evening there had occurred a terrible scene of brutal violence. Early the next morning the Earl had ridden forth, no one knew whither, evidently still in furious wrath. Shortly afterwards the Countess had been seized with a coughing-fit, which had ended in the breaking of a large blood-vessel. As soon as she recovered strength enough to whisper an order, she had sent off an express for Grace Beauclerc, who chanced to be staying within a few miles. She and her husband came instantly; but it was only to find Helen's state hopeless. You know the rest.

Alan listened to all this, but answered never a word; indeed, he scarcely spoke, except to ask some question about the road, or to give some order about increasing or moderating their speed. Once Algy heard him mutter aloud,—"If we are only in time!"—and when they had to halt for some minutes, while a sleepy lodge-keeper was opening the park-gates of Clydesholme, his ear caught the fierce grinding of Wyverne's teeth.

The broad front of the mansion was as dark as the night outside, for the windows of the Countess's apartments looked over the gardens, but several servants came quickly to answer the summons of the bell. There was a scared, puzzled look about them all. Beauclerc whispered to one of them, and then turned to Alan with a gleam of satisfaction on his face.

"We *are* in time," he said; "thank God for that, at least. Stay here one minute, till I have seen Gracie."

Wyverne waited in the huge gloomy hall, with scarcely more consciousness or volition left than a sleep-walker owns. He allowed a servant to remove his drenched overcoat, and thanked the man, mechanically; but he never knew how or when he had taken it off.

Beauclerc soon returned and led the way through several passages into a long corridor; at the further end of this, light gleamed through a half-open door. Algy did not attempt to enter, but motioned Alan silently to go in.

It was a large, dim room, magnificently furnished after an antique fashion, and Grace Beauclerc was sitting there alone. She looked wan and worn with grief, and she trembled all over as she locked her arms round Alan's neck, holding him for a second or two closely embraced, and whispering a warning in his ear.

" You must be very quiet and cautious. She has hardly strength enough left to speak. Call me if you see any great change. I shall be here. The doctors and nurses are close by; but she would not allow any one to remain when she guessed you had come. She caught the sound of hoofs before any of us heard it."

She pointed to where a heavy curtain concealed an open doorway opposite. The gesture was not needed. Wyverne knew very well that in the next chamber Helen lay dying. His brain was clear enough now, and he was self-possessed, as men are wont to be when they have done with hope, and have nothing worse to fear than what the next moment will bring. He walked forward without pausing, and lifted the curtain gently, but with a steady hand.

The entrance nearly fronted the huge old-fashioned couch, shadowed by a canopy and hangings of dark-green velvet, on which the Countess lay. Her cheeks had scarcely more colour than the snowy linen and the lace of the pillows which supported her, and, till just now, it seemed as though her heavy eyelids would never be lifted again. But, at the sound of Alan's footfall, the eyes opened, large and bright, and the face lost the impress of Death, as it lighted and flushed, momentarily, with the keen joy of re-cognition and welcome.

He was kneeling, with his head bowed down on Helen's hand, that he held fast, when the first words were spoken.

"I felt sure you would come," she murmured. "I have been so still, and patient, and obedient—only that I might live long enough for *this*. I heard you, when you rode up, through all the wind and the rain. I am so glad—so glad. I can die easily now. I could never have rested in my grave if we had not said—'Good-bye.'"

Wyverne tried twice to speak steadily, but there came only a miserable, broken moan.

"Ah! forgive—forgive! God knows, I thought I was right in keeping away. I did it for the best."

The thin, transparent fingers of the hand that was free wandered over his brow, and twined themselves in his drenched hair, with a fond, delicate caress.

"I know you did, Alan. *I* was wrong—I, who would have risked all the sin and the shame. But I have suffered so much, that I do hope I shall not be punished any more. See—I can thank you now for standing firm, and holding *me* up too. And, dear, I know how good and faithful you have been from the very beginning. I know about those letters, and all the truth. I am content—more than content. I have had all your love—is it not so? You will look at my picture sometimes, and though she was wilful and wicked, no woman, however good or beautiful, will win you away from your own dead Helen. Ah! it hurts me to hear you sob. I feel your tears on my wrist, and they burn—they burn."

Let us draw the curtain close. Even where sympathy is sure, it is not lightly to be paraded—"the agony of man unmanned." It was not long before Wyverne recovered self-control. They spoke no more aloud; but there were many of those low, broken whispers, half of whose meaning must be guessed when they are uttered, but which are remembered longer than the most elaborate sentences that mortal tongue ever declaimed.

For some minutes Helen's eyes had been closed. Suddenly, though not a feature was distorted, Alan saw a terrible change sweep over her face, and rose to call in assistance. It seemed as if she divined his purpose, and wished to prevent it. The weak clasp tightened, for an instant, round his fingers, the weary eyelids lifted, enough to give passage to one last, loving look, and the slow syllables were just barely audible—

"This once—only once more."

He understood her, and, stooping down, laid gently on the poor pale lips his own—almost as white and cold. Then, for a brief space, there was a great stillness—a stillness as of Death. An awful sound broke the silence—a dull, smothered cry, between groan and wail, that haunted the solitary hearer to her dying day—a cry wrung from the first despair of a broken-hearted man, who, henceforth, was to be alone for evermore.

Grace Beauclerc shivered in every limb, for she knew that all was over. But even then she had presence of mind enough to refrain from summoning any one from without. Helen was past human aid, and Grace knew that she could not serve her better now than by keeping for awhile curious eyes and ears away.

She found Alan standing, with his head resting on his arm that was coiled round one of the pillars of the canopy He did not seem aware of his sister's entrance, and never spoke or stirred as she cast herself down by the side of the dead, pressing kiss after kiss on the sweet, quiet face, and weeping passionately.

How long they remained thus neither could have told. All at once the door of the outer room opened quickly, and Beauclerc lifted the curtain and stood in the doorway. The first glance told him the truth. He walked straight up to the foot of the bed, and gazed steadily for a few seconds on the wreck of marvellous beauty that lay there so still; at last he muttered between his teeth,

"It is best—far best—so."

Then he passed round to where his wife was lying, and wound his arm round her waist and raised her gently.

"Darling Gracie, you must rouse yourself. It seems hard, I know, but this cruel night does not even give time for mourning. We must leave this instantly. I have ordered the carriage, and, Alan, I have ordered your horses too. You can find lodging within two miles, but you must not stay here five minutes longer. It is no place for any of us. Clydesdale is in the house at this moment."

For many hours Grace Beauclerc's nerves and strength had been sorely tried, but had never given way up to this moment. She broke down utterly now, marking the ghastly change in her brother's face, and the murderous meaning of his eyes, as he moved slowly and silently towards the door. She wrenched herself out of her husband's clasp, and threw herself in Alan's way with a wild cry of terror.

"Heaven help us! Have we not suffered enough to-night without this last horror? Alan, you shall never meet while I have sense to prevent it. Algy, won't you stop him? Don't you see that he is mad?"

Beauclerc strode forward and laid his strong grasp on Wyverne's breast.

"Yes, you *are* mad," he said, sternly. "You shall not pass out of this room, if I can prevent it, to work such bitter wrong against that dead woman, who loved you only too well. Cannot you see that if you retaliate on her husband to-night, her name will be dishonoured for ever and ever? She has suffered enough for you to sacrifice your selfish vengeance. Alan, listen now; you will thank God on your knees that you did so hereafter."

Wyverne gazed in the speaker's face, and as he gazed the devilish fire died out of his eyes. He passed his hand over his forehead twice or thrice as if bewildered, and then walked aside to the darkest corner of the room, leaning his face against the wall; when he turned round again it was settled and calm.

"You are quite right," he said, slowly. "I *was* mad, and forgot everything. You need fear nothing now. I only ask you to trust me. I will see Clydesdale before I go; but I swear I will not speak one angry word. We will go down directly. Leave me here only three minutes, and I will follow you."

They did trust him; they went into the outer room, and never thought of listening or lifting the curtain. It is an example that we may well imitate.

All this while the Earl sat down-stairs alone, in such an agony of remorse and shame that, in spite of his past brutality and tyranny, his worst enemy might have spared reproach. He knew that Helen's state was hopeless, though he had not heard yet that the end had come. He thought of her, as he saw her first, in the radiant bloom of her imperial beauty. He thought of her, as he saw her last, pale and exhausted and death-like after his savage frenzy had vented itself. He *did* repent heartily now, and felt as if he would have given 10 years of his life to undo the wrong and make ample amends. And still, the voice that none of us can stifle for ever kept whispering, "Too late—too late!"

He was musing thus in miserable anticipation of the next news, when the door opened slowly, and Wyverne entered, fully equipped for his departure.

What passed between these two will never be known. Beauclerc, who stood outside within earshot, ready to interfere in case Alan's self-control should fail, heard absolutely nothing. At first the Earl's harsh, rough voice, though subdued below its wont, sounded at intervals; but Wyverne's deep, sombre monotone seemed to bear it down, and even this eventually sank so low that not an accent was distinguishable.

At last the lock turned softly, and Wyverne came out. He just pressed Algy's hand in passing, and went straight to the hall-door, where his horses were waiting. Immediately afterwards the hoofs moved slowly away.

It was five minutes or more before the carriage was ready. Beauclerc had put his wife in, and was standing in the hall, making his last preparations, when Clydesdale came up behind him, and took his arm unawares.

The Earl's face was convulsed with grief; his eyes were heavy, and his cheeks seamed with tears; and his voice was broken and low.

"I hardly dare to ask you to stay to-night," he said; "but if you would—— Only consider the fearful weather, and your wife's health. If you knew how bitterly I repent! I only heard the truth 10 minutes ago."

Algy Beauclere could preach patience better than he could practise it. He shook off tho detaining hand with a force that made Clydesdale reel, turning upon him the wrathful blaze of his honest eyes.

" I hope you *do* repent," he said, hoarsely. " My wife is not strong, but she should lie out on the open moor, sooner than sleep under that accursed roof of yours."

If he had looked back as he went out he might have seen the Earl recoil helplessly, covering a stricken face with shaking hands.

Wyverne remained at tho village inn, not a mile from tho park gates, just long enough to rest his horses and men, and then rode back to the Abbey as fast as blood and bone of the best would carry him. His strained nerves and energies were not relaxed till he got fairly home. There was a sharp reaction, and he lay for somo time in a state of half-stupor; but he was never seriously ill. It was no wonder that mind and body should be utterly worn out: the dark ride through such wild weather was trying enough, and he had scarcely tasted food or drink for 20 hours. Twice within the week there came a special messenger from Clydesholme; it is to be presumed that the errand was one of peace; for, eight days after Helen's death, Alan Wyverne stood in his place among the few friends and relations who travelled so far to see her laid in her grave. But it was noticed that neither at meeting nor parting did any word or salutation pass between him and the Earl. Alan arrived only just in time for tho funeral, and left immediately afterwards, without setting his foot over the threshold of Clydesholme.

No one saw anything of Wyverne for somo weeks. When he reappeared in society he looked certainly older, but otherwise his manner and bearing and temper remained much the same as they had been for the last four years.

That night left its mark on others besides him. It was long before Beauclerc recovered his genial, careless elasticity of spirit; and for months his wife scarcely slept a night without starting and moaning in her dreams. Judging from outward appearance, Clydesdale was the person most strongly and permanently affected by the events just recorded. He was never the same man again; his temper was still often harsh and violent, but the arrogant superciliousness, and intense appreciation of himself and his position, had quite left him. The lesson, whatever it was, lasted him his life. Very few of the many who were pleased or profited by the alteration in the Earl's character, guessed at what a fearful cost the improvement had been made.

It seemed as if poor Helen had felt for some time before her death that the end was fast approaching. They found not only her will, which had been executed when she was last in London, but divers letters, not to be delivered till after her decease. There was a very large legacy to Grace Beauclerc, and some minor ones to old servants and pensioners. All the residue of the vast sum at her disposal was bequeathed to her father, without condition or reserve. Her jewels—with the exception of Lord Clydesdale's gifts before and after marriage, which reverted to him—were left to Mrs Brabazon. There was no letter for Wyverne, and no mention of his name; but Maud sent him a casket which had been in her hands for some time past. It contained three of Alan's letters, a few trifling relics of their brief engagement, a thick packet in Helen's handwriting, bearing a comparatively recent date, and a small exquisite miniature, taken before her beauty had begun to fade. That casket was the crown jewel of the testament.

The void that her death made in society was not easily filled up; but after awhile the world rolled on, as if she had never been. The Squire looked broken and grey, and more careworn than when his affairs had been most desperate. He knew scarcely anything of the terrible truth, but a vague remorse haunted and bore him down. Lady Mildred's face was inscrutable as ever, but her smiles grew rarer and more artificial day by day. Max Vavasour, after the first emotion of sorrow, troubled himself little about what was past and gone. If he ever realized his sister's sacrifice, he looked upon it as a great political necessity— to be deplored but not to be repented of. Maud Brabazon felt as if she could never bring herself to wear the jewels that she inherited; but she got over these scruples in time; and, at the first drawing-room of the following season, her sapphires and diamonds were generally envied and admired.

When I said that in Alan Wyverne there was little outward alteration, I ought to have limited the assertion. Men would have told you so; but maids and matrons are sharper-sighted, and their report would have been very different: *they* knew how utterly he was changed. Their society still had an attraction for him; and he was frank, and kind, and gentle as ever, when a woman was in presence; but a word never escaped his lips that could be construed into anything warmer than friendship and courtesy. The most intrepid coquette refrained instinctively from wasting her *câlineries* and seductions there: she might as well have sought a lover in a deserted statue-gallery of the Vatican.

How Alan fared when he was quite alone it would be hard to say. Such seasons were rare, except at the dead hours of night, when sleep comes naturally to any constitution, unless some powerful momentary excitement is at work; for he mixed more in general society than he had done for years. I doubt if he did not suffer less acutely than when Helen was alive, and in her husband's power. He was at least free from the torments of anxiety and apprehension. If in this world of ours we can defy these two enemies of man's peace, we have gained no mean victory over Fate

CHAPTER XXVII.

MORITURI TE SALUTANT.

It is a clear breezy night, out in the midst of the Atlantic, the mighty steam-ship, *Panama*, ploughs her way through the long, sullen "rollers," steadily and strongly, as if conscious of her trust, and of her ability to discharge it—the safe carriage of 300 lives. A few wakeful passengers still linger on deck; amongst them is Alan Wyverne; the restless demon, ever at his elbow, has driven him abroad again, to see what sport may be found on the great Western prairies.

Suddenly there is a trampling of hurrying feet between decks, and a sailor rushes up the companion and whispers to the officer of the watch, who descends with a scared face; in five minutes more a terrible cry rings from stem to stern, waking the soundest sleeper aboard—"Fire!—fire!"

Can you form any idea of the horror and confusion that ensue, when hundreds of human creatures wake from perfect security, to find themselves face to face with death? I think not. No one can realize the scene, except those few who have witnessed it once, and who see it in their dreams till they die. No man alive can say for certain if his nerve will stand such a shock, and the bravest may well be proud, if he emerges from such an ordeal without betraying shameful weakness. I speak of a mixed and undisciplined crowd—not of trained soldiers; we have more than one proof of what *these* can do and endure. I think that those who died at Thermopylæ were less worthy of the crown of valour, than the troopers who formed up on deck and stood steady in their ranks, till every woman and child was safe in the boats, and till the *Birkenhead* went down under their feet.

Nevertheless, at such emergencies, a few are always found who single themselves out from the rest, as if determined to prove what daring and devotion manhood can display at extremity. First and foremost among these, on this occasion, was Alan Wyverne. He never lost his presence of mind for an instant. Yet he had accidentally become possessed of a secret that few on board had any idea of. English powder was at a high premium in America just then; and the captain had shipped, at his own private risk, and against his orders, enough to blow all the fore part of the vessel to shivers. Alan reached his cabin before the first upward rush came, and made his preparations deliberately. They were very short and simple. He opened a certain steel casket and took out a packet and a miniature, which he secured in his breast; then passing his arm through the port-hole, he dropped the casket into the sea; a sharp pang of pain flitted across his face as he did so, but he never hesitated; that one fact told plainly enough his opinion of the crisis. Then he buckled round his waist a broad leather belt, from which, among other instruments, hung a long sheathed hunting-knife; he put some biscuits and cakes of portable soup, and a large flask of brandy, into the pockets of a thick boat-cloak, which he threw over his arm; then, after casting round a keen hurried glance, as if to assure himself he had forgotten nothing, he left the cabin, and with some difficulty made his way on deck.

It was a ghastly chaos of tumult and terror—a babel of shouts, and cries, and groans, and orders to which no one gave heed, while over all rose the roar and hiss of escaping steam, for they had stopped the engines at the first alarm, and the *Panama* lay in the trough of the sea—a huge, helpless log; though the weather was by no means rough, the "rollers" never quite subside out there in mid-ocean. The flames, beginning to burst out of one of the fore hatchways, threw a weird, fantastic glare on half-dressed, struggling figures, and on white faces convulsed with eagerness or fear; and all the while the clear autumn moon looked down, serenely indifferent to human suffering; even so, she looked down on Adam's agony, on the night that followed the Fall.

Personal terror and the consciousness of guilt, had made the captain utterly helpless already; but the chief officer was a cool-headed Scotchman, a thorough seaman, and as brave as Bayard; he was exerting himself to the utmost, backed by a few sailors and passengers, to keep the gangway clear, so as to lower the boats regularly. In spite of their efforts, the first sank almost as soon as she touched the water, stove in against the side through the slipping or breaking of a "fall." At last they did get the launch fairly afloat, and were equally successful with the two remaining cutters.

There was manhood and generosity enough in the crowd to allow most of the women and children to be lowered without interference; but soon it became terribly evident that fully a third of those on board must be left behind, from absolute want of boat-room. Then the real, selfish struggle began, some of the sailors setting the example, and all order and authority was at an end. As Alan stood in the background, a man came up behind him and touched his arm, without speaking. It was Jock Ellison, whose father and grandfather had been keepers before him at the Abbey; he had accompanied Wyverne through Africa and India; his constitution and strength seemed climate-proof, no peril disturbed his cheerful equanimity, and he would have laid down his life to serve his master any day, as the merest matter of duty.

It did Alan good to see the handsome, honest, northern face, and the bright, bold, blue eyes close to his shoulder. He smiled as he spoke.

"We're in a bad mess, Jock, I fear. Keep near me, whatever happens. You've always done that so far, and we've always pulled through."

The stout henchman was slow of speech as he was ready of hand. Before he could reply, Wyverne's attention was called elsewhere.

A few steps from where they were standing, a pale, sickly-looking woman sat alone, leaning against the bulwarks. She felt she was too weak to force a passage through the crowd, so she had sunk down there, hopeless and helpless. She kept trying to hush the wailing of her frightened child, though the big, heavy tears were rolling fast down her own cheeks, moaning low at intervals, always the same words—"Ah! Willie, Willie!" It was her husband's name, and the poor creature was thinking, how hard he had been slaving these three years, to make a

home for her and "Minnie" out there in the West, and
how he had been living on crusts to save their passage
money—only to bring them to *this*. Alan had been attracted
by the pair soon after he came on board, they seemed so
very lonely and defenceless, and so wonderfully fond of each
other. He had been kind to them on several occasions, and
had made great friends with "Minnie," a pretty, timid,
fragile child of five or six years.

He went up now, and laid his hand gently on the
mother's shoulder.

"Don't lose heart," he said, "but trust to me. You
shall meet your husband yet, please God. You will be
almost safe when you are once in a boat. The sea is not
rough, and you are certain to be picked up by some vessel
before many hours are over. The only difficulty is to get
to your place. We'll manage that for you. Don't be
frightened if you hear an angry word or two. I can carry
Minnie on one arm easily; let me put the other round you;
and wrap yourself in this boat-cloak—there's enough in
the pockets to feed you for days at a strait, and it will keep
you both warm."

He hardly noticed her gratitude, but whispered a word
or two to Jock Ellison, and moved steadily towards the
gangway with both his charges. The gigantic Dalesman kept
close to his master's shoulder, rather in his front, cleaving
the crowd asunder with his mighty shoulders, utterly regardless of threat or prayer. Some of the better sort, too,
when they saw the white, delicate woman, and the little
child nestling close to Alan's breast, till her golden hair
mingled with his black beard, yielded room, not unwillingly, muttering,—"Let *them* pass, at all events: there's
time enough yet." So, Wyverne had nearly reached the

gangway, when a haggard, wild-looking man thrust himself
violently forward, evidently determined to be the next to
descend.

"You shall have the next turn," Alan said, firmly. "Let
these two go first; you see how helpless they are. They
are not strong enough to fight their own battles."

The other turned upon him furiously.

"Who the —— are you, that give orders here?" he
screamed. "I've as much right to my life as the woman or
any of you. I'll have my turn in spite of you all;" and he
began to open a clasp-knife.

Alan's face grew very dark and stern.

"I haven't time to argue," he said; "stand clear, or take
the consequences."

His adversary sprang at him without another word.
Wyverne's arms were so encumbered that he was perfectly
defenceless; but just then Jock Ellison's hand came out of
his breast, grasping a ponderous revolver by the barrel:
the steel-bound butt crashed down full on the man's bare
head, and he dropped where he stood, without even staggering. The crowd drew back instinctively; before they
closed in again the mother was safe in the boat. Even in
her agony of terror she found time to kiss Alan's hand,
crying "that God would reward him." In truth he *was*
rewarded, and that soon.

It was strange—considering their brief acquaintance—
to see how the poor child clung to her protector, and how
loth she was to leave him, even to follow her mother; it
almost needed force to make the thin white arms unloose
the clasp of his neck. Young as she was then, "Minnie"
will be a woman before she forgets the kind grave face

that leant over her, and the soft voice that said " Good-bye,
little one," as Wyverne let her go.

He was turning away, when the man that grovelled at
his foot began to stir and moan.

" It's hard on him too, poor devil ! " some one grumbled
in the background; "his wife is in the boat; she's five
months gone with child, and she'll have to starve if she
ever gets to land."

Wyverne stooped down and lifted up his late adversary
as tenderly as he had supported the woman.

" Hold up for a minute," he whispered. " You brought
the blow on yourself; but I promised you should have the
next turn. Your wife has hardly missed you yet. And
take care of this : it may help you some day."

He drew a note-case from his pocket as he spoke, and
thrust it into the other's breast: no one attempted to interfere as he put the guiding ropes round the half insensible body, and passed it carefully over the ship's side.
One determined man will cow a crowd at most times; and
remember, there were two to the fore, just then.

" He has *my* place," Alan said, simply—as if that were
the best answer to any objections or murmurs; and then
he made his way back again to the clear part of the deck,
his trusty henchman following him still.

The dreadful struggle was over at last; the boats, fully
freighted, had pushed off, and lay at a safe distance; those
who were left on board knew that they had only to trust
now to their own resources, or to a miracle, or to the
mercy of Providence. There was scarcely any wind, and
what there was blew in a favourable direction, so that
little of the smoke or flame came aft.

Suddenly Wyverne turned to his companion, who sate near him, apparently quite cheerful and composed—

"You had better look to yourself, Jock. She won't hold together another quarter of an hour. It's no distance to swim, and they may take you into a boat still, if you try it. You've as good a right to a place as any one now the women are gone."

The Dalesman's broad breast heaved indignantly, and there was a sob in his voice as he replied,

" I'll do your bidding to the last, Sir Alan; but you'll never have the heart to make me leave you. I haven't deserved it."

Wyverne knew better than to press the point.

" Shake hands then, old comrade," he said, with a sad smile on his lip. " You've served me well enough to have your own way for once. I fancy you have few heavy sins to repent of, but you had better make your peace with God quickly; our minutes are numbered."

Just then a boat ranged up close under the ship's quarter, and a smothered voice called on Wyverne by name. It was the chief officer's, who had determined to make this last effort to save him.

"Let yourself down, Sir Alan, there are ropes enough about, or drop over the side. We'll take *you* in; you have well deserved it."

He never hesitated an instant—he had withstood stronger temptations in his time—but leant over the side and answered, in his own firm, clear tones,

" Thanks, a thousand times; but get back out of danger instantly It is useless waiting for me; I don't stir. I have given up my place already, and no power on earth would make me take another man's. If a ship comes near, we may all be saved yet; if not, we know the worst, and I hope we know how to meet it."

When the cutter had pushed off, Wyverne sat down again, burying his face in his hands, and remained so for some minutes. Suddenly he looked up, and drew the miniature out of his breast, gazing on it steadfastly and long, with a love and tenderness that no words can express, and a happiness so intense that it savoured of triumph. One of the survivors who chanced to be watching him (unconscious of the catastrophe being so near) said afterwards that a strange light shone out on Alan's face during those few seconds—a light that came neither from moon nor fire, but as it were from *within*—a light, perchance, such as saints may, one day, see on the faces of angels.

"Helen—darling Helen," he murmured, "I always thought and hoped and prayed that I had acted rightly; but I never knew it till now."

He pressed the picture to his lips, and kissed it twice or thrice fervently. Let us hope that in that impulse there mingled nothing of sinful passion; for it was the last of Alan Wyverne's life.

In a moment there came an awful smothered roar—a crash of rending timbers and riven metal—all the fore-part of the vessel seemed to melt away, scattered over air and water in a torrent of smoke and flame; the after-part shook convulsively through every joint and seam, and then, with one headlong plunge, went down, like a wounded whale "sounding." Some half-dozen strong swimmers emerged alive from the horrible vortex, and all these were saved. Brave Jock Ellison, after recovering from the first stunning shock, never attempted to make for the boats, but swam hither and thither, till his colossal strength failed him, hoping to find some trace of his master. But Alan Wyverne never rose again, and never will—till the sea shall give up her dead.

And now my tale is told.

I have attempted to sketch, roughly, what befell a man very weak and erring—who was often sorely tried—who acted ever up to the light that was given him, at the cost of bitter self-denial and self-sacrifice—who, nevertheless, in this life, failed to reap the tithe of his reward.

Alan Wyverne was strong, up to a certain point; but he had not faith enough to make him feel always sure that he had done right, in defiance of appearances; nor principle enough to keep him from repining at results. He could neither comfort himself nor others, thoroughly. He was a chivalrous, true-hearted man; but a very imperfect Christian. He dared not openly rebel against the laws of God; but he was too human to accept, unhesitatingly, the fulfilment of His decrees. Throughout Alan's life, Honour usurped the place where Religion ought to have reigned paramount: he shrank from shame when he would perhaps have encountered sin.

Just see, how complete was the earthly retribution.

To that one principle—sound enough if it had not been the ruling one—he sacrificed love, and friendship, and revenge, and life. Yet the happiest moments that he knew for years, were those when he stood face to face with a terrible death—a dead woman's picture in his hand.

THE END.

JOHN CHILDS AND SON, PRINTERS.

TINSLEYS' MAGAZINE:

AN ILLUSTRATED MONTHLY

PRICE ONE SHILLING.

CONDUCTED BY EDMUND YATES.

Published on the 16th of every Month.

CONTAINS:

NOVELS BY EDMUND YATES,

Author of "Black Sheep," &c.

WILLIAM HOWARD RUSSELL, LL.D.,

Of "The Times."

BREAKING A BUTTERFLY;

Or, BLANCHE ELLERSLIE'S ENDING,

By the Author of "Guy Livingstone," &c.

A HOUSE OF CARDS,

By a New Writer.

AND VARIOUS ARTICLES OF GENERAL INTEREST.

LONDON:

TINSLEY BROTHERS, 18, CATHERINE STREET,

STRAND.

www.ingramcontent.com/pod-product-compliance
Lightning Source LLC
Chambersburg PA
CBHW051518100726
47898CB00005B/1502